The Secret Path

Karen Swan is the *Sunday Times* top three bestselling author of twenty books and her novels sell all over the world. She writes two books each year – one for the summer period and one for the Christmas season. Previous winter titles include *Christmas at Tiffany's*, *The Christmas Party* and *Together by Christmas*, and for summer, *The Greek Escape*, *The Spanish Promise* and *The Hidden Beach*.

Her books are known for their evocative locations and Karen sees travel as vital research for each story. She loves to set deep, complicated love stories within twisting plots, sometimes telling two stories in the same book.

Previously a fashion editor, she lives in Sussex with her husband, three children and two dogs.

Follow Karen on Instagram @swannywrites, on her author page on Facebook, and on Twitter @KarenSwan1.

Also by Karen Swan

The Secret Path

KAREN SWAN

PAN BOOKS

First published 2021 by Macmillan

This edition first published 2021 by Pan Books
an imprint of Pan Macmillan
The Smithson, 6 Briset Street, London EC1M 5NR
EU representative: Macmillan Publishers Ireland Limited
Mallard Lodge, Lansdowne Village, Dublin 4
Associated companies throughout the world
www.panmacmillan.com

ISBN 978-1-5290-0626-1

1 3 5 7 9 8 6 4 2

Visit **www.panmacmillan.com** to read more about all our books
and to buy them. You will also find features, author interviews and
news of any author events, and you can sign up for e-newsletters
so that you're always first to hear about our new releases.

For Wallcoot
No one laughs like we do

Part One

Part One

Chapter One

March 2011

'Tell me a secret,' Tara whispered into the silence.

'A secret?' Alex echoed, sounding sleepy.

'Yes. Something you've never told anyone before.'

'Oh. That type of secret.'

She smacked his chest. Immediately kissed it. He smelled of her shower gel – jasmine and vanilla.

'Hmm.' The sound reverberated against her ear, travelling through her and into her. She felt suffused with him – his breath, his smell, his kisses, his love.

There was a silence, and then his chest inflated, the thought assuming a physical shape. 'Well, I've always wanted a pet goat.'

She lifted her head and pinned him with a look. 'That is not what I meant!'

He grinned back at her. 'No?'

'No!'

'But I've never told anyone that before. I feel very . . . vulnerable to have admitted I love their flicky little tails and hairy chins and little prancy jumps.'

She smacked him again, laughing. 'No! That doesn't count and you know it doesn't.'

'Huh.'

She gazed at him, wishing he wasn't so handsome. Or funny. 'Tell me what frightens you most in the world.'

'Oh well, that's easy. What frightens me most in the world is what we're doing to the world.'

She groaned. 'Ugh. Can you just stop being an eco-warrior for one minute? We're in bed!'

'I'm a biologist,' he corrected her. 'And biology never sleeps. Unlike you.'

He arched an eyebrow; they were beautifully shaped – thick and straight, but finishing in a sharp point – and their very boldness highlighted the paleness of celery-green eyes that sometimes looked grey in weak light.

'What can I say? My body and brain just need a lot of rest and repair.'

'Well, it's not beauty sleep you need, for sure.'

'Charmer,' she grinned, nudging him with her shoulders, but pleased. 'Do you ever think what might have happened if we hadn't met in the coffee shop that morning?'

'No.' And before she could protest, he smiled. 'Because if it hadn't been there, it'd have been somewhere else.'

'You're a fatalist?' she gasped with mock-horror. 'But how can you say such a thing? You're a scientist.'

'I say it as a good son. My mom always told me, the people who are meant to be in your life, you'll meet them twice without trying.'

She raised an eyebrow. 'And you believed that?'

'Of course. I believe everything my mom ever told me.' A small smile whickered in his eyes, so hers too, and she let the lack of rigorous adherence to scientific principle go. He loved his mum. There was a lot to be said for that.

4

'Do you . . .' She thought for a moment. 'Oh! Do you believe in never going to sleep on a fight?'

'I believe in going to sleep on a mattress.'

'Stop it!' she laughed. 'Be serious! I am learning about you!' She peered at him through narrowed amber eyes. 'I am studying you! You are my specialist subject.'

'Huh.' He inhaled deeply, but a smile tickled his lips.

'So do you?' she prompted. '. . . Believe in never going to sleep on a fight?'

'I've never thought about it. But I guess . . .' He lapsed into thought. 'No.'

'*No?*'

He seemed surprised by her surprise. 'What? I don't think it's about the speed of how you resolve something. In my experience, talk can be cheap and apologies are meaningless if you're just rushing to get them in before a deadline. Sometimes, yeah, it's better to go to sleep on the fight.'

'Said no one *ever*,' she protested.

He shrugged. 'You've got to have conviction if you want to have integrity. All the people I admire most in the world have principles they would die for.'

She took his hand, which was lying inert over his chest, and distractedly slotted her fingers between his, feeling the size of his palm against hers. There was a tiny moon-shaped scar on the side of his hand from where he'd been hooked by a fishing fly when he was a little boy. She loved stroking it, the ridges satisfying under her thumb. 'So, like who, then?'

He gave her the side-eye. 'Do you know the artist Peter Beard?'

'Sure. Did all the Africa collages. Smeared them with his blood.'

'Right. He was one of the first to recognize species

decline in the wild and really do something about it. Back in the sixties and seventies, this was. He's a pioneer, even though everyone just thinks of him as a playboy.'

'Like Attenborough, but with sex appeal?'

'Yeah, he had a *lot* of that back in the day.'

'So you admire him because he's a conservationist?'

'Not just that – I admire him because he has the power of conviction and if he believes in something, he backs it up, a hundred per cent.' He looked at her. 'Whenever he's done the wrong thing, it's always been for the right reasons.'

'Like what? Give me an example.'

'Okay then.' He thought for a moment. 'Okay. There was this one time he caught a poacher on his land – and do you know what he did?'

She shook her head. 'Nope, not a clue.'

'He put the guy in his own snare.'

She stared at him. *'What?'*

'Yep. Left him there for hours. Didn't kill him, but . . . he made him think twice about ever doing it again, let's put it that way.' His voice had become velvet – thick, soft, like a big cat's purr. 'When I read that, I thought he was fucking A! He became my hero there and then. Finally, here was someone actually doing something!'

'But he put the guy in a *snare*.'

'The guy was putting lions in snares. Is that any better?' He blinked back at her, his eyes shining with their own fierce light. 'Sometimes talk isn't enough, Ta. You have to act. Be prepared to cross the line to get things done.'

'Well,' she said finally. 'That's good to know. Remind me not to fall out with you,' she teased, her arm brushing over him in long, languid strokes. She loved the feeling of their skin-on-skin.

'It's not looking especially likely at the moment.'

'I'm hoping for a lot longer than a moment,' she said, hoisting herself up onto her elbows so that she was able to look at him clearly, at the beautiful face that had captured her even before their first hello. She felt the attraction zip between them, his fingertips pressing a little more firmly against her flesh. She tapped her index finger against his chest, one of her nervous tics he found endearing. 'So. Don't you want to ask me if I've got a secret too?'

He looked back at her, a flicker of bemusement in his eyes. 'I don't know. Do I?'

'Well, I thought you would. Now I'm not sure.' Her tone sounded tart in the face of his seeming indifference. What if he wasn't as curious about her as she was about him? Did he feel the same need to possess her – body, soul, every last memory?

'So, you're not sure if I'm sure I want to hear your secret,' he murmured drily, sinking back into quietness again.

The silence in the room deepened. 'What are you thinking?' she whispered, when he offered nothing further. No curiosity, no wonderings.

'I'm thinking I'm not sure we should be having this conversation.'

She pulled away, stung by the comment, but his hands clasped her and held her firmly. 'I'm teasing,' he grinned. 'Of course I want to hear your secret.'

'I don't think you do,' she mumbled, feeling thrown.

He flipped her onto her back in a fluid motion. 'Twig, I do,' he said, leaning on his elbows and kissing her lightly on the tip of her nose. 'I do. Tell me your most secret secret. The one thing you've never told anyone else.'

She stared up into those green eyes, her mouth parted for

the words to come. But the moment had gone, and her big secret with them. '. . . I hate mushrooms.'

He deflated, looking visibly underwhelmed. 'That's it? You hate mushrooms?'

'Mm-hmm. Detest them,' she nodded. 'But I've never told anyone. So I always eat them when they're served up. To be polite.'

'You Brits and your politeness,' he tutted, looking baffled. 'Why can't you just say when you don't like something?'

'Well, as you just pertinently pointed out, it's a British thing. We apologize when other people walk into us. We wait for permission to leave when we've paid for something with the correct change. I'll probably end up marrying the first guy who asks me, just to be polite.'

He arched an eyebrow. 'Twig, will you marry me?'

'Absolutely. Thank you so much for asking. How kind.'

They both laughed, Alex burying his face in her neck, his silky dark hair tickling her cheek. She felt his teeth graze her skin lightly, mock-biting her and sending a flush of goose-bumps up her body. He sank back again, lying on his side, resting his head in one hand as he began tracing swirls on her stomach. 'Baby, you have got to learn the power of "no". I'm going to Americanize you. Repeat after me. No.'

'No.'

'Bit stronger. *No.*'

'No.'

He frowned.

She tried again. 'No!'

'Okay, it's passable. You're a quick learner,' he shrugged. 'Now let's apply it to some real-life scenarios. Twig, would you like a puppy for your birthday?'

She laughed. 'No.'

He nodded, looking impressed. 'Twig, let's go to Kabul for Christmas.'

'No!'

'Excellent. Most excellent . . . Twig, you should definitely wear the red shoes in bed, with nothing else.'

She laughed louder, her body arching off the sheets. 'No!'

'Damn. Own goal.' He pulled a face, but his eyes were dancing with merriment. 'Twig, would you like some garlic mushrooms with your steak?'

'No!'

He held an arm out in amazement. 'I believe my work here is done.'

'You're a truly great teacher, Alex Carter. What a magnificent professor you're going to be.'

'Thank you. But there's still one final test.' He took a slow, deep breath and pinned her with a stare that could have made the stars leap down from the sky. 'Twig, will you marry me?'

'Absolutely. Thanks so much for asking. How kind.'

'No!' he wailed, pressing his face into the crook of her neck again, shaking his head as she laughed beneath him, feeling especially ticklish, the midnight hysterics beginning to get her. 'You were so close. *So* close.' He looked back at her. 'But now look – instead you're going to be stuck with me for eternity, all because you're a polite Brit who couldn't say no. I'm really sorry, baby. That's some hard cheese right there.'

Her laughter faded as she looked up at him, seeing past the jokes. '. . . Huh?'

'You didn't say no.'

'No.'

The eyebrow went up. 'No, you agree you didn't say no? Or no, you don't want to marry me?'

He was bamboozling her. 'No, I . . . agree I didn't say no.'

His smile widened as he pulled her towards him. 'So at least now you'll have the rest of your life to learn.'

'Yes,' she whispered, feeling her heart begin to quicken.

'Yes,' he echoed, his gaze locking with hers. 'I like that word better.'

'Yes.'

'Twig, will you marry me?'

'Yes—' His mouth was upon hers, his body weight pushing her deeper into the mattress, all jokes forgotten as they submitted to the chemistry that had shocked them both at their very first meeting, only four months earlier. Glued to their phones during the morning rush, she had inadvertently picked up his soy filter and he had chased her halfway down Queen's Gate with her caramel macchiato. So much of it had slopped over the sides as he ran that it was half empty by the time he caught up with her and as their eyes had met over his breathless explanations, he'd insisted on buying her another. She'd ended up missing her lecture on pharmacodynamics that morning and he'd missed a meeting with his PhD supervisor. Coffee had become lunch, then they'd met up that evening for dinner and they'd not spent a night apart since.

Within the space of a week (but really, within that first day), he had become her life system – he was her oxygen, her sunlight, her beating heart. Even just the thought of being without him was insupportable. She'd never known passion, yearning, lust like it and sometimes the strength of their feelings frightened her. It wasn't healthy, surely, to want another person so entirely? He was a drug she simply could not do without. And now she wouldn't have to?

The excitement escaped her as a little laugh.

'What?' he asked, nudging her legs apart with his knee.

'Mushrooms to a marriage proposal. That was . . . un-expected,' she breathed as he began kissing her neck.

'You're telling me.' His voice was muffled.

'So you didn't plan it?'

He pulled his head up, his cheeks flushed, his eyes bright. 'No. But now I've told you my deepest, darkest secret about my love for goats, I'll have to keep you close. Can't have that getting out.' He winked at her, forever teasing.

His mouth was on her skin again, her body already crying out for him. She closed her eyes, sinking into the splendour of knowing she would have this for the rest of her life.

'Of course you know what this means,' he murmured, his voice a hot breath on her tummy.

'What?' she smiled, eyes still closed.

'You'll have to introduce me to your parents,' he said, that signature wry smile on his lips.

'Oh God . . . I guess I will.'

He looked back up at her with a bemused expression. 'Well, you don't have to sound so unhappy about it.'

'I'm not. They'll love you.'

'But . . . ?' he prompted. 'What is it? They hate Americans?'

'No!'

'Well done. Good no. Forceful. Believable. Emphatic.'

She laughed, exhausted by his verbal games.

'Is it because no one could ever be good enough for their darling daughter? Are they those guys?'

'Maybe a bit,' she conceded.

'Relax. Parents love me.'

'Oh? Met many of your fiancées' parents, have you?' she asked archly.

It was his turn to laugh. 'You are the only fiancée I have ever had or ever intend to have.'

'Fiancée,' she repeated. 'It sounds funny even just hearing it.'

'Wait till we swap it for wife.' He kissed her tummy again, just once, lightly, as though a butterfly was landing on her, resting his head in one hand. 'Tell me, what are you more worried about – introducing them to me, or me to them?'

She bit her lip. 'You to them.'

He pulled a worried look. 'They don't have two heads, do they?'

'No!'

'Again, very good application of the no there.'

She smacked him lightly on the shoulder.

'It's all gonna be fine. They're gonna love me and I'm gonna love them. You know why I know?'

She shook her head.

'Because all three of us love you. It's really that simple.' He hauled himself up the bed again so that he was nose to nose with her. 'But I gotta meet your dad so I can do this right.'

She swallowed, feeling tears prick her eyes, the happiness beginning to overflow. 'You're going to ask him for my hand?'

'Ideally the rest of you too. But yeah, we'll start with the hand.' He took her hand and kissed it. 'Anything I should know before I go in?'

She opened her mouth to tell him her secret – not the one she had never told anyone, just the one she had never told him. But staring into his clear eyes, it didn't feel like the right time. For weeks now she had been waiting for just the right moment to tell him everything, the whole truth and not just a portion of it. But this moment was so pure, so joyous, she didn't want to sully it with anything crass, overwhelm him with background details that were nothing to do with the two of them.

She shook her head. 'Not really,' she demurred. 'Daddy's a sweetheart.'

'What's a safe topic to start on? Don't tell me, he's a golf man?'

'Actually, he's big on environmental issues, so I reckon you two will get on like a house on fire.'

'Yeah? Great,' Alex shrugged, looking pleased. 'So then, when can I meet him?'

Chapter Two

Pigeons pecked and strutted a few steps ahead of them in the sandy avenue of Hyde Park's North Ride, the early morning sun pale and bright as it streamed through the budding horse chestnut canopies. The first crocuses and primroses were already dotting the park with yellow and purple splashes like Monet brushstrokes, the background hum of London traffic on Bayswater Road superseded every few moments by the heavy, rhythmic breathing of runners overtaking them. The mornings were getting brighter, the frosts not quite so furious as they laced the grass.

Tara took another sip of her coffee, the steam swirling in the cold air. Holly was having her signature hot chocolate with whipped cream and chocolate sprinkles, the first of her many daily sugar hits.

'And what did he say then?' Tara asked, as Holly drew breath. Her friend was in the midst of a protracted breakup with Dev, a radiographer in Oncology. What had started as a drunken hook-up in the Irish bar just down from St Mary's hospital had become a more regular arrangement, and it had all been going well for several months till Dev had surprised her by clearing a drawer for her. Holly had reacted by walking out. Cue reams of anguished texts and some excellent make-up sex. The drawer had been hurriedly restuffed with mismatched sports socks and the tall can of athlete's foot spray, but the damage had been done – Dev wanted commitment, and Holly wanted out.

'He said I've got abandonment issues!'

'Huh.'

'I mean, please. I said to him, don't you push your clichés onto me. Not everyone whose mother walks out falls apart, you know. Some of us pull ourselves up by the bootstraps and do even fucking better than we would have done if she'd bloody stayed.'

'Quite.'

Holly muttered something unintelligible under her breath. 'I really mean it this time. I told him in no uncertain terms last night that we are done.'

'Your terms are never uncertain, Hols.'

'Right?' Holly asked indignantly.

'But you still slept with him?'

'Yeah, of course. He looked really sad. You know those puppy-dog eyes he gets . . .'

'I do. So cute.'

Holly sighed. 'But anyway, he knows that's it now. I can't be distracted by this kind of drama. I swear – no more men for me for a bit.'

'Good idea. Take some time out, let everything settle.'

Behind them, coming up the sandy path, the Household Cavalry was going through its drills, the clatter of brass breastplates and highly polished weaponry and the steady drumbeat of hooves drawing ever closer.

Tara took another sip of coffee as they turned down West Carriage Drive, heading for the rush-hour stampede along Kensington Gore.

'And I suppose you had another night of beautiful love-making with Pretty Boy?'

Tara grinned. 'Pretty much.'

'Ugh, you're nauseating. It's completely contemptible, all this unblemished happiness. And . . . and it's boring, actually. Where are the highs, if there are never any lows?'

'In bed,' Tara shrugged.

'Oh shut up! Come on, you've got to give me something – a chink in the armour. No one's life is this perfect.'

Tara thought for a moment. 'Well, he cooked me chicken risotto for dinner and if I'm being really honest . . . it was a little dry.'

Holly's lip curled. 'That's it? That's your chink?'

'Make way for the Blues and Royals!' The warning call from the Horse Master meant the cavalry was almost upon them now and they automatically moved out of the way, standing patiently on the sidelines as several hundred tonnes of glistening horses trotted past, the soldiers dressed in full regalia of shiny buttons and sharp spurs, red full-length cavalry coats, extravagant gold silky plumes swaying from their helmets. It was the same routine every morning, a part of their commute to lectures, but the thrill never diminished. This was also a wholly British thing – that and the torturous politeness Alex found so baffling – and a smile escaped her as she remembered his proposal last night. How a joke had turned into something profound and life-changing . . .

'What are you smiling about?' Holly asked, noticing how her friend was staring into space, biting down on the rim of her KeepCup. 'One of them tip you a wink, did they? Rascals!' she laughed as the soldiers passed by, stares dead ahead and impassive.

Tara turned to face her. 'Alex proposed last night.'

Holly's jaw dropped open. It was like watching a trapdoor fall. '. . . *What?*'

Tara nodded. 'I know, I can't believe it either. It was all such a surprise. For him too. He hadn't planned it.' Holly was staring at her, open-mouthed. Carefully, Tara pushed her friend's jaw back up again. 'Well, say something!'

'What the actual fuck?' The teasing quality in Holly's voice had disappeared and now reverberated, hollow with shock.

Tara hesitated. '. . . Say something else.'

'Tits!'

One of the gold plumes twitched in their direction. Tits was her friend's unique nickname for her, combined from her initials, TT, and not because she was especially well endowed. No one else called her by it – they didn't dare – and it was reserved for moments of either extreme happiness or extreme annoyance. From the look on Holly's face . . .

'He asked you to marry him?'

'Yes.'

'But you're *twenty*.'

'You make that sound like twelve.'

'It basically is.' They stared at one another, the moment becoming ever more awkward as Holly's lack of instinctive joy grew more apparent. She gave a short, hollow laugh as she realized it too. 'I mean . . . I'm happy for you, of course I am.'

Tara blinked at the weak lie. Her friend sounded like she was being strangled and even her distinctive fiery red cork-screw curls were beginning to look a little limp.

'A-and you . . . clearly fancy the pants off each other,' she stammered. 'And he makes you laugh. You're always laughing.'

Tara frowned. 'But?'

Holly's shoulders slumped. 'Why can't you wait? Even if you weren't going to be a child-bride, you've still only been together a few months.'

Tara could only shrug. 'Neither one of us ever planned on

17

getting married so young. I totally expected to be in my thirties, but it's turned out how they say in books – when you know, you know. Really, the question to us is – why wait?'

'Because you're *twenty*.'

'You said that already. I don't think our age is that big a deal,' Tara said calmly, but her heart was pounding. Holly's reaction had been completely unexpected. She had known it would be a shock – as it had been for her – but her friend's clear reservations about it, her inability to convincingly pretend that this was a good idea . . .

They walked in silence for a while, each lost in their own conflicted thoughts. 'And there you were, letting me bang on about *Dev*,' Holly muttered. She gave a little frown. 'How did he take it when you told him he's going to be Mr Tara Tremain? And don't tell me he's completely fine with it,' she said sternly. 'He might have that sexy, dishevelled vibe going on, but the guy's also got ego.'

Tara swallowed. 'Well, actually, I haven't told him that bit yet.'

'*Still?*' Holly's voice scaled up two octaves. 'I don't get it! What exactly are you waiting for?'

'The right time.'

Holly raised an eyebrow again. 'And that moment where the two of you decided to join your lives together for all eternity – that wasn't the right time?'

Tara winced. 'I know. I fumbled the bag, I should have told him then.'

'Duh!'

'It was just all happening so fast. I didn't want to . . . spoil the moment.'

'Yeah, because discovering your future father-in-law is actually a billionaire is what everyone calls having a bad day.'

Tara jogged her friend with her elbow just as Holly went to take another sip, so that a smudge of whipped cream moustached her top lip. 'I've told you before, it complicates things.' Although she'd never told Holly just how much. She preferred not to remember the time her best friend at boarding school had been selling stories about her to the press, or how the girls in her dorm had thought it funny to steal an item from her every day because 'she could afford it'; their own parents were well off too, of course, but the B-word still had a rare cachet even in those circles. 'It can overwhelm people – as I recall you didn't talk to me for three weeks when I told you.'

'That was very different. You lied by omission when I was clearly never out for anything from you.'

'You mean, apart from my stash of peanut butter, magnum of rosé and any fresh bread?'

'Excuse me, I was – *am* – a starving student.'

'And my favourite navy cashmere V-neck. You've still got that, by the way.'

Holly shrugged. 'Statute of limitations. It's mine now.'

'But it's my favourite!'

'Bite me, bitch.' Holly stared at her, that small characteristic glint in her eye, and Tara felt the momentary chill between them begin to thaw. 'Anyway, the boy's besotted. He's clearly not out for anything from you, except getting into your pants.'

'Except that,' Tara agreed, allowing herself a small smile. 'In a weird way, it's almost the fact that he's *so* uninterested in money that makes me worry about telling him. I mean, his parents were Californian hippies. He grew up on biodynamic farms and communes.'

'Christ. It's like they actively chased poverty!' Holly muttered, looking away.

They were almost at the Serpentine Bridge, the lake looking mercurial in the frigid temperatures, a couple of red-beaked black swans gliding towards the boathouses. The last of the early morning swimmers were ploughing rhythmically up and down the lido. They stopped to cross the road, waiting for a black cab to rumble past, its light on.

'But I know I can't keep putting it off. He was always going to have to meet my parents sooner or later, and it looks like it's going to be sooner. He says he wants to ask my father for my hand.'

'Huh. How old school.' Holly's tone had cooled again, disappointment butting at her, as though knocking her off balance.

'I know, it surprised me too.' Tara bit her lip distractedly as they walked across the bridge. 'But it'll be fine. He'll be fine with it. I'll just . . . mention it in passing tonight. I'm probably making it into a bigger deal than it actually is.'

'You think?' Holly quipped.

'I mean, maybe . . . maybe I don't even need to explicitly say anything about it at all? I could just . . . imply that we're—'

'Rich as Croesus?'

'I was going to say affluent.'

'No one says *affluent*. Apart from sociologists doing surveys.'

'Fine, then. Comfortable.'

Holly choked on the dregs of her drink. 'Comfortable? Well, so long as you get there *after* the helicopter's dropped your folks off, or *before* the chauffeur hops out of the Bentley, Alex will be none the wiser and then yeah, you can pretend to be . . . y'know, comfortable.'

Tara mouthed a silent, sarcastic *ha ha* at her friend's tease. Holly had been raised singlehandedly by her father on a school caretaker's income after her mother had walked out when she was four. For some reason, this entitled her to unlimited sarcasm any time the subject of money (or more specifically, fortunes) came up.

Holly sighed, as if sensing the cruelty in her jibes. 'Listen, if that boy doesn't accept you as you are – private jets and all – then he isn't worth holding on to anyway. But I doubt it's going to be a problem.' She gave a small mocking laugh. 'He'll probably be on a mission to impregnate you straight away to seal the deal.'

Tara stopped walking.

Holly looked back, a look of regret already plastered all over her face. 'Too much?' She took in Tara's look of horror. 'Sorry.' She gripped a hand through her red hair and angled her face to the sky. She looked strained and tense. 'That was a shitty thing to say. You've just got me . . . jangled, that's all. I'm misfiring arrows.'

But Tara's feet wouldn't move. Her mouth wouldn't close.

'Look, you know I didn't mean it,' Holly said, walking back to her and placing a hand on her arm. 'He's a good bloke. Of course that's not what he'll do.' She arched an eyebrow. 'I mean, like you'd let him anyway! No chance! You're not going to fuck your life up doing something *that* stupid—'

For the first time, she saw the tears shining in Tara's eyes. Her face fell. 'Ta, oh please . . . don't look like that. I didn't mean . . .' But something in the way Tara was standing, the rigidity in her shoulders . . . Her gaze fell to Tara's hand, placed instinctively over her stomach. Slowly, she looked up at her, open-mouthed. 'Oh no,' she whispered.

Tara tensed further, bracing for the next onslaught. For the past twelve days, since she'd taken the test, she'd vacillated between joy and despair, clarity and confusion – until Alex's pledges last night. Without even realizing, he'd pushed aside her doubts and talked her into keeping the baby. Clearly, this wasn't the path she'd set for herself, but she had somehow persuaded herself it meant a deferral, not an abandonment, of her plans. As he'd slept beside her, she had lain awake growing ever more convinced that this was what she wanted, that she could make it work, so that when she'd woken this morning, she'd been so excited to finally share her news with her best friend. Now, instead, she waited for the words to come . . . *But you're twenty.*

None came. Not immediately. A silence stretched between them, Holly's eyes swimming with emotions that for once – for the first time ever – she wasn't articulating. The silence was worse than any harsh rebuke. Tara felt it was like watching a rainstorm sweeping over distant fields, seeing it coming her way, knowing that she couldn't outrun it.

'So what about this?' Holly asked quietly, carefully, her arm sweeping in an arc around them, gesticulating to the park but meaning London, their medical degrees, their lives here.

'Well,' Tara said slowly. 'I've been thinking it all through and I'm going to take a sabbatical after our summer exams. The timing will work quite well. I'll be seven months along by then. I can rest up for the last few weeks before the birth and then come back in September next year.'

'But you won't.' Holly's voice was abrupt, her tone flat, the words final.

'Hols, I will.'

'You're telling me you're going to go straight from months without sleep, into night shifts, ward rounds, fifteen hours on your feet?'

Tara swallowed. 'Yes.'

'No. It's not gonna happen. Face facts – this is an either-or situation. If you have this baby, then you can't have that career. It demands too much of you. You can't have both, no one can.'

'That's not true. Plenty of women are doctors and mothers.'

'Not at twenty they're not.'

There they were – the words that repeated again and again why this was all wrong. Doomed to failure. A disaster of epic proportions.

'. . . Five years down the line – fine, if that's your bag. But you're not even out of the starters' block.' Holly stared at her flatly. 'What does Alex say about it?'

Tara could hardly bear to see the disappointment in her friend's eyes; she couldn't think of the counter-arguments she had rehearsed in her head. She hesitated. 'He doesn't know yet.'

'Fucking hell, Ta!' In a flash, Holly sounded angry. 'So you've agreed to marry the guy but he doesn't know who you really are, *or* that you're pregnant with his kid?'

Tara felt panicked. Everything was going wrong. She hadn't imagined it going like this. Surprise, yes, but then hugs, excited squeals, a rush of plans. 'I didn't know he was going to propose!' she replied defensively. 'I told you, it all just happened on the spur of the moment. I'd been building up to telling him about the baby last night, but then when he asked me to marry him . . . it was sort of a joke, but then *not* . . . I worried that telling him I was pregnant too, there and then, might have made it feel a bit . . . shotgun?'

'But he asked you without knowing about the pregnancy,' Holly said flatly. 'Ta, you are making this harder than it needs to be and you should be asking yourself why. Either you trust the guy or you don't.'

'I do! There's no question of it.'

'Then stop keeping secrets from him! These are things he deserves to know!'

Tara's shoulders slumped. It was all true. 'You're right. I'll tell him about the family tonight and the baby later in the week.'

'What's wrong with doing it all tonight? He's about to find out his future parents-in-law are billionaires. You may as well throw imminent fatherhood into the mix as well.'

'No, I . . . I want to be sure he's marrying me because he loves me, not because he feels trapped by me.'

'So you don't trust him.'

'I do! It's just . . .' She felt exasperated. 'Ugh. I know it's hard to understand but I just instinctively feel I need to deal with one thing at a time – my family isn't normal, no matter how much I wish it was. It'll be a shock for him to find out who we are. He should meet my parents first and have the big chat with my dad. Get that done and out of the way. Then we can deal with the rest.'

Holly leaned on the railings, her gaze on the parked-up pedalos on the opposite shore. She was biting her lip, looking pale.

Tara took her arm gently. 'Please be happy for me, Hols. You're the only person I've told.'

Holly looked back at her. 'I want to be, really I do. But how can I lie when I think you're making the biggest mistake of your life? What sort of friend would I be?'

'You could be a lying friend.'

Holly turned to face her. 'No, I can't be that. You're being naive about what this will mean for you. Getting married's one thing – I think you're mad to be committing the rest of your life to this guy you just met when you haven't even properly left home yet! – but hey, it's reversible. Things don't work out, you get a divorce, carry on.' She shook her head. 'But you can't do that with a baby. This is a deal-breaker. You're going to have to give up the one thing that you said defines you.' Holly leaned closer to her now. 'When we first met, you told me medicine was your way to give back *and* be separate from your family.

24

You said it gave you purpose and that it's all you've ever wanted to do since you were six. You never once said you wanted to be married with a kid at twenty-one.' She paused to draw breath. 'Alex is cute – but, Ta, no one's *that* cute.'

Tara felt her stomach swoop and fall at her friend's brutal frankness. It was everything she had told herself since that dark blue line had shown up on the pregnancy stick; all her own doubts voiced.

'You had that plan, remember? You wanted to get your dad to help you build those mother and child health clinics in every country that had communities living off grid – no power, no running water. You said if you could protect and empower the women—'

'I know what I said,' Tara interrupted, not wanting to hear it.

Holly stared at her with a look of sadness. 'Coming from anyone else, it was pie in the sky. But you? You actually could have done it! You told me it was your way of justifying being so lucky; you said your mother couldn't understand why you'd want a career and that you had to fight to get them to allow you to go to uni at all. And now you're just giving all that up for a guy you've known for less than six months?'

Tears pricked at Tara's eyes. She felt there was a weight pressing on her chest. 'We love each other.' It was a feeble argument, but all she could muster. She could feel Holly already withdrawing from her, as if they were two boats on separate tides, and she realized how much they had been bonded by their mutual ambition: the princess and the pauper who both wanted the same thing.

'Yes, I know you do. But just answer me this – is he giving up everything for you? *Would* he be giving up his dreams, and his career, for you?'

Every question was like a body blow. Tara was struggling

to keep a lid on her emotions. 'Look, all of this will change *both* our lives, not just mine. It's just happening sooner than we had thought . . .'

It wasn't an answer. She knew it. Holly knew it.

'Oh, so you'd discussed starting a family, then?'

'Well, no, not yet, but—'

'But . . . ?'

Tara swallowed. 'It was . . . understood.'

Holly's eyes narrowed. 'Understood. Right.'

Tara looked down, feeling the first tear fall. It made her furious to be crying, as though this was the first sign of her disintegration into someone lesser – evidence of her changing hormones and new life path. 'Life doesn't always run to a timetable, Hols.'

Holly sighed as a sob escaped her; she could never bear to see anyone upset. She stepped in and roughly gave Tara a hug. 'No, I know it doesn't.' They embraced in the morning chill, but it was awkward and stiff, neither one of them finding resolution in the rapprochement. 'But – oh shit! That anatomy module does – and . . .' She pulled back sharply and double-checked the time on her phone. 'I'm going to be late. I've gotta run.'

'Oh God!' Tara automatically went to jog beside her too, but Holly stopped her with an outstretched arm.

'No, don't run, you should take it easy. I'll tell them you got delayed en route.'

'But—'

'You mustn't exert yourself now. And anyway, you'll only be a few minutes behind me. I'll save you a seat.' She gave a shrug as she sped off, but Tara knew what that shrug meant: what did it matter now, how late she was? She was never going to be a doctor. Anything done after this point was just lip service to a dream she had tossed aside. She was going to be Mrs Alex Carter instead. Wife and mother.

Chapter Three

The front door closed with a slam, followed a second later by the thud of a bulging leather satchel hitting the encaustic-tiled hall floor.

'God, that smells good!' Alex came through and planted a kiss in the curve of her neck and shoulder. His nook, he called it. She turned her face towards him and he kissed her on the mouth. 'I missed you.'

'I missed you too,' she murmured, and she felt him hesitate, knowing that to kiss her again would inevitably lead . . .

He pulled back, indecision in his eyes, the vestiges of his working day still clinging to him like sticky buds. 'Man, what a day.' He tossed his jacket over the back of the chair and walked across the small kitchen. It was a perfect square, with eighties orange pine cabinets and white ceramic knobs. The splashback tiles were decorated with hens – incongruous for a kitchen in Kensington – and four rushback chairs were set round a small painted table that had once been turquoise but was now white, with just flecks of the old colour peeping through in places. Even stressed, Alex looked horizontally relaxed in his rumpled shirt, sleeves rolled up to the elbows and jeans that hung low on his hips.

'Busy one?' she asked as he pulled a bottle of wine from the fridge. The cork had been replaced at a jaunty angle after he'd opened it at dinner last night. It released again with a soft pop.

He sighed. 'No, just . . . frustrating. MacLennan's paper got picked up by *Proceedings* so he's been strutting about all day like the cock he is—'

Proceedings was the Royal Society's flagship publication and was to him what *The Lancet* was to her.

'He reckons it'll get the attention of that donor he's been chasing and finally some—' He rubbed his fingers together, meaning money. Funding.

'Ah.' There was no love lost between her boyfriend – fiancé! she corrected herself – and James MacLennan, the other PhD student in their department. Though Alex was brilliant – gifted, passionate and instinctive about his work – his rise through academia had been unorthodox. His love of biology had started in the fields of the farms and communes they lived on as his family travelled through the Golden State and he'd been entirely home-schooled, with no formal qualifications whatsoever. He had been seventeen when a botanist visiting the farm they were living on at the time offered Alex the chance to assist him on a research trip to Honduras in Central America. Six weeks had turned into five years as his carefree childhood quickly found a focus in the field. From Honduras, he went on to Nicaragua, Brazil and Costa Rica, at one point studying only twenty miles from where Tara and her family had holidayed every year since she was a little girl. Along the way he became an expert on tropical forest habitats, and particularly on the effect of species decline on biodiversity. He had made a chance comment – on the abundance and range of butterflies in a given area as a marker of biodiversity health – to a professor, Robert Hamlyn, whom he'd met while changing a flat tyre on a jungle road on the way back to San José. Hamlyn was on his way home from an expedition for Imperial College London and, intrigued by Alex's observation, had eventually invited him to study for a doctorate there, without even a bachelor's degree to his name. Hamlyn had even offered to oversee his research.

It was the unorthodox nature of Alex's induction into the world of academia that rankled with James MacLennan and made him such a thorn in Alex's side. As James saw it, he had grafted and gained access to Hamlyn's inner sanctum the hard way – picking up degrees first at Edinburgh and then Cambridge – whilst the 'American hipster' had simply curried favour to get there.

'Here.' Alex held out a glass of wine for her.

'Oh. I've already got a drink.' She reached for her glass of Purdey's. 'Sorry.'

'So you don't want it?'

'No. I'll have another night off tonight, I think. More tests coming up. I need to keep a clear head.'

'Okay.' And he sank her glass whilst still holding his own.

She watched, seeing anger still in his movements. He definitely looked wired, his eyes a bit too bright, and she knew he'd had a tough day. He never moaned, not really, but he often struggled with the politics of academia; it frustrated him, a self-titled 'farm boy' who just wanted to leave the world a better place than he had found it. He didn't engage in power plays, didn't care which of them Hamlyn bought a coffee for. Tara had never met anyone with more passion to learn, act and make a difference – not even Holly could match him for drive – and it was one of the things she loved most about him. But she was beginning to sense it wouldn't always make him easy to live with. There was still so much they had to learn about one another, and a tiny voice in her head wondered if Holly been right. Were they rushing into this? Was it all far too much, far too soon?

He caught her watching him as he drained his own glass too – a very tough day, then – and he startled, as if embarrassed, remembering himself. He leaned forward to kiss her again, his lips soft against hers, tasting now of Chablis. She felt his tongue lightly against her lips and her stomach fluttered, butterfly-like, in response. It was always so easy to fall into one another. A default option. Their 'factory settings', he had joked once.

She put her hand on his chest, pushing him away lightly. 'Why don't you go and have a shower? Unwind a bit. This'll be ready in five.'

His smile was grateful. 'Thanks, baby. I just need to . . .' He gave a shudder as though trying to physically cast off the day's tests. He was trying so hard to be his usual loving self, but he was as tightly wound as a spring.

'I know.'

He kissed her once more lightly, before walking through to the bedroom at the back. She watched him go, loving the breadth of his shoulders, the narrowness of his hips. He was always so unaware of the physical impression he made – growing up without TV or internet meant he had no interest in how he looked; good or bad, it was all the same to him – and Tara was pretty sure part of James MacLennan's rancour towards him was thwarted lust. Alex Carter had the charisma to make anyone fall in love with him: man, woman, young, old.

The extractor fan had stopped working at some point in the noughties, and she opened the window to let the steam escape as the steak sizzled on the heat, pausing a moment to glance over the patchwork of gardens below. A wooden swing with red abacus beads hung limply from the branch of a crab apple tree in the garden opposite theirs; Bumpy, the cockapoo two houses up, was racing around the small garden in frenzied loops; a grey squirrel leaped from the branch of a horse chestnut to a silver birch, straddling No. 24 and No. 26 Tor Gardens in one graceful jump. She gave a small smile. The Sumatran rainforest it might not be, but they still had a mini paradise outside their window.

She caught herself. *Their* window. So would she move in here with him, then? They hadn't discussed specifics yet, but that was the intimation. The flat she shared a mile and a half away in Bayswater with Holly was a study in student grot. It looked onto a laundrette at the front and the bins of the Chinese restaurant at the back, and she was woken every morning by the dawn delivery lorry to the Polish store four numbers down. There was mildew in the shower, the kitchen sink was stained, the tap leaked – dripping noisily all day and night – and the cracks in the walls seemed more substantial than 'settlement' to her eye. Nonetheless, it had been her choice to live there and, in an odd way, she loved it. She and Holly had chosen it together, before Tara had admitted the truth about her family's wealth, and it was all Holly could afford. Once she did find out, Holly had spent a year alternately pleading with her not to 'sacrifice herself' to their subpar accommodation and berating Tara for not having come clean earlier and put them up in a Hyde Park penthouse. She had been fully incredulous at Tara's insistence that she *wanted* to be there. That she *liked* being normal.

Alex's flat – a grace-and-favour residence in the gift of the university – was still tiny but it had two bedrooms at least (although one was so small she was certain she'd received bigger Amazon boxes) and it came up well after a clean. But perhaps they would get somewhere new, somewhere they would start afresh as a family?

Her hands fell to her tummy again – a fresh habit. She smoothed it tenderly, still so flat. She wasn't showing at all although her breasts were more tender and the nausea was beginning to steadily dial up. Alex hadn't noticed yet that she'd found excuses not to drink alcohol for the past couple of weeks – a test the next day, a headache – but he soon would. He had an eye for detail, and she felt a twinge of guilt to be keeping it a secret from him still. It felt like a deception somehow, almost a theft, but Holly's reaction that morning had startled her. There was no guarantee he would take the news of imminent parenthood well and she had to be prepared for another bad response. She had to judge the right moment to tell him.

She was dressing the salad when Alex came back a few minutes later, towelling his wet hair and wearing just his jeans – the cold never bothered him – his t-shirt tucked into the waistband and hanging down like a window-washer's rag. Everything hung loosely on him, his body spare, lean and finely muscled, though he never worked out. He was just active.

She relaxed under his touch as he kissed her in the crook of her neck again – his place. 'Let's try again,' he murmured, taking the salad servers out of her hands and turning her towards him. 'Hello, love of my life.' He smoothed her long dark hair off her pale face. 'You look especially beautiful today.'

She smiled, feeling the day's tension begin to rise off her too. 'Hello. You're not too shabby either. Had a good day?'

'Excellent. I spent it thinking up ways to impress my future parents-in-law.' He arched an eyebrow, looking pleased with himself.

'Intriguing. And what did you come up with?'

'Well, you said your father was big on environmental issues, right?'

She nodded.

'I'm thinking a trip to the Aquarium? I know a guy who works there. He could get us in after closing time, take us around the tanks round the back, show us their protection and breeding programmes in place? Then I thought drinks at . . .' He wrinkled his nose. 'Well, not sure on that bit yet, but somewhere fancy. And then dinner at this new Korean place in Notting Hill Gate, they've got a pioneering recycling scheme which, if that's his thing—'

Tara laughed. 'You're a nut! Alex, you don't need to do anything fancy to impress my parents. They'll love you. How could they not?'

'Uh-uh. Fathers-in-law are different. They never like the guy who's taking away their little princess.'

'My dad isn't like most other dads.'

'Said every girl ever.'

'No, I mean it. We're . . . not like other people.'

'Ha! Say that after you've met my folks!' He clasped her face with his hands, kissing her tenderly, blocking out the world. 'Another Purdey's?' He picked up her empty glass and waggled it in his hand.

She smiled weakly, knowing she'd just missed a chance to tell him. Why couldn't she just say it? *You either trust him or you don't.* 'Lovely.'

She plated up the steak and took it, with the salad, to the table. She sat as he poured them fresh drinks. He came and sat opposite her, his knees touching hers under the table as he tonged the salad onto her plate. 'So tell me what you've told them about me.' He paused. 'You have told them about me, haven't you?'

'Of course! They know that your name's Alex, that you're American, twenty-three years old, a PhD biology student at Imperial.' She shrugged. 'Uh . . . yeah. That's pretty much it.'

'That's *it*? That's the sum total of what they know about me?'

'I—' Her mouth opened, looking for excuses. 'I don't like giving them too much detail early on! We've only been together a few months, after all, and trust me, my mother would need no encouragement to start planning a wedding. She's been waiting since the day I turned eighteen. No, scratch that, twelve.'

'Hmm. So then it sounds like it's your mother I need to get on side.' He cast a sidelong glance, winking at her and making her stomach somersault. Just like that.

'She actually cried – not tears of pride, mind you – when I told her I was going to be a doctor, can you believe that?'

He considered for a moment, a morsel of medium-rare steak perched on the tines of his fork. 'No. That is odd.'

She leaned in towards him. 'So what have you told your parents about me?'

'That you're a stone-cold fox, shit-hot at anatomy.' He winked at her. 'And that once you're a doctor and I'm a professor, our letters are going to look really cool on the doormat.'

She felt her smile falter as Holly's predictions continued to echo through her mind. Was she right? Would it really be too hard for her to pick up the reins a year from now and continue on with her dream?

He noticed her absent look and gave her a quizzical look. 'You okay? You're a little pale.'

'Mm-hmm,' she nodded, knowing that now was the time to tell him. She had to do it before the moment slipped away again, a silk scarf in the wind. 'But actually, there is something I've been wanting to tell you. For a while, actually.'

'Sounds ominous.'

'No, it's nothing bad. I'm just . . . not sure how you're going to take it.'

'You're not already married, are you?' He looked around the room mock-apprehensively, as though he expected someone to leap from the larder.

'No, I'm not married; I'm just . . . rich.'

His apparent confusion deepened. '. . . You're *rich*?' He looked sceptical and she knew she looked anything but in her vintage jeans and Zara jumper; that was partly the point, after all.

'Yes, I'm afraid so.'

He stared at her, a long silence opening up. 'Sorry, I'm not getting why . . . why's that a thing?'

She felt her cheeks redden. 'It's just the stuff that comes with it, that's all. It can be overwhelming.'

A light came into his eyes. 'What, you mean the jets, the yachts, having to remember which clothes are in which homes . . . ?'

He had been joking, but she nodded. 'Exactly.'

'Oh!' His smile faded as he ran a hand through his hair. His forehead was two shades lighter than the rest of his face, his fringe always flopping down over it. 'Okay, so then you're rich,' he said finally. 'But what's it got to do with *us*?'

She gave a relieved laugh, putting her hand over his on the table. It was the perfect response. 'Nothing. Exactly, nothing.' She wanted to cry with relief. 'It's got nothing to do with us at all. I try to . . . pretend it's not even there, as much as I can. I just want to live my life and be me and be liked and loved for who I am and not because my family's got money.' The words came out in a jumbled rush.

'Okay.' Alex still looked baffled. He took another sip – gulp, actually – of his wine. 'But you were nervous about telling me because . . . ?'

'I was worried you'd feel I'd lied to you – by omission, I mean. We've been together four months now and things have moved pretty fast between us. Clearly. I know I should have brought it up before now but I just didn't . . .'

His eyes narrowed as he watched her. 'Trust me?'

'No! Of course I trust *you*.'

'So then . . . ?'

She sighed. It was always so hard to explain. For all those with not enough – which was almost everyone – they didn't want to hear that wealth could be a burden. 'Look, I've been raised in a certain way which means not trusting anyone, at first. As kids, my brother and I had to have security because of the kidnap risk.'

'Kidnap?' He looked shocked. 'Jesus, just how rich are you?'

'*I'm* not anything. It's all in trust till I'm thirty. Like I said, I try to live as normally as possible, and just be like everyone else. Which is why I never said anything before. But now that we're engaged and you're going to meet my family . . . well, it's a big thing not to mention. I didn't want you to meet them unprepared and feel ambushed.'

'Ambushed,' he echoed, looking exactly that.

'Alex, I hate even having to talk about it, making it a thing. I just don't want it to change things between us.'

He looked at her sharply, offended. 'Why would it change things between us? You think I'm impressed by money?'

'Of course not. What I meant was, everything's been so perfect between us, I just didn't want to change a single thing.'

'In case with one turn of the dial we fall apart?'

She shook her head quickly. 'I don't want to take any chances of losing you. My family's rich. So what? Everything goes on just as it has been for us.'

He looked into her eyes, and then away again. 'But that's naive, isn't it? What about your engagement ring? I'm a student, I can't afford some massive rock.'

'I don't want a massive rock! I want you.'

'But your parents—'

'Aren't impressed by material things. Believe me. If there's one thing they know, it's the value of people and experiences over things. They only want to see that we love each other. That's it.' She picked up his hand from the table and kissed the back of it, staring deep into his eyes. 'They're going to love you. As I do.'

He was quiet for several moments, digesting the revelation. 'Well, not *exactly* as you do, I hope.' A glimmer of amusement made his eyes sparkle. 'That really could be awkward over breakfast.'

She burst out laughing. 'You're incorrigible!'

He grinned too and she felt the low-grade tension that had pulled between them for a few moments slacken again. It was done at last. He knew! He knew and he didn't care.

'Incorrigible, yes,' he agreed, lifting his arm up so that, holding his hand, she rose to standing. He pushed his chair back and pulled her towards him. 'Also indefatigable. And inescapable.' He pushed his knees between her legs. 'And, when it comes to you, Twig Tremain,' he murmured, pulling her down onto his lap so that she was straddling him. 'I am most definitely . . . insatiable.'

Chapter Four

Tara peered through the crack in the door. A riot of *stuff* met her eyes – ski medals were hanging on ribbons from hooks and mirrors, a jug-eared silver trophy for eventing was on the bookcase. None of the books had ever been read, or even opened, the spines completely uncreased and as smooth as marble. A small suitcase was open on the floor, half-packed with clothes that had been precision-folded. A wet towel and yesterday's Calvin Klein boxers were strewn on the floor.

Her little brother Miles was lying on the bed on his stomach, wearing a pair of jeans and a striped shirt wrongly buttoned up. He was watching something on his laptop, the sounds coming from it dubious enough that she felt impelled to give a little cough before entering.

The screen was slammed down and he twisted onto his side as she came in.

'Ah, so you're in here,' she said breezily, seeing it was safe to enter. 'Why am I not surprised?'

He rested his head in his hand as she came in and jumped on the slouchy sofa opposite, putting her feet up on the arm, legs crossed at the ankles. 'What's brought you back so soon?' he frowned. 'Weren't you only here two months ago?'

'Haha. Nice. Good to see you too.'

'You really need to send over an up-to-date photo before these visits, so that we can recognize you. Wouldn't want Tamba thinking you're an intruder. Those are some sharp incisors she's got.'

She tossed a scatter cushion at him. 'All right! Point made. But I have been busy, you know. Medical degrees don't just earn themselves. And anyway, it's not like you've been around much.'

'I've been back two and a half weeks.'

She was surprised. 'Really?' Term dates, once the pin around which her entire life pivoted, had ceased to register the moment she left school.

He shrugged, reaching his arm for a rugby ball that was, randomly, on the pillows. He fell onto his back and began lackadaisically tossing it in the air. What was it about boys and balls, she wondered? They simply couldn't leave them alone.

'So, is it all going okay at school?' she asked.

'S'pose, if you don't include my mocks.'

'Tough, huh?'

He looked across at her. 'Put it this way – there's only gonna be one doctor in this family.'

'Oh good – well, Mum will be pleased.'

He had to chuckle at that. 'Yeah. I'll do what you won't and find me a good man and settle down. Only I don't think that would please her either!'

They both laughed. Miles had come out a year earlier, although Tara (and her father, she suspected) had always known. 'Poor Mum,' she grinned. 'Having such problem kids.'

'Have you seen them?'

'Not yet. Mum's having her hair done and Dad was on a call when I arrived.'

'Surprise of the century.' Miles threw the ball so high into the air it almost touched the ceiling rose – an intricate froth of Regency plasterwork that she'd barely ever noticed.

She squinted at it for a moment, then looked around the room, trying to see it with fresh eyes, trying to understand what Alex would see when he arrived here in an hour's time.

This had been home for most of her life. They had lived in the Mayfair townhouse for thirteen years, upgrading from the Virginia Water mansion when her father had sold his pharmaceuticals business and made his second fortune. The building was reasonably understated from the kerb – handsome but muted, built in red brick with a super-glossy black door and a cloud of box balls neatly arranged in a parterre out front. Inside, though, was a different matter. Marble floors, grand chandeliers that weighed as much as a small car, and Ionic columns testified to the historic grandeur of the house, and the roll-call of former residents read like a Who's Who of London power players, including former prime ministers, Napoleonic-era ambassadors, a Nobel Prize-winning scientist and the scandalous mistress of King Edward VII.

Miles's room was much like any other eighteen-year-old boy's, with empty beer bottles proudly stacked in a pyramid in the empty fire grate and a Chelsea poster stuck to the walls, slightly off plumb. Mrs Titchenor, their housekeeper, was under strict instructions to leave Miles's room 'as is' and not to tidy or clean in there more than once a day. 'Teenage boys need some chaos,' her father had proclaimed, although it was impossible to imagine him ever having been a chaotic teen. Nonetheless, it was still a room bigger than her entire Bayswater flat, with deep coving, highly polished oak parquet and an eighteenth-century statuary marble fireplace, and it occurred to Tara now that for a man who'd grown up hobo-style on farms throughout Southern California, this might be something of a shock.

Perhaps they ought to have gone out for the first meeting after all. Neutral ground would put Alex more at ease, surely? It wasn't like it was going to be a relaxing experience for him, asking her father for her hand, moments after they met. *Here*.

But it was Alex who had insisted. 'I want to know your life – warts and all,' he had joked, and she knew she couldn't hide this from him. At some point he would have to come face to face with the reality of her background; better to get it over and done with early. She wasn't good with secrets.

'So why *are* you here?' Miles asked curiously, watching her scan the room. 'Marge is insisting I wear a collared shirt.'

She looked back at him, knowing her brother already suspected more than just a meet and greet. He had good instincts – about people as well as situations.

'So that you can all meet my new boyfriend, Alex.'

'How new?'

'Four months, thereabouts.'

'Box-fresh, then. Is there much point?' he groaned. 'Surely he's not going to last another four with you. Any minute now he's going to know what I've been saying for years: that you're an uptight goody two-shoes who wouldn't know a good time if it hit you in the—'

'Oi!' She threw a cushion that hit *him* in the face.

Miles laughed. 'Where is he, anyway?'

'Arriving shortly. He had some things to finish at work first. And I wanted to get here beforehand and warn you to *be nice*.'

'Why? Is he fragile?'

'Yes, actually, he's precious – to me. And I don't want you scaring him off.'

'Me? Scare him off? I think you're overestimating my powers.'

'He's an impoverished student. Doing a biology PhD at Imperial. *This*' – her hands vaguely gesticulated around the grand room – 'isn't his bag.'

Miles looked bemused, still tossing the ball rhythmically above his head. 'So we've got to pretend we *don't* live here?'

'Just tone everything down. Don't mention the boat, the cars, definitely not the plane. Not the houses.'

'What? Not even Gstaad?' he pouted, taking the mickey.

'Nothing,' she said in her best warning voice. 'Nada. Zip.'

He gave a dramatic sigh. 'This will be *so* dull.'

'Actually I can guarantee you're going to love him. He's incredibly handsome and he's got a very dry sense of humour.'

'Hmph, well, that's the oldies' needs covered. But I still don't see what's in there for me.'

Tara smiled. 'He's a die-hard Chelsea fan.'

'I thought Mum said he's a Yank?'

'Californian, actually. But he got taken to Stamford Bridge his first week in London and he's been a True Blue ever since.'

'Yeah? What's his view on Drogba?'

'I don't know. Probably that he's a god or something?' she shrugged.

'Like, duh! No one can touch him for pace, power and skill on the ball.'

'Yeah. That's what he said,' she fibbed. She had never had a conversation about Chelsea with Alex, other than to mention in passing that her brother was a fan – there were far more fun things they could be doing – but if it brought Miles onside . . . Holly thought *she* was reserved with new people, but Miles could be positively hostile. Her hard time at school had been nothing compared to his – the only boy who'd received more tackles on the rugby pitch had been the son of the exiled prince of Greece.

He sat up. 'What time's he getting here?'

She grinned and checked her phone. 'Twenty minutes or so.' She took her feet off the sofa and stood up. 'So I'd better check in with Mum, at least. Do you know who Dad's on the phone to? Can I look in?'

'Gerard.'

'Oh,' she groaned. 'Better leave it then.' Gerard was their father's investment manager and as such almost the third wheel in their parents' marriage. 'I'll go see Mum. But come down when you hear Alex get here . . . and remember what I said.' She brought a finger to her lips.

'I know, I know. We're humble peasant farmers and all this is a figment of our hallucinatory imaginations.'

She went down the hall, chuckling to herself.

Her parents' suite was on the next level up and took over the entire floor, her progress along the corridors silent as she walked over the plush mohair ivory carpet.

'Hey, Marie,' she smiled as she passed the young assistant housekeeper on the stairs. 'How's Jack getting on?'

Marie straightened up from sweeping the treads to allow her to pass. 'So well, Miss Tara. He is top in his class for fractions.'

'Oh that's amazing, I'm so pleased! Tell him congratulations from me,' she beamed as she carried on up the stairs.

Her parents' rooms were roughly divided into his and hers sides with a drawing room connecting them in the middle. Her father had the east side, on account of being an early riser; her mother the west, for the flattering evening light when her make-up was being applied. Tara knocked on the door at her mother's side, already able to hear her voice over the sound of the hairdryer, and peeked her head around. 'Hey, Mumma.'

'Tara, darling!' Her mother, arms outstretched, remained seated in her hairdresser's chair as Jakob, her stylist, did some backcombing with a fine comb. 'Come here, let me see you.'

Tara walked in, aware that her midnight needlecord flares and pretty new H&M blouse looked woefully undercooked beside her mother's Valentino. 'You need a haircut, darling. Doesn't she need a haircut, Jakob?'

Jakob – who was to her mother what Gerard was to her father – nodded. 'I could take three inches off and it would freshen you up, like that.' He snapped his fingers together.

Idly Tara threaded her long dark hair through her fingers. She supposed it had grown too long. She'd not bothered with her 'maintenance' as her mother called it, for months. She had even taken to shaving her legs in the shower each morning, something that would no doubt put her mother in a full swoon.

'Let me see you. I feel I haven't seen you in so long. Have you lost weight?'

Tara felt her nerves flutter under her mother's close scrutiny. 'I'm not sure. I don't think so.'

'Hear that, Jakob? She doesn't *think* so.' Her mother tutted. 'Youth's fast metabolism is wasted on the young.'

Tara went and perched on her mother's dressing table. It was pale pink onyx, underlit, and decorated with a few black-and-white photos in silver frames; a bespoke bottle of perfume, made by a Nose in Florence and enclosed in a commissioned crystal bottle, sat to one side.

Tara picked up the bottle and began fiddling with it. Now that she was here, she felt an overwhelming urge to reveal her happy secrets, as though they were birds inside her that she needed to set free. Her mother had always struggled to understand her, it was true; Tara's nature was far more akin to her father's, but that didn't mean she didn't value or seek her mother's opinion, and she knew news of her engagement would surely delight her mother. It would be everything she'd been waiting for, a return to the path her mother had mapped out for her . . . Was that why she felt so nervous about it, too? Was it confirmation that Holly had been right – that she was turning her back on her dreams?

She felt another stab of nerves, her stomach pitching and swooping in anticipation of the ride tonight was going to bring. 'How was Milan?' she asked instead, knowing she had to allow Alex to take the lead on this. He had specifically asked for it.

'Milan was Milan,' her mother sighed happily. 'I can't believe we'd left it so long. Songs at La Scala, dinner with the Sevezzas. It was so good to see them. Did I mention their daughter's getting married?'

'A few times, yes.'

'Lovely girl. Lives in New York now. She's on the Met Ball Committee this year, does a lot for the homeless. Her fiancé's a prince, although that doesn't count for much of course, they're ten a penny over there; but he's high up at Cazenove.'

'Always helpful.'

Her mother must have caught her wry tone because she gave her a look. 'Of course, we're tremendously pleased to be meeting your new beau too, dear.'

'Mumma, no one in the world has a beau anymore. And Alex is looking forward to meeting you too. But as I've just said to Miles, can we please keep the . . .' She circled her hands in the air vaguely. 'To a minimum.'

'What's . . . ?' her mother asked, also circling her hands in the air and almost taking Jakob's eye out with her cushion-cut pink diamond ring.

'You know perfectly well. He's a student like me. He doesn't have any money. It's going to be daunting enough for him coming here to meet you, without . . .' She circled her hands again. 'Too.'

Her mother sighed. 'Fine,' she said disappointedly, and Tara suspected she was thinking that Senora Sevezza hadn't had to tone things down for her daughter's prince. 'So tell me about him. What are his interests?'

Tara felt her smile grow. Just to get to talk about him made her feel happy. 'Well, his big love is butterflies.'

There was a long silence. Even Jakob's eyebrows shot up, his hands momentarily stilled above her mother's head.

'Butterflies?'

'Yes.' She rolled her eyes, knowing exactly what her mother was thinking. 'Don't worry, he's not interested in them because they're *pretty*. They are excellent indicators of the health of any given ecosystem and a predictor of the biodiversity that is likely to be found there. The future of this planet rests on flourishing biodiversity, Mumma. It's actually cutting-edge stuff.'

'*Butterflies?*' her mother repeated.

Tara sighed. 'Anyway, I'll leave him to explain it to you. He makes it sound much more interesting than I can.'

'I don't see how.' Her mother's eyes narrowed interestedly. 'Still, you must really like him to be introducing him to us.' For all her social flightiness, she could still drill down to the nub of a matter more succinctly than any other person Tara knew. Years of tolerating sycophants had taught her how to read people and know whom to trust; if she was her father's daughter, Miles was his mother's son.

'I do.' Tara felt the secret bubble in her throat again – she wanted to shout it out and swallow it down all at once; it was the same curious feeling she'd had as a little girl when she would laugh so hard, she'd tip over into crying, her body confused about what her mind felt.

'He's only the second boy you've ever brought home to us.'

'I'm not sure the prom date even counts, does he?'

'Well, I still don't understand when proms became a thing over here,' her mother said disapprovingly. 'But talking of all things American, have you met his parents?'

'Not yet. They're . . . in America,' she shrugged.

'Where exactly?'

'Southern California.'

'San Diego? Santa Barbara? I wonder if they know the Palmers?'

'They won't,' Tara said quickly. 'They moved around a lot when Alex was growing up. His parents were . . . farmers.'

'Ah. Arable? Livestock?'

'. . . Smallholdings, mainly.'

'Ah.' Her mother's smile faltered as all potential avenues for conversation seemed to lead to dead ends. 'And how did you meet him? Did you tell me that already?'

'Yes. He's at Imperial too, studying for a PhD. We met in the coffee shop down the road from the campus.'

'Uh-huh.'

Jakob picked up a can of Elnett and shook it violently. 'Samantha, just close your eyes for a moment.'

Her mother shut her eyes as the room was misted with hairspray. It was one of the scents of Tara's childhood. She looked at her mother's face in repose – rosy skin with only a few deepening lines down the sides of her mouth, owing (in spite of her 'little tweaks') to her readiness to laugh; champagne-blonde hair styled in a long bob; the deep-set hazel eyes she shared with Tara, which flashed like amber in candlelight (her preferred lighting setting). Samantha had never been the most beautiful woman in a room, but she was always one of the most sought-after, her warmth and flair for recounting anecdotes bringing friends to her side like moths to the flame.

Tara went to put the bottle back on the dressing table but it slipped from her fingers and fell with a clatter onto the shagreen tray. Thankfully, nothing was broken. 'Oh!'

'You seem . . . nervous, darling,' her mother said, regarding her through slitted eyes again, and not – Tara suspected – on account of avoiding the hairspray.

'Nervous? No. I'm fine. Just a bit tired, perhaps.'

'And that's all?'

The secret expanded like bellows in her chest. 'Of course.' She got up again, not wanting to lie outright, not wanting to linger in case Jakob was drafted in to 'do something' quickly with her hair. 'I'm going to find Daddy before Alex gets here. He was on a call to Gerard when I arrived.'

'Well, when you see him, remind him not to be . . .' Her mother twirled her hands in the air, almost clocking Jakob again. 'You know how he gets.'

A tiny smile danced in her eyes and Tara laughed as she left the dressing room. She appreciated her mother's soft, subtle humour – her father was understated to the point of invisibility. Unlike his wife, who wore couture at breakfast, he had more than once been mistaken for the driver, which he loved. It wasn't that he was shabbily dressed; there was just nothing about what he wore that broadcast he was worth £2.4 billion (or whatever the most recent estimate was; it shifted with the markets) – not his shoes, not his watch. In fact, Holly had a fancier iPhone than he did. Tara was convinced he downplayed his status markers in order to lull his opponents into a false sense of superiority. Mark Zuckerberg hadn't invented the concept of the t-shirt-wearing chairman; Bruce Tremain had.

She found him in his study on the ground floor. His desk, always so neat, was dotted with a small stacked pile of papers. He was writing something but looked up as she came in, his expression still stern as his concentration lagged a moment behind his gaze, and she glimpsed him for a moment as the rest of the world saw him – an immensely powerful man, self-made, almost unlimited in his reach. As predicted, he was wearing clothes that, to the casual observer, could have come from Gap or L. L. Bean.

'Twiglet.' He dropped the pen and rose to hug her. 'How's my piglet?'

'Twiglet the piglet' had been his nickname for her since she was a little girl. He stepped back to take a better look at her, as though looking for changes since their last meeting six weeks before. No doubt she had bags under her eyes but if so, they wouldn't be from overwork for once. Now that he'd come round from behind the desk, she could see he was wearing his gold-monogrammed navy velvet slippers – an annual Christmas present from her mother. 'I'm fine, Daddy. How are you? Is this a bad time? You look busy.'

'Oh, it's nothing. Just one or two things to sign off on for that pledge business.' He frowned, checking his watch. 'He's not here already, is he?'

'Alex? No, not yet. He's coming straight from Imperial so I thought I'd take the opportunity to see you all alone first.'

Her father gave a knowing look, crossing his arms in front

of his chest and leaning against the desk. 'Oh, I see. So you mean this is a briefing.'

She grinned. He had always understood her horror of ostentation; she got it from him. 'If that's what you want to call it. I've simply asked Miles and Ma to maybe just not mention . . . the toys.'

'The toys, I see.'

'And of course to do a slipper check.' She cast a quick look down at the slippers again, one eyebrow lifted.

He laughed, squeezing her shoulder like he was pinching a toddler's cheek. 'Outrageous! And what have you told him about us? Knowing you as I do, I imagine you've said almost nothing? Or has he had time to read up on me and now he thinks I'm the big bad wolf?'

'Of course not. I told him you're a sweetheart.'

'Sweetheart. Dear God.' He groaned, amused. For a man with all the responsibility that came with running a giant corporation, he had somehow maintained a light-hearted approach to life. For her, at least, he was ready to smile, laugh, listen to a story, tell a joke.

Tara grinned as her father went to his chair beside the fire and slipped off his slippers, reaching for his shoes. She wandered slowly around the room, her hand trailing over the familiar furniture and artefacts. Her father's study had always been comforting to her: walls lined with books, that faded rug, the sun-bleached striped chair by the fire, its arms worn bald over the years. Her mother rarely ventured in here and as such, it had a worn-in, slightly nibbled look.

She went and stood by the window, looking out onto the street, scanning for the lean lope of her fiancé. Gleaming dark cars were parked along both sides, the streetlamps already shining as daylight faded fast. The days, though growing longer, were still too short for her liking and the glow of lights inside their neighbours' houses was contained by heavy passementerie-trimmed curtains, spilling out only in half crescents through fanlight windows above old Georgian doors. Not a person was to be seen. They were in the centre of London, only a few hundred metres from Piccadilly, Park Lane and Regent Street, but it may as well have been a village in the Dales for all the footfall after dark here.

'Well, just so you know,' he said, tying his laces, 'in the interests of transparency, I've had a profile worked up on our guest.'

'Daddy!' she admonished.

'Only a short one,' he replied, shaking his head quickly. 'I wasn't looking for skeletons in the closet or anything like that – although you may be pleased that I can confirm he's not been married before or got any kids,' he added with an amused glint in his eye. 'Relax, I just wanted to find some common ground with him. Your summary of "twenty-three-year-old American botanist" didn't exactly give me much to go on. But I like what I see. He appears to have gone about things in an unusual manner and he's a doer, gets his hands dirty. I like that.'

'Well, I knew you would. He's a bit of a maverick, but so passionate about his work.'

'And he's written some interesting articles. I particularly liked that one on reforestation and food waste.'

'With the orange peels?' she asked, pleased. She was pretty sure she had begun to fall in love with Alex in the course of that conversation. He had explained to her how, back in the mid-nineties in Costa Rica, an agreement between an orange juice manufacturer and a conservation-inspired landowner had led to 12,000 metric tonnes of orange peel and waste being allowed to biodegrade on scrub land within the landowner's park. A rival juice manufacturer had taken a case to the Costa Rican Supreme Court a year later, successfully arguing the waste had despoiled a national park (but really wanting to trim their rival's expanded profit margin, as their waste disposal costs were slashed) and nothing further was allowed. For fifteen years it was forgotten, until a Princeton biologist friend of Alex's happened to look in on the site and saw with his own eyes a flourishing, thriving forest so thick with trees and vines that the road wasn't visible even a few feet away. 'Can you just imagine,' Alex had asked her, his eyes shining, 'how many problems could be eradicated if we could get the private sector to work with environmental communities? Imagine if we could bring back tropical forests by using the leftovers from industrial food production?' The way his eyes had glittered at that question, his passion for the subject, his need to not just do good by the planet but to do better by it . . .

'It's amazing, isn't it? He's got so many ideas. His mind is just alive to possibilities, getting different industries to link up and offset one another. He knows the future is about collaboration, re-engaging communities at the grass roots.'

'Mmm.' He looked thoughtful suddenly and went over to the desk, beginning to rifle through the slim pile of papers. 'Hmm . . . I wonder if . . .'

'What is it?'

'Hmm, no,' he murmured, reaching the bottom of the pile. The rest of his desk was bare but for a solid gold nugget paperweight shaped like a bird's egg, and a selection of ink pens in a pot. 'I thought I wrote a small cheque a while back to a charity in central America doing something similar, but I can't see it. I'll ask Patsy tomorrow, she'll know.'

'Tomorrow's Saturday.'

He looked at her blankly for a second before getting her gist – he might work every day of the week, but his PA didn't work the weekends.

'Oh well, Monday then. But I'm keen to get into the detail of it with him tonight. It sounds like it's got legs.' He smiled, his eyes softening. 'Not to mention, he clearly knows a thing or two about *our* favourite place.'

Tara smiled. Her father had been taking her and Miles to a small cove on the Costa Rican Caribbean coast since they were small children. It had been his way of reconnecting with them when building his business had consumed him; weeks could go by in which they never saw him, he was always in a meeting, on a plane . . . but their month in the Central American tropics was ring-fenced every summer and nothing – absolutely nothing – was allowed to impinge upon it. Costa Rica had been the place where they rewilded, escaping the gilded cages they lived in throughout the year; it was where they ran about like normal kids, the only place where they had no security. It was an arduous journey in and out of the region; no one knew who they were, or cared, so he employed just a local man and his son to provide them with adventures and local knowledge and to keep a beady eye on them. Tara and Miles had learned to surf there, abseil, zipwire, scuba dive, go on jungle safaris . . . and their mother would fly in from Jamaica, 'just across the water', at the weekends. She preferred to visit a detox clinic there whilst the rest of them 'went feral'.

'It was one of the first things we connected over,' she said. 'He spent eleven months recording butterfly populations in Limon.'

'Yes. I see he's doing his PhD on how they're a marker of the health of an ecosystem.'

'Precisely,' Tara smiled. Her father was nothing if not thorough. 'Did you know the species found there make up about ninety per cent of all Central American butterflies and eighteen per cent of all the world's species?'

'Well, I do now,' he smiled, regarding her intently.

She shifted under his gaze. He had always been able to read her so well and she didn't want him to guess her secrets yet, to ask the one pertinent question and steal Alex's thunder. If it had been hard keeping quiet with her mother, it would be harder still with him—

As if on cue, they heard the heavy knock of the bronze lion's head on the door. Her father waggled his eyebrows at her the way he had always done when she was little, to make her laugh (usually at inopportune moments, like a parent–teacher meeting). 'Aha. The great moment is finally upon us.'

It was a joke but Tara swallowed, feeling her nerves skyrocket. So this was really it? She looked back at her father with a sudden sense of an ending. He didn't know it yet, but their family was about to change shape; he was going to be asked a question he had probably assumed was another decade off. They would no longer be a family of four, but of five. It wasn't just her life that would change with tonight's news, but theirs as well, to an extent. Should she have given him – them – some more warning?

Or *any* warning? For the first time, a thought occurred to her: what if her father actually said *no*? He'd never met Alex before. He had no way of knowing that Alex really wasn't after her money. He might well say it was all far too early and tell them to wait. Oh God, had she fully conveyed to him what Alex meant to her? Her father's refusal wouldn't stop them, of course – this was a gesture of respect, not an actual request for permission – but it would throw a shadow over their happiness if things didn't go the way she hoped.

'Piglet?' Her father clicked his fingers to get her attention, motioning for her to move towards the door. 'We should go and put a face to the brain?'

'. . . Yes . . . Okay.'

Her father held the door open for her, regarding her shell-shocked expression with bemusement. She stopped in the middle of the doorway. 'You know, Daddy, he's a really special person. One of a kind, really, I've never met anyone like him. I think you're going to find him fascinating.'

'Well, unlike the other friends you've introduced us to I imagine this one will giggle less.'

'He's definitely not a giggler.'

He shrugged. 'Then I like him already.'

Chapter Five

His footsteps were hurried on the stairs behind her, as her key slid into the lock and she flung open the door.

'Oh, you're still up!'

Tara was surprised to find Holly and Dev sprawled on the sofa, legs intertwined, an almost-empty bottle of red on the table in front of them. They were watching an American murder documentary on Netflix and Dev had pressed pause at a particularly unfortunate moment. Even as a trainee doctor, Tara grimaced.

Her eyes slid over to Holly. They hadn't seen each other since their tiff a few days earlier. Tara had been lying low at Alex's flat ever since and she was pretty certain Holly had been avoiding her at uni, too; she hadn't glimpsed her in the cafeteria, and Holly could always, always be found by a vending machine.

Alex caught up with her at last and she felt him come and stand behind her as Holly met her gaze with a look of recrimination and, worse, disappointment – before looking away again. 'Wasn't expecting you back tonight,' she said shortly, reaching for the wine bottle and emptying the dregs into her glass.

'We . . . we just came back from dinner with my parents.'

'Oh.' Holly nodded, getting it immediately, understanding

what that meant. Operation Domesticity was underway. Little did she realize that they were mid-argument; that Tara had only come back here because she didn't want to stay at Alex's, and he was only here because he'd followed after her in another cab. If she hadn't been so surprised by the vision of her flatmate clearly reconciled with the guy she had been so adamant on rejecting, she would have closed the door on Alex and thrown over the chain, leaving him abject in the corridor. Instead, she felt his hand press lightly on the small of her back. She tried to arch away but it was impossible to escape his touch without leaping from the spot, and she didn't want Holly to see –

'Go well, did it?' Holly looked over at Alex.

Tara could feel his smile behind her head, feel his body heat like a glowing coal at her shoulder. 'Fantastic. Twig's parents were so welcoming.' He glanced at Tara as if for corroboration, but she kept her gaze dead ahead.

'Yeah, they're sweet, aren't they?' Holly agreed with a tone that Tara – and only Tara – knew was mocking. 'If you didn't know, you'd never know.'

'Know what?' Dev asked, but Holly just kicked him with her leg as a shushing gesture.

The poor guy frowned. 'What'd I say?' He had such a hapless expression, Tara felt a rush of sympathy for him. He deserved better than the rollercoaster ride Holly was putting him through, saying one thing, wanting quite another. She was all bravado and independence at breakfast, but three glasses in at the pub and she was speed-dialling him from the toilets. Tall and skinny, bespectacled with a small goatee, he didn't exude any obvious raw sexual energy, but there was something in his quiet, easy-going manner that had hooked her ambitious, outspoken friend.

Former friend? Holly was staring at the TV screen again, her head resting in one hand, as though she could flick it off 'pause' through sheer willpower alone.

'Wanna join us?' Dev asked, the remote poised in his hand. 'It's about a paedophile in the seventies who abducted this girl – twice. *Twice!* He'd befriended her parents so, the first time, okay, they could be forgiven for not seeing what he was. But the second time . . . ? Come on, dude!'

The word quivered in the room for a moment; Dev really wasn't someone who could pull off the word 'dude'.

'Fool me once, shame on you. Fool me twice . . .' Holly muttered.

'Thanks, Dev, but we've got early starts tomorrow.' Tara gave an apologetic smile. She couldn't stand here for much longer without Holly sniffing something was off between her and Alex. Her friend had unerring instincts and lived by her hunches, be it for choosing the Grand National winner in the annual sweepstake, predicting the Oscars or diagnosing rare conditions. She was rarely wrong – which was precisely why her words on the Serpentine bridge had been so bruising. 'You still coming to Sophie's this weekend?'

'Of course. Why wouldn't I?' Holly replied, looking aggrieved by the question. Sophie, who'd been in halls with them in the first year, was celebrating her twenty-first with a girls' weekend at an Airbnb near her parents' farm in Shropshire; it had been in the diary for weeks.

'No reason. Just checking. I'll drive, shall I?' It was a rhetorical question and she instantly regretted it – they both knew perfectly well Holly didn't have a car – but nerves were making her jumpy.

'Sure.' Holly gave a resentful shrug. 'What time do you wanna leave?'

'Eight?' They were both answering every question with another question. Holly was on edge too.

'Cool. Night then.' Holly's voice was clipped and dismissive. Tara swallowed. '. . . Night.'

'Night, guys,' Alex said, raising a cheery hand back to Dev. Tara walked down the narrow corridor to her room. Space was so pinched, she could easily place both palms flat on opposite walls at the same time and tonight, for the first time, she felt the gulf between her family life and this one. Was that because she was seeing it through Alex's eyes? He'd come straight from a Mayfair townhouse to this. The contrast was marked.

He shut the door behind him with a soft click. She was aware they were both trying to be extra-quiet and not betray their discord to Holly and Dev, as though it in some way undermined them. A chink in the armour after all.

She sat on the bed and stared back at him, her heart pounding both from the conversation she'd just had and the one she was about to have. Alex remained with his back to the door; his hands were pinned behind him and the pose struck her as boyish and young. He was such a clash of contradictions – all guileless innocence at one turn, passionate orator at another; puppy-dog eyes, wolfish grin. How was anyone ever supposed to stay angry at him? Say no to him? But then she remembered what he'd just put her through.

'So?' The word was hard and accusatory.

'Twig, I'm sorry. It just didn't seem like the right time.'

The laugh escaped her body like a jet of steam. She'd had a wretched evening, sitting in apprehensive silence, waiting for him to ask for a private moment with her father, trying to catch his eye over the dinner table as the minutes and then hours slid past and still no mention was made . . . 'Not the right time? You were right there, in the same room as my father. What more did you need?'

'*More* time! That's what I needed.'

'Why? You're not marrying him, are you?' She felt close to tears, disappointment flooding her bones that the big moment she'd been preparing for all week had simply . . . not transpired. She had felt distracted and nervous for days, and for what? To watch her father and fiancé fall into some weird mutual love-in where Alex had seemingly forgotten the entire reason for their get-together?

He walked across the room, but her body language was closed and he stopped a few metres short. 'Look, your father's not like . . . most fathers. He's just not.' He pinned her with a look that said he wasn't being unreasonable. 'I didn't get it before, what you were trying to tell me, but I do now and there's no point beating about the bush – he's a very rich, powerful man who is going to be protective of his daughter.'

'So?'

'So I need to get to know him better. I don't want him thinking that I'm with you because of . . . his money.' He looked exasperated, flustered.

'He wouldn't think that! He knows I'm cautious.'

'Yes, he knows *you* are – but he doesn't know me! It's about self-respect, Ta; I don't want him thinking I'm on an easy ticket here. Look, it wasn't till I walked into that house that I got the "scale" of what you'd been trying to tell me. I mean, I know you didn't want me to be ambushed, but nothing can really prepare you for that.' His eyes were wide at the memory. 'And if I'd just strutted in there and asked for your hand . . . well, why the hell would he agree? He doesn't know me from Adam.'

He was right, of course. Why would he? It was precisely the question she'd asked herself in the study. Looked at objectively from her parents' standpoint, they'd been together just four months; it wouldn't have crossed their minds – not even her mother's! – that she had gone over there to tell them she was getting married and forfeiting the career for which she had fought so hard. And her father had referred to Alex as her 'friend', she remembered; he really hadn't got it at all. For Alex to have gone ahead and asked, as planned . . . her father would have been blindsided.

But none of that made her feel any better. She wasn't yet ready to be placated. She still had another secret of her own that she needed to offload, and she couldn't, not until this one was unburdened. Disappointment made her angry. 'Actually, that's not true,' she replied evenly. 'Daddy knows plenty about you. He had a report done up.'

Alex paled. 'What?'

'It's standard. He does it to pretty much everyone.'

'Pretty much?'

'Not Holly.'

He looked genuinely shocked, so stunned she felt almost sorry for him. Almost. 'He had a report done on me?' he repeated.

'Yes. That's how he knew about the Princeton project. It wasn't me who told him.'

'B-but . . .' His mouth kept opening and closing like a guppy fish, questions forming and being discarded before he could get the words out. 'What – did he get in a PI? Has he been having me *followed*?'

She rolled her eyes. 'No, nothing like that. Just paperwork. It's really not a big deal, he wasn't dishing for dirt. He was just trying to find out your interests to put you at ease,' she said, watching the shock flicker across his features like shadows. 'So he already knows what you're all about, is what I'm saying. He knows you've got integrity . . .' She realized she was mollifying him and resentment crept into her tone. Why was she having to make him feel better? 'Although *I'm* not quite so sure now.'

'What does that mean?' His voice broke slightly with the emotion, rendering him boyishly young at a stroke.

'You told me you're a Chelsea fan,' she said simply, watching as the confusion cleared to understanding.

His shoulders slumped. '. . . Oh. You're talking about Miles.'

'He told me you'd never heard of Drogba and that you kept calling it *Stan*ford Bridge.'

'Yeah, it wasn't my greatest moment. Or ten. Why did you even tell him?'

'Because you had told me you supported them!'

'Ta, I'm American. I've seen, like, five soccer games my entire life!'

'Then why lie about it?'

He sighed, looking stressed. 'Because in one of our first conversations, you said your brother was a fan and I wanted to find a way to . . . bond with him. For you.'

'So, what? You were going to start suddenly supporting Chelsea? Start swotting up on their team, their past record?'

He shrugged. 'Why not? I live here now. I've got to pick a team if I'm ever going to be allowed into your pubs. I hadn't really thought it through.'

'Well, it backfired. Miles is now decidedly *not* a fan of yours. My parents might think you're the greatest thing, but he doesn't. He doesn't like liars. You blew it with him.'

'Okay, well then, I'll put it right. I'll . . . I'll—'

'No, stop! Just stop faking it! He'll see right through you.

Miles can spot a bullshitter twenty miles off. He's already texted me twice, asking what the hell I'm doing with you.'

'He has?' Alex's face fell. He looked bewildered and she suspected it was an unfamiliar feeling for him – being disliked.

'Just stop trying so hard. You can't pretend to be someone you're not.' In spite of her determination to the contrary, she felt her anger thaw at the sight of him so crestfallen. She gave a groan of exasperation. 'Look, you thought that was a shortcut to bonding with Miles, I get it. And I know you're trying to do things properly with my dad . . . but this is the twenty-first century. My family knows I'm no fool and that I make my own decisions. It's you and me getting married, not them. Just keep it simple. You'll get to know them in time, and they'll get to know you.'

'But now your brother hates me.'

She sighed. 'He doesn't hate you. He just doesn't trust you yet. I told you, we don't trust easily, it's how we were brought up. But he'll come round.'

He nodded silently, but there was tension in his jaw. He looked unhappy. 'So you're saying I should just go ahead and ask your dad?'

There was a tense silence for a moment. 'Look, I'll set up a Skype with them—'

'Skype?' He looked shocked. 'No. No way. I wanna do this right. Face to face, man to man.'

'But you missed your chance, Alex! That was what tonight was for; they're flying to Geneva early next week.'

'So then we'll go over again tomorrow.'

'I've got Sophie's this weekend, remember?'

His blank expression suggested he didn't. 'Shit . . . Well, when will you be back?'

'Late on Sunday night. I can hardly rush off. And they're

going Monday first thing.' He just didn't get it. He didn't know what it was like, pinning down people like her parents. They had commitments to honour, committees to sit upon, charities to chair, functions to host, multinationals to run. 'My mother mentioned something about Paris on the way back, and she likes to be in Harbour Island for Easter, so . . . that's that for the moment.' She shrugged, well used to her parents' globetrotting ways, although boarding school had protected her and Miles from a lot of it.

He bit his lip, a deep frown furrowing his brow. 'Okay. Okay. We can make this work, I know we can.'

'Alex—'

'No, let me just think . . . I can do this.'

She sighed as he began to pace, knowing full well that ship had sailed. It might be weeks before she saw her parents again. This was futile. 'Look, it really doesn't matter that much you asking him for my hand. It's me you're marrying, and I've already said yes.'

He wheeled round, suddenly angry. 'But it matters to *me* to do this right, don't you get it? Everything about my life up till coming to London was . . . weird. I didn't have roots. I didn't have a family in the conventional sense. I didn't go to school, didn't go to prom. For once in my life, I want to do something the right way. And whether you see it or not, it matters to me that I have your father's respect.'

'But you already do! The two of you didn't stop talking all night. Trust me, that doesn't happen. He's polite and friendly but he's reserved. He isn't usually like how he was with you tonight.'

Alex's face brightened a little. 'Really?'

'Really! Trust me, you're in with him. He respects you. You've got nothing to worry about.'

'That's pretty cool. I liked him too.' His mouth spread into a wide, delighted smile that flipped her stomach over with it. Annoyingly. He stared unseeingly at an anatomy poster on her wall, lost in thought. 'Hey – could we go back for breakfast tomorrow? *Before* you go to Sophie's thing?'

'I'm leaving at eight.'

'So then leave later.'

'My mother does not receive anyone before double digits and I can't wait till then.'

'So, what? Your father fasts till she's ready?'

Tara snorted at the thought. 'Absolutely not.'

'So then couldn't I join him? Just him? Better yet, I could take him to breakfast – to the Wolseley or Claridge's.'

'You can't afford that,' she tutted. 'And it wouldn't impress him and he wouldn't let you pay anyway. Besides, it would be odd for you to suddenly turn up there on your own tomorrow, having only left at midnight.'

'But if *you* were to text him now and suggest it? You said yourself we got on like a house on fire, so why should it be odd? You could say you're going away for the weekend – true – and I'm home alone – also true – and you thought it would be nice for us to do more . . . bonding. True, true, true. And then boom, as soon I get there, I'll ask him.'

She stared at him, seeing the desperation in his eyes, the urge to be conventional for once and not the irreverent maverick getting by on his charm alone. He wanted to do this properly, to win her father's respect when it had never occurred to her that might be important to him. It was a matter of honour and, in spite of her own disappointment, she loved him all the more for it.

'Well . . . I suppose I could suggest it to him,' she said

slowly. 'But wouldn't it be odd, you asking him for my hand when I'm not there? Not even in the next room?'

He looked anxious. 'I'm not sure, is it? I've never done this before.'

'Well, I don't know! I've never been proposed to before either.'

He pulled a face as they looked at one another. 'I feel . . . literally paralysed with fear of making a faux pas. You Brits, with all your manners and goddam politeness—'

'Hey! It's the goddam politeness that's getting you hitched in the first place. Don't forget that.'

A light lit up his eyes as he walked slowly back over to her, knowing he was forgiven, knowing she could never stay angry with him. 'Don't I know it. I owe it a lot.'

'Yes, you do,' she murmured as he leaned towards her, over her, forcing her down onto her back until she was gazing up at him.

'You're the best thing that's ever happened to me,' he murmured, his lips inches from hers now, their fight almost forgotten. 'I just want to do this right.'

She stopped him with a hand on his chest, knowing she would be lost in the next moment. 'Alex, I just want you to do it.'

Chapter Six

'Are we nearly there yet?' a breathless voice panted.

'Yes! Keep going! We're so nearly there!' Sophie said encouragingly, bounding ahead of their group like an enthusiastic PE teacher. Or Labrador.

The strong gusting wind was blowing them all sideways, flattening the grass and streaming their hair across their faces, making it hard to look up or see. But Tara was aware the horizon had dropped in her peripheral vision as she walked in breathless stomps, listening vaguely to everyone chatting around her.

She still felt tired from their early start and three-hour journey up the motorway. Holly had slept most of the way, her pillow pressed against the seatbelt and still wearing her pyjamas; Tara had packed them a thermos of tea, a packet of dark chocolate digestives, two bottles of water and a phone charger. They had barely spoken and when they'd arrived at the cottage Sophie had rented, to Tara's surprise, their hostess had put them in rooms with . . . other people! She had assumed that as flatmates and best friends, they'd be rooming together, but perhaps Sophie had wanted to separate them on purpose, so they weren't too cliquey? Tara didn't think they were cliquey, though, and surely Holly hadn't *asked* to be put in a different room?

'Look! We've done it!' There was a victorious whoop as Sophie held her arms out wide and turned a circle on the spot beside a cairn. 'Isn't it beautiful? This is my favourite place in the entire world.'

Everyone staggered up to the plateau with relief, hoping the view was worth the hurried hike. They had barely dropped their bags in the door before Sophie had bustled them back out again, wanting to 'make the most of the day' before the light went.

There were several moments' silence as they took in the sight of fields parcelled below them like a patchwork quilt, thick hedgerows like wonky, bushy borders, lone ancient oaks like elder statesmen amid the furrows. The land rolled back for miles, tightly tucked beneath a billowing grey sky, occasional drops of moisture dotting their faces. Fresh droppings on the ground suggested the flock of sheep they'd passed a few moments earlier had only just vacated the area.

'It's very . . . green,' Charlie said suspiciously. A born and bred Londoner, she needed to be equipped with good reasons for ever leaving the city.

'It's fabulous, Soph,' Tara panted, trying to get her breath back and wishing, treacherously, that a helicopter could be summoned to bring them back down again. She couldn't believe how drained of energy she felt. With every passing hour, it seemed, her body was changing in silent, secretive ways.

Holly, the straggler in the group, crested the summit to find the lot of them – except Sophie – sitting on their bums, elbows on knees, heads hanging. Sophie still had her arms outstretched like Rio's Christ the Redeemer. 'Isn't it glorious?' she grinned with an almost evangelical glee. Tara wondered how her friend coped with living in the city when she clearly belonged out here, in nature.

Holly sank to her knees. 'Fuck me! I am cream-crackered! A gentle stroll, you said.' She gave Sophie an accusing look.

Sophie laughed, falling down beside them in a joyous heap. 'Sorry. I tend to forget not everyone has grown up with these hills. This used to be my run with my dog.' She began picking absently at the long grass and looking out, every few seconds, over the far-reaching view.

'You *run* up that?' Holly wheezed.

Annie, in reply, laid flat out in the grass, as if just thinking about the notion exhausted her. 'I despair.'

'Ugh, and we've still got to get back down again,' Holly moaned. 'It's my Saturday afternoon, fuck's sake. I should be on a sofa right now. Eating Doritos. Watching *Hollyoaks*.'

'You and me both, babe,' Charlie muttered. Like Sophie, she was a veterinary student, but if it was clear Sophie was going to be returning to her roots as a big animal, farmyard vet, Charlie would be tending to urban customers, 'treating talking parrots for laryngitis and chihuahuas for crush injuries when they hide beneath scatter cushions. That kinda thing.'

Liv was a medical student too, on the same course as Tara and Holly, and Annie was reading politics. They'd all been friends since their first year, when they'd been on the same corridor and shared a kitchen in the student halls.

'I don't suppose anyone thought to bring us some sustenance?' Charlie asked as she finally got her breath back. 'I definitely burned off at least a scotch egg on the way up.'

'Actually, I've got some tea and biscuits,' Tara said, reaching into her backpack and pulling out the thermos. She had just had time to refresh the hot water when they'd got in.

'*Or* . . . I've got some whisky!' Holly said with a devilish wink, pulling a hip flask from her jacket pocket.

'Ooh!' Charlie said, her arm literally swerving from left to right as she went, last moment, for Holly's offer instead.

Everyone had a tot except Tara. Whisky was the last thing she could drink and she couldn't explain why. Instead she fussed with pouring herself some tea, pretending this was what she really wanted, dunking the teabag repeatedly as her friends watched on in bemusement.

She took a sip – it was both tepid and too strong – and defiantly stared out towards the distant town, a dark smudge on the horizon from here. For the umpteenth time, she wondered how Alex's breakfast had gone with her father; she had assumed one of them would ring when he'd done the deed – Alex, elated; her father, choked; her mother (when she was finally up and dressed), emotional and teary that her only daughter was getting married and when could they meet to start pinning down details? Instead, radio silence.

She checked her phone again for signal. Two bars. Decent. Decent enough.

'Missing lover-boy?' Liv asked with a knowing tone as she put her phone away with a supressed sigh.

'Of course.'

'I'd miss him too if he was mine.' Liv gave one of her signature dirty laughs, followed by a wink and a nudge of her elbow. 'Although I have to say you seem very relaxed about leaving him.'

'Well, it is only for an overnight stay, so I think we'll survive.'

'Oh, don't be so sure – lives have changed in shorter time frames than that,' Liv countered. 'And I wouldn't give him too long a rein if I was you. He's the sort of guy who attracts attention, know what I mean?'

Tara knew exactly what she meant, but she resented the intimation. 'Not really.'

'Liv means that if he was her boyfriend, she wouldn't leave him for a single second in case another woman made a move on him,' Sophie explained unnecessarily. Sophie wasn't really an expert on men yet; she was still more interested in large mammals of the four-legged kind.

'Huh. What a relaxing way to live,' Tara replied with cool sarcasm.

'Hey listen, I've only been cheated on by every guy I've ever dated,' Liv continued. 'But yeah, call me paranoid, why don't you?'

Everyone laughed as the hip flask was passed around again, and Tara took another pointed sip of her tea. She felt off form, isolated somehow from the others. She couldn't put a finger on it, but she sensed a distance between herself and them, starting when she and Holly had been put in different rooms. For the first time, she wondered if Holly had told the girls her secrets. On the one hand, she passionately didn't believe her friend would betray her like that; but on the other, Holly clearly considered her decisions a betrayal of their friendship, and with her enduring anger and the palpable chill between them, the others couldn't have failed to notice it.

'You've had some rotten luck, I know. But Alex really isn't like that.'

'Hon, he's a man,' Annie drawled. 'They're *all* like that.'

Tara gave a puzzled smile. Why were her friends pushing the issue? 'Well, Alex isn't.' Tara automatically looked to Holly for some backup. Her best friend knew that she and Alex were far beyond the petty jealousy stage – only she knew that he was in London right now asking Tara's father for her hand; that their child was already growing in her belly. And besides, she knew Alex well enough to defend him against these slurs – but Holly looked immediately away again. She plucked a long strand of grass and began threading it through her fingers.

Tara felt like she'd been slapped.

'What about Dev? D'you think he's the cheating type?' Annie asked, following Tara's line of sight and looking across at Holly too.

Holly looked surprised. 'No!' she scoffed. 'But only because I'm the only female this side of Moscow to find him attractive and that's only when I've got my beer goggles on.'

Tara frowned. Holly hadn't been drunk last night when they'd been enjoying their cosy night in together on the sofa. She had looked languid and settled. She'd looked happy.

'Oh, poor Dev!' Sophie cried in his defence. 'No, you can't talk about him like that. He's . . . got his own charm. He's sort of bookish-looking and sensitive.'

'I think he's lovely,' Annie agreed.

'Lovely,' Holly repeated. 'Yeah, because that's what we're all looking for. Killer in bed and . . . lovely.'

'I think you make a great couple,' Tara ventured.

Holly looked back at her with angry eyes. 'But we're not a couple. I keep telling you, it's just a sex thing when there's no better option.'

'And there's nothing wrong with that,' Liv sighed. 'Sometimes it's better the devil you know than . . . no devil at all.' She gave another dirty laugh. 'We can't all be players like Annie here.'

Annie gave a small sigh of coquettish contentment – slightly built, with a sweetheart-shaped face and long, straight light brown hair, she had a pretty girl-next-door look that men couldn't resist. 'What can I say? You've either got it or you don't.' She squealed as Charlie and Liv kicked resentfully at her feet.

'Yeah? Well maybe *you* don't,' Charlie said provocatively. 'Sounds to me like you've found a guy *not* that into you. He's got you dangling like a puppet on a string, girl.'

'Gay?' Liv suggested.

'*So* not.' Annie arched an eyebrow and gave them a knowing look. 'James was just playing hard to get.'

'Wait – James? Who's this? I thought you were seeing George?' Tara asked. 'What have I missed?'

'Keep up, Ta!' Sophie admonished.

'George is dead to her now,' Liv said in a dramatic voice. 'This week – for one week only—'

'Hey!' Annie protested.

'—It's all about James. A mature man.'

'Mature student, there's a difference. He's only twenty-four, for Christ's sake.' Annie pouted prettily.

'So what's happened, then?' Charlie asked, looking peeved that Annie had got her man after all. 'Last I heard, he kept blowing you off for work.'

Annie leaned herself up on her elbows, eyeing them all like the cat who'd got the cream. 'I went up to his office on Thursday and we had a carpet picnic.'

'A what?' Charlie frowned.

'Smoked salmon, strawberries, prosecco. It was lush.'

Charlie looked on with a wry look. 'And did James take well to eating his lunch on his nylon carpeted floor? He doesn't seem the type.'

Liv spluttered with laughter; Holly too. But Tara felt sad that she had missed out on her friend's latest love-life twist; she'd been too busy with her own to take notice, increasingly abandoning drinks with the girls for cosy nights in with Alex. She watched her friends laughing and teasing one another and felt another sharp pang at what she was leaving behind – girlish stuff and nonsense, doomed love affairs, dramatic heartbreaks, hilarious nights in. She was barely twenty and that was already behind her.

'Actually, he loved it,' Annie insisted, with a sly look. 'It was Alex who looked shocked.'

Annie looked across at her and Tara startled as she absorbed the intimation. '*My* Alex?'

'Yes, *your* Alex,' she laughed. 'Didn't he tell you? They do work together!'

The penny dropped. 'Oh my God, you mean James is James MacLennan? But he's such a dick!'

The words burst out before she could stop them; months of hearing Alex's complaints about James's rivalry, power politics, smear campaigns and dirty tricks had left her with a low opinion of a man she'd never met. But why hadn't Alex mentioned that James was seeing Annie? He knew they were good friends. Did he assume she already knew? Or did he just not care who his colleague was dating?

True, Alex wasn't an undergraduate and never had been; he'd not been inculcated into student culture in the same way, and his unconventional upbringing and life experiences rendered him older than his twenty-three years. He was passionate about his work and he displayed no interest in gossip of any sort – be it about celebrities or friends. It was one of the things she liked best about him. His discretion, too. And yet . . . it felt like such a glaring omission not to have brought this up. Annie was her friend, James his colleague and rival. Did he think she was going to suggest double dates with them?

Annie's smile faded at the bald insult. 'Well, Alex would

say that. He's pissed off because he didn't get published and James did.' She gave a shrug. 'Your guy seriously needs to take a chill pill. James says he is way too intense. He says you'd think he was plotting world domination, the way he gets. Can't you have a word with him or something?'

Tara blinked, feeling a rush of indignation gathering in her. She'd been with Alex for four months; Annie had been with James a week! Who did she think she was to start lecturing her about her boyfriend's ambition? But, as ever – the lessons she'd learned in childhood about public restraint were too strongly inculcated to override – Tara said nothing.

No one spoke for a few moments, no one came to her or Alex's defence, and the tension thickened as the silence lengthened. Sly looks passed between her friends and, yet again, Tara had the feeling of words not being spoken, of secrets being kept. Were they jealous of what she had with Alex? Was that it? Or was she being paranoid? Was she touchy because of the stiffness between her and Holly? Not to mention the enduring silence coming from Alex himself; still no text, no missed call. It was almost five o'clock. What the hell was he doing? Had 'the right moment' eluded him again? Had her father cried off at the last moment? Or had something else happened? Had he been hit by a bus on the way over? Had Professor Hamlyn called him in? *What?*

She felt a rush of despair. Why was everything proving so hard? It felt like the world was against her when all she wanted was to get on with living happily ever after. Instead, she was tired, emotional and hormonal, and stuck up a windy hill in the Shropshire dales with friends who were bordering on bitchy. She felt caught between two lives, with no one to talk to. She was immersed in secrets, and the only person who knew about them had made her feelings perfectly clear.

Tara watched as Holly passed around the hip flask again, the flash of bitterness between her and Annie seemingly forgotten by the others already. Everyone was already getting looser as the amber spirit shot into their veins. There'd be singing on the way back down, no doubt, a takeaway curry and more drinks back at the house. What excuse was she going to use to avoid them then?

It had been a mistake coming away this weekend, she realized that now. Like Alex pretending to be a Chelsea fan, she hadn't thought it through. She'd thought she could pretend that she was still one of the gang for a bit longer – deny that she was already changing course – but she was already an outsider. She could feel it, and so could the others, even if they didn't yet know why.

'Come on. Let's head back before it gets dark and open some booze,' Charlie said, scrambling to her feet. 'I've not come all the way up to bloody Shropshire to spend it getting windburn on a mountain.'

'Technically it's only a hill,' Sophie corrected her. 'It has to be over—'

'Shuddup. I don't care. If I'm leaving London it's only on account of a damned good pub. I've done my good deed of the day, now it's time for my reward. First round's on me.'

'Actually, my father's running a tab for us,' Sophie said with a hitch of her eyebrows.

Charlie's mouth opened wider. 'Then what the fuck are we doing up here with sheep?'

The girls all gathered in their legs, pulling each other up by outstretched arms and swiping grass off their bottoms. Tara simply smiled – and did her best to blend in.

*

Tara stood at the bar, watching as the barman pulled on the ale lever, the glass angled precisely to create just the right amount of froth. Behind her she could hear her friends, laughing loudly as Annie regaled them with a tale about her ex, George. From what she had picked up, it involved thorny bushes, torn, bloodstained boxers and having to sleep on his stomach for a month.

Her eyes rose to the clock, willing the hands to be further round than they had been last time she checked. Ten thirty-four. It was something, she supposed. She had blagged her way through this evening by laughing even when she wasn't amused, suggesting a game of Ibble Dibble and fulfilling her Mother Hen duties by taking the seat closest to the bar and insisting on being the one to get each round of drinks – this was their fifth, and she had been passing off her elderflower as vodka tonic all night. Only Holly had sussed her game, disappointed looks scudding her way across the table every so often.

The phone in her jeans pocket vibrated suddenly and she whipped it out with impressive fluidity, her heart rate rocketing up. 'Alex?'

'Twiggle! My Twiglet!'

She frowned at the uncharacteristic bounce in his voice. 'You're drunk?'

'No. I'm . . . what's that word you use? . . . Sozzled. I'm sozzled.' He laughed, the sound soft and indistinct, like his words had rolled onto their sides.

She heard the sound of traffic rushing past him, London in her ear. 'Where are you?'

'Going home . . . Taxi!' There was a pause. 'Fuck.' The word was a whisper, muttered below his breath. He hiccupped. She had never heard him hiccup before. It seemed such a frivolous sound for him. 'You should have warned me your father takes no prisoners.'

'*Dad*? You mean you're still together?'

'All day. All day long,' he said, sounding as proud as a boy with his first sandcastle. 'We had the best time.'

'Where are you right now?'

'I'm not entirely sure . . .' he said slowly, sounding baffled. She could practically hear his brow furrowing – as though this were the first opportunity he'd had to consider his surroundings. 'I think St Jays,' he slurred.

St James. They were at her father's club. She groaned as another thought followed on the heels of that realization. 'Oh God. Not the port.'

'*Yesh* the port!' There was a small silence, then another hiccup.

Her father had a very serious wine collection, kept in his various cellars, but he was a particular aficionado of port, and rare was the man who could keep up if he was treated to a tasting session.

'So you've been with Dad all day?'

'We've been bonding.' Another short silence, another hiccup.

'And . . . ?' she prompted, as he offered nothing more. She wondered if he had gone to sleep standing up, right there, in the middle of St James.

'Oh. Yes. And we're playing golf tomorrow. At his club. Another club.'

She rolled her eyes, and not only because he'd completely missed her point. Getting to Wentworth meant taking a helicopter – and what had she specifically asked her father to do? Hide the toys. Hide the bloody toys. 'Alex, do you even play golf?'

'No,' he chuckled. It sounded like it would have been a giggle except that his body couldn't muster the requisite muscular strength. 'But I know the concept of the game – get the ball in the hole in as few hits as possible.'

Tara shook her head; it was hard to believe this was a PhD student she was talking to right now. She caught sight of her friends in the foxed mirrored wall. Holly was staring into space, looking a world away from here.

She brought her attention back to the very drunk man breathing heavily in her ear. 'Alex!' she hissed, snapping him to attention; she heard his breathing change.

'Huh?'

'Did you ask him for my hand?'

The guy standing beside her and nursing his pint overheard and looked at her with a curious mix of surprise, distaste and pity. Tara gave an embarrassed smile.

'No!' His 'ew' tone was clear and she knew his brain was translating her words literally. She waited. 'Oh . . . No, wait . . .' The word was stretched out as the drunken fog cleared momentarily and the penny dropped.

No. No, he hadn't. She felt too upset to even ask why not, resentful that she was having to push on it – as though all this marriage business had been her idea and he was the reluctant groom.

'But I will. We've just been *bonding*,' he repeated.

Bonding. That word again.

She didn't say anything, but just rubbed her temples with her hand. It had been a long day. Actually, it had felt like a long week. What should have been one of the happiest times was feeling somehow contorted and forced. She was beginning to feel her engagement was like a car out of fuel, sputtering down the street, wholly unable to get to its destination. She shouldn't have to beg for her parents to be told she was getting married. His insistence upon adhering to some old-fashioned notion of etiquette was doing more harm than good. Couldn't he see that?

'Twig? My Twiggle?' He had never called her Twiggle before. It irritated her.

'Go to bed, Alex.' Her voice was flat and weary. She felt exhausted by all these balls she had to keep up in the air; today with her friends had been a case in point of why keeping secrets only led to confusion and pain.

'Twiggy.' His voice was plaintive, so unlike his usual commanding, self-possessed tones. She didn't like him this drunk. It diminished him somehow, robbed him of all the strength and purpose she found so attractive. 'Tomorrow, I promise. I absolutely promise.'

'Night, Alex.' She hung up on him, unconvinced. She'd heard that before.

Chapter Seven

'Bugger, we've got no bread.' Charlie stared disconsolately into the larder. 'I swear we brought a loaf?'

'We did,' Liv said, from her spot sprawled on the worn armchair beside the royal-blue Aga. 'But then we had munchies when we got in last night, remember?'

Charlie had to concentrate very hard to remember. 'Oh yeah.' She looked back at the almost empty larder again. 'Bugger.' They had a tub of Philadelphia cheese, a jar of jam, some butter, a pack of sliced honey-roast ham and an aubergine. No one quite knew what meal had been planned around the aubergine – they were all hopeless cooks – but apparently nothing at all could be eaten without bread.

They were significantly the worse for wear after last night; much to Tara's dismay, the celebrations had continued long after the pub had thrown them out and, despite the fact she'd been secretly sober as a judge, she looked as convincingly battered and hungover as everyone else on only four hours' sleep.

'I'll nip out and get some,' she said, reaching for her jacket and grateful for the excuse to escape for a bit and have some fresh air. 'We need more milk anyway.'

'No, we've got milk. We've got four pints, in fact,' Sophie said proudly, showing her the carton in the fridge door compartment.

'Yes, but Hols likes full-fat,' Tara shrugged, aware of Holly's gaze coming to rest upon her. She was sitting slumped at the pine kitchen table, stretched out on one elbow, her head in her hand as she listlessly read the local businesses directory. It had a picture of a red squirrel on the front and an ad for oven cleaning on the back page.

'And she couldn't, this one time, have semi-skimmed?' Charlie asked. She had a rabid dislike of anyone being 'precious'.

Holly pinned Charlie with a look. 'Hey! In Yorkshire, tea is a serious business. Don't mess with my tea.'

Everyone was scratchy, irritable and exhausted, and the teasing tone was only half an octave away from being war.

'Do you want the bread or not?' Tara asked, checking that the car keys were still in her pocket. Her phone was – sixteen per cent battery left. She had left it downstairs accidentally last night and by the time she'd realized, the house was in darkness and Annie was already beginning to fall asleep (or rather, pass out) beside her.

She could charge it in the car on the journey back later. Listlessly, without much hope, she checked for messages or missed calls, but there was nothing. Naturally. They would be on the second hole by now anyway. Her father always teed off at nine sharp.

'Sure. And Nutella, if they've got any,' Charlie said, too hungover to argue for once.

'And the Sunday papers, please,' Liv said, clasping her hands in a weak prayer position. 'I need to see my horoscopes for the week.'

Everyone simultaneously tutted. 'And you call yourself a scientist!' Charlie scoffed.

'Annie calls herself a vegan but she eats halloumi!'

'Only because I like the way it squeaks,' Annie protested, as though that was a logical defence.

Tara had to smile. Her friends might be a fractious, useless motley crew, but she supposed she loved them. 'I'll be back in ten, then – don't murder each other before I get back. Bread, milk, Nutella, papers.'

'And some chocolate Hobnobs!' Liv called after her. 'If they've got them.'

'Chocolate Hobnobs,' Tara nodded, slipping through the kitchen stable door into the garden.

There was still a chill in the air, but the skies were clear and a tendril of mist draped over the shoulders of the hills like a scarf. The valley was a palette of hesitant greens, gentle greys and browns, sheep dotting the fields like cotton flowers. A distant river tumbled over rocks, bringing a chattering babble to the otherwise pervasive silence.

She unlocked the car and was clicking on her seatbelt when the passenger door opened and Holly slid into the seat beside her. She was still wearing her striped flannel PJs – her 'old man pyjamas', as Dev called them – with socks, Birkenstocks and a borrowed wax jacket thrown on top. It smelled like wet sheep, which was not helpful to either of them. Tara had felt her nausea increasing over the last few days, and Holly had been throwing up all morning.

'. . . Hi!' Tara said in surprise. She had begun to adapt to the idea that Holly was actively avoiding her.

Holly glanced at her as she too clicked in her seatbelt. 'Annie needs tampons.'

'Oh. Okay.' She didn't reply that Holly could have just

texted her that request – or indeed Annie herself. Was this an opportunity for the two of them to make up?

They pulled out of the short cobbled drive and onto the lane. It was single-width with only occasional passing places and Tara sent a prayer to the travel gods that they wouldn't meet any tractors coming in the opposite direction. The village was two and a quarter miles away, but it felt longer than that as they drove in silence. Tara wished she'd put the radio on first, just for some background noise.

'So how are you feeling now?' she ventured, glancing at Holly, who was looking out the side window, her jaw pushed sullenly forwards. She was pale, with dark bags under her eyes, her red corkscrew curls scraped back in a ponytail and secured with a green wire toggle that looked like it should be holding up staked sweet peas.

'Rough.' Even the word was a croak.

'Yeah. What we'd give for a saline drip right now, huh?'

Holly frowned at her. 'You don't need one. You were on the tonics all night.'

'Well no, but I'm still feeling . . . meh.' Her voice was quiet, the words small as though she didn't dare to give them a solid shape; she felt a sense of shame, as though her pregnancy was something she was not allowed to acknowledge. Holly stared at her with an inscrutable expression. Tara kept her eyes on the road, her grip tightening on the wheel. '. . . Do you think anyone clocked that I was faking?'

There was a pause. 'No. They were all too busy getting hammered themselves. I don't think it would cross their minds that anyone would willingly *not* drink themselves into oblivion at a twenty-first, much less that one of us might be pregnant.'

'Yeah. It wasn't much fun having to pretend like that.'

'So then don't. Just tell them.' Holly gave a bored shrug, as though it was no big deal telling people she was dropping out of her studies, abandoning her high-flying career before it had even begun, becoming a mother by twenty-one. 'Don't make it more complicated than it needs to be.'

Tara felt stung by the words. Her situation was complicated and to suggest otherwise was facetious – but she bit back her indignation, not wanting to get into another argument. Holly on a hangover was the proverbial bear and sore head. 'It's too early,' she mumbled instead. 'I'm only nine weeks . . .'

A red kite suddenly shot past the car, giving them both a fright, and Tara slammed on the brakes. 'Oh holy shit!' she cried, feeling her heart rate shoot up.

Holly didn't say anything, her silence somehow withering as Tara tried to collect her wits. She was jumpy and anxious. They drove along again, past the low mossy drystone walls.

Holly shifted in her seat, and Tara noticed she still looked green around the gills. 'So what's Alex up to this weekend, anyway?' she asked flatly.

'Um, well . . . bonding with my father, mainly.'

'You what?' She could seemingly only manage to hitch up one eyebrow in response.

'Yeah. They're playing golf together right now.'

Tara glanced over as a silence stretched again and she saw her friend looking at her with an expression that suggested she'd sprouted a second head. 'Alex? Alex is playing golf?'

'With my father. Yes.'

'Where?'

'. . . Wentworth.'

Holly spluttered with sudden laughter, the sound erupting from her like a volcanic eruption, surprising them both. Tara cracked a tiny smile.

'Does he have the right clothes? I mean – the socks alone! Does Alex even have a matching set?'

'Probably not . . . He's never played before,' Tara grinned. 'Dad will have to get him kitted out.'

Holly tipped her head back against the headrest, clearly amusing herself with a visual montage. 'Ah God,' she mumbled. 'The thought of him hacking those greens in Fair Isle socks . . .'

Tara felt her grip relax around the wheel as the tension between them slackened somewhat. Ambition hadn't been their only bond; they shared a wicked sense of humour too. 'What's Dev up to?'

Holly's smile disappeared in a flash. Seemingly even Dev's name was now off limits. 'Why would I know?'

'You didn't ask him on Friday?'

Holly shook her head. 'Nope. His comings and goings are none of my business.'

'Oh.' Tara offered nothing more. There was no point. If her friend was going to be adamant that they were not a 'thing', that they merely slept together and what he did during daytime hours was none of her concern, what could she do? Seemingly nothing she could say was right.

They passed the village sign, white-painted with a flower-bed of crocuses planted around it. Someone had left a Coke can on the top. Weathered stone cottages stood barely a hip-width's pavement back from the road, fresh eggs – blue, brown and white – left in an honesty box on a deep windowsill. A noticeboard fluttered with pinned memos for babysitting services, the upcoming Spring Fayre, requests for lambing help, cars for sale . . . A decommissioned red phone box stood on a grass verge opposite the Snooty Fox pub where they had caroused last night, and the village store was housed in a pretty whitewashed building with wooden crates of fruit and vegetables stacked in tiers outside. But for the fact that the carrots looked stringy and there was some obscene graffiti inside the bus stop, it could have been a Richard Curtis film set. It felt like stepping back in time, to an age of innocence and decorum, and it certainly explained a lot about their friend Sophie. Were they all products of their upbringing, Tara wondered? Alex certainly was – free-spirited, irreverent, independent. Holly was grounded, loyal, plain-speaking and fiercely ambitious. In which case, how did hers manifest in her? Especially when she always went to such lengths to hide it?

They parked and staggered out of the Mini, Holly hung-over and Tara deeply nauseated.

'Papers, bread, milk, Nutella and . . . what else?' Tara asked, as she held open the door for Holly.

'Tampons,' Holly said flatly as an elderly man in a flat cap went to pass by them, a roll of Sunday papers fastened under his arm. Holly gave him a blank nod in greeting but he seemed flustered, whether by her comment or her clothes. 'And chocolate Hobnobs.'

'Oh yes.'

They looked around the store. It was tiny, no bigger than the sitting room in the Airbnb cottage. A woman in her mid-fifties was standing behind the counter labelling tins with a hand-held sticker device. She glanced over at them as they got their bearings.

'Mornin'.'

'Morning,' Tara smiled more cheerily than she felt as she picked up a wire basket and turned down the aisle. Holly did the same.

'So, they're bonding, huh?' Holly scanned the shelf of breads.

Tara took a moment to process her meaning and pick up the threads of the conversation again. 'Oh, yes. Ritual humiliation for Alex, to get into my father's good books.'

'Funny. He doesn't strike me as the sort to care about what parents think.'

Tara glanced at her as she reached for the Best of Both loaf. 'Why'd you think that?'

'Well, he told me one time – I think you were in the shower – he grew up smoking joints with his folks and calling them by their first names. Seems weird that he's suddenly prepared to play golf, of all things, just so your dad'll like him.'

Did it? 'Well, I guess when you're getting married and joining a new family, these things matter more. He wants to start out on a strong footing; he's paranoid about not wanting my parents to think he's with me for the money. It's important to him to do this properly.'

'Do what properly?'

'Ask my dad for my hand.'

Holly looked surprised. 'You mean your parents still don't know? But I thought you were telling them at dinner the other night?'

She winced. So had she. 'That's the purpose of this weekend – bonding with Dad, before he asks him.'

Holly's eyes narrowed. 'While you're *here*?'

'Well, this was in the diary for ages. I couldn't exactly duck out on Sophie, could I? And besides, it doesn't matter. It's not like he'd ask with me right there in the room anyway.'

Holly looked shocked. 'Why not? Because your future has to be decided between men in your absence? What are you – chattel?'

'*I* decide my future, thanks very much. This is just . . . etiquette.'

Holly gave a snort of derision as they stopped in front of the biscuits. 'It's just bullshit, is what it is.'

Tara gave a small smile at her friend's feminist indignation. 'I don't disagree. Still, my father will like being asked. *I* just want Alex to get a damned move on with it.'

'And there I was thinking you'd be onto the bridesmaid flowers by now,' Holly sighed with trace sarcasm, reaching for a packet of Hobnobs. 'And how did he take the news he's gonna be a dad himself?'

Tara hesitated. 'He still doesn't know.' She saw Holly's eyes widen further. 'But before you freak out, there's no great conspiracy, it's just a timing thing. Once he gets asking my father for my hand out of the way, then I'll tell him, them and fricking everyone.' She rolled her eyes, not wanting to meet Holly's gaze. She knew the look she'd find there.

'So I'm the only person who knows?'

'Yes.'

'The only one in the world?'

'Yes.'

Holly was quiet for a moment. 'God, the power I wield.'

Tara laughed. 'Huh?'

'I could totally blackmail you right now. One million pounds to keep your secret.' Her eyes narrowed. 'You'd probably pay it too.'

Tara just shrugged. 'It wouldn't do much for our friendship. And you'd definitely be off the godmothers list.'

Holly's mouth opened in surprise and then closed again. She looked quickly away. '. . . Are you frightened?' Her tone had changed.

Tara frowned. 'About the birth?'

'Giving up your entire life?'

There was a pause. 'I told you. I don't see it that way.'

'No.' Holly was quiet for a moment. 'Well, I guess that's what they mean about the rich being different from the rest of us.'

Tara frowned, not sure what to say to that. She didn't want to get into another argument about it, not when they'd just thawed the ice. 'Hols—'

But Holly was already moving off, her back turned. 'You do you. I'll get the tampons. See you out at the car.'

They drove back towards the cottage at twice the speed of the journey out, the shopping in a brown paper bag on Holly's lap. But Tara's gaze kept falling to the other bag between her friend's ankles – it contained a box of tampons and, beside it, a pregnancy test. At the mere sight of it, Tara felt her hackles rise. Was that what this journey had been about? Holly was going to bully her into providing *proof* that this was actually happening? Tara's anger was immediate. She didn't need to prove anything to anyone, not even her best friend.

She had switched the radio on with the ignition and turned up the volume, determinedly drowning out the possibility of further conversation – but the words hovered unsaid regardless, creating a tension they could both feel. The cottage was in sight when Holly angled towards her. '. . . Twig, I need to ask you something.' Her voice was uncharacteristically stiff. Nervous, even. She knew what she was about to ask was outrageous, unacceptable . . .

Tara straightened up, glancing at her with a hard look and feeling her indignation swell. 'Oh yeah?' she said, her fingers tapping on the steering wheel to the song playing on the radio. She was not taking that pregnancy test, and she couldn't believe Holly would even ask her.

'. . . Do you trust him?'

Tara frowned. It wasn't the question she'd been expecting. 'What?'

'Is that why you still haven't told him about the baby? You don't trust him?'

'Hols, we've talked about this before. I've told you I do. Why would you even ask me that?'

There was a hesitation. 'Because of something Annie said.'

'*Annie?*' Tara spluttered, as the memories of yesterday's awkward hilltop encounter flew back into her mind. 'She knows nothing about Alex, so don't even think about listening to anything she's got to say. She's only met him a few times.'

'Actually, it was something James said to her.'

Tara frowned. 'James MacLennan?'

'Yes.' Holly looked pained. 'Apparently he . . . Look, this is really hard to say . . . but apparently he told her that Alex is using you, that he's cheating—'

'Stop.' Her voice was flinty but Tara felt like the breath had been knocked out of her.

'She's had been worrying all weekend about whether or not to tell you.'

Just Annie? Or all of them? Was that what the conversation yesterday on the hill had really been about – bringing up the suggestion that Alex might cheat on her under the guise of Liv's bad luck with men and Annie's great wisdom about them?

'Obviously she has no idea about the . . .' Holly continued, gesturing in Tara's direction and clearly meaning the engagement, the baby, everything.

'I said stop!' Tara slammed her foot on the brake so suddenly they both slumped forward from the force. They were ten metres from the driveway. 'Stop talking! I don't want to hear it.'

Holly stared at her. '. . . You don't think it's important to know if your boyfriend's cheating on you?' Her voice was quiet, trying to be calming, even as she knew that every word she uttered was a bomb to Tara's happiness.

'I know he's not.' Tara could feel the chill from her own glare.

There was a pause as Holly faltered, before she staggered on. '. . . Annie said James was adamant about it, that he saw something on his computer . . . Why would she lie?'

'I'm sure she wouldn't, not intentionally, but she's been with the guy for all of a week! Does she have any clue that James *hates* Alex? That he's riddled with jealousy over the fact that their professor favours Alex and not him, that he'd say anything to try and tear him down? He probably thinks breaking us up would distract Alex just enough to give him some kind of edge! I think there are a few people who would like to see us break up.'

There was no disguising the pointedness of her words and Holly looked at her for a long moment with sad, questioning eyes that only made Tara angrier. 'So then, you don't think there's any truth in it at all? You've never had any suspicions—'

'None! I trust Alex completely.'

'And you believed him when he said he was bonding with your father this weekend?'

Tara stared at her, open-mouthed and furious as she finally realized why Holly had come back repeatedly to the topic of conversation. 'It would be a pretty fucking stupid cover story, let's face it! One phone call to my parents and I'd have the truth.'

'I guess that's true,' Holly conceded.

'Of course it's true,' Tara snapped.

'Twig, I just don't want to see you get hurt, that's all. Alex is a good-looking guy and he knows it. He knows he could have anyone.'

The Secret Path

'Really? Anyone?' Tara sneered.

Holly's eyes widened. 'Oh God, not me! Fuck no! I just mean he's no innocent. He's charming, but he's not . . . fluffy. He's got a ruthless streak. I've seen it in him sometimes when he talks. He's so uncompromising.'

'And you? Are you compromising? Have you been supportive and flexible over the changes I've got coming? Or have you been cutting me out because my plans no longer align with yours?' Tara glowered at her with an anger Holly had never seen before. She was always so good at keeping her emotions under control, hiding parts of herself from the public gaze with a dance between shadows and light. She was a pleaser, forever the good girl, the mother hen, a product of her upbringing in which she tried to temper her outrageous good fortune with self-effacement and steadfast placidity. 'What other people *think* they know is of no interest to me. Annie knows as much about Alex as I know about James, so you know what, Hols? Next time Annie brings it up, tell her from me, to tell James to go fuck himself!'

Holly's mouth dropped open at her language. Tara had never spoken to her like that before.

Tara looked away, but she could feel herself shake, the adrenaline tearing through her body. She moved the car clumsily back into gear and rolled them forwards the last few metres. Taking the bag of groceries from Holly's lap, she got out of the car. 'And don't even think of insulting me with that bloody test either!' Holly's gaze followed Tara's to the bag between her ankles. She looked shocked and then shame-faced.

'Twig, I'm sorry—'

But Tara didn't hear it over the slam of the car door. She had already turned her back.

93

Chapter Eight

London sparkled like a cut diamond, glass towers reflecting the sun as she turned off the motorway and headed in on the arterial roads, slowing to a crawl alongside black cabs and delivery vans, trundling past smoked Victorian terraces, dark with soot and exhaust fumes. She didn't notice as the narrow red-bricked houses were replaced by wider, taller Georgian stucco villas, as the red buses became more numerous and she never moved beyond second gear. Her mind was on the tense end to Sophie's birthday weekend.

Nothing had been said outright, but it was clear from the watchful looks thrown her way as she had angrily set down the bag of groceries, and the weighty silence that had accompanied Holly's arrival several moments later, that this 'talk' had been planned. Hols had just been the messenger. They had evidently all discussed it between themselves and come to their conclusions: Alex was deceiving her and she was a pitiful fool if she refused to see it.

Unable to meet their eyes but refusing to let them see her cry, she had left within the quarter hour, citing a family emergency that no one believed and she didn't even try to make sound convincing. Sophie had made a feeble attempt to try to make her stay but Tara wouldn't be placated, knowing what they really thought. She had thrown her bag in the boot of the car, not even zipped up, and left Holly to sort out her own transport back. Tara wouldn't even look at her. Any of them.

She hadn't cried all the way home, as she had wanted to, but her body had been held as tense and tight as a metal drum, her ribcage scarcely moving as she breathed in shallow sips, like a swallow skimming a pond for water. Her shoulders were up by her ears and she'd not heard a word or song on the radio, for if her body was still, her mind was racing.

It was all lies. Alex wasn't cheating on her, she knew that for certain. She knew what they had. The chemistry between them was more real, more visceral than the skin on her hands. Passion like theirs couldn't simply be made up or faked. When they were together, she felt his appetite for her; quite literally it was *appetite* – he would bite her, graze his teeth on her skin, nestle his face in her hair, squeeze and pinch her; she would dig her nails in his skin. Mere touch wasn't enough. Sometimes she felt they wanted to swallow each other whole.

So why, then . . . why couldn't she shake off the feeling of unease? Even as she had shut down Holly's words, the tiny doubts that had been picking threads at the furthest reaches of her mind all week had begun to pull. The impulsiveness of his proposal, which had seemingly surprised him as much as her: was that guilt? The dragging of his feet afterwards: was that regret? His odd insistence upon etiquette as a form of respect to her parents: was that just something useful to hide behind as he procrastinated and looked for a way out? Did he have doubts?

Did he have someone else?

It seemed so impossible, to her. But what if Annie was right and men were different? She'd never been in love before. He was her first love, but she wasn't his: she knew there'd been other women, lots of them. His teenage years had been so much freer than hers; for one thing, he hadn't had a security detail tailing him every time he went out till he was eighteen.

She parked outside his flat, the little cream car seemingly having driven there itself as she continued staring out over the steering wheel, not even seeing the familiar street, or his bike chained to the black railings. She just sat there, blind and lost in her thoughts, the minutes dragging past as suspicions presented themselves and contradicted each other by turns.

Was she the one being disloyal to him for even having these thoughts? He'd never done anything to make her doubt his feelings for her, so why would she attach weight to the comments of a man she knew despised him? Was threatened by him?

No. This was madness. With a shake of her head, she pulled the keys from the ignition and clambered out of the car. For the first time, she took stock of her surroundings and looked up at the third-floor windows of his flat. They were in darkness, no lights shining from within. She checked the time – it was just gone four. If he and her father were playing the full eighteen holes, they'd be finishing around now. Allowing for time to get back to Battersea heliport . . . she estimated she had a good hour to herself, to calm down and settle – and to charge her phone. After the night spent in her coat pocket and then the three-hour journey back through the hills and down the motorway – the charging cable remembered too late in her overnight bag in the back – it had given up the ghost a third of the way down the M6.

Reaching for her things, she walked up to his door and used the spare key he had given her in their first week together. She let herself into the flat and dropped her bag with a sigh of relief as his usual untidy carelessness presented itself – shoes in a kicked-off pile under the hall console, papers spread in a messy heap across the kitchen table, the milk carton left out on the worktop, a shirt and several pairs of boxers drying on the clothes airer. It was hardly the scene of a seduction in her absence.

Feeling her doubts cast off once and for all – feeling guilty that she'd even given the suspicions airplay – she began tidying up as she plugged her phone in and got the bath running; she opened the windows to air the flat, sniffed and put the milk away, folded his clothes and laid flat the airer in the cupboard. She put the kettle on and began tidying his papers left out on the table. Most of it was colourful jargon to her – pie charts and bar graphs depicting . . . she wasn't even sure what. She shuffled them into a vaguely neat pile and made herself a decaf coffee, sinking into the chair to drink it whilst keeping an ear out for the sound of the bath filling up.

Outside, she heard the murmur of conversation on the street below, voices carrying but their words indistinct from here, the whine of leaky brakes from Ken Church Street. A pigeon was cooing from a nearby tree; planes coming in to land at Heathrow, not so very far away. Everything suddenly had a comfortingly humdrum familiarity to it and she felt her nerves begin to settle. A quiet Sunday afternoon in the city was exactly what she needed after the duplicity of her countryside weekend, the betrayal of her friends . . .

She picked up the topmost report and read idly, her gaze catching on words like *reforestation*, *vegetation structure*, *cost-negative carbon sequestration*. It was the orange peel report, she realized, the one her father had picked up on. He must have dug it out again to remind himself of the facts, determined to impress his future father-in-law.

She thumbed to the next report, below it, to see her family name spread loud and proud across a headline. And the next.

And the next . . . She smiled. Her father might have commissioned a summary report on him, but clearly Alex had decided to do some research of his own too. No wonder they got on so well.

There was a print-out of an *FT* article, complete with a picture of her father. It showed him in a boardroom somewhere, gripping the hand of another grey-haired man, both looking suitably pleased about some deal. Beneath that was a *Forbes* profile on her father; it was a year or so old and she remembered it well, coming out shortly after the announcement that the Tremain family was signing up to the Giving Pledge – the new initiative by Warren Buffett and Bill and Melinda Gates, it had immediately become the world's most exclusive club in which billionaires pledge to donate the majority, if not all, of their fortunes during their lifetimes or upon their deaths. But that wasn't why she remembered this journalistic piece. Her father never gave interviews, but the reporters had found some sources prepared to talk, and someone had even supplied a photograph of her and Miles as teenagers. It was the fact that the photograph had been printed without copyright permission that meant her father had been able to threaten to sue unless they made a sizeable donation to his foundation and printed a written apology in the next issue.

Parts of the text had been underlined in blue ink – the nuggets Alex wanted to bring out in conversation and use as part of his charm offensive. She remembered him coming in the other night, saying he'd been trying to find ways to impress her father and if there was one thing he – as a PhD student – could do, it was research. She read the notes with a wry eye; it was always strange to read about her family in the third person, observed by strangers who wrote in a tone that suggested they knew them.

She read it through once, then again, leaning in more closely. Something had caught her attention on the first skim-read, a detail that snagged in her mind . . .

The phone rang suddenly, vibrating loudly against the table and jolting her from her concentration.

She went over to it. Four per cent battery? Still not enough to unplug it. 'Hello?' she asked, crouching down on her heels; the cable wasn't long enough for her to stand.

'Piglet?' a voice shouted down the line.

'Dad! Hi.'

There was a lot of background noise, the line indistinct, and she wondered whether he was in the chopper. 'Where are you?' he called. 'Not still in the sticks, I hope?'

'No, I've just got back. I'm at Alex's flat.'

'Good! Because we're on our way back now. Get over to the house and keep your mother calm till we get there.'

Calm? Tara felt her heart catch. She hardly dared ask the question. 'Dad . . . do you mean Alex has talked to you?'

'Absolutely he has!' he laughed. 'You've found a good one there, Piglet! But I don't want to talk about it here. Get back home double-time. We've got some celebrating to do!'

Tara put the phone down, her hands over her mouth as her excitement suddenly ricocheted. 'Oh my God,' she whispered to herself, giving a squeal. 'He's only gone and done it!'

'Darling!'

Her mother looked surprised as Tara walked in, not least because for once, she had dressed up. She had put on the Ganni dress she'd been waiting months for an opportunity to wear. It was slim-fitting aubergine silk with a waistband that wasn't going to be an option for long.

Her mother was sitting on the sofa, a gin and tonic on the

table beside her and a magazine on her lap. 'I didn't know you were coming over.'

Tara walked to the bar cabinet and poured herself a tonic water, adding a slice of cucumber for visual interest. 'I know. Twice in one weekend, the world's going mad,' she quipped.

Her mother cast an up-down gaze over her. 'Are you going on after here?'

'No. I don't think so,' Tara smiled. 'Why? Are you going out?'

'I hardly think so,' her mother tutted. 'I've barely seen your father all weekend. He's been playing golf today, with your Alex.'

Tara's smiled widened. Her Alex. 'Yes, I heard. They should be back any second apparently. Dad called.'

'He called you?'

'Mm-hmm.'

'And asked you to come over here?'

'Yes.'

Her mother blinked, no fool. She sat a little straighter. 'Why would he do that?'

Tara felt her stomach fizz with happiness and excitement. She didn't know how he and Alex wanted to tell the happy news, but she would have to wait till they got here. 'Why not? Can't we enjoy an impromptu Sunday night supper all together before you go off?' Tara looked around the space. 'Is Miles in?'

Her mother sank back a little into the cushions. 'No. Gstaad, remember? Left yesterday morning. He's back Tuesday night.'

'Oh yes. I forgot.' It was probably just as well. She would need to talk Miles around first and carefully engineer the next meeting between her brother and boyfriend. She took a sip of the drink, needing to cool down. She had run her bath too hot and, adding on the hurry to get over here before the others, she was now flustered.

'Weren't you off on a jolly somewhere too this weekend?'

'Yes, Shropshire. For Sophie's twenty-first. I just got back this afternoon.'

'Now, Sophie . . . ?' Her mother looked blank.

'Vet, slight buck teeth.' Tara knew to reduce her friends down to their compound parts for her mother's ease of attention. It wasn't her usual style to be so blunt, but she was still smarting at the way they'd treated her; they'd clearly said far worse about her behind her back and though Sophie hadn't said anything derogatory outright, she hadn't stepped in either.

'Oh yes, Sophie! Lovely girl. Is she really twenty-one already?'

'I know.'

'She looks so much younger. I think because she hasn't mastered her *maquillage* yet.'

'Sophie doesn't have any make-up.'

'Well, that's her problem, right there,' her mother said with a pitying look. 'Of course, we shall have to start thinking about your twenty-first.'

'I don't want a party.'

'So you always say, but we really must mark it in some way. It's far too big a life milestone to just let slip by.'

'Well, I'll think about it,' Tara lied; she had bigger life milestones coming up than a birthday party. She took another sip of tonic as they heard the front door slam and the low timbre of male voices echoed down the hall. Talk about timing!

Tara felt the butterflies in her stomach take wing. Finally, the moment she had been waiting for all week – if not quite all her life – was here. Alex had rung her seven times too since she'd put the phone down to her father, but she'd been in the bath for three of them and missed the rest driving over.

She didn't want to hear half-stories, anyway; she wanted him to tell her everything when he got here. She wanted to know every last detail of his bonding weekend and to forget every single moment of hers, to see the look in his eyes . . .

The door opened, her father filling the void and looking uncharacteristically ebullient in an emerald-green diamond-knit cashmere sweater; for some reason, dressing for golf meant casting off all sartorial sobriety and going all out on colour. 'There you are!' he boomed. 'I was hoping we'd find you together.'

'Were you, Brucey? And why was that?' her mother asked with outright suspicion as he strode into the room and kissed her on her powdered cheek. 'Hello again, Alex.'

'Samantha, it's lovely to see you.' Alex had followed in after him, wearing navy chinos and a button-down shirt and jumper, not his style at all and clearly freshly bought at the club. Tara's smile widened at the sight of him – too handsome for his own good; awkward and preppy-looking in his new clothes – before he was blocked from sight again by her father coming over for his hug.

'Piglet.' Her father bent down to kiss her cheek too, rising with a wink. Tara could feel her eyes shining with happiness. He turned back to his wife, his movements energized with the vigour of a man thirty years younger. 'To answer your question, Sam-Sam, I asked Piglet over here because we've got some celebrating to do, that's why.'

Tara always smiled when her father called her mother by her pet name. It was so . . . unlike her.

They all watched as he walked over to the drinks cabinet and pulled a magnum of Bollinger from the chiller. Samantha Tremain shifted forwards in her seat again, glancing across at Tara. 'Bruce, what exactly's going on?'

Bruce looked over at Alex, clearly enjoying building the suspense. 'Do you want to tell her, or shall I?'

'Uh . . .' Alex's gaze slid over to Tara. For the first time, she noticed how pale he looked.

'Stage fright?' Bruce chuckled, popping the cork and letting it fly through the room, hitting the frame of a small Vermeer on the opposite wall. 'Fine, I'll be the master of ceremonies.'

Tara looked back at Alex again as her father poured them each a flute. He looked . . . ill. Feverish, almost.

'Alex . . . ?' she asked in concern. Was he still hungover? Had the port done for him last night? She'd certainly never heard him drunk like that before.

'Yes, Alex – the man of the hour! The man we have been looking for.'

We? Tara glanced at her father as he placed a glass in her hand. Alex was the man *she* had been looking for, surely?

Everyone had a glass now. Her mother was perched on the very edge of her seat as though preparing to either jump up or lie down.

Bruce Tremain stuffed one hand casually into his trouser pocket. It was the stance he often adopted when he was making a speech – relaxed, confident, loquacious.

'I'll be honest, when he first walked through that door on Friday night, I had no inkling whatsoever that this young man was going to become such an important part of our family's life. Samantha and I try to be approachable and welcoming to all our children's friends – possibly especially to our Piglet's, as she is so very prickly about all . . . this.' He gave that vague gesture her family always used when talking about their surroundings. Tara's gaze slid back to Alex's again and she gave him an encouraging smile – but he didn't smile back. In fact, he looked away.

Tara felt a bubble of fear begin to roil in the pit of her stomach. Something was wrong, she could feel it. Was he regretting it already? Had she pressured him, after all, into doing this before he was truly ready?

'But I did not expect the exciting revelations that have developed over the course of this weekend. Sam-Sam, I know you've been annoyed with me for not spending the time with you here that I promised I would, but when I tell you our announcement, I think it will all make sense.'

'Then get on with it, please.'

Bruce went over and rested a hand on Alex's shoulder. 'Alex here came to me with a question, a proposal if you like—'

Her mother's hands flew to her mouth and she looked across at Tara with bright eyes.

'—And after many deep discussions over the course of this weekend, I have agreed.' He looked at the younger man, nodding with an earnest sincerity that, for some reason, didn't comfort Tara. 'I've made some calls and got the ball rolling on plans to buy nine thousand square miles of land in Costa Rica.' His grin widened. '. . . We're setting up a national park together.'

Silence echoed like a gunshot. Tara felt the room spin and tilt, her life beginning to slide away under her feet.

'You're doing *what*?' Her mother's voice sounded a hundred miles away. 'Oh for heaven's sake, Bruce! That wasn't what I was expecting you to say at all!' She glanced towards Tara and then away again, pursing her lips. 'I mean, why did you have to make such a fanfare over something like that?'

'Because this is the project we've been looking for, Sammy, don't you see? Ever since we signed to the Giving Pledge, I've been wondering how the damned hell I'm going to get rid of the money. Seems to me it's easier to make that sort of money than it is to get rid of it. Then Alex here came along and started talking about his ideas for a huge conservation project in Central America. It's all about scale! That's the secret to making a meaningful difference. All these other projects and charities that come to us . . . they're just tiny islands of endeavour and good intentions. But as Alex here has pointed out to me, islands never thrive, darling! They're too small, with too many middlemen taking their piece of the pie. I mean, you know what the egos of these guys are like. "My foundation this, my foundation that." Fifty years from now, they'll all be defunct! Lasting success means having a long-term vision, getting rid of the middlemen, streamlining the process to a single source of funds – and thinking big. If we want carbon stability then that requires biodiversity and abundance, and that can only be delivered on scale.'

Tara felt a ringing in her ears, a shrill high-pitched tinnitus that filled her head as the room spun around her in ever faster circles.

'But why Costa Rica?' her mother asked. 'I mean, it's so far away.'

'I like that we have a connection with the place, for one thing.' Momentarily, her father looked across at Tara and winked at her, oblivious that with every word, her world was collapsing around her. She could actually hear Alex's voice in her father's words; they were words he had said to her countless times over dinner, on the sofa, lying in bed . . . But now it was her father saying them, his eyes glittering with pride and excitement, a look Tara had seen so many times before. He loved nothing more than cutting a deal, so to save the planet at the same time . . . 'But more than that, six per cent of the planet's biodiversity lives within its borders and through this project, we now have an opportunity to protect that in perpetuity. Alex, our man with a plan, has thought it all through! He's drawn up a comprehensive ten-year programme for developing the park, with a view to gifting it back to the Costa Rican people at the end of that time, although clearly with caveats attached. Lots of caveats. But I don't envisage any problems – a quarter of the country is already in private protected ownership; conservation is their thing. Did you know that Costa Rica is on course to be the world's first nation powered entirely by renewable energies?'

'Bruce, you know I don't keep a track of these things.'

'Well, to be honest, neither did I. I didn't even remember that I'd already written Alex here a cheque for five million dollars for his butterfly conservation initiative! I think Patsy must have handled it for me.' He frowned, as if still baffled that he could have overlooked such a thing. '. . . But doesn't that sum up the problem? There's too many people doing lots of little things, when the time for that has passed! It's already too late. The natural world is in crisis and what's needed now is bold vision and big fortunes. There's only a handful of people in the world who, like us, can make a difference on the scale that's needed now.' He looked at Alex proudly, placing a hand on his shoulder like he was his son. 'I'm still not entirely sure how it's all come about, but somehow over the course of our conversations this weekend, Alex has leveraged that little five mill donation into a billion-dollar endowment instead.'

How it had all come about? Tara knew.

'A billion? All at once? Oh Bruce, don't you think that's a bit much?'

'Darling, what have I just been telling you? Saving the planet can't be done piecemeal. Growing populations, spreading human civilizations and climate change are overwhelming the earth's resources. It's no good breaking up our donations into a few million here and there; we can only make a meaningful difference by working at scale. By buying a vast chunk of land to actively foster reforestation projects *and* preserve the existing forest regions; only then can we lock down vast swathes of land into a permanent carbon storage state.'

Her mother was finally silenced. Tara hadn't said a word. She wasn't sure she'd even breathed in all that time. She felt removed not just from the conversation, but her own body.

'Do you know . . .' her father laughed, suddenly amused by something as he jabbed a finger in her direction. 'I had thought you were introducing us to Alex because you two were an item! It never crossed my mind you were bringing him to me with an agenda!' He wagged the finger affectionately, like he was indulging her mischief. 'First it was the mother and child clinics, now this.'

'Tara—' Alex's voice was like a blade glinting in long grass. It flashed, making her wince and draw back as finally, her eyes connected with his in a way she knew they never would again. He stared back at her with regret, and yet no regret either, and she remembered the conversation they'd had only this week about conviction. *Be prepared to cross the line to get things done.*

'Excuse me,' she said, setting down her glass with a visibly shaking hand and running from the room.

'Piglet?'

She left the room in a whirl, her skirts blowing back against her legs as she grabbed her keys from the hall table and made for the front door. Alex's footsteps were right behind her, his hand on her arm, stopping her.

'Tara, this has nothing to do with us—'

She spun round and slapped him hard on the cheek, stunning

them both. She could feel the gaping great hole already opening up inside her as she let his lie settle. Because it was a lie, she knew that as fact. This was everything to do with them. It was not just why he had chased her down the street that morning, but why he'd been in that very coffee shop. They hadn't met by chance, he'd planned this from the start. He had known all along who she was, and when she hadn't shown any signs of introducing him to her parents, he had proposed marriage to accelerate the process. His surprise over dinner when she'd finally told him who she was? A charade. His prevarication over asking her father for her hand at dinner? He needed more time alone with him to make his pitch. James MacLennan had been right. Alex was cheating his way to the pinnacle of his career ambitions by using her as a Trojan horse to get to her father.

And she knew exactly how it had all gone down. Thanks to that *Forbes* article – the only one that had ever carried a photograph of her – he had realized the opportunity she presented and he had ruthlessly exploited it. She thought of his hands upon her body, his lips on her skin . . . his baby in her belly . . . Oh God!

'I know what you're thinking,' he said urgently. 'But you don't understand—'

She stared back at him with a contempt she had never known possible. She understood far more than he knew, her mind returning again and again to the profile he'd printed up and specifically, the faint line which her eye had snagged on, just as her father rang.

You last visited this page on 18/03/2010.

A year ago. Eight months before he'd met her. There was simply no other way to spin it – everything he'd ever said to her had been a lie.

Part Two

Chapter Nine

Ten years later

Holly set down her tray with a clatter, sinking into the chair and letting her limbs splay like a rag doll's, her head lolling back in a moment of stolen relaxation. 'Tell me it's nearly over,' she groaned, her curly red ponytail almost brushing the floor.

'It's nearly over,' Tara replied, biting into her sandwich like she was a lion sinking her teeth into an antelope. She had been on her feet for ten hours and counting, and she'd yet to finish a can of Coke. Was it any wonder she was plagued with almost-permanent headaches?

Holly pulled herself back into a semi-erect form, taking in Tara's own quiet exhaustion. 'Remind me again why we do this?'

'Job satisfaction, apparently.' Tara arched an eyebrow as she chewed.

'Oh yeah – that's it. I've had *so much* of that today,' Holly quipped, a glint in her eyes. 'So far, I've been puked on, put in a stranglehold, called a "fucking bitch" three times and had someone threaten me with a needle.'

'Huh. Quiet shift.' The lowdown on Holly's shifts as a registrar in A&E often read like horror stories. Tara watched

111

as her friend sucked coffee through a straw, trying to avoid the 'bad tooth' she had been avoiding going to the dentist for.

'Busy one for you?' Holly asked out of the corner of her mouth, continuing to suck.

'One sub-cranial bleed, one ruptured spleen, two resusc, and a fourth-degree burns admission. No strangleholds though.'

'See? You're missing out. A&E's where the excitement is.'

'Not to mention the glamour.' Tara nudged her friend's foot lightly, signalling with her eyes the regurgitated carrot remains still stuck to the top of her shoes.

'Eewww! For God's sake . . .' Holly grimaced, immediately pushing her plate of spaghetti Bolognese away. She reached for the Chunky KitKat instead. It was a constant wonder to Tara that Holly wasn't permanently shaking – she survived on caffeine and sugar and weighed about the same as Tara's left leg. 'It's your big night tonight, isn't it?'

Tara took another bite of sandwich. 'Ugh, don't. I hate awards things,' she said, her mouth full.

'I wouldn't know. I've never been invited to one.' Holly's tone was arch, but her eyes were dancing. As she had once told Tara, she was in this game 'for the guts, not the glory'.

'Well, have you built any international paediatric clinics recently?' Tara's tone was wry.

'Not *recently*, no.' She groaned. 'I can't even afford to do my side return.'

Tara offered no comment. Her friend would never allow her to help out, even if she was daft enough to offer.

'So don't tell me, you're already packed for the trip?'

'You mean you're not?' Tara quipped.

'We both know I'm going to be sitting on that plane in my scrubs.'

'Mmm.' Tara took another deep bite of sandwich. She wasn't sure anything had ever tasted so good, but even chewing felt exhausting.

'If I'm held up, they'll wait for me, right?'

'No. They'll have filed a flight schedule.'

'I thought that was the point of having your own plane. They work around you.'

Tara shot her a stern look.

'What?' she grinned. 'Am I wrong? Tell me I'm wrong.'

'It's about attitude.'

Holly tutted. 'Your fortune is wasted on you, d'you know that? God, the things I would do if I was in your shoes! Instead you build baby hospitals and vote Green and recycle the shit out of things. Why do you always have to be so good?'

'Why do you say that like it's a four-letter word?'

'Technically it is a four-letter word.'

Tara grinned, letting her mind wander to the promise that the coming week was bringing – getting out of these clothes, this hospital, these shores, back to the place of her childhood dreams, the land of lush rainforests and exotic birds and pristine beaches. She planned to eat hourly and sleep in ten-hour shifts and finally look after herself. Sun, sand, sleep – it had become her mantra, especially on night shifts.

'*Doctor Tremain to ICU.*'

They both tensed at the sound of the voice on the tannoy. Tara stared at the half-crescents in the tuna sandwich, the scant evidence that she had had lunch today. Without even a sigh, she dropped it to the plate and pushed her chair back, her tired eyes meeting her friend's.

'Catch you later then, maybe,' Holly nodded with a resigned expression. 'Airport for eight thirty tomorrow, right?'

'*Eight*,' Tara corrected, knowing her friend knew the ETD perfectly well. 'Sharp.'

Tara picked up her KeepCup and took a large swill of what passed as coffee here before breaking into a jog. She nodded at familiar faces as she ran with careful haste. She never usually ran; it panicked the patients to see doctors sprinting. But as her pager went off once, twice, three times more, she sped up through the too-familiar corridors and tore up the stairwells; there was no time for lifts.

She could have run it blindfolded, knowing the layout of the hospital better than her own home. She could locate swabs from the tiniest store cupboard or grab the defibrillator on any ward; she knew which vending machines were tricky, the nicest porters to ask for help, but she had no idea of the names of her neighbours or where the stopcock was in her Pimlico flat, and Rory had pointed out to her only last week that the protective blue film was still stuck to the front of her fridge; she had thought it was supposed to look like that. She'd had it for eighteen months.

She was there in under three minutes, flashing her ID card against the ICU entry screen, waiting impatiently for the two seconds it took for the doors to swing back with a brushed whisper. Her heart plummeted as she saw one of her F2 team duck her head out of Room Three with a wild-eyed expression, as though looking for someone. Looking for her.

'Talk to me,' she said, automatically reaching for the stethoscope around her neck as she walked in, the other juniors straightening up and moving back slightly from the bed, revealing the tiny, crushed form of a four-year-old girl. In spite of her training always to be objective, her usually implacable mask slipped and she inwardly reacted with shock and horror again at the sight of the child. No one should endure what that little body had: sixteen broken bones. A ruptured spleen. Fractured skull. Hearing loss.

'BP crashed. Sixty over forty. Fluid, stat!'

What? Tara's eyes scanned the monitors, making sense of the digits that told her an accelerating story, a subplot to the simple Happy Ever After Tara had thought she'd given her in theatre nine hours ago. Everything had been fine all day, but now her blood pressure was 60/40, far too low; her oxygen saturation levels were 85; and her pulse was 140 and rising as her heart desperately tried to pump enough blood and oxygen to her organs. She was going to crash again, her system insistently shutting down, her tiny body wildly swinging towards death like a monkey looping between the trees.

Tara frowned, trying to make sense of the riddle. Something was glitching inside that little body – but what? What was she missing? The surgery had been a success. Admitted just after 6 a.m. – her parents now in custody – the scans had been unambiguous, her stitches had been clean and neat. It had been a textbook procedure, the girl had come through without any complications; Tara had done her job well. She'd been anticipating a quiet day and night's rest for her small patient and then a move to the paediatric ward tomorrow morning, followed by the inevitable visit from social services. She hadn't been worried about her prognosis, though it had broken her heart to think that no one, absolutely no one, was sitting in the waiting area, tearful and pacing, desperate to hear how that little girl was doing. Surviving? Dying? No one cared. She was four years old and as alone in this world as anyone could ever be.

Tara put her hand on the slender arm, feeling the small girl's warmth, her flickering aliveness like a candle in the breeze. What chance did she have? Born to parents that never wanted her, parents barely more than kids themselves, parents who only knew the rule of the fist and the escape of the bottle. She felt the familiar groundswell of dismay – guilt – rise up in her that she should have so much and others so little, but she drew herself up an inch, reminding herself this was what she lived for. This was how she made the difference and gave back. She could do this, at least.

The child's body stiffened suddenly beneath her touch, then relaxed, monitors beginning to blink and flash, numbers to shout at her.

'Call theatre,' Tara said, her voice setting hard as logic, fact and a rigorous education took over. Sentiment wouldn't save the child. Only medicine. Only calm. Her eyes tracked the changing stats, deciphering now the meaning behind the digits and converting them to flesh and blood catastrophe. 'She's haemorrhaging. We need to get her back on the table. Now.' She must have missed something when she went in the first time. She must have done.

One of the nurses ran out of the room to make the call as the sides of the bed were raised up and the brakes taken off. Tara blocked it all out – the noise, the flashing colours, the adrenaline like a metallic tang in the air. She felt held in a cloud where the world beyond its feathered edges ceased to exist, where *she* ceased to be or feel. Her feet moved automatically, lift doors were closing but she could see only what was in front of her. A child, dying.

'Stay with me, Lucy,' she said, squeezing the tiny forearm. 'You're safe. We're going to look after you.'

She moved instinctively into the surgical theatre, walking arms-first into her outheld scrubs and soaping her hands rhythmically, methodically, her brain scanning through for the most likely areas of breach. She had to find the point of egress quickly. She was opening up that little body for the second time in nine hours, a little body that should, right now, be playing in a garden in the sunshine or splashing in a pool or eating cake. She was even more vulnerable now than the first surgery, even weaker, and Tara knew there was a precarious tipping point when the interventions made to save her would become the intrusions that endangered her: hands shouldn't be inside a chest cavity no bigger than a ball, that healthy growing heart shouldn't need to be assisted by a ventilator . . .

She blinked hard once, banishing all emotion and pushed the door with the back of her shoulder, rejoining the team in theatre. Their small patient had been prepped but Tara knew the crash was still coming. It was a race against time.

She stood motionless and took a steadying breath, feeling her mind clear.

'Scalpel.' The word was a command, like the first note of a song. She held out her hand and the nurse placed the instrument carefully in her palm.

The incision was clean and decisive, the blood dark and thick, telling her at a single glance that her patient's oxygen levels were low. Her world narrowed further. It was like looking through a telescope, her field of vision trained solely on the radial field immediately before her. There was order in what she saw; it was one of the reasons why she loved medicine – the fundamentals were always identical, it was just disease and trauma that needed to be rooted out as anomalies. But she was blind here. Blood was filling everything, too quickly, a glistening dark red sea flooding around organs. The suction pump could only do so much.

She didn't panic. She trusted in the training she had had at the side of the world's best. She trusted in her abilities.

Even with a mortality rate as inevitably high as ICU's, she had never had a child die on her table and this four-year-old girl, utterly alone, was not going to be her first.

She put her hands in, making minute movements with her fingers and feeling for the tiny tear that could wreak such devastation, her fingers pressing lightly against tender tissue, brushing against the proud neat and tidy stitches she had put in herself early this morning.

The monitors were screaming at her in an orderly manner, telling her – as if she didn't already know – that she was losing the race, running out of time, not good enough.

'BP fifty-four over thirty-five.'

She felt the team's eyes upon her as the tension tightened. She worked faster, her fingers deft, trying to 'see' where her eyes could not. She was known for her calm under pressure, her ability to rise above a crisis and do what needed to be done. But she wasn't rising right now and she felt the first shot of panic, like a fluttering frill around the periphery of her vision. There was so much blood. This couldn't be from a single breach, surely? Where was it? What . . . ?

What was it?

What was that?

There was something, hidden below the scarlet surface; as thin as a hair but the tip sharp enough to prick against the pad of her index finger—

'Suction.' She directed the nozzle herself and saw it – a flash of silver embedded in tender tissue. Tara felt the walls press in, the ceiling drop an inch.

A *blade*?

In the next blink, it was hidden from sight again, blood refilling the cavity, that strong little heart doing its job too well. It was her own that was struggling to beat. She felt completely blindsided by the discovery, her mind racing to find explanations even as her hands moved automatically, fingers blindly probing for the tiny metal shaving again.

She found it, and started to stitch, but her time was up. The charts on the vital signs screen – already wailing and flashing red – were interrupted suddenly by a steady bold line that raced from left to right, like some early 1980s computer racing game. Flatline.

'She's crashing!' the nurse said.

'Moving to one hundred per cent oxygen,' the anaesthetist said.

Tara removed her hands as they began manual massage. She stared down in a disassociated state at the tiny body, bright white and dark red. It felt like the world had stopped spinning, the tiny scalpel blade glinting jewel-like in the kidney dish. She felt frozen in time, holding her bloodied hands up like spiked crowns, as the drama played out towards an inevitable end, telling a single story.

This was all her fault.

Chapter Ten

Her dress swished as she walked, a long black taffeta column with a flat bow that looped at a jaunty angle across the shoulders, and her hair swept up in a bun that would have had a prima ballerina wincing. She was grateful the hotel had a carpeted lobby; it made walking in heels so much easier after a bottle and a half of red. She reminded herself to keep putting one foot in front of the other. That was all she had to do. Just get through tonight. Keep walking, keep smiling . . .

'Tremain.'

The man stopped in front of her, handsome in black tie – and aware of it.

'Charles! Goodness, I didn't know you were here.' Her voice was composed, but it had a hollow ring to it, like she was speaking into a barrel. 'How are you? It's been a long time.'

'I know. What – five years? Six?'

She shrugged. 'Something like that.' Their relationship – if it could be called that – had been more stop than start. She tried to remember the name of his wife. '. . . How's Caroline?'

'Great. Great. Expecting number two.'

'Two? Wow. Congratulations.' Every other person she met was pregnant these days, it seemed.

'Thanks.' His eyes crinkled at the sides when he smiled

now, and he looked tired. (Didn't they all?) 'And I hear congratulations are due to you too?'

Her smile slipped, all the way to the floor. 'Sorry?'

'I heard you made consultant.'

She gave a wan smile. 'Oh that, yes. Very pleased.'

'I'll bet. Did I hear right that you're the youngest consultant at Tommy's?'

'Well, I wouldn't know about that.'

He gave a lopsided smile. 'You always were too modest.' A blonde woman in ivory draped silk viscose came and stood beside him. 'Ah, there you are, darling. I was just on my way back to the table,' he said. 'You remember Tara Tremain? We were SHOs together at St Mary's.'

'Of course,' Caroline smiled blankly, her bump as neat as her hair. 'How are you?'

'Tremain's made consultant in ICU at Thomas's,' Charles offered, before Tara could even open her mouth.

'Oh. Congratulations.' Caroline, Tara seemed to recall hearing somewhere, was head of a Montessori nursery that had a waiting list as long as the Rheumatology department's.

'And to you. Your second, I hear?' It was one of those circular conversations, the same material being passed around with faux cheer and insincere wishes. No one actually saying anything meaningful. No one actually connecting.

Caroline's hand instinctively went to her stomach. 'A little girl. Rollo's so excited he's going to be a big brother.'

Tara nodded. 'So lovely. Well, you look wonderful, pregnancy suits you.' She began stepping away. 'Great to see you both. I'd better get back to my table.'

'Absolutely. Let's grab a coffee sometime. I want to hear how you did it,' Charles called after her. 'Give me some tips for the top.'

'Haha!' she replied, as though he was joking. 'You never did need my help, Charles,' she said with a wave, turning away.

She slid into her seat, casting a vague smile at their table. Rory, listening in on a conversation with Mark Wu, sat back and squeezed her knee. He draped an arm over the back of her chair, watching as she fiddled with the skirt of her dress.

'I thought you'd left me,' he murmured in her ear.

'You should be so lucky. No, I got caught by Charles Miller, know him?'

Rory thought for a moment, his face falling into that familiar look of concentration. 'Over at Guy's?'

'Yeah. I did my SHO training with him.'

Rory smiled, an eyebrow lifting, knowing how tangled medics' relationship histories tended to be . 'And . . . ?'

'And his wife is expecting a little sister for Darling Rollo.'

He chuckled and leaned over, kissing her on the cheek.

'How much longer before we can get out of here?' she whispered.

His blue eyes twinkled. 'Well, bit rude before coffee, don't you think?'

'Mmm,' she concurred reluctantly, looking around them and wishing he wasn't always so polite. As Holly had said on more than one occasion, she had managed to find her perfect match. 'You, but with a willy,' had been Holly's exact words.

She sighed restlessly as she watched people beginning to mingle. Now the awards and speeches were done, now the wine had been drunk, the evening was going to slip its stays. People would begin to dance and flirt with people who weren't their spouses . . . It all suddenly felt endless, airless, the small talk stupefying. She had a fear she might lose control of herself and suddenly *do* something – scream, laugh, cry, rip her clothes off; that worst of things, make a scene.

'Everything okay?' His hand was on her knee. 'You went pretty hard on the cab sauv, I noticed. Has something happened?' Rory was watching her keenly.

She gave a careless shrug, looking away as a lump gathered in her throat. 'Everything's fine. I'm just tired.'

'Yeah,' he sighed in weary agreement, running a hand through his hair and holding it there for a moment. 'Okay, fine. How about we make a French exit in five minutes? I'll just extricate myself from this conversation.' His head angled slightly towards Mark Wu, holding court. 'Can you last that long?'

Could she? She felt an agitation that was down to far more than just wine. It felt like her soul was turning over from a long sleep.

'Five minutes?' She narrowed her eyes as she caught sight of someone familiar. 'I think I can manage that. I've just seen a face from the past.'

'Who?'

'An old uni friend. I've not seen her in ages.' She kissed him on the lips and got up again. 'Rescue me in five. You'll find me by the ice penis.'

'It's clearly modelled on a syringe.'

'Yeah-yeah-yeah. You say tomato . . .' she said, tossing the words over her shoulder like a scarf.

She crossed the ballroom, although that was too grand a word for what it actually was. No balls had ever been held here, at least, not of the crinoline and wigs sort. They were in an executive hotel off the Edgware Road, whose conference room had been draped in white chiffon swags. Giant cardboard hoardings of their sponsors – a medical equipment company – showed saccharine-sweet images of people hugging and children running on grass, strangely at odds with the bow-tied stiffness of the awards ceremony.

The object of her attention was leaning against a mock-marble pillar, texting with one hand, holding a glass of red wine in the other. The droplets from the revolving glitter ball were falling upon her like crystal rain.

'Don't tell me. Man trouble,' Tara said, coming to stand by her and taking the glass from her hand. She took a sip as Liv looked back at her in surprise.

'Fuck! Twig!'

They hugged, before Liv stepped back and gave her the full once-over. 'Look at you! My God, when did you become such a grown-up?'

Tara groaned. 'I hardly think so. I feel I'm the only woman in the room not either wearing a ring or carrying a bump.'

'You and me both,' Liv drawled, resuming her slumped position against the pillar again. She looked at Tara through narrowed eyes. 'Congrats on your award, by the way.'

'Thanks.'

'A teaching hospital in Senegal, huh?'

Tara shrugged. Her family's standing was no longer a secret from anyone thanks to the media fanfare that had greeted her father's 'Costa Rica project' (as her mother called it) and which, of course, had proved correct her friends' fears for her. The girls had rallied around her in the wake of events, but their pity at Alex's treachery had been heightened by their excitement at her newly revealed heiress status and there had been something mawkish in their attentions. She had found it hard to forgive them fully for the sly way they had behaved at Sophie's birthday and things had never been quite the same between them (except with Holly, of course, who had always known and never cared). Perhaps it was because they were so inextricably linked to that fateful weekend that Tara hadn't tried to stay in touch with them after graduation, instead letting the friendships slowly drift, and it had been at least seven years since she'd last seen Liv. But little had changed, it seemed. Even standing here now, she could sense Liv's beady-eyed fascination with her life, and even now, Tara still felt a glint of anger. More than a glint.

Nonetheless, she smiled. 'Well, if you ever fancy a sabbatical, we're always on the lookout for medics to train up the staff. Between yellow fever, typhoid and hep A, we've got our work cut out for us there.'

'Don't jest – I might take you up on that,' Liv groaned. 'I've got a wait list that would go four times round the block. I think I could work till I'm eighty and still never clear it. I used to fantasize about my dream man. Now I just fantasize about running out of patients.'

'I know what you mean. The other day, I went eleven hours without even peeing. My bladder was like a bowling ball. I swear a junior actually opened his mouth to ask me when the baby was due.'

Liv chortled. 'And to think we chose this.'

'I know. Last laugh, right?' Tara glanced casually around the room, aware she was on autopilot. It seemed to her that much of being a doctor involved boasting to other doctors and 'civilian' friends about how exhausted and overworked they were. Like it was a competition.

Everyone was up and mingling now, a few people even beginning to dance. Charles Miller was one of them and Tara watched him for a minute. That was some advice she could have given him for getting to consultant: *don't*. She was firmly of the view that throwing shapes at an event like this had a direct negative impact on promotion chances. Seeing some people dance made it seem like a moral imperative to remove all surgical implements from their hands.

The snatched glimpse of the blade flashed through her mind's eye again and she turned sharply away.

She looked back at her old friend and took the glass from Liv's hand again, almost draining it. 'So who's the guy?'

Liv pulled a face. 'Ugh, just a fling. Flingette, actually. A waiter I met at this fancy pizza place in Soho.'

'Well, so long as it was a *fancy* pizza place,' Tara quipped.

'He's very hot.'

'I should hope so. Age?'

'Mid-to-early twenties.' Liv hesitated. 'What? Don't judge me! Like I said, it's a flingette. No strings.'

Tara shrugged as Liv gave a half-hysterical wail. 'It's your life, your choice, Liv. Who am I to judge?'

'Yeah, but I bet you're with some shit-hot Master of the Universe type.'

'Because that's really my type,' Tara deadpanned.

'Well, you always did get the gorgeous ones.'

'Not always.' Tara looked around the room before Liv could catch her gaze. She sensed *his* name hovered like an aura around her whenever she saw any of the old crowd. She could tell they wanted to know if she'd seen him, what he was up to now working for her father, whether they were in touch . . . For all his two-faced duplicity, he still exerted a pull over her friends and in spite of Holly's warnings never to mention his name, it was always there nonetheless, just unspoken. She felt her soul tremor and twitch again, deep inside her bones, and she suppressed a shudder.

'. . . Huh. A really shit DJ,' Tara tutted as 'Ice Ice Baby' came on.

'So who are you with now? Are you married?' Liv remained on topic, still watching her, and Tara could detect a coldness in her gaze. Her family's wealth made her an object of constant scrutiny. People wanted to know what that kind of wealth looked like, close up. Even people who had known her once.

'God, no. I'm seeing a guy called Rory. He's a senior reg in cardio at Chelsea and Westminster.'

'Younger too?'

'No, two years older than me.'

'But you're a consultant already.'

'Yes.'

Liv's eyebrows shot up. 'And he's cool with that?'

Tara shrugged. 'Well, I guess he has to be. I'm not getting a demotion for him.'

Liv looked bemused. 'Is it serious?'

'Define serious.' Tara gave one of her signature dismissive shrugs. 'We've been together a year or so now. We've talked about us getting our own place.'

'I sense a "but".'

Tara wrinkled her nose. 'No, no "but". Things are just pretty good the way they are and I'm of the "if it ain't broke" school of dating.' Rory had suggested moving in together enough times to prove he was serious, but if there wasn't an overwhelming reason to do it, there also wasn't one why they shouldn't. They got on so well, shared the same interests, understood the demands of each other's jobs; the sex was good. He liked having money but wasn't consumed by it; he'd come from enough affluence to live in a certain way without really having to think about it. Life with him would continue to be uncomplicated and steady. Perfectly, quietly happy.

'Oh, I hear ya. I moved in with Ben, the dentist – remember him?'

'Just about.' Strawberry blonde, jug ears. She was her mother's daughter after all.

'Three years we were together before we took the big leap. I was convinced he was The One – my mother had chosen her outfit, I was all ready to order the flowers. Then two weeks with the same front door key and it was over. Never again.'

'It's not for everyone,' Tara sighed. 'We can't all be like Sophie.'

To everyone's astonishment, Sophie had married at twenty-three to a small livery yard owner and was now back living in Shropshire with three black labs, a Welsh cob and a flock of ducklings.

'I swear to God, I thought she'd be the last of us to get hitched, not the first!'

'She did too, no doubt,' Tara shrugged. 'Have you seen anyone else recently?' 'Anyone else' specifically meant their old uni group.

'Annie and I text, meet up for a drink whenever she's in town, which isn't all that often.'

'Last I heard she was in Brussels?'

'Yeah. Conducting a torrid affair with a Euro MP who's married with four kids.'

'Nice,' Tara said flatly.

'How about you? You still see Hols a lot, don't you?'

'Yes, we're at Tommy's together.'

'Of course. Nothing will break you two up.'

Tara smiled, hearing the edge in Liv's words. 'And Charlie lives in Chalk Farm, so we see her occasionally – when our shifts allow us something as incredible as an evening off.'

'Well, quite. Is she still with her girlfriend?'

'Yep, that's been a while now actually. Three, four years?'

'So maybe they'll be the ones walking down the aisle next.'

'Could be.' Tara felt something on her shoulder and turned, just as Rory slid his hand over her bare skin and gently squeezed the back of her neck.

'Your five minutes is up,' he said to her with a wink, before looking over at Liv. 'Hi. Rory Hutchings.'

'Olivia Manley.' Liv shot Tara a knowing look as they shook hands and Tara tried to appraise her partner with fresh eyes; she didn't consider him Master of the Universe material. He looked as good in a white coat as in a DJ, true; and she'd always liked tall men; and of course he had a good career, great prospects . . . It was sweet he'd brought her bag over, holding the sequin clutch casually in one hand like it was a sweater, her award for the Overseas Enterprise sticking out the top.

'Liv and I were at Imperial together.'

'That would explain the dirty laughs I could hear over the music. You two look like you're hatching a plot.'

'Old habits die hard, I guess,' Tara sighed, sliding her arm around his waist and putting her head upon his shoulder. 'Is it really time to go?'

'I'm afraid so.' He knew the drill.

She looked back regretfully at her old friend. Part of her felt bad for leaving her here on her own. 'Liv, it's been so lovely bumping into you.'

'And you! Let's stay in touch, okay?'

'Definitely. Are you on social?'

'Are you kidding?' Liv quipped. 'It's the only way my family knows I'm alive!'

'Nice to meet you, Liv,' Rory said, beginning to lead Tara away.

'Listen, next time Annie's in town, we could all meet for dinner perhaps?' Liv called after her. 'Get Charlie and Hols along too.'

'That'd be great!' Tara said back over her shoulder, one hand raised in acknowledgement.

They meandered through the crowd, heading for the exit.

'Sounds fun,' Rory said, his hand on the small of her back.

'What does?'

'Dinner with the girls.'

'Oh. That. It'll never happen,' she muttered, looking in her bag for her coat ticket.

'Why not?'

'Because that time has gone.'

'I thought you said you were old friends?'

'Back then, at uni, yes. But we're different people now.'

Rory looked bemused. 'Only superficially, surely? You're fitter now for sure. Better dressed. You have more expensive tastes in wine. But fundamentally you're the same person you were back then.'

She shook her head, one eyebrow arched as if amused by his nostalgia. 'No.'

'No? You're not the person they knew?'

She found the ticket and handed it to the clerk. 'I'm not the person *I* knew. Thank God!'

'Why d'you say that?'

'Because I was an idiot back then. I almost threw my entire life away on . . .' Her voice snagged. 'Pipe dreams.'

He frowned. 'So what changed?'

'I grew up,' she shrugged. 'I focused on what I wanted and became the person you see before you now.' She walked over to him, still feeling the effects of all that wine, pressing a hand against his chest, her face angled coquettishly towards his.

'Any complaints with that, Dr Hutchings?' she asked in a lowered voice.

He smiled. 'Definitely not.'

'Good. So then take me home.'

Rory stirred, lifting his head momentarily from the pillow as though he sensed she had gone, before turning onto the other cheek and succumbing to sleep again in the next moment. His skin looked pale in the moonlight, with just a faint tan line on his thighs and lower back from their break on Harbour Island at New Year; by contrast, it had taken a good few weeks for his ski-goggle tan to go down in March after he refused her suncream on a cloudy day in Zermatt; the nurses had taken the mickey out of him every time he did his ward rounds and kept paging him to the burns department.

He always slept so soundly, it amazed her. Sometimes she watched him, just to see how he did it. It was like everything inside him just . . . switched off. When she closed her eyes, it was the complete opposite: everything switched on, loud, neon bright, wide awake; voices ran through her head, memories surfaced like bodies from ponds, her heart sped up. And even when she did drop off, invariably she woke again with a start, like klaxons were ringing in her head for her attention.

She was largely used to it. Being an ICU doctor hardly sat well with eight-hour sleep cycles anyway. She had spent years being dragged from snatched sleep by a pager, but tonight had been worse than usual. Her mind wouldn't switch off at all and the wine she'd drunk at dinner to try to . . . dim the day's horrors, had left her agitated and restless. Her headache was worse than ever.

From her spot on the window seat across the room, she stared out over the sleeping city. Never fully dark, the sky was a dusty charcoal; there were no stars that she could see even though she knew they had to be there. All the birds were asleep, no owls resident in the horse chestnut and limes here, and even the neighbourhood cats were prowling elsewhere tonight. She had a feeling not just of aloneness, but of nothingness. Like existing in a vacuum. She wanted to cry but couldn't. She wanted to sleep but couldn't. She wanted to run away but couldn't. Not quite yet anyway . . . There was another day to get through, somehow.

She closed her eyes as the physical memory of the small blade pressing her finger reasserted itself. She thought she would always feel it now, when her thumb pressed that particular part of her finger pad – this statistical loss not just part of her clinical record now, but her body.

She still couldn't work out how it had happened. The nurse had counted the implements into the sharps bag, all present and correct. If she had only noticed the blade was missing, there would have been time to go back into that tiny body and fish for it. Instead with every move, every breath, every peristaltic squeeze, it had cut the child a little deeper, a little longer until there were too many to count. Quite literally, it had been death by a thousand cuts.

Tara wanted to blame someone else – to believe it was the nurse's fault, or the scalpel manufacturer's – but she knew it was hers. As the consultant on duty, the buck stopped with her. That was what it meant to be the boss, her father had always told her that. 'You take the rough with the smooth, Piglet.' A child had died because of her negligence and she would have to live with that knowledge.

She turned to get back into bed. Her shift started at nine and it was now four. Somehow, she needed to find rest, go hunting for it. She picked her way carefully over the plush carpet, her hand brushing the evening dress that now lay carefully draped over the back of a bedroom chair. Rory's dinner suit was equally considerately folded and laid out. Surgeons, by nature, weren't messy types – they liked order, knowing exactly where everything was, so that the hands could move and the brain could work automatically. On autopilot. She was good at that.

She slid down the sheet and pulled the covers back over her. She looked at Rory asleep. He looked younger, his features almost toddler-soft as his lips slackened, a flush in his cheeks. She wondered why she hadn't told him about her day and the trauma it contained. She had simply come down to the taxi and greeted him with a smile, her 'face done', as her mother would have said and the new dress on. Perhaps if it had mattered less, she might have been more inclined to share. They usually talked about their days and what they'd done; he was a doctor, after all, he got it. People died all the time, it was part of the job. But this felt different, like she'd failed. Because to lose a child . . . There was nothing in this world worse than that.

Chapter Eleven

Holly's hand gripped Tara's arm tightly as she came and joined her in the terminal building. Tara was standing stiffly in front of the large window, blindly watching the pilot run through checks for the plane that was going to take them away from here. It was eight on the nose and, as feared, Holly had come straight from the hospital, albeit scrubs off and back in the clothes she had rolled out of bed and picked up off the floor this morning. Her trainers thankfully no longer had specks of someone's regurgitated carrots on them.

'I heard about the girl.'

Tara felt the lump in her throat swell again as she stared out over the runway with studied intensity, her muscles rigid. She had called in sick for the first time in her career. She knew the disruption it would bring, her colleagues forced to cover for her, another consultant drafted in on call, her patients waking to find themselves with a new doctor – but to work after a night of no sleep at all would have been as bad as operating drunk or high. She was used to broken sleep, but seven hours of staring at the ceiling was another level altogether and she had spent the day on the sofa, exhausted and unable to rest. Sleep fluttered around her head like an angry crow, diving at her but never quite making contact. Every time she closed her eyes . . . And now her glands were up and her head felt clamped in a vice that was being ratcheted ever tighter. A holiday had never been more needed.

'It's always worse when it's a kid,' Holly murmured, getting it.

Tara nodded again, her reply needing a few more seconds of focus before the word could be formed. 'Yes.' If she could only erase the sight of that small, punished body on her operating table, if she could only forget that stinging sharpness against her blood-soaked fingertips.

'I remember my first. Mohammad Parveneh; seven and a half. Hit and run.' Holly's voice cracked on 'run'. 'They caught up with the bastard within the hour. He got three years for careless driving, was out in half that.' She swallowed. 'It really made me question whether I was cut out for it; I didn't think I could hack it. Sometimes this job makes you feel like you only see the worst of people—'

'Mum!'

They both turned as the drumbeat of trainered feet rolled down the tile floor.

'Most excellent boy!' Holly grinned, instantly sinking to her heels, her arms outstretched just in time for a skinny, long-legged, dark-haired, ultra-fast torpedo to spin into them. Her nightmare cast off by a dream.

Tara smiled as she watched Holly kiss Jimmy's head, tousling his silky hair as if to rough it up.

Dev brought up the rear, towing two large suitcases and Jimmy's enormous Liverpool holdall strapped across his body. He hadn't put on a pound in ten years and looked like he might crumple in half from the weight of his load, his glasses slipping down his nose but with no free hand left to push them up.

Holly stood again and did it for him, greeting him with a casually affectionate kiss. 'Did you turn off the immersion?'

'Yes. And changed the cat litter,' he said, before she could ask. 'And watered the basil and put it by the window.'

'With the little gap open at the top?'

'Yes, and the safety locks tightened.'

Holly visibly relaxed. 'Good.' Her signature enormous smile spread across her face, and it really was like a dawn. 'Well, then in that case I'm defo ready to go on holiday.' She leaned into Tara and squeezed her arm again, dropping her head on her shoulder, both sympathetic and encouraging at once.

Dev shot Tara his usual bemused look. 'Hi Twig.'

'Hey Dev,' she smiled.

Jimmy looked up at her. He was a beautiful boy, seemingly having inherited the best of both his parents – caramel-coloured skin, his father's fine bone structure, his mother's light eyes. 'Aunty Twig, is it true we're going on a private plane?'

She looked down at him and wrinkled her nose. 'I'm afraid so.'

'Do they have Dr Pepper?'

'Absolutely not,' Holly said firmly, turning away to double-check for the passports in Dev's bumbag. She was outrageously hypocritical and was firmly of the 'do as I say, not as I do' school of parenting.

Tara winked at him and pressed a finger to her lips. 'Lots of fresh juices.'

'And still water, I hope?' Holly asked over her shoulder. 'Carbonated is shit for their teeth.'

'Mummy potty-mouth!' Jimmy cried, as Dev had taught him to every time his mother swore.

'Ugh,' she groaned, reaching into her jacket pocket and giving her son a pound.

Jimmy looked at it, pleased. Tara suspected he was probably quite well-off if Holly paid up every time she was supposed to.

The stairs were being lowered to the tarmac; it was time to go.

'Where's Rory? I thought he was coming?' Dev asked, looking worried. He relied on Rory's calm presence as an antidote to the two women together.

'Don't worry, he is. He got stuck in traffic on the A40. More worrying is, where are Miles and Zac?'

'Oh God,' Holly groaned. 'Please don't tell me I'm going to be the only person with hairy legs on this holiday?'

In spite of her misery, Tara chuckled. Dev shook his head and huddled his wife in close, kissing her on the temple. 'Well, we may as well wait for them on board. At least we can sit down and have something to drink.'

'Ooh,' Holly said, her tired eyes brightening.

'I'm starving!' Jimmy almost shouted.

Tara picked up her small, neatly packed bag and led them through the automatic doors, from the air-conditioned cool of the terminal to the sizzling heat of the runway. London was baking in the hottest July on record – and it was still only the seventeenth of the month. The tropical rains of Costa Rica were going to be a welcome respite.

Two steps behind her, the Motha family bickered over bags, until Jimmy sprinted ahead and straight up the steps into the plane.

'Jimmy, no! Come back here!' Holly yelled. 'Fuck.'

'Hols, it's fine,' she said reassuringly. 'He's not doing any harm.'

'Now, technically we don't know that. He could be up to anything.' She looked at Dev. 'Did you search him for Sharpies?'

'Hi Sandy, how are you?' Tara said with a tired nod to the flight attendant as they climbed the steps.

'It's a pleasure to welcome you on board again, Doctor Tremain,' the attendant said, taking her travel bag.

Jimmy was already standing by the bar, his hand plunged up to the wrist in a bowl of chocolate eclairs. Holly just burst out laughing at the sight of all the cream quilted leather and burred wood tables. Everything was so plush and mani-cured, it had the effect of making *them* look untidy. 'Oh God,' she gasped. 'It actually is just like you see it on the Kardashians!'

Dev was dumbstruck.

'Now, just explain to me again, why we've been friends for over a decade and I've not been on this before?' Holly asked slowly, turning a full 360.

'Because I hardly ever use it myself . . . Sit wherever you like, Dev,' Tara said, patting his shoulder comfortingly. 'There are no set places. It's very relaxed.'

'Yeah?'

Tara dropped into the nearest seat and checked her phone for messages. Rory was three minutes away. She closed her eyes as Holly, giddy with choice, immediately began fussing about which seats they should have. She dropped her head back, trying to summon her fantasy about the feel of the sand between her toes, tropical waters lapping by her ankles. She reminded herself she could be barefoot all week; flip-flops would be her only concession to shoes, and that was only on account of the ants. Everything was going to be fine. In spite of the feelings to the contrary, she would one day sleep again and her head was not going to explode. She just needed to get away from here, a little time and space away from her everyday life—

'Sorry, sorry! Bastard traffic through Bayswater.'

Her eyes opened to the sight of her brother coming down the aisle, looking Monaco-ready in pale buff narrow chinos rolled at the ankles, tobacco suede car shoes and a pale blue shirt, accessorized with a vintage Colombian stitched polo belt that had been their father's – back when he wore a thirty-two-inch waist – and a pair of sleek gunmetal Porsche sunglasses.

Zac, right behind him, was no less impressive in his Brooks Brothers suit. 'Hey Twig.'

Both of them kissed her and greeted the others; no one seemed to notice that she was fundamentally altered, the black spot on her soul seemingly leaving no trace.

'Please tell me we're not the last for once?' Miles asked, looking delighted by her lack of Plus One.

'You're not the last,' she replied obediently. 'Rory got stuck in traffic too. He's a minute away.'

'See? What did I tell you?' Zac said, slapping Miles once, hard, on the backside. 'Plenty of time.'

Miles cracked a grin that was all his own – it somehow occupied only the right side of his mouth, tipping it up boyishly. He smiled a lot these days. After several years in the dating wilderness, when he'd been chased and seduced for all the wrong reasons, life had changed for the better when he'd met Zac, a corporate lawyer. Miles loved to recount how their eyes had met over the conference table . . . Tara just loved to see her little brother happy. Zac was seven years older and comfortingly protective of him, and they kept their social circle small and intimate these days. 'Well fuck me, that's a first.'

'Pottymouth!' Jimmy cried, racing back down the aisle with the hand that had been only moments before up to the wrist in chocolate eclairs outstretched in front of Miles, awaiting a fine.

'Say what now?' her brother asked, bewildered.

'No swearing in front of my nine-year-old godson, please. Kindly cough up a pound.'

'Seriously?'

'Every time,' Tara nodded, as the attendant came round with a tray of flutes of champagne. She flinched as she took hers. Celebrating was the last thing she felt like doing. Drinking to the point of oblivion on the other hand . . . 'Hols has had to take out an overdraft.'

'He's saving up for an electric scooter,' Dev said proudly. 'He's almost there, too.'

'Well, he certainly will be by the end of this week,' Zac laughed, loosening his tie and reaching for his glass of champagne.

'Cheers!' Holly said, taking one for herself and holding her glass aloft until the others clinked it too. She drank deeply, with the zeal of someone released from a fifteen-hour shift; someone who had started her day pulling a Coke bottle from a man's rectum and was ending it seated on a stitched-diamond cream leather plane seat, heading for a tropical paradise with her best friend and family.

Tara's own day hadn't followed that upward trajectory and, try as she might, she couldn't click out of this sense of isolation; she felt set apart from everyone, locked behind a glass wall and unable to reach even the people she loved most in this world. A little girl had died because of her negligence and oversight. Why couldn't she cry or talk about it? Why couldn't she feel anything?

She looked out of the window and saw Rory stepping out of the terminal building, half-running, half-walking across the tarmac, a copy of *The Times* clutched in one hand and his bag rolling behind him. His suit jacket was flying open in the wind, his tie flapping over his shoulder. He didn't look dressed for the tropics (unlike Dev, who was already in a tropical print shirt and Jesus sandals) and she felt a rush of relief at the mere dependable sight of him. He would make her feel better. As soon as she told him, he would know what she should do.

She waited expectantly for him to come up the steps, for his face to appear in the doorway. She smiled as everyone cheered at his arrival and watched as he threw his arms in the air jubilantly in response, playing the part. Zac put a glass in his hand before he'd even taken off his jacket. There was a party feeling on board, and the engines weren't even on yet.

'Hey, you,' he said, sliding into the seat beside her and kissing her lightly on the mouth. 'Sorry I'm late. Good day?'

'I called in sick, actually. Wasn't feeling so great.'

He looked surprised, then frowned. 'Another headache?'

She gave her shrug. 'Can't shake it off. Can't sleep through it.'

He squeezed her knee sympathetically in reply. 'I've got some heavy-duty ibuprofen if you want?'

'Sure. Why not?'

Rory opened his bag and rifled for the little silver packet as Miles brought up his Ibiza playlist and Holly began dancing in her seat. Tara gave a wan smile. She was going to be stuck on this plane for the next twelve hours with her best friend and her brother calling the shots, neither of whom believed that less was more, or that good things come to those who wait. 'I might be better off with a tranquillizer than headache pills,' she said, as he handed her a couple.

The stairs were pulled up, the engines fired and she looked out of the window, watching as the tarmac began to roll by, seeing how the horizon leaned to a tilt and the houses became small, until eventually the clouds wound around the plane in tatty rags and they emerged soaring into the blue.

She felt like a ball shot from a catapult as she stared from the windows at the world below. Everything looked peaceful at this distance. She had a feeling of having escaped from something terrible down there and that she would be safe if she could just stay up here, suspended in time, as well as space—

'Oh bugger!' Rory startled beside her, so violently he almost sloshed his champagne over his lap.

'What?' she cried, alarmed.

He looked back at her with wide eyes. 'I forgot the electric toothbrush charger adaptor plug.'

'The—' She stared at him, her heart beating at triple time.

Jimmy came and stood in front of him with a hand outstretched. 'Pottymouth. One pound, please.'

A helicopter was waiting on the tarmac a short distance from the plane, its headlights shining into the darkness and ready to whisk them straight off to Talamanca. Tara stood at the top of the steps and stared out, but not even the San José Highlands were visible on this inky night, and the stars remained obscured from sight by the intense blaze of city lights. She took a lungful of the warm air instead, as if the foreignness of her new environs could be tasted, even if not seen. It seemed woody compared to the granular minerality of London, somehow heavier and more dense, and she felt her blood gently warm.

'Chop-chop,' Rory said, patting her on the bottom to nudge her forwards. 'Wide load coming through.'

She glanced back and saw Dev struggling to carry a very long, sleeping Jimmy. He was as limp as a noodle. She jogged down the stairs and stepped out of the way on the tarmac to let him and Holly pass. Holly was looking fairly wild, as anyone might after a fifteen-hour shift and a magnum of champagne on a transatlantic flight. They'd all drunk far too much.

'Wow, it's actually *not* raining!' Miles exclaimed, sticking his head out of the plane after them. 'I thought they only had two settings here: rain, and more rain.'

'Ror, it's best to check messages here while you still can,' she said, sounding as hungover as she felt. 'The signal at Talamanca's shocking.'

He frowned. 'Really?'

'By which I mean . . . non-existent.' She watched the look of panic bloom across his face. 'On the plus side, we'll get to properly switch off and relax.' She gave an approximation of an optimistic smile as he began to look anxious.

'Hmm.' He pulled his phone from his pocket and began scrolling quickly through his emails. At some point in the journey, she saw now, he had changed out of his suit and was now in chino shorts and a polo shirt. She didn't remember exactly when. She had succeeded in drinking herself to distraction and had slept fitfully for a few hours. But at least she had slept.

Tara flicked through her emails too – the usual mix of marketing rubbish she never opened but couldn't be bothered to unsubscribe to, and medical news. She saw she had a missed call, which was something of a novelty. Did people still use phones to actually . . . make calls?

She dialled her voicemail and listened in, watching blankly as Holly clambered inelegantly into the helicopter and reached back down to take her sleeping child from her husband's arms. Tara turned away.

'*Tara?*' The voice was clipped, efficient. Instantly recognizable. '*It's Helen McPherson calling. Ring me back, would you? I understand you're on annual leave for a week but I want to go over a few things with you with regard to the Miller case. Just a quick chat. Okay thanks.*'

The Miller case. That little girl was a 'case' now?

Tara disconnected, feeling light-headed and like she wanted to throw up. Helen McPherson was the hospital's clinical director, and a ruthless bureaucrat. She didn't suffer fools or egos, and she was a slave to AI, especially when it promised to save money or lives, or both. The mortality rates under her stewardship had dropped seven per cent in eighteen months and Tara had heard whispers she was being lined up for a place on the Trust's Board. This was no mere quick chat she wanted – the hospital's youngest (and most newsworthy) consultant had left a blade inside the body of a four-year-old girl and that made *her* look bad. No, that message was the verbal equivalent of throwing a grenade across the floor – leaving Tara waiting for the bang.

Chapter Twelve

Everyone always seemed to react in the same way when they stepped into a tropical forest for the first time. First their gaze went up, looking for a star-freckled sky that could now only be glimpsed in small pieces; then their arms went out as they slowly revolved on the spot. It seemed almost a spiritual response, as though for once, the body was being driven by the soul.

Even if it hadn't been the middle of the night, there wasn't much to see here; only the lights of the helicopter gave them any visibility at all. There was no terminal building (or even a hut), no giant H painted on the ground. The helipad wasn't visible from the road and was nothing more than a rogue bare patch where some old trees had once fallen. And yet Tara watched as Holly, Dev and Jimmy went through those motions of awe, an expression of wonderment on their faces beneath the giant ceibas.

Holly looked back at her with big, shining eyes. 'I like what you've done with the place.'

Tara laughed. Holly could always bring a smile to her face.

Rory didn't seem to have noticed yet; he was being useful and helping the pilot bring the bags out. Miles and Zac were on their phones, pointlessly checking for wifi in case things had changed since their last visit seven months ago. It was one in the morning, and they were all exhausted after over twelve hours of travelling.

'For the record, I'm never going back,' Holly said, staring up at the jagged patch of sky; it looked like a caterpillar-nibbled black leaf.

Tara smiled tiredly. 'Tell me that when you're a fortnight into the wet season. There isn't enough serum in the world could make you stay here then.'

Holly looked suitably perturbed by the thought of the frizz.

Tara looked around, trying to see this place with fresh eyes too, but it was like unknowing the twist in a thriller film. It couldn't be done. Innocence, once lost, was lost forever. She had been coming to this pocket of Costa Rican jungle since she was nine years old and Miles was seven. For eleven years, it had been her place of refuge, the holiday she looked forward to all year, a time-out from the world where boarding school was far away and the management boards couldn't reach her father . . . They could all be themselves here in a way they couldn't anywhere else. She felt it was the only place where she truly lived freely.

That had all stopped abruptly, of course, when the national park project had been announced. It was too tied up for her now with Alex Carter's betrayal and the way he'd used her to get to her father. She couldn't think of one without the other, and for almost a decade it had been easier not to think of either by simply not visiting. But she had missed coming here and it had forced her to deny a part of herself. It had been another loss on top of loss, she realized, as she stood there feeling the forest breathe around her. She could smell the sweet scent of orchids and the rich, woody earth; she could hear yellow-throated toucans yelping, thought she glimpsed a flash of bright feathers as a parakeet flew between canopies, heard the chatter of monkeys not too far away. She felt the forest vibrate and hum in her bones, staking its claim in her heart again and telling her she shouldn't have stayed away so long; not because of *him*.

Two sets of headlights were bouncing along the dirt track towards them.

'Jed!' Miles cheered, reaching into the leading white open Jeep as it came to a stop and gripping the driver's hand. 'I thought we said one sharp?'

'Shar*pish*. You're on Tico Time now, buddy,' Jed grinned. 'Time to get out of your straitjacket.'

Miles laughed, doing exactly that as he shrugged off his unlined linen blazer and swung himself into the front seat. Zac slid into the back, doing a fancy-grip handshake with Jed that proved they had met several times over the years now. Tara felt another pang of regret over time lost. Memories wasted.

'Tara. It has been too long,' Jed said, kneeling on the seat and looking back at her, leaning his arms on the roll bars overhead. 'What took you so long?'

Tara felt Miles's stare become heavier upon her. He knew what had kept her away; he alone in their family knew what Alex had done, and had been adamant their parents should know the full scale of his betrayal. But in spite of their mother's lingering misgivings, to this day their father still believed she and Alex had been 'just good friends' and that the introduction had been facilitated for the purposes of the conservation project alone. She had had to beg her brother to stay quiet. Neither she, nor he – nor Alex too, no doubt – were under any illusions that if the truth was to become known, her father would pull support immediately. And as much as she had fantasized about striking back and stripping him of his prize, she also knew the potential of this project was far more important than avenging her single shattered heart.

But that didn't mean she didn't dream of it. In ten years there had never been an apology and he had never made a meaningful attempt to win her back. No midnight phone calls. No pleading texts. Perhaps he thought it was to his credit that he didn't muddy the waters any more than he already had? He had got what he'd come for and he just let her slip away. She had been collateral damage, that was all; it was unfortunate, but also inevitable. Besides, he knew what he'd done was unforgivable. Irreversible. He'd even tried warning her. *'He has the power of conviction and if he believes in something, he backs it up, a hundred per cent.'* He'd said that to her once, lying in bed, her believing this was intimacy, never dreaming it was a confession. *'Whenever he's done the wrong thing, it's been for the right reasons.'*

The right reason was all that remained now and the memory of their relationship was just a distant twist of smoke, somewhere out of sight, over the horizon.

'What can I say? Med school was *hard*, Jed,' she shrugged. 'And it's not much easier now I'm qualified, either.'

'That's why you should have come here – to relax!' he smiled back at her, with simple rationale. Even the way he said the word 'relax' made her feel relaxed.

'Well, at least I've brought my friends at long last. That's my partner, Rory,' she said, pointing to where her boyfriend was hauling their luggage into the backs of the Jeeps; Rory waved a hand in greeting, looking more like a baggage handler than a heart surgeon. 'And Dev, Holly and their son Jimmy.'

'How old are you, Jimmy?' Jed asked, looking over at the shy, sleepy boy.

'Nine.'

'Tall for nine!' Jed remarked, looking impressed. 'Do you surf?'

Jimmy shook his head.

'Would you like to?'

Jimmy nodded.

'Then we'll have you surfing by the time you go back,' Jed grinned, giving him a thumbs up.

'Jed taught me and Miles how to surf,' she added to her godson. 'He's the best.'

'Come on, then. You must be tired. Let's get you to your beds,' Jed said, swinging back down into his seat.

'You go with these guys. I'll sit with the others,' Rory said to her, immediately seeing how the seating arrangements were going to be restricted and Jimmy would need to sit on one of his parents' laps.

'Sure?' He was always so considerate.

He winked and joined the Mothas in their Jeep.

Jed opened up a coolbox and handed out cans of beer, beads of condensation trickling down the sides. Tara opened hers and took several long, thirsty gulps; the effects of the humidity were immediate, her skin already beading with sweat even at this time of night.

Jed put the steering wheel in full lock and turned them out of the landing area, the other car following just behind on the bumpy track. Tara liked the way her hair lifted off her neck as they drove fast through the trees. It felt so good to be outside again. Over twelve hours had been spent in state-of-the-art, climate-controlled air-conditioned spaces but this felt like the luxury, cutting through the night, below the stars, towards the sea.

She glanced at Jed in the mirror, looking for changes in her childhood friend, but any differences were as subtly evolved as the forest's – he still had the same heavy eyebrows and black hair worn long and shaggy, an ever-ready smile that dominated his broad face. He was a little heavier, but no grey hairs yet. His father had owned the bar and row of huts set along the fringes of the beach when they first started coming here, gradually expanding his operations to include surf hire and bike rental too, local tours and expeditions.

Everything she and Miles had done, Jed had done with them – as a friend, but as a mentor too. He was seven years older than her – old enough to look after them, still young enough to be fun. And he had been fun! He knew the area intimately and had grown up doing all the things they now learned as adventurers – he kept them safe as they dived the reef, taught them what to look for as they learned to track ocelots. Father and son had proved their loyalty as well as friendship over the years and had become the Tremains' gate-keepers on Costa Rican soil – they fixed whatever needed fixing, did the helicopter pickups, organized moonlit treks, put extras of her favourite papayas in the fruit bowl. And once the conservation project had swung into action, Jed's father had been rewarded with a senior role in the running of it, tasked with co-ordinating the rangers who ran the midline between the biologists, ecologists and the local communities.

As if sensing her scrutiny, Jed's dark eyes met hers briefly in the mirror. He smiled back at her warmly, her old friend.

'Hey! Was that a jaguar?' Zac asked excitedly, twisting in his seat beside her. 'Did you see that, Twig?'

She shook her head apologetically. 'Afraid not.'

'I just saw a pair of, like, yellow eyes, between the trees.'

Tara looked back but, even if it had been there, the creature was already lost in the trees. Like putting a foot in the river, the rainforest never stood still.

'Sorry to disappoint but it was a margay, more likely,' Jed said over the wind, glancing at Zac in the mirror. 'The jags don't come this close to the coast.'

Zac sat forward in his seat, gripping the back of Miles's headrest. 'Shame. I'd love to see one.'

'Well then, we can arrange that for you, for sure.'

'Really? You could find me a jaguar, just like that?'

'They're getting harder to find but we know their most common routes. It's just about knowing where to look, and being patient.'

Miles twisted back to look at his husband. 'I keep telling you – whatever you want, Jed can make it happen. He's the man.'

Jed kept his gaze dead ahead. They were approaching the junction where the track met the single main road. 'Of course. Nothing's a problem. Whatever you need.'

Jed looked in both directions and pulled out. Tara knew they were only a few minutes from the town and that soon the strains of music would become audible and her holiday would begin.

They accelerated, Jed's eyes flicking quickly between the road and the rear-view mirror as they picked up speed. He was watching someone behind them, his eyes instinctively narrowing to slits as a dazzling brightness suddenly washed over their vehicle. She glanced around to see the beam of headlights from the other Jeep. Only it *wasn't* the other Jeep – these were higher up, and advancing fast.

Too fast.

She looked back at Jed, seeing how his grip had tightened around the wheel, hearing the engine growl as he pushed his foot flatter to the floor. They sped up so that her hair blew about her face, making it hard to see anything clearly.

But the other vehicle was still gaining on them, catching them up. What was happening?

'Jed?' she asked, a tremor in her voice that made even Miles turn around. As if in response, the lights behind were flicked

151

to full beam and he winced, automatically raising his arms to his face.

'What the fuck?' her brother cried.

The vehicle behind honked loudly and insistently, bearing down with frightening speed and compressing the distance between them to just a few metres. Tara gasped, unable to process what was happening. The lights were blinding. In the space of mere moments they had gone from holiday vibes to being run off the road. They would hit the trees! She screamed as she saw the truck get to within six feet of the back of them, before it suddenly, violently, swerved. In the next instant, it was overtaking them so closely that the truck's running board missed the side of the jeep by mere inches.

'Holy shit!' Zac yelled, his eyes wide and mouth open wider as the truck sped past and into the distance. 'Who the hell was that?'

In her panic, Tara had clocked nothing but the set profiles of two men in hats in the front seats. Jed was quiet for a moment, his grip still tight around the wheel so that his knuckles blanched. 'No one. Just some local fools,' he said finally, in his calm, steady voice. 'Not everyone here knows how to drive properly.'

'That's putting it *lightly*,' Miles muttered, looking and sounding shaken.

But Tara, watching him still in the mirror, saw how Jed had looked away before speaking. One of the clearest signs he was lying. All doctors were trained to read the clues by which people give themselves away, in preparation for dealing with the teenage girls who would swear blind they were virgins even as they heard their baby's heartbeat on the monitor, to winkle out the abusive partner speaking on behalf of a 'shy' patient . . . Why would he lie about who those people were? And why had they tried to run him off the road?

Everyone was quiet now, their initial excitement at being here suddenly diminished by the unsettling incident. Jed turned on the radio, the songs drifting into the night as they sat in uneasy silence.

Within minutes they were coming into Puerto Viejo, long-familiar wooden shacks lining the road, brightly painted signs advertising beers or beans and rice bowls, craft stands shuttered up for the night, bars dimly lit with hanging lanterns, surfboards outside hire shops stacked in storage racks like whale ribs, ready for the first dawn riders . . .

Over the wind, Tara could hear reggae beats, glimpsed people seated on rickety chairs and smiling at them with easy hospitality as they sped through the small town. It had only six streets in total, which was precisely why her family loved it here. Low-key and off the well-heeled track, its isolation had been almost entirely protected until 1979 when the road had been built, opening it up to the rest of the country some-what. But progress had been slow – electricity had only come in 1986, and internet (such as it was) in 2006. As teenagers she and Miles had been appalled by the slow broadband speeds, but now . . . it was the perfect place to be. Refuge. Escape. She had come to the edge of the world. She had always liked it here because in this tiny pocket she was invis-ible, her family insignificant; but now she felt unaccountable too. Suddenly Helen McPherson and *the Miller case* felt very far away. If she tried really hard, she thought she might be able to believe that they weren't real. That it had never even happened . . .

Jed turned down one of the streets and she caught her first glimpse of the sea, lying in heavy, inky quietude. The moon was waxing, perhaps two or three nights off fullness and throwing a milky haze onto its surface. She caught a splash as something breached before disappearing again, the waves gently hushing onto the shelved black sand beach. Palm tree fronds hung like splayed fingers, large boulders dotted along the cove with sculptural frequency.

Jed pulled up outside their digs, a short run of heavily weathered, brightly painted huts right on the beach. Blue, yellow, red, green, they were flimsier than most sheds and yet for her, they were a home. The crucible of her childhood happiness, their imperfection and sense of gentle decay were strangely reassuring; their long-standing presence suggesting things didn't always collapse in a storm of dust.

'Yes!' Miles swung himself out of the car before Jed had even cut the engine and tipped his face to the sky. He kicked off his shoes and ran onto the beach, burrowing his feet into the cool sand.

Zac joined him, standing with his hands on his hips as they looked out to sea. 'Never gets old, does—'

'What the *hell* was going on back there?'

The anger in the man's voice made them all turn and Tara was startled to see Rory marching across the sand towards Jed, looking like he was going to beat ten bells out of him.

'You racing that truck like that? They could have been killed!'

'Whoa!' Miles interjected, physically inserting himself between the two men as Rory bore down upon Jed. He had to press hard against Rory's chest to stop him from grabbing him. 'Mate, it's all cool. It wasn't Jed's fault.'

But Rory wouldn't be appeased. 'That driver—!'

'Was a fucking idiot. Yes, we know. Jed wasn't *racing* the guy. But he handled it. We're fine.' Miles swept an arm round to where Tara was standing. 'Look, she's fine.'

Rory, his eyes ablaze, stared at her, his chest heaving with emotion.

'I'm fine,' she repeated, somewhat amazed by his reaction. The incident had frightened her too, but it had all been over in ten seconds. Exactly how bad had it looked from where they were sitting?

'*Fine?* You know they had guns?' Rory asked, looking from her to Jed again, accusation in his eyes.

Guns? Even Miles and Zac looked concerned by that.

Jed was quiet for a moment. 'Yes. But as I told Miles and Tara, I know who they are, and I will deal with it. Nothing would have happened . . . They just like to puff their chests, that is all.'

'Who are they?' Miles asked.

'Just some guys who work on a ranch round here. Hoodlums. They like to believe they own the place.'

Miles gave a short laugh, his hands on his hips. 'Well, if that's the game they want to play . . .'

Jed gave a small smile. 'Exactly.' He looked at Rory. 'Please do not worry. I will deal with it.'

Tara went over to her boyfriend and put her hand on his arm. 'Listen to Jed, he knows what he's talking about.'

There was a reluctant silence, the men seemingly speaking without words. Something about the ranchers' show of strength signalled a message she seemingly didn't quite get; a machismo thing that had rattled Jed and Rory's cages.

Tugging Rory by the arm, she started walking over the sand again. 'Let's just leave it now and go to bed. We're all tired. It's been a long journey and we need to sleep.'

'But—'

'Come on. Let's sleep. Red hut for us, yes Jed?'

Jed nodded, never taking his eyes off Rory. The new man

was but a guest of the Tremains; he didn't get to throw his weight around like that.

Reluctantly, Rory allowed himself to be pulled away, but he continued muttering under his breath. 'That was fucking ridiculous . . . You didn't have to watch. From where we were, that truck was going to ram you off the road.'

'It must have just been perspective,' she fibbed, reaching for her bag from the back of the Jeep. 'It didn't feel that bad to us. Really.' She saw the astonishment in his eyes. 'But I'm sorry, it must have been horrid for you.'

'It was. You didn't have to see it. Poor Jimmy screamed.'

She winced at that. 'I really am sorry.' She wasn't quite sure why she was apologizing – it wasn't any more her fault than Jed's. 'Come on, we're in here.'

She pushed on the latch and opened the door to the red cabin. It was the second of four and had always been hers. Miles was always in the green one next door; her father had the yellow one flanking her far side and the blue one was kept free in case of guests (although in all those years as kids, they had never invited anyone along; they liked keeping it for themselves, a cherished secret).

Rory stopped in the doorway.

'Like it?' she asked, hoisting up her bag and setting it on its side on an upended banana crate.

'It's very . . . basic.'

'Well yes, I told you that. Rustic vibes.' She unzipped the bag, desperate to find her toothbrush.

He peered around the minimal space. 'I thought when you said basic you meant . . . no spa, no Sky package. Not . . .' His eyes fell to the colonial fan on the ceiling, the mosquito net hanging over the bed. 'No air con.'

She stopped what she was doing and scanned the room

with a fresh gaze. A loosely woven rattan lampshade dangled from the centre point of the apex roof; a long-forgotten beer can nestled in the crux of the rafters, where the roof met the walls. The space was small but felt spacious on account of there being no furniture apart from the 1970s cane bed, which had peacock-tail head and footboards and was dressed with faded turquoise cotton sheets that were years old and as soft as hankies. Clothes had to be hung from the hooks nailed along the walls and, if you wanted to sit, you just sat on the bed. Some old wooden Coke boxes had been set on their sides and stacked three high to form a type of console, which was at least useful as somewhere to set down a book, or glass or phone; and on the wall, as a solitary nod towards decoration, there was a brightly painted 1950s kitsch oil of a pneumatic woman in an off-the-shoulder red dress.

Tara had been sleeping in this room since she was nine years old and that painting had been hanging there even then. To her pre-pubescent self, the woman's glamour and obvious sex appeal had been enthralling. She would stare at her for hours wondering, wishing, hoping that she too would one day look like that: seductive, enigmatic, alluring, dangerous. But standing here now, the only thought in her mind was trying to work out exactly when (and why) she had gone from desperately wanting to look like that woman, to desperately not. And how sad that was, because it illustrated as a fine point that every last vestige and wish of the person – child – she had once been, had vanished. No trace remained.

'Don't worry, it'll grow on you,' she said, patting his stomach as she passed him into the bathroom. She kicked the door to.

'Is there even hot running water?' he called through.

She hesitated as she sat on the loo. '. . . There's running

water,' she conceded. 'But don't worry, everything's hot around you instead.'

She flushed, washed her hands, began brushing her teeth.

Rory walked through a few moments later, stripped down to his boxers. He stopped at the sight of the tiny space. 'Please tell me there's a shower?'

'Of course . . . Outside.'

His shoulders slumped. It was half one in the morning.

'Relax. Shower in the morning. We just need to sleep.'

Rory began splashing cold water over his face. He looked at his reflection in the light of the exposed bulb. Bags pouched beneath his eyes; the light flattered neither of them. 'Jesus.'

Tara stripped off as she walked back into the bedroom, collapsing into the bed naked.

Rory pulled the mosquito net closed around them and slid down the sheets beside her. She lay still as he fussed with the pillows, punching them into fluffiness and turning them over. They were finally here, back in the land she loved, on the holiday she had been dreaming of – the one that was going to be filled with lots of sun, sand, sea and sex. But not just yet. Right now, all she wanted was sleep.

'How's your headache?' he asked, his voice already growing thick with incipient unconsciousness as he allowed his limbs to become heavy.

'Still there.'

'Need a Nurofen?'

She was quiet for a moment as her thoughts caught up with her again. 'No, I think I'll be fine. I can sleep through it.'

But she didn't close her eyes, too scared of what she might see behind her eyelids. She watched the ceiling fan whirr and spin. He watched her from one open eye.

'Hols mentioned you had a patient die?' he asked after a moment.

Her hair rustled on the pillow as she turned to face him. 'Did she?'

'Asked if you were all right. I had to tell her I didn't know anything about it.'

'No, I . . .' She gave a tiny shrug as it settled on her again, the memory like a rock on her chest. 'There wasn't much time; we had the awards thing straight after.'

'Right.'

'Yes.'

'We could have cancelled.'

'Hardly. Not when I was a recipient.'

She felt his hand find hers under the sheet and squeeze it. 'Well, I guess that explains the raid on the Medoc.'

She fell still. 'Her name was Lucy. She was four.'

She heard his breathing halt . . . then resume again. 'Shit, that's hard. What happened?'

She squeezed her eyes shut, not even wanting to say the words. 'She'd been beaten up by her parents, was admitted just before seven. I did a routine splenectomy. It all went fine. Then in the afternoon, she crashed. I opened her up again . . .' Here her voice snagged.

He was watching her now, in the dark, sensing calamity.

'A blade from one of the scalpels from the earlier surgery had . . . slipped out. It embedded in her large intestinal tract.'

He could guess the rest of this story.

'There were multiple incisions. We couldn't close them up in time. She bled out on the table. Four sixteen p.m.'

'Ta . . .' But there was nothing he could say to make it better.

'There's going to be an investigation,' she said after a pause.

159

He hesitated. 'Well, that's routine, I guess. But nothing for you to worry about.'

'How can you say that? I should have checked the sharps count. I should have double-checked.' She blinked back at him in the darkness.

'Ta, stop right there.' His voice was suddenly firm. Calming. 'This is not your fault, you hear me? You did everything you could. But sometimes, even in spite of your best efforts, you're going to lose a few.'

'But she was four. She was saveable. I *had* saved her! And then I—'

'Ta, if a blade fell from the scalpel, then the equipment was faulty.' His voice was steady. Logical.

She blinked back at him, feeling a rush of self-hatred. 'Or the surgeon was in a rush and tired and thinking about what dress she was going to wear that night. I should have double-checked, Ror.'

'No. I won't let you talk like that. You have to accept that you cannot save everyone. It's just not possible and you'll go mad trying to hold yourself to that account. We are not superhumans. We do our best and then let it go. That's all we can do.'

Tara stared into the darkness, finding no comfort in the words. She couldn't just settle for 'doing her best'. As far as she was concerned, surgeons had to be held to higher account. The stakes were too high for them to be slack or relaxed about what they did. 'What if they take my licence?' she whispered.

'That won't happen.'

'It might. They could decide I was negligent. That I *should* have double-checked before I closed her back up.'

'Ta, you are their show pony. Their flagship consultant. That's not going to happen.'

Tara blinked in the darkness, feeling a sudden vibration in her bones at his words. '. . . What do you mean, show pony?'

There was a pause. 'I mean that you're the youngest ever consultant they've had in ICU. They believe in you. They wouldn't let you go over something like this.'

She fell quiet, reading the subtext: no, he had meant that she was a Tremain. That was why she'd got so far, so fast, in her career. She'd always wondered if, deep down, he resented her greater success. Now she knew. He believed what she'd got, she'd got by favours, influence, prestige. She felt a profound loneliness whistle through her like a cold wind. 'I can't lose my career. It's all I have.' Her words were barely a whisper now.

'No. You've got me.'

She stared into the dark room, into the void.

It was all she had.

Chapter Thirteen

She came to, in chunks of sensory processing: first she heard the rhythmic crash of the waves, then occasional voices passing by the huts, a distant shout. Opening one eye, through the gauzy haze of a tented mosquito net, she saw sunlight slanting through the cracks, striping the room. It was morning, then? She'd actually slept?

She sighed and reached for her phone. 11.09.

Eleven? She felt a wave of relief that she had slept through the night; she couldn't remember the last time she'd slept so long, or so deeply. It made her feel strangely . . . well.

She stretched, feeling her muscles engage, sliding her legs across the sheet, looking for Rory . . .

She turned her head. The bed was empty.

She looked towards the bathroom: the door was ajar, no sounds coming from within. She pushed herself onto her elbows, leaning back with a general feeling of befuddlement. Sleep was still a shroud upon her and she let her gaze absorb – properly this time – the little red hut, her home for the next week. One of Rory's shirts was hanging from a hook, his bag zipped up and standing on its end on the floor. A towel dangled over the bathroom door. He would be swimming, she knew.

With a sudden desire to join him, to start her day – her

holiday! – by plunging herself into the Pacific, she threw the sheets back and got up, catching sight of her own outline sketchily drawn by sweatmarks through the night. The humidity was oppressive, making the air feel almost solid, and her skin was clammy. She walked naked through to the bathroom, catching sight of herself passing by the mirror. Had she lost weight? She stopped to examine herself more closely. Never as skinny as Holly, she was nonetheless a slim build, albeit soft and unathletic – her hours never left time for the gym, much less the energy. But now the nub of her shoulders looked polished and shiny, the upper curve of her hipbone pressing lightly against the skin as though trying to break through. Her face was definitely thinner, a newly sharp angle of her cheekbone throwing a shadow over the hollow of her cheek. But her eyes were puffy and almost slitted as sleep lay settled upon her still, like a little storm cloud. She sighed at her reflection, as she so often did. Usually she had bags from too little sleep but now it was puffiness from too much. Her face appeared to be a finely tuned instrument that had to be held in balance.

She still had her headache – obviously – but it was a dim, glowing pain this morning, rather than the usual full-wattage glare. The power of sleep, she supposed.

And to eat – that was the next wellness challenge to conquer. When had she last had a decent meal? She tried to think back, but everything felt woolly and indistinct. Too much travel, too many time zones.

She would eat first, then swim. If that didn't clear her headache, nothing would.

She found an olive bikini in her bag, twisted her dark hair into a rough bun and stepped into a pair of denim cutoffs. She opened the door and blinked. It always took a moment to register that the sight before her was actually real – the charcoal black sand, cerulean sea, green macaws sitting in the palm trees, the sun-bleached striped hammocks slung between slanted trees. If it looked like a stock screensaver image, it was because in fact it was her screensaver image. If she was having a bad shift or a rough day, it always gave her a lift to be reassured that this place was real, to know that she could actually come here and escape. Like now.

She could see a couple of surfers sitting on their boards on the water. They appeared more interested in chatting than catching waves, legs astride as they bobbed on the surface. No sign of Rory though, that she could see. The doors to the other huts were closed and although she was tempted to knock, she didn't. Everyone needed to recover from the journey.

She stepped onto the sand, feeling it crush between her toes as she began to walk slowly along the beach. The sunlight was dazzling, the sky unremittingly clear, and she kept to the shade, the sand already too hot for bare feet at this time of day. She watched the surfers bob, not a care between them. This wasn't the main surfing beach; that was a little further down the shore, two bays away. Here, the cove was too small to really travel any distance, but some of the locals liked to come here for an easy ride before or after work and she liked that it was quieter.

Jed's beach shack was only a couple of hundred metres away and she found him unpacking crates of rum and beer as she walked up. He had his back to her, a triangular sweat patch on the t-shirt between his shoulder blades as he worked, but she knew he'd seen her. The coloured huts were in eyeline from here and she knew he surreptitiously 'kept an eye' on them. Always had, always would.

'Morning, Jed.' She placed her forearms on the bar. It was just old gangplanks nailed together, but they had long ago been worn marble-smooth by generations of people doing exactly the same.

He turned, his eyes meeting hers with a smile. 'Morning, T-t. Sleep well?'

T-t. One of her childhood nicknames, rarely used these days. His voice had a skip to it, as though both a joke and a song lay curled within its folds.

'Like a log,' she smiled, perching on the bar stool. 'I didn't realize how tired I was.'

'Yes,' he nodded deeply. 'The others said you've been working hard.'

'Are they still asleep?' She twisted on the seat, looking back to the water. The surfers were on their tummies and paddling out to deeper waters now.

'No. Miles and Zac and Rory have gone on a bike ride. The others are on a walk to the big beach. Little Jimmy was keen to see the surfers doing their thing.'

She turned back again with a pout. 'They're all up? Oh, I wish they'd woken me! I'd have liked to have gone with them too.'

He chuckled. 'Oh, they tried. A few times. You were fast off, they said.'

She sighed. 'Oh dear. I guess I was pretty tired.' She closed her eyes, feeling the ocean breeze ruffle the baby hairs that escaped her bun, tickling her neck. It was good to be out of clothes, to feel the wind and the sun on her skin.

'And hungry now too?'

As if on cue, her tummy grumbled. 'Funny you should mention that . . .' She leaned in closer on the counter. 'What have you got by way of scoff?'

'Scoff.' He repeated the word as though trying it out for

size, softening her vowels so that the word became different but the same. *Scaff.* 'I can do you some Gallo Pinto.'

She smiled gratefully, knowing perfectly well he would. Gallo Pinto – beans and rice, with plantains and egg – was to the Costa Ricans what eggs and bacon were to the English. Jed and his father had been cooking it for her since she was little; it was instant comfort in a bowl. 'Great,' she sighed, feeling cared for, her needs already met. She was well rested, she was warm . . . This was going to be a good day. She could feel it.

'You want some coconut water?' He held up a coconut questioningly.

'Oh my God, yes.'

Reaching down to below the counter, he pulled out a machete and with one practised swipe, took off the top. It was still as exciting as when she'd been a kid. He stuck a straw in it and handed it to her, watching as she drank.

'Oh. My. God,' she said as she came up for air. 'That is literally better than saline.'

He raised an eyebrow. 'Saline?'

'What we doctors use for a rapid recovery.'

'Ah.' He chuckled as he walked off towards the kitchen area at the far end of the bar and began slicing up some plantains.

'So, tell me your news,' she said to his back, finding comfort just in watching his familiar routines. 'What's been going on over here?'

There was a short pause as he put a pan on the heat. 'Well, they gone built the new school at last,' he said over his shoulder.

'Finally!'

'Yeah. Only took eight years in the end.'

Only eight? He wasn't joking, and she felt a shot of anger. How many children had grown up here without a formal education in the meantime? Her father had given the money in a lump sum years ago, so it wasn't funding that had been the issue. It wasn't even that corruption was rife; she just knew that when it came to the Indigenas – the native people – their needs were at the very bottom of a long governmental to-do list.

'And ol' Sam finally perished.'

'Oh no, I'm so sorry. Was it his heart?' She quickly calculated that he must have been in his late eighties by now. He had been on statins for years. She was the one who had diagnosed his symptoms on her last trip out here, when she was a first-year in med school. The summer before she'd met Alex.

'Yes. He died happy though, Bertha said.'

Bertha was a kindly, larger-than-life figure in town, who sat on her stool making baskets by day and was the town prostitute by night. She had to be in her mid-sixties. 'Well, that's . . . nice to think he . . . had a smile on his face.'

Jed laughed, his muscular arm stirring the rice and beans as the plantains sizzled and softly charred. 'He had that all right,' he chuckled.

She watched him move, so loose-limbed and easy in his bones. He looked like there wasn't a knot of tension in his entire body.

'And how about you? What's happening in your life?' she asked, as he cracked two eggs and spilled them into a clearing in the pan, leaning back as the fat began to spit.

He didn't look back. 'I've got four little ones now. They're six, five, two and eight months.'

'Wow, Jed! I didn't know! . . . Your wife must be very busy.' And Tara had thought *she* was tired!

He gave an easy shrug. 'They're good kids.'

'How could they not be? What's your wife's name?' She had heard he had married several years back but she'd not heard about their growing family. Or perhaps she had just never asked. She had covered her ears and averted her eyes so that she never had to think about or remember Alex Carter, who had made this place his home now too.

'Sarita.'

'That's so pretty. I'd love to meet her while I'm here.'

He glanced back with a smile. 'You will.'

'And is your dad around?'

'No. He's up at the Lodge.'

The Lodge was the large plantation-style house her father had built high up in the hills, several hours from here – or so she was told. She herself had never visited it; it had been built during her self-imposed exile, but she had seen the plans and photographs, heard it lauded over family dinners . . . The official handing-over ceremony of the park, back to the Costa Rican people, was going to happen on Friday in the nearest town to the Lodge, and a small fiesta had been planned.

'He's getting the last bits ready for the launch,' Jed continued.

'Ah yes, of course. The launch.' She rolled her eyes, her fingers tapping lightly against the glass as the spectre of coming face to face with her past ran an icy chill down her spine. 'How *could* I have forgotten about that?' she muttered.

Jed chuckled and shook his head, prodding the eggs with a spatula and watching as they whitened before his eyes. 'Now that I don't know.'

The plan was for her and Miles and their group to fly up there on Thursday evening in time for the handover on Friday, and do their duty hobnobbing with the government bigwigs; there would be press and much pressing of the flesh for the Tremain family members. For Miles that was the worst of it, but she had a far more dreadful fate to contemplate – Alex Carter would be on that stage, by her father's side, and for those few hours there would be no avoiding him. But there was no question of ducking out. This wasn't just their father's project, it was his legacy, and for his sake, they had to be there. Besides, she wouldn't need to speak to Alex. Miles, Holly and (unwittingly) Rory were going to be her defensive wall, she had privately decided, and once the ceremonies were over, their happy group could then spend the rest of the weekend relaxing at the Lodge before they flew home on the Monday. It was far from ideal, but it would be absolutely fine.

She watched as he spooned several large dollops of chilled rice and beans into the pan to warm it through and mix with the egg. He gave the pan a final shake, then slid the contents into a shallow yellow-painted ceramic bowl.

So quick, so good.

He set it down before her and the aroma hit her like a slap. She closed her eyes, feeling her mouth instantly water. 'Oh my God,' she moaned. 'That smells *so* good. I'm absolutely starving. I've not had a proper meal in days.'

'Why not?'

She shrugged. 'Work.'

His eyebrows raised to a single point. 'T-t, if you haven't got time to eat, then you're working *too* hard.'

'Yeah, probably,' she said, taking the fork he was holding out for her and beginning to eat. And once she began . . .

she felt a sort of desperation wash through her, as though she couldn't get the food into her body fast enough. She hadn't realized how much she had neglected herself. It felt so normal back home to – literally – run on empty. No sleep, no food.

He watched in bemused silence as she chased the last grain of rice around the bowl, pushing it onto the fork with her finger, before finally setting down her cutlery and sitting back with a satisfied smile. His gaze went from her face to the licked-clean bowl to her face again. 'Seriously. Maybe don't work so hard?' he repeated, an eyebrow arched.

She laughed and nodded, looking back with affection at that kind face with quietly wise brown eyes and a mouth that knew when to stay shut. It had always been easy talking to Jed. 'Oh, I've missed you.'

'I've missed you, T-t. Why *did* you stay away so long? Surely they give doctors holidays back in England?'

'Yeah, they do,' she sighed, looking away and desperately not wanting to bring up Alex's name. She had never brought him out here, so unless Miles had blabbed, Jed wouldn't know about her relationship history with the conservation project's big boss. What was his title – technical director? Something like that. To bring it all up now, to try to explain how devastating his betrayal had been . . . How could she explain that Alex's presence here had contaminated this place for her? That her place of childhood refuge had become inextricably linked with the man who had destroyed her life? 'Time just . . . slips past, I guess, when you're not looking. I've been pretty focused on my career.'

Jed nodded. 'So, the boyfriend . . .' He picked up a crate of glasses and one by one, began pulling them out and stacking them on the shelves.

'Rory.'

'Yes. Rory.'

His guarded tone reminded her of their run-in last night. 'He's a good man,' she said reassuringly. 'A doctor too.'

Jed nodded, not making eye contact. 'You been together long?'

'About a year?' She didn't know why she said it as a question. Jed wouldn't know how long it had been. She ought to know, she just wasn't big on marking dates. Her hand went to the gold locket at her neck – his gift to her for their first anniversary together. 'Just over.'

'It must be serious, then.'

'I guess. We're both . . . settled, very happy together. It works well, us both being doctors. He's a good man.'

'Yeah, you said that.' He winked, teasing her lightly. 'You thinking marriage? Babies?'

'No.' She shook her head. 'Definitely not. My focus is my career for the moment.'

Jed glanced at her, but said nothing. But she knew what lay in that silence; he knew she was thirty years old; he assumed her biological clock was ticking . . .

'You want a coffee?'

She smiled. She had always loved the way he said it. *Kaffee*. 'I'd love one, thank you. You always look after me so well.'

'Somebody got to look after the doctor doing all the looking after.'

'Ha!'

She turned in her seat to watch the surfers catching the waves now, their shouts carrying to her ear as they carved over the water's surface in meandering arcs, like musical notes on a manuscript.

'Mean rip out there yesterday,' Jed said warningly.

'Yeah?'

'It's better now but be careful if you're going in.'

'Don't worry, I remember – swim perpendicular to the current. You taught me well.'

He nodded, pleased. 'We'll need to keep an eye on little Jimmy, though.'

'For sure. He's my godson.'

'He's fast. Does he like football?'

'Do you know a boy who doesn't?' she quipped.

They watched as the surfers tipped backwards into the water, their run already over, the waves closing over their heads.

'How long ago did they all leave?'

'An hour and a half ago. 'Bout that.'

'Gosh. An early start, then.' Jet lag, she supposed. Plus kids. Poor Holly. There was no rest at all, ever, for her. It wasn't a problem Tara suffered from.

The surfers were walking out of the water now, their boards tucked under their arms, exhilaration infusing their strides. She could see the droplets of water falling off their bodies like crystals, hear the cadence of their laughter over the waves. That was what it was to be happy. To be rooted. To be here.

Pura Vida, the locals called it.

She watched on with emotions she couldn't quite describe, an ache deep inside her she couldn't understand. She had a nagging feeling she was doing this Life thing all wrong.

'You're awake!'

Holly ran over the sand towards her, already touched by the first kisses of a tan. Her freckles were blooming, her hairline damp. Brightly coloured net shopping bags bulged in her hands. It had clearly been a morning well spent, in every sense.

'Only just.' Tara watched her lazily from the old striped hammock, one leg dangling idly over the side. She'd been trying to read a book for the best part of an hour now but she'd yet to turn the page. Lying about made her an easy target for her thoughts, it seemed.

'Right?' Holly laughed. 'We kept going in and checking on you. I actually checked your pulse at one point.'

'Told you I was tired.' She nodded towards the shopping. 'Find any treasures?'

Holly's smile widened. Twelve hours in and she was already a different animal from the pale, exhausted medic living off sugar in the hospital canteen. 'Sure did. Got me some—' She reached into the bag and pulled out a long string and shell necklace; it was all bleached colours and intricate knots, and would jangle when she walked.

'Nice,' Tara smiled. She had bought an almost identical one when she was fifteen. It was an intrinsic part of the boho beach look, the Blue Lagoon fantasy everyone ended up chasing out here.

'Plus, some of these babies,' Holly said, presenting a pair of faded red leather thong sandals.

'Love those,' Tara nodded, knowing she would get blisters from them. 'Let me guess, did you get a basket?'

'Not yet, but I'm gonna! How did I *not* know that I needed baskets? They've got so many!'

'So many baskets,' Tara concurred. 'My mother bought one once that was just big enough to carry a single egg.'

'A single *egg*?' Holly's jaw dropped open.

'A single egg. It was beautiful, don't get me wrong. Exquisitely crafted. But a single egg.'

'Wow.' Holly said wistfully, lapsing into silence for a moment and musing on the whimsy of a basket woven by hand for such a singular task. She seemed to be tapping into the Tremains' obscure definitions of luxury – ramshackle huts on a pristine beach, fresh coconut water, single-egg baskets.

'Did Jimmy like watching the surfers?' Tara asked, watching as he and Dev, silhouetted, ran straight down to the water's edge, the hot sand burning their feet.

'We had to drag him away. Somehow he's managed to come back with a new Liverpool kit, I mean, how . . . ?' She shook her head wearily.

'Have you seen the others? What's their route?'

'Dunno, they said they were going to go inland.'

'Oh dear. That means mountains. Did anyone tell Rory that?'

Holly shrugged. 'They said they'd be back sometime after lunch.'

'Right.' Tara felt a twitch of irritation. Okay, so she'd slept late – but did he really have to take himself off for a half day?

'Don't look like that!' Holly warned her, knowing the nuances of her tone only too well. 'You're the one who overslept. Anyway, he's bonding with your brother. You should be pleased.'

Bonding. How she hated that word.

'Well, we should do something too, make the most of our time while we can,' Tara said, kicking her leg and beginning to rock. 'I'm keen to get over to the clinic today and give them the supplies we brought over.'

Holly gave a sigh that suggested she wasn't quite so keen to return to a medical setting so soon. 'Sure, whatever you want.'

'But I can go on my own if you want to hang out here, it's really no problem.'

'Listen, you're the expert on this place; we'll do whatever you want, but don't feel you need an itinerary. We're cool just hanging out here.' Holly sighed happily, looking out over the water and watching her family frolic in the shallows. 'Jed's so amazing. He's going to teach Jimmy to surf.'

'I know. He taught me. He's the best.' She watched the look of contentment on her best friend's face. A family beach holiday. Simple pleasures. She felt an unexpected stab of pain again and looked away. 'And your hut's okay?'

'I want to live there forever. What more do we need? Beds, beach. Outdoor shower. And there's just something so . . . romantic about a mosquito net, isn't there?'

Tara smiled, hearing her falling for the illusion of the simple life. She had followed the same curve herself over the years. It was easy to fall for the paradise sell, but this stripped-back aesthetic was an illusion. What was charming on day one could be wearying by day thirty. Not to mention the realities of the wet season, when the rain fell like glass spears and the humidity meant nothing – not clothes, hair nor skin – could ever quite dry . . . And the second Holly ran out of anti-mozzie spray, shit would get real, real quick.

For the first time, Tara noticed a large coconut poised among the palm fronds above her head. She tried to remember the statistic for the number of people killed by falling coconuts each year. Was it a hundred and fifty? Something like that.

She sank into her thoughts. One hundred and fifty people killed every year by a falling coconut. It was such a . . . random way to die. Ridiculous, really. Like the two killed per annum by vending machines falling on top of them. Or the two and a half *thousand* left-handers who died from using right-handed products. The medical world was littered with anecdotes about inane deaths and oversights. They were taught in med school that more than seven hundred patients every year (an average of two per week) were sewn back up after surgery with some part of surgical waste left inside them – a swab, a forceps; one time she'd heard of a pair of pliers. Maybe even that would have been better than a teeny-tiny samurai-sharp scalpel blade. Less lethal.

'. . . waterfall!'

Tara was torn from her thoughts. 'Huh?'

'Jed mentioned a waterfall yesterday. We could go there, after the clinic?'

'Yes, that sounds fun.' She swung her leg out of the hammock and struggled up to standing, feeling a sudden urge to move and escape her thoughts. 'I'll go and speak to him about it if you want to tell the boys?'

Holly looked surprised. 'Okay. I hadn't meant *right* this second, but sure.' She got up – her bottom all sandy – and ran down to the water's edge.

Tara turned towards the bar, towards Jed's comforting shape in the shadows, when she heard a heavy thud behind her that vibrated through the ground. She turned and looked back. The hammock was now twisted on its strings so that it bellied out upside down, a coconut in the sand beside it. It was the coconut that had been right above her head a moment earlier.

She stared at it in shock. One hundred and fifty people in a global population of seven billion.

Suddenly she wasn't sure she liked those odds.

Chapter Fourteen

The open-top Jeep rumbled through town, the shadows of trees casting lacy patterns on their faces. Jimmy was strapped into the boot and waving at all the stallholders and street vendors as they passed. Most waved back at him with fleshy palms and gappy grins, encouraging him further.

Tara had forgotten the sheer vibrancy of the place, the weather-boarded buildings painted in nursery colours of yellow and blue, hot pink and turquoise. People sat in pairs and small groups along the sides of the buildings, perched on stools, leaning on countertops, sprawled over car bonnets. There were no pavements; pedestrians and drivers shared the tarmac in a way that would be impossible in London; telephone wires were looped slackly overhead. People parked where they liked – sometimes it wasn't clear if they were parked or in fact just stopped – driving around in open-sided fruit trucks, Vespas, bikes, Jeeps, no one in a hurry, brown arms stretched casually along open windows.

Some children were playing around a yellow fire hydrant, running through the spray, the water droplets catching the lunchtime light. Sides of buildings were painted with Coca-Cola signs and hand-decorated hoardings were layered in piles on signposts, pointing the way to surf hire shops, cabanas, hostels . . .

Tara kept an eye out for three out-of-breath cyclists, but saw no sign of them. She hoped Miles and Zac weren't showing off and taking Rory on some ridiculous overly long ride, though she wouldn't put it past them. Rory was in decent shape but his long hours meant he couldn't – and didn't – give the same dedication to the gym as her brother and his husband.

'Nice work if you can get it, Jed!' Holly called from her seat in the back as they sat at the rudimentary traffic lights, people calling Jed's name and hailing him from the streets. 'What are you? Mayor?'

'I wish!' Jed laughed, nodding his head in amusement, but Tara noticed the way people's eyes slid from him over to her in the next instant, as though they knew who she was too. It was an easy enough calculation to make – everyone knew he and his father worked for her family – but she realized now that the relative anonymity her family had enjoyed on her childhood trips over here had been superseded by their profile as the largest single private landowner in the country. The new national park was big news, and her father's face probably had the same recognition factor as the President's now. But hers too? She had made a point of keeping herself out of this project.

She kept her gaze as light and flitting as a moth, not hovering anywhere too long, not making eye contact. She admired the stalls selling baskets of every size and shape, all intricately woven from grass; she smiled at the sight of brightly coloured ceramics displays, pineapple stalls, tourist shops flogging lilos and postcards, beach shacks pegged with tie-dye t-shirts and cotton pareos.

The sea was to their left, a high tide covering the dark gold beach, and she watched as some surfers caught the barrels, scudding in on white waters and silhouetted against a clear sky. Jed turned a sharp right, waiting for a banana truck to come past before heading down one of the long, straight back roads that led inland and towards the distant hills. The sky looked turbulent over there, dark clouds twisting and bumping into one another, a mist falling to the ground like a privacy screen.

The buildings became steadily more spread out and lower to the ground, high, dense hedges marking the start of the residential district. The houses were mainly single-storey, some topped with sheets of corrugated metal. They passed the elementary school, beside it a large unmanicured, unmarked playing field, a group of boys playing football, their rucksacks in a forgotten heap.

The treelines started to became more dense as they rolled further on, the road no longer tarmacked as they headed for the hills. They stopped at lights again and she swept her gaze over the only house on the opposite corner. It was largely hidden behind a concrete-panelled wall which had been defaced with graffiti and it was several moments before her gaze focused to read what it said in Spanish: *Foreigners out! Costa Rica for Costa Ricans!*

The meaning was clear. She immediately looked at Jed and one glance at his terse expression told her he had already seen it, that he had hoped she wouldn't. He had wanted that light to be green and not red. He had wanted to shoot through it before she could read it.

The lights changed and Jed pulled away. She glanced back at the house, just in time to see around the concrete wall and into the yard. A man in jeans and a hat was reaching into a pick-up and he happened to look up as they passed. His eyes locked with Tara's. In the next instant, they had driven past and he was gone again but something in the way he had looked at her, the way his body had tensed as he had seen who she was . . .

'Who was that?' she asked quietly, knowing Jed had seen the interaction.

There was a short pause. 'One of Miguel D'Arrosto's men.'

'And who's he?'

'Just a cattle rancher who doesn't like being told no.'

Tara hesitated. '. . . Same rancher whose men almost ran us off the road last night?' she asked, lowering her voice.

Jed glanced at her. 'Don't worry. He's all talk.'

Tara wasn't sure that was true. That truck bearing down upon them at speed, threatening to tail-end them at eighty miles an hour, hadn't felt like 'talk'. It had been action. Open threat.

She automatically rubbed her temples, knowing it made no difference to her headache, knowing this wasn't the time to discuss it – her friends were in the seats behind, their young child sitting between them; and besides, they had arrived at their first destination. She gave a small gasp as they pulled into the parking lot of the clinic she had only ever seen on a computer screen – her 'baby', loved from afar, it had been the first of her award-winning international mother and child clinics, and unlike real babies, she definitely had favourites. This would always be the one she loved most.

Seeing it in three dimensions was surprisingly emotional and immediately she sensed the energy about the place. It was so much bigger than she had imagined, for one thing. It wasn't an object of beauty – a bright white concrete hulk, single-storey, with lots of windows, a red medical cross sign hanging above the door, the universal language for medical help. But a couple of young mothers were sitting on a bench, one breastfeeding a baby while toddlers played with a hoop around them.

They parked up, and Jed and Dev went round to the back to start lifting out the boxes of supplies she had brought over from England. It was a stocking-up of basic kit – syringes, sterilizing solution, dressings, antibiotics, saline, blood pressure monitors – but she'd also managed to get her hands on some Doppler ultrasound scanners.

'Pretty decent,' Holly nodded casually at the clinic. It was hard to impress her friend.

They walked into the air-conditioned cool. For all the bucolic calm outside, inside there were people everywhere – doctors in white coats moving officiously, nurses running between rooms, parents and children and babies sitting on plastic stackable chairs. The noise level was high – babies crying, toddlers shrieking, but also the hum of conversation too, the punctuation of laughs as mothers talked among themselves as they waited to be seen.

Tara looked around with a critical eye. In spite of the seeming chaos, there seemed to be a patient registration system in place and everything looked clean, from what she could see. The antiseptic smell was reassuring.

'Ah, home sweet home,' Holly quipped. 'I can feel my cortisol levels rising already.'

'Shuddup,' Tara grinned. 'This won't take long.'

She saw the reception desk and walked over. A young woman looked up and smiled at her, asking her something in Spanish.

Tara replied in kind, saying she was looking for Dr Morales, and the receptionist pointed towards an office in the far corner. '*Gracias.*'

'You speak Spanish?' Holly asked her as they walked across to it. *Now* she was impressed.

'Just enough to get by.'

She knocked on the door and leaned forward, waiting for a voice to tell her to enter. Instead, the door swung open and she found herself almost at eye level with an enormous bosom.

There was a moment of mutual surprise, and then the owner of the bosom gave a huge smile. 'Dr *Tara*? You are finally here?'

'In the flesh. How are you, Yorleny?'

She was swept into a hug by way of reply and it was like hugging pillows, everything soft and warm.

'It is good to see you,' the woman said. 'We have waited a long time for this moment.'

'I've waited a long time to get back here. I've missed this beautiful country.' Tara stepped back to introduce the others. 'These are my friends, Holly and Dev Motha. They are doctors too. And their little boy, Jimmy.'

'Welcome, welcome,' Yorleny said in English, greeting them all with double-hand clasps, including a cheek-chuck for Jimmy. She lifted her head and called out in Spanish: 'Hey, everybody – this is Dr Tremain, our clinic's founder and benefactor.'

Tara's face burned as suddenly all faces turned towards her – doctors, nurses, patients – and people began clapping.

'Oh God, you really didn't have to do that,' Tara said, mortified, under her breath and smiling back politely. She could hear Holly laughing beside her as a train of people came over. Some wanted to shake her hand, others just to look at her – seemingly – and she understood for sure that her family's name had resonance here. People knew her for reasons other than just this clinic.

'Oh no, I'm not anyone,' she heard Holly bluster as her hand was reached for too, her curly red hair touched like it contained magical powers. 'Oh, well yes . . . how do you do . . . uh-huh . . . Okay yes, you can stroke my hair . . . Yes, *hola*.'

Tara laughed as the crowd swarmed around, mobbing them. Even Jimmy found himself caught up in it, mothers cooing over his limpid eyes – so like his father's – children showing him their toys, pointing at his trainers.

'We've got some supplies for you,' Tara said in her best Spanish, when the numbers finally subsided. 'I'd have called ahead, but I didn't want you to go to any trouble and start laying on some kind of welcome.' She could only imagine what they might have done with forewarning.

'Tara, you are so good to us,' Yorleny said in halting English, so that Holly and Dev could listen too.

'It's the very least I can do. I'm sorry I couldn't bring more. But I will next time, definitely,' she promised, knowing she would be back again soon. She'd cut off her own nose to spite her face by refusing to come back here for so long. She had let Alex Carter drive her out as though this country wasn't big enough for the both of them. But of course it was.

'Do you mind if I have a look around? I'd like to see what you've got and what you don't. I can write up a sort of inventory for what to bring next time.'

'Tara, this is your clinic, you do not need to ask.' She looked at Holly and Dev. 'You are doctors too, yes?'

'That's right. I do trauma. My husband is a radiographer. X-rays,' Holly said, enunciating every word with comic effect.

A gleam came into the clinical director's eyes and Tara knew what she was thinking. There had to be fifty patients in the waiting area, and so far she'd counted only four doctors in white coats, including Yorleny, the clinical director. 'Then perhaps . . .'

'We've got a free hour or so, if you'd like some help?' Tara offered on all their behalf. 'And actually, we've brought a couple of ultrasound scanners for the pregnant mothers, so Dev could set them up for you?' She looked over at him.

'Sure,' Dev shrugged, easy-going as always.

'I don't know what to say,' Yorleny said, looking amazed.

'Just point us where to go. We can work out the rest.'

An hour passed in what seemed like fifteen minutes. Tara and Holly were set up in adjoining rooms and between them they assessed and cleaned wounds and scrapes, took temperatures and palpated swollen stomachs, measured blood pressure, took bloods, administered inoculations and gave out iron tablets . . . It was like being medical students again, going back to basics and dealing with the business of life, not death, of connecting with patients without the high-octane drama that characterized their roles back home. It was all a long way from her intensive care unit, where everything flashed and beeped and there was more machinery to see than patient. She felt in her element here.

Jimmy had been tasked with tidying the toy crates and putting the right bits of jigsaw back in the right boxes. Dev had moved on from setting up and explaining the Dopplers to seemingly running his own obstetric clinic as he scanned the expectant mothers himself, giving them printouts of their foetuses and explaining what they were seeing. Jed was unpacking the boxes and stacking the shelves – and seemingly repairing them, too.

'Jed, where are the gauze swabs we brought?' she asked him, popping her head out of her room. He was working in the cupboard opposite, down on his hands and knees and hammering something into the back wall.

'Down the corridor, in the office second door on the left,' he said, his voice muffled. 'Beside the speculums. I'll get them for you.'

'No, don't worry. It'll only take me a sec,' she said, patting his shoulder as she passed. She saw Holly holding up her fingers and getting a young boy to follow them as she went past her door. She was smiling, her eyes bright. No sugar required. She never looked like that on the A&E ward.

Tara found the office and knocked. There was no reply, so she went in. Jed had stacked the supplies conscientiously so that all the labels were facing forwards.

She took two boxes, her gaze falling to the view outside the window as she closed the cupboard. It had begun raining. She could see the patch of scrubland at the back where the local kids played football around the thick tufts of grass, heavy-headed trees bowing low as the cloudburst passed over with casual, familiar ferocity. Two women were walking with bags in their hands, not bothering to run; they knew the rain would be gone within another few minutes, that there was nowhere actually to run to. She could see Jed's Jeep parked up in the lot, surrounded now by several other trucks. She frowned. They were all clustered together, like sheep huddling for warmth. She made a mental note to have parking lines painted – something else to go on her list – but she would have thought logic would dictate where and how to park?

She walked back up the corridor.

'Jed.' She waited for him to crawl backwards from the cramped space. He looked up at her, flushed; he was far too big a man to fit into something of that size. 'You might want to ask around and see if some people can move their trucks? We're a bit hemmed in.'

'Oh. Okay.' He frowned, seeming puzzled.

'It's not a problem, but I reckon we'll be good to go in ten minutes or so, that's all. It's a holiday after all, and remember we've promised Jimmy a swim in a waterfall.'

'Sure.'

She went back in to her patient, a seven-year-old boy with an infected leg wound. 'Right. Now, where were we?' she smiled.

Tara lay on the rock, out of breath and still laughing at Holly's wedgie on her last 'run'. Jed had taken them to the waterfalls she remembered visiting as a child. They weren't as high as in her memory, nor as azure as Instagram led everyone to believe, but the river feeding into them was wide and fast and the falls fanned round the pool in a crescent. In the far corner, a short sequence of smooth-bouldered runs acted like chutes and it was possible to slide down them – which was what they had been doing for a couple of hours now. Jimmy couldn't get enough, and Holly and Dev had been taking it in turns to 'cannonball' with him. They were all feeling very waterlogged.

'Anyone hungry?' Jed asked.

'Me!' Holly's arm shot up like she was in school.

'I would murder for a coffee,' Dev panted, wading through the pool to where Jed was sitting on the rocks and opening up his large rucksack.

'Not got coffee here, but how about some fresh papaya juice and some mangoes?'

'Oh my God yes,' Holly said, hurriedly wading over too, elbows out like she was a sales shopper. 'This is like one of those posh spas – waterfalls. Mangoes. Papaya juice.'

Tara lay flat out on her rock, basking like a seal, her eyes closed and listening to the sounds of the jungle all around them. It was so much *busier* than her sleep apps suggested. The air positively thrummed with noise, it dripped with scent, even her own skin quietly beaded with sweat as though that too was brimming to overflowing. It felt like sensory overload and she had a feeling of becoming grounded and settling back into her own body again. Even her headache was on a dim setting.

She heard a distinctive shriek and opened her eyes in time to see a keel-billed toucan flying between the trees. She smiled, still able to remember the first time she'd seen one. She'd been ten.

'Here, T-t.' Jed was squatting on the rock beside hers, reaching over with a glass of juice.

She scrambled up onto her elbows and took it gratefully. 'So this is heavenly.'

'I sure think so,' he grinned.

'Having fun, Jimmy?' she called over. He was still clambering over the rocks and shooting down them without stopping, but he couldn't hear her over the thunder of the falls.

Dev was watching him with an unwavering gaze and Tara felt a rush of love for her old friend. He was such a good father, such a patient husband. Tara didn't think there were many men out there who would or could put up with Holly; she was strong, demanding, generally uncompromising. She always shouted longest and loudest – and yet, somehow, Dev steered her to where she needed to be. They made a good team. She couldn't imagine either one of them without the other and yet she remembered a time when Holly had been so determined to cut him out of her life. It seemed inconceivable now. 'He frightened the hell out of me,' Holly had admitted years later. 'I had this sense he was going to be The One and it really pissed me off. I thought I was going to get a lot more shagging around in first.' The revelation that Holly had been pregnant at the same time as Tara had been just one of many shocks for them both in that period. It was the only one she could look back on with warmth.

'So, Jed,' Holly said, settling herself on the rocks, her elbows resting on her knees. 'Twig told me you've known her since she was a little girl . . .'

Tara grinned at her friend's tone of voice. Uh-oh.

'. . . That means you must have some dirt on her.' Her blue eyes twinkled.

Jed laughed. 'Well now, if I did, it would be more than my life's worth to share it.'

'Huh, that's very disappointing, Jed,' Holly quipped. 'I think you and I are going to need to crack open a bottle of rum sometime soon and see what you have to say then.'

Everyone chuckled.

'I can't believe we've got this place all to ourselves?' Dev said, looking over at Jed. 'I assumed it would be overrun with tourists.'

'Well, there are some much bigger falls than this a few kilometres away. They usually go there and mainly it's the locals come here, 'cos it's close by. But it will all get busier once the new park opens. What is it they call it? Eco-tourism?' He gave a wry smile.

Dev grinned. 'I still can't believe your family owns a national park, Twig.'

Tara blushed. 'Well, technically it's still just a private conservation project until the weekend. Only once it's gifted back to the Costa Rican people will it become a national resource.'

'Oh, just call a spade a spade,' Holly scoffed. 'It's a goddam national park!'

Dev looked back at Tara. 'It's an incredible thing, what your family's done.'

'It's really nothing to do with me.'

'But for your family to use their money like that, to realize such a bold vision. I mean, how many other people in your position would have committed to something of that scale? It's all very well and good signing up to the notion of good causes but actually following through on it . . .'

'Dev – stop talking?' Holly muttered, seeing Tara's frozen expression. It was several seconds before he caught up and remembered the background story. Realization ran openly over his face. He had been there, back then; he remembered the fallout from this Great Idea, the sacrifice to the Grand Scheme . . .

He looked at Jed instead, flustered. 'How is it regarded by the Costa Ricans?' he asked, looking for safe ground.

Jed gave a cautious nod. 'Most people are pleased.'

'Only most? Not all?'

'Well, not the mining or the logging or the oil companies, nor the ranchers, or the farmers or the plantation owners. All the ones who have to cut back the forest for their profits, they don't care about saving the planet.'

'Mmm. I guess this is the problem, isn't it?' Dev said. 'These high-minded ideals of preserving the forests, protecting wildlife, reducing carbon emissions – they come with the best intentions, but for the guy on the ground who's lost his livelihood . . .' he shrugged. 'It's a kick in the teeth.'

'Yes. Some people have been very unhappy.'

Tara watched Jed. She knew him too well. He was a born diplomat, careful with his words, but she knew that often the truth lay in his silences. There was something he wasn't telling them. Or rather, her.

'At least *you're* on the right side of the fence,' Dev continued. 'Holly told me you and your family are very important to Tara's family.'

Jed smiled, glancing at Tara almost shyly. 'Well, that is good to hear. They are very important to us. We feel honoured to work for them.'

'What is it your father does exactly?'

'For the moment, he is based at the rangers' lodge in the middle of the park. He manages the rangers. It is a varied job – maintaining boundaries, catching poachers, illegal farmers.' He gave an amused laugh. 'He caught one of the villages illegally trying to build a road not so long ago. It would have run across one of the main breeding areas for jaguarondi, which are endangered, of course.'

'Oh dear.'

'Yes. So he is very busy. And of course there has been much to do to get ready for the handover.'

'It sounds a mammoth task,' Dev sympathized. 'And here you are, looking after us and bringing us to waterfalls!'

'I caught the long straw, for sure!' Jed laughed. 'But it is important, making sure you are happy.'

'Jed, I'm not sure I've *ever* been happier,' Holly murmured, lying down to bask on a warm rock, her eyes already closing.

'Does your wife work?' Dev asked.

'She does. She is a teacher in our village.'

Tara frowned. 'Village? But I thought you lived in Puerto Viejo?'

'Not anymore. You see? Much has changed since your last visit. My wife is Indigena – she is of the Bribri. They live past Manzanillo, in the mountains.'

'But I thought . . . do you mean you travel over here, every day?'

'Only when your family is here. Otherwise I help my father, usually at the rangers' base station.' He smiled, seeing her expression. 'It is not a problem for me to come to the beach, T-t.'

Tara said nothing, but she knew that journeys here weren't like they were at home. It wasn't a matter of hopping on buses or trains, of walking down roads or even through fields. This was a land of tropical forests – rainforests, cloud forests, dry forests. Moving even ten metres could be a challenge in some parts. To get to the beach in time for her family to wake up every day, he must be leaving his home well before dawn.

'Wouldn't it be easier to stay in town in the week and go home at weekends?'

'Easier? Yes,' he grinned. 'But for my wife left with the babies? Believe me, my life is easier if I am there too.'

'Oh I hear you!' Dev nodded. 'And amen to that.'

Jed chuckled, understanding the joke as Holly looked on with a mock-peeved expression. His smile faded. '. . . Sadly our second boy is sick. It takes two of us to be there at night. One to look after him, and one to look after the others.'

Tara frowned. Something in Jed's tone of voice, his altered speech pattern, put her on high alert. 'Sick how?'

'Bad stomach pain. Fevers. He cannot eat. His skin itches all the time.'

'Any joint pains? Swellings?' Holly asked, turning her head on the rock, a deep frown on her brow. Briefly, her gaze met Tara's.

'Yes. In his hands. And a lot of nosebleeds.'

'*Nosebleeds?*' Tara echoed.

'Is he jaundiced? Have his bloods been taken?' Holly pressed, propping herself up on her elbows.

Jed looked taken aback by the rapid-fire questions, but Tara knew exactly where her friend was heading.

'Has he seen a doctor, Jed?' she asked gently.

'The Awa is treating him.'

'Awa?' Holly echoed.

He reached for the word in English. 'The shaman. The doctor in town will not visit the village, and anyway my boy is too weak to travel. It is safer to keep him at home.'

Holly and Tara shared a knowing look. If he was too weak to travel, that was proof alone that he needed to be in a hospital. Tara's gaze slid over to Dev and Jimmy. This was their trip of a lifetime; it had been one thing helping out at the clinic for a couple of hours, but Holly couldn't start trekking cross-country on a busman's holiday.

'Jed, would you allow me to take a look at him?' she asked, treading carefully.

He blinked, looking suddenly nervous. 'Thank you, but it is not necessary. The Awa is treating him.'

'Of course. And I respect that. What does the Awa say is wrong with him?'

'That he has the spider sickness.'

'Spider sickness.'

'The sickness is a thread that goes through the veins and around the body, like a spider walking on a web.'

'Right, yes, of course.' Tara plastered a smile on her face; she had never heard a potential case of hepatitis being called that before. 'Well, would you let me take a quick look at him anyway? Just to offer a second opinion. I would like to help if I can. You always do so much for my family, it would be the least I could do.'

Jed hesitated, the fearful parent suddenly visible in his happy-go-lucky face.

'Please. Whatever I might recommend would be entirely for you and Sarita to decide if it was what you wanted,' she added. 'There would be no pressure from me. He's your son.'

'. . . Okay,' he said finally.

'Great. What's his name?'

'Paco.'

'Paco, lovely.' She kept her voice deliberately calm, her cadence slow. 'So then, maybe I could travel back with you tonight?'

'Tonight?'

'Mm-hmm,' she said casually, hoping he wouldn't be alarmed by her urgency.

There was a hesitation. 'But it would be very dark. You would not be able to get back until the morning.' Jed looked concerned by this.

'That's fine – as long as there's somewhere I could sleep for the night?'

He thought for a moment. 'There is a bed I know of. Our neighbour's son went to San José for work.'

She nodded, not exactly relishing the idea of sleeping in a complete stranger's house. 'Uh-huh. Well, if you're sure your neighbour wouldn't mind, just for the night . . .'

Jed looked back at her. 'Of course not. If you really think it will help?'

'I do, Jed,' she nodded. 'I really do.'

The sun was beginning to sink when they finally made their way back. The original plan for a quick excursion to the waterfalls had led to an all-afternoon escape as they took it in turns napping, sunbathing and swimming with Jimmy. At one point, Jed took the boy off to see some rarely sighted grey-crowned squirrel monkeys which he spotted nearby.

Now, with dusk falling, the forest was becoming even louder – emerald cicadas scratched, sending a deafening hum into the sky, monkeys shrieked, parakeets flapped and cawed, tapirs shuffled heavily through the undergrowth. Everything could be heard, but almost nothing was seen; life teemed and pulsed just out of reach – a flash of colour here, a slow blink in the leaves there.

They walked in a line behind Jed, below the giant ceiba trees, watching – as per his instructions – where they put their feet. If there was beauty here there was also peril – coral snakes, Brazilian wandering spiders; although not much was as nasty, according to Jed, as the red caterpillars that would get them if they sunbathed in the shade of almond trees.

It was a long walk back towards the road, where they'd left the Jeep – there was no car park, of course, just a break in the trees where the locals knew to stop – but Tara could tell something was wrong just by the shift in Jed's shoulders. He stopped, still a way from the road, hidden by the trees. Instinctively everyone else stopped too, watching him as he stared at the seemingly innocuous scene. The car was where they had left it. It was not on fire. There wasn't a jaguar sitting on the roof. And yet something had caught his attention.

Slowly, he began walking forwards again, emerging from the tree cover and going to stand by the front wheel arch.

That was when Tara saw it too. The tyre was flat, the car now sitting at an angle different to when they'd left it. Only by a few degrees, but still – Jed had clocked it immediately.

'What's happened?' Jimmy asked curiously, as Jed crouched down on his heels to examine it more closely.

Jed looked up at him. 'Nothing serious,' he smiled after a

moment. 'We must have hit a rock on the way over here. Some of them are pretty sharp. They're not like them smooth roads you got back home.'

Holly guffawed. 'Oh trust me, you've clearly not seen the state of our roads lately! There are potholes you could bathe your granny in!'

Jed chuckled at the idea. 'Not to worry. We got a spare. We'll get it changed and be heading back in no time.' He looked across at Jimmy. 'You want to help me, big man? I could use your muscles.'

'Yeah!' Jimmy said excitedly, as though this was every bit as exciting as shooting down waterfalls.

Tara watched as Jed sprang up. She knew for sure now that he was hiding something from them, something that had been going on since they'd landed here – that incident on the road last night, the contempt in that man's stare as they had driven by . . . even those trucks all parked around their Jeep at the clinic – was that really innocent, or another warning too?

Jed patted Jimmy on the shoulder. 'Good boy. This way, then. We're going to need to get it out of the back and there's a nut that can be stiff. I hope you've got some strength left.'

Jimmy pulled a muscle pose.

'That should do it!'

They went round to the back of the car; Holly was getting Dev to hold the rucksack while she refolded the wet towels. Tara crouched down by the tyre, examining it closely herself. She put a finger to the hole. It was small and neat, precise almost. This hadn't been done by a sharp stone. This was no accident. As a surgeon, she knew exactly what a cut by a knife looked like.

This wasn't just talk, and it was more than a threat.

This was a statement of intent.

Chapter Fifteen

'Where have you been?'

Rory sat up on the bed. He was wearing just a pair of shorts, a bottle of beer on the side table. His face was flushed, though she didn't know if it was from the beer, the sun or even his earlier bike ride.

'Sorry.' She shut the door behind her with a sigh. 'Turned out to be a bigger afternoon than we expected.'

'And you couldn't text? Let me know where you were?'

Tara was amused. 'We're in the rainforest, Ror! How good do you think phone signal is around here?' She went and sat on the end of the bed, falling back with a groan. The mosquito net was knotted above the bed and tucked behind the headboard. The ceiling fan whirred, pushing the hot air around the room, but creating a breeze at least. She closed her eyes, feeling the heat of the day still in her bones.

'. . . So?'

She twisted to look back at him. 'Huh?'

'Where were you?'

'Oh. We went to the clinic to drop off the supplies, ended up helping out a bit, and then took Jimmy to the waterfalls. It was only supposed to be a quick thing – but he was having so much fun. Jed took him off to see some rare monkeys and we had a picnic. It was really amazing actually.' She reached for his leg, rubbed it affectionately. 'I wish you'd been there.'

'Ha! So do I.' His voice was testy.

'Ror, you'd gone cycling. I had no idea how long you were going to be.'

'So you thought you'd just take off for the day?'

She sighed. 'I just mean, I wasn't sure how long you were going to be and I felt a sense of responsibility to make sure they all had a fun time. Jimmy's never even left the UK before. They spend every summer in Suffolk. I wanted it to be an exciting first day for him.'

Rory swung his legs off the bed, draining the rest of his beer. He got up and put the bottle on the makeshift console table, reaching down to a bucket on the floor which held another three bottles of beer, sitting in ice. He was moving stiffly and she suspected that bike ride was going to come back to bite him tomorrow.

'Look, I'm sorry,' she said, watching him. 'It really wasn't intentional to be gone so long. We'd have been back an hour ago but . . . on top of everything, we got a flat. Jed had to change the wheel.'

Rory rolled his eyes. 'Really? Tracking down endangered monkeys. Changing wheels. He didn't perform open-heart surgery on a leopard too, did he?'

Tara gave him a look but let the comment pass; he was irritable and a little bit hurt. 'Tell me about your afternoon. What did you do?'

'Not a huge amount. I hung around here in case you came back.'

'Oh, well that must have been nice surely? Getting some downtime. When did you get back?'

'About two.'

She winced. She and Jed and the others had only left around one-ish.

'Your brother and brother-in-law decided it would be the perfect day to climb the Cordillera.'

'Oh no, they didn't.' She winced again. The highest mountains in the range rose above 11,000 feet. 'I'm sorry. Was it awful?'

'Put it this way – getting back to you felt like a wholly justified reward. Only . . .' He spread his arms wide. 'You weren't here! And I had no idea where you were! Or when you were going to be back!'

'I'm sorry.'

'That's our first day here, wasted. Gone. And I've scarcely seen you.'

'I'm sorry.' She rubbed her temples automatically, feeling the vice tighten around her skull a little more.

'Could you please stop apologizing?'

'Sor—'

They stared at one another. They were arguing. They never argued.

'Since when do you even sleep like that anyway?' he sighed, one hand on his hip as he walked and swigged.

'I've always slept well here,' she shrugged. 'I'm not sure why.'

'I got bitten to buggery.' He scratched at an angry bite on his shoulder.

'Oh no. The mozzies always go for you, don't they?' she said sympathetically.

He glanced over, hearing her appeasing tone. He blew out through his cheeks, his body slumping. 'Well, I guess the day's not a complete write-off,' he said finally. 'We can still go for dinner, just the two of us. Get some time together at last.' He took in her expression. '. . . What?'

She winced again. 'I'm afraid I've got to go.'

'Go?' he frowned. 'Go where?'

'To Jed's village. It's about ninety minutes from here.'

'What – *now*?'

She nodded. 'He's waiting outside for me.'

Rory looked towards the door and back at her again. '*Why?*'

She put a finger to her lips, trying to get him to keep his voice down. 'Something came up in conversation earlier about his son. He's sick and has received no medical help whatsoever, no official diagnosis.'

'Well, I'm sorry to hear that, but why is it your—'

'From what he's said, it sounds like cholestatic hepatitis. Holly thinks so too. But I'm worried – from some of the other symptoms he listed, there's a chance it could be AML too. Maybe.'

Rory blinked. Acute myeloid leukaemia was a tough diagnosis even in a hospital setting. 'And so you're going now? *Right* now?'

'I don't think we can afford to put it off. He's six years old, Ror. And anyway, it's just for the night. I'll be back before you're awake tomorrow, I promise.'

'Tomorrow,' he echoed, looking dumbfounded.

'I'll make it up to you then.' She got up from the bed and kissed him lightly on the lips. 'I double promise. Pinky promise, whatever it is.'

He watched as she got up and unzipped her travel bag. She pulled out the small kit she took everywhere with her – stethoscope, thermometer, blood pressure, tranquillizers, some plasters and bandages – and put it in her rucksack, along with a t-shirt to sleep in and some hardcore insect repellent.

She pulled off her jean shorts and grabbed a towel. 'I'm just going for a quick shower,' she said, padding out in her still-damp bikini.

Rory followed her around to the shaky clapboarded stall around the side of the hut, watching over the top as she stripped off and let the water run over her skin. She could see he wanted to get in there with her, that it was crossing his mind to be impulsive, romantic—

'Jed's waiting for me,' she said, lathering her hair quickly and looking back at him through one closed eye. Even a quickie couldn't be quick enough. 'I told him I'd be ten minutes. But I'll make it up to you in the morning – I promise.'

The Jeep rumbled over the rutted tracks, Tara having to hold on to the roll bar overhead as they travelled through the giant trees. The raucous cacophony of dusk had settled but sleep had not yet come to the denizens of the rainforest and she felt eyes upon them from high perches and low, hidden dens.

The air was still hot, impregnated with moisture and swollen with the scent of ylang ylang trees; she remembered Jed telling her an obscure fact once that it was the main scent used in Chanel No. 5 and it had made her laugh to think of a Parisian couture house smelling of the Costa Rican rainforest. The scent felt like a physical thing to cut through, as real as the leaves they would have to push back and the tree roots they would have to clamber over when they parked up. Jed had told her there was then a twenty-minute walk from the 'road' to the village and she wondered how he did this in the dark, every morning and evening. In spite of her cold shower, the sweat was rolling off her again.

He stopped the car in a small clearing and they walked in

single file again, Tara planting her feet in the spaces where he had put his. They didn't talk much. They were both tired and she needed her concentration, her senses on high alert. Jed's body language was relaxed, yet attuned, his head moving fractionally in the direction of every twig snap, every brush of leaves, but there was no tension in the swing of his arms. He knew exactly where to go, even though markers seemed non-existent to her.

The lone song of a dusky nightjar pirouetted in the air, soaring above the canopies and heading for the stars. The sky was almost blocked from view but when it did peep through, it seemed salted, more bright than dark as galaxies twisted through endless space. Occasional birds, silhouetted in dramatic shapes, pitched past in silence.

'There.'

She looked up. Jed had stopped walking and was pointing to two carved terracotta statues, positioned either side of the path like a gateway. Beyond them lay a cluster of buildings, not so much houses as huts – they were larger than she had expected, some conically shaped, with pitched, rush-covered roofs that skimmed the ground; others were rectangular and built on stilts, with large hatches that pulled down to serve as windows for light and airflow.

She could see a rusty child-sized bike abandoned below one house; beside it, a plastic play pit on legs that had once been red but had faded to a gentle pink. But that was as far as Westernization went – a snakeskin was drying on a wooden rack outside one hut, some carved wooden staffs were propped against a wall. She could smell wood smoke and hear the low murmur of voices. Someone was singing.

It was almost ten now and she still hadn't eaten since

they'd had the mangoes at the rock pools. Her tummy grumbled as if in realization of the fact.

'Should I wait here? Let you go in first?'

But Jed shook his head. 'No. You are very welcome.'

She followed him in, hearing first the shouts of joy of his children as they heard him approach, then seeing their faces as they leaped into his arms. Tara felt a rush of emotion as a young girl with eyes as bright as a squirrel's flung her arms around his neck – then saw her. She stared at Tara with an unabashed curiosity. Tara smiled back, almost shy herself.

She saw his wife, Sarita, stand up from a low stool; she was carrying a baby in a papoose and had been feeding another child, a toddler, from a couple of banana leaves fashioned as a bowl.

Jed said something to her in Spanish and she nodded, looking over at Tara with a curious, clear-eyed gaze, like her daughter's. She came over to where they were standing. Jed was still talking to her.

Sarita reached a hand and clasped Tara's in her own. She said something in a low voice and gently tugged her arm.

'Sarita says it is an honour to meet you. Please sit down, she would like to make you comfortable.'

'Thank you,' Tara replied, nodding exaggeratedly to convey her own pleasure. 'But please tell her not to go to any trouble. I've come to see Paco, remember? *I've* come to help *you*, for once.'

Jed shrugged and in the gesture she understood it was important to honour the wishes of his wife. On their drive over here, Jed had explained the Bribri tribe's culture – how men were allowed to take more than one wife, though he never would, that marriage was granted through common understanding, that their society was matrilineal – so Tara allowed herself to be taken to the wooden stool where Sarita had been sitting only moments before. Knowing it would be rude to refuse, she obediently sat.

The space was imposing, surprisingly impressive. The ceiling was high, supported by massive timber poles and struts. It was like being in a wooden Big Top. The roof was covered with splayed hands of dried rushes; she could glimpse the sky through tiny gaps – not so good in the wet season – but right now, tonight, she was grateful for any extra breeze. Some rope hammocks swung off the ground, and bags filled with what seemed to be clothes were knotted and tied to the vertical support poles.

She watched as Sarita crossed the space, talking animatedly to her husband. The children – the little girl and the toddler boy – stood by their father's legs, staring at her. Where was Paco?

She twisted slightly and saw, in the far corner, a large mattress on the floor. But only one. There was a shape under a sheet and it shifted suddenly, as if sensing it was being observed. Tara flinched as she saw the traces of the boy lying there. He was tiny, little more than skin and bone, eyes appearing to bulge in a sunken face, his teeth oversized in his head. His hair had been razed short as he sweated, febrile.

Instinctively, forgetting her manners, she went over and crouched by the mattress. Dimly, she heard Jed's voice, talking again in Spanish – so not to her.

'*Hola*, Paco,' she smiled. '*Me llamo Tara. Soy tu amiga*,' she said in her basic Spanish.

She received a blank stare in return.

'*Soy medica. Como estais?*'

Slowly, as if asking his permission, she held up her hand to him and when he didn't protest, placed the back of it to his forehead. By touch alone she knew he was above thirty-nine degrees. She took his pulse; it was racing. There was some swelling in his hands at the finger joints that she could feel, and a bucket to the side of the mattress suggested he was routinely being sick.

'How long has he had symptoms for?' she asked Jed as he moved closer.

'Seven months.'

Seven months? She could see the fear in his eyes from across the room. Sarita was holding a small wooden bowl in her hands, but she had seemingly forgotten she was holding it, her gaze pinned to Tara.

She swallowed down her alarm. 'What were his initial symptoms?'

Jed thought back. 'Uh . . . his stomach hurt. His fingers as well. And he kept scratching his skin. The Awa says it is his liver.'

'Awa?' She remembered. The shaman. 'Oh, right.' She looked back at Paco again. He was regarding her as though from a great distance, his gaze focused but blank. 'May I examine him more fully?'

Jed translated for Sarita and she nodded, her hands going trepidatiously to her mouth.

Tara checked his glands.

'Paco, can you breathe in for me?' she asked him, and though he didn't understand her words, he innately caught her meaning, copying her exaggerated inhale. Gently, she slid her hands over the right side of his abdomen, palpating for the liver. It felt enlarged, the spleen too. She looked for yellowing to the whites of his eyes but the light was too dim to see clearly. What she could see were some dark stains blooming like old roses on the sheet by his head. She looked back at him with concern. She had various suspicions, but there was little more she could do without running diagnostic tests. She needed a full battery of blood screens, ideally a liver biopsy.

She smiled at him as reassuringly as she could, clasping his hands in hers. 'Well done. You are very brave.' Her Spanish was rusty and not particularly idiomatic but she hoped he could read her meaning in her eyes, her intention to *do no harm*.

She rose slowly, knowing she needed to convey her concern with calm.

Sarita rushed towards her, pressing the cup into her hands, as though the hospitality would be inducement to alter her findings, as though this was something to be negotiated.

'*Gracias*,' Tara said softly. And she took a long sip of the drink. It was some sort of juice, sweeter than she anticipated. 'Mmm. *Bueno, gracias*.'

Sarita smiled, loosening with the compliment.

'Jed, Sarita . . .' She looked at them both. 'Paco is very sick. It is my opinion that he should be taken to hospital so that they can run further tests.'

Jed translated her words quickly. Sarita looked away, pained herself.

'It is not possible. He is too weak to travel,' Jed said after a silence, speaking for his wife, knowing her wishes. 'He cries in pain every time he moves.'

Tara blinked, knowing there were no easy options. The trees were too dense for a helicopter to land, and if he couldn't move without anguish, she didn't see how he could cope with being stretchered for thirty minutes, before then enduring the rough car journey along those roads.

'Jed, I understand the pain of moving might hurt him – but it wouldn't kill him.' She stared at him, willing him to understand what she wasn't saying: that just lying here might. 'He needs to be in hospital.' She hated seeing the anguish on her old friend's face. 'I'm sorry. I know what I'm asking is hard. But it is for his benef—'

The door behind Jed opened and a man came in. He was not big but he had presence; he was not wizened, but she knew he was wise. He looked like a coffee or plantain farmer, wearing plain trousers and a shirt, but she instinctively knew he was important.

Sarita immediately began speaking to him in a language Tara didn't understand – Bribri? – gesticulating with her arms towards Tara. She understood who the man was just from the way they deferred to him.

After several minutes of indecipherable back-and-forth conversation, Jed turned to face her.

'Tara, this is Don Carlo, the Awa. He has been treating Paco for us all these months.'

Tara nodded respectfully. 'It is a pleasure to meet you, Don Carlo,' she said in Spanish.

Don Carlo nodded slowly in return, regarding her intently, and she had a sense of being absorbed, like she was ink and he was blotting paper.

Jed began speaking again in Spanish and Tara noticed that wasn't the language the Awa used when he spoke to Sarita. Even Jed was an outsider here.

The Awa looked back at her again; there was no malice in his gaze as Jed continued to speak. Then he fell quiet.

There was a prolonged hush and Tara wondered whether

she should step into the void and just get the ball rolling. It was clear they came from opposing medical disciplines.

But the Awa spoke first, his voice deep and low and sonorous. Sarita repeated his words in Spanish to Jed, and Jed looked back at her. 'He says there are over fifteen hundred plants in the jungle he can use as medicine. That there are fifty in the gardens right here.'

'Great. Okay.'

'He trained as an Awa from his uncle. From the Guetares tribe.'

'Oh, really?' She was interested, of course. But how was this relevant?

'Their ancestors have been living in the Alto Uren mountains for three thousand years. Their wisdom and knowledge has been passed down through their families. It has never been written down. What the Awa knows, cannot be found in a book.'

'I'm sure. And it is something I would love to know more about. I'm personally very interested in natural medicines and the botanical world and where that could intersect with Western medicine.' She realized she was using her 'work' voice, the one she used for communicating terrible news to strangers, when she had to be a doctor and not a flesh-and-blood human too. 'But Jed, your son needs urgent help that can get guaranteed results. He needs a thorough diagnostic workup and probably some full immunosuppressive therapy. I can't say for sure without running complete tests but from his history and presenting symptoms, he could very well be suffering with—'

'Hepatitis.'

The word had come straight from the Awa. He spoke English?

'Hepatitis, yes, it's a possibility,' she agreed, turning to him. 'But it would need further tests to establish for sure.'

'Hepatitis,' the Awa repeated. And he walked over to the small stool and picked up the bowl Sarita had been working at when they'd arrived. He lapsed into Bribri again.

Tara waited for the information to be relayed – Sarita, to Jed, to her. 'These leaves, when ground up, make a juice,' Jed said. 'For seven months so far, to purge the blood. No food.'

Tara's eyes widened in alarm. Seven months with no food? Even manners couldn't hold back her shock. He would die of starvation and malnutrition long before the disease got him. Little wonder he was skin and bone!

'He needs nourishment, Jed, or he will die.' Her voice was more urgent now, more insistent.

'He says all the medicine we need is right here. The earth will heal us, we just need to know how.'

She watched as the Awa reached into a cloth sack she hadn't noticed he had brought in with him. He pulled out a variety of leaves, still green, still fresh. He held them up as he began speaking again.

'These ones – coffee leaves . . . are for headaches,' Jed said, translating dutifully.

He put the coffee leaves back in the bag.

'Oh God,' she thought, watching in dismay as he brought out some others. Another perceived display of strength? He could show her the leaves of every plant in this jungle, but it wasn't going to make that little boy better.

'These . . . this is the Clorox.' The Awa rubbed it between his hands and presented it to her to sniff. 'We use this for washing our clothes,' Jed translated.

'This leaf . . . with the red spots . . .' Tara waited as it was held up to show her. 'Is for the woman's menstruation cramps.

You cook it up and drink it as a tea. See? It even smells like blood.' Tara didn't want to smell these leaves, but being polite, being British – an old joke, she vaguely recalled – she did. It did, curiously, have that ferrous tang to it.

'And these ones . . .' The Awa held up some glossy green leaves, shaped with three dips, and said something directly to Jed. 'He does not know the word in Spanish. In Bribri is called *curyho diwhipa*. For curing the diabetes.'

'Diabetes? Really?'

'Bu he calls it men's underwear.'

Tara frowned, as the Awa laughed suddenly, the sound cackling and ancient. 'Men's . . . ?'

'Yes. It looks like men's underwear. He says.'

Tara looked at it more closely. She supposed the shape might, possibly, bear a relation to Y-fronts although she couldn't be a hundred per cent sure, as she didn't know any men who wore them. She gave a small, polite smile. This was a waste of precious time. None of it changed the fact that a young boy was slowly dying in the corner of this hut in the jungle.

'Don Carlos—' she began, just as the Awa stepped towards her and reached forwards, putting his hands on her ringing head – one hand over her forehead, the other behind, at the base of her skull. He closed his eyes.

Tara, though startled, fell still at the firm hold. It was so profoundly surprising and unexpected and . . . comforting. She listened to the hush grow like a suspense.

She waited . . . and began to feel a curious rush, as though something was shifting in her, unblocking dammed-up waters. Anger breaking past her manners at last, perhaps? It was a giddying sensation, but she didn't stir. For half a minute, maybe more, no one moved at all. Then the Awa stepped back, his hands lifting off her and leaving heat imprints on her skin. The rushing sensation immediately stilled. He said something to Sarita, who passed it to her husband.

'. . . He says the heart vibration is weak.'

'Hearts don't vibrate, Jed,' she said in a quiet voice that refuted the assertion.

The Awa spoke again. This time, when Jed listened, then looked at her, he seemed both shocked and awkward.

'He says you have lost a child. That is why you are here.'

The statement was startling, images of little Lucy Miller flashing through her mind, of blood in water—

She swallowed. 'I am here to stop you losing *your* child.'

The man spoke again and Tara waited as the message was conveyed down the line to her. 'He says you carry it in your heart,' Jed murmured.

Memories clawed at her like spitting cats, the white noise of a fast-gathering headache turned up to maximum volume.

'Of course I do. Who wouldn't? The death of any child is devastating.' But her voice was choked and she stepped back, out of their orbits, turning away. She didn't want to be 'read' again. She didn't believe in . . . this. 'Which is why it's so important we get Paco somewhere he can be treated.'

The Awa spoke again, but Tara felt her patience beginning to fray. This was ridiculous. Paco needed to get to a hospital, as quickly as humanly possible.

'He says what Paco needs is the black star leaf.'

Tara blinked. 'What?'

'It is the plant which can truly cure him. But it cannot be found here, only in one spot of the sacred Alto Uren mountains. It is a two-day journey from here and the leaves must be picked by a woman at dusk.'

Oh, for heaven's sake! A woman at—? Tara stared at him,

struggling to contain her frustration. 'Jed, your son could be in a hospital in San José in a few *hours*. If you could just steel yourself to get him to somewhere a helicopter could land, we could get him to full medical help tonight. Won't you let me do that for you? Please.'

Jed stared back at her, hearing the glint of steel in her words. He could recognize the logic of what she was saying, she could see it, but he was conflicted, a husband and father torn. After several moments of protracted silence, he turned to talk to Sarita. Tara watched as she began shaking her head, stepping back and away, her eyes down, refusing to make contact with Tara again. Tara heard the shrillness in her voice, saw the way the Awa frowned at Jed's words.

Tara felt her stomach drop as she listened to them argue; she understood it was a lost cause. Jed couldn't convince his wife and she got to have the casting vote. Her culture didn't recognize the help Western medicine could give to her son; she didn't see it could save his life.

Jed looked back at her, an expression that she couldn't quite read on his face. 'Tara,' he said slowly, picking his words carefully. 'We thank you for coming here tonight and offering to help. It is a great honour to us that you have shown so much friendship and compassion to our family. You, whose family has done so much to help protect our country. Sarita wishes you to know she sends you many blessings.'

He didn't even sound like her old friend, but a stranger, a humble employee demurring politely to the boss. Tara gave a weak smile. 'I see. Well . . .' She looked at Sarita and nodded in acknowledgement, but she didn't want blessings or thanks or honours. She wanted that boy to live.

'Come, you must be hungry. We will eat.'

'Actually—' She stopped him, defeat crashing over her like a wave and taking her energy with it. 'I'm so tired still. The flight last night and the jet lag . . . If I can't help here, would it be terribly rude if I went to bed?'

'Of course not, please . . .' He turned and spoke rapidly to Sarita again. She nodded and began moving quickly, gathering things from hidden corners. She returned a few moments later with some sheets.

Jed took them and went to lead Tara outside.

'*Gracias. Buenas noches*,' Tara said, stopping at the door, her gaze flitting one last time to the sight of the thin boy labouring on the mattress. It was almost more than she could bear.

'*Buenas noches*,' Sarita said with the Awa, both of them watching her go.

She followed Jed into the night. It was black as pitch but he walked, sure-footed and clear-sighted, to a small hut just a few metres away.

'This is empty,' he said, handing her the sheets. 'You will be perfectly safe here.'

'Of course. Thank you.'

'Just remember to check for ants. They give a nasty bite out here.'

'Sure. Jed, I—'

But he stopped her with a firm smile. His wife's word was final.

'Good night, Tara.'

Chapter Sixteen

She felt a tickle, light as a hair, over the back of her hand. A breeze had found her and fluttered over her skin. She gave a soft moan, feeling herself slowly rise up from the depths of sleep. She felt heavy, heavier than she had ever been, like an anchor listing on the seabed. Vaguely, behind closed eyelids, she detected skeins of light. The tickle came again, crossing to her wrist, getting closer to her f—

She jumped up with a gasp, her eyes focusing just in time to see a beetle the size of a plum skittering across the floor. It was a dazzling electric blue, actually beautiful. Just not to inhale.

'Jesus!' she hissed, sitting back on her heels on the mattress and trying to bring her heart rate back down. She sat there, inert, her head hanging, for several moments. She had a vague sense of despair in her bones but she couldn't put a shape to it, couldn't quite cast off the confusion of sleep until she looked at the rudimentary bed she had been lying on and remembered where she was – and why.

Oh God. She rubbed her hands down her face. That boy, that poor child. How long had she slept for? How many hours had he been lying in suffering, while she'd slept soundly here? She remembered her failure to do anything about it. Her losses were coming thick and fast at the moment.

With a sigh, she looked around her more keenly. The room, no bigger than a few square metres, was softly lit, daybreak tumbling through numerous wooden splits so that the room felt covered in golden splinters. There was a small hatch in one wall and she got up to open it.

She peered out – and instinctively smiled. The greenery was dense and lush, massive banana tree leaves splaying like parasols; a line of washing strung up between two trunks and hung with dull-coloured sheets. She saw a couple of small pigs truffling along the ground. Smoke was twisting from the top of one of the huts. It was an extraordinary scene, so completely tropical and different in every way to the rooftops-and-terraces vista from her Pimlico flat. Back home, nature was something to clip, tame and suppress into submission with perfectly clipped box balls, artful sprays of lavender and erect tulips. Here, everything ran riot, sprang up, toppled over, spread out, fought like toddlers, for air, rain, light . . .

She heard chickens pecking somewhere just out of sight from here and thought how much it sounded like waking up in an aviary, to the sound of wing flaps and trills and squawks.

Steadily, she felt nature acting as a balm to her frazzled nerves, the bright light of day dousing the emotional passions of last night. This was not her tragedy; it wasn't, and she had to maintain her boundaries. She could try to help her friend, yes, but if he would not be helped . . . What was it Rory had said? *You can't save everyone.*

She pressed her fingers to her temples, a long-worn, completely unscientific habit for gauging the strength of her headache. Today's was low-to-medium.

What time was it, anyway? There was no way of telling. Her phone was out of battery, with no way of charging it out here – she resolved to go into town later and buy a solar battery pack if she could – but from the light and the angle of the sun, she guessed it was early morning still. Five, maybe six o'clock? Had it not been for her run-in with the beetle, she might have slept for hours yet. She yawned, thinking of her promise to be back before Rory woke. At least that was something she could do – under-promise and over-deliver.

She picked up the sheets and pillow Jed had given her last night and carefully folded them into a neat pile. Her sleeping t-shirt had remained in her bag; it was far too hot for night-clothes and she'd slept in her bra and knickers – much to the mosquitoes' delight, she realized, noticing some bites and scratching them before she could catch herself.

She stepped back into her denim cutoffs and soft khaki waffle shirt, a new raspberry-pink bikini doubling as under-wear. Her hand brushed against the smooth mini doctor's kit in her bag and she felt another kick to the stomach at the thought of Paco, languishing. Suffering . . .

She straightened up and headed outside. To her surprise, there was a tiny package just outside the door. She might have trodden on it if she hadn't happened to be looking down. She picked it up carefully – it was something soft, wrapped in leaves and secured with a young vine. Unsure what to do with it, she kept it in her palm and walked over to Jed's hut, setting her bag down against a banana tree. She could hear voices coming from within, now that she was closer. It sounded like they were talking in hushed tones and she wondered whether that was for her benefit – as the 'honoured' guest – or Paco's.

Should she knock? Wait out here? She turned a circle on the spot, wondering what to do – and almost jumped six feet into the air. A man outside a neighbouring hut was watching her. He was sitting astride a large dug-out wooden trough and grinding some grains beneath a giant whittled pestle.

'*Hola*,' she stammered, recovering herself as he continued to grind, watching her impassively.

The man nodded and she gave a nervous laugh as a silence stretched. Her Spanish didn't extend to anywhere near good enough to shooting the breeze with a tribesman in the Costa Rican jungle.

'Oh, Tara.'

She turned, to see Jed standing behind her. He was holding a small basket.

'You've met Juan, I see.'

'Juan. Yes. We were just saying hello.' She nodded awkwardly in the tribesman's direction again.

'And you received the ointment from Don Carlos?' He looked down at the parcel in her hands.

'Oh. Yes. I wasn't sure—'

'It's for the mosquitoes. Best to put it on before you get dressed.'

'Oh, right. Thanks.' She gave a small laugh, as if to say, 'Bit late now.' Besides, she had some commercial-grade Deet that could have nuked the dinosaurs. She didn't want to cause offence, however, and she opened her bag and carefully set it on the top of her clothes.

'Come. I'm just going to feed the chickens,' Jed said, beginning to walk away. 'How was your night? Did you sleep well?'

'So well. How about you?'

'Fine, thank you.' But she had heard the hesitation before the word. How was it possible for them all to share a bed, much less with such a sick child?

'You look tired.'

'Me?' He shook his head. 'No.' They had stopped at a small pen constructed a short distance from the huts and watched as several skinny black chickens scratched at the ground. Jed reached into the tub and began scattering some feed, sending the birds into a frenzy. 'We can leave soon if you are ready. We must not leave your guests unattended.'

She watched the chickens peck and flap, then looked back up at him. 'Sure, yes. Whenever you're ready.'

He turned back towards the huts without looking at her and she realized he had barely made eye contact with her. 'But Jed, before we go back—'

He stopped walking, his gaze on the ground. 'Don't, Tara. I know what you want to say and it will make no difference. She is my wife.'

Tara ran around and in front of him, determined to make him look at her. 'And he is your son. This is about what is best for him, surely? He's *suffering*. At the very, very least, we could get him somewhere they can make him comfortable.' Her voice was rising, pleading, her concern an anxious wheedle.

Jed stared back at her, implacable, unreachable. 'Sarita trusts the Awa, and I trust her.'

He walked away, leaving Tara staring at his broad back. She wanted to scream, cry, block his path again. But it was hopeless. She had no rights here. That child was going to suffer and, in all likelihood, die a slow, drawn-out death and she could do nothing about it.

She followed him back, stepping disconsolately into the hut a few moments after him and taking in the scene from the door. The children were sitting on the ground eating from banana-leaf bowls. They ate with their hands, chattering happily.

'Please.' She looked across and saw Sarita beckoning for her to come in. Tara crossed the room and sat obediently on the stool Sarita pointed to for her. A 'bowl' of fruit was placed in her hands and Tara could see the anxiousness in her hostess's eyes that she accept their hospitality, having ducked out last night. She knew her behaviour would have been considered rude. What did jet lag mean to these people out here?

'Mmm, wonderful,' she smiled as best she could – but her gaze kept returning to the inert form on the mattress in the corner. To just *leave* him there . . .

'*Para usted.*' She looked up to see Sarita holding out a carved coconut cup. Inside was a drink she again could not recognize, but which manners compelled her to accept. She watched curiously as Sarita placed two banana leaves curled towards one another by her feet.

'To balance the cup,' Jed explained, nodding to the coconut in her hands.

'Ah.' She drank – it was stronger and more bitter than the one she had received yesterday but she swallowed it anyway, setting it down on the 'brackets' Sarita had set. The system worked.

At least something did.

Twenty minutes later, she and Jed were just reaching the car, when he asked her how she was feeling.

'Fine,' she replied, somewhat confused by the enquiry; they'd exchanged pleasantries first thing this morning and he knew her well enough to know that a short hike through the jungle wouldn't faze her. 'Why d'you ask?'

'The Awa brought the coffee leaf remedy over for you this morning,' he shrugged. 'He said it would help, that's all.'

'Help with what?' But even as she asked, she realized something was . . . missing. She blinked in concentration, then blinked again. She watched him throw his bag in the back of the car, a small smile playing on his lips.

For the first time in five days, she realized, she didn't have a headache.

'I'm back,' she whispered, shutting the hut door quietly behind her and tiptoeing across to the bed.

Two things immediately struck her before she got to Rory's sleeping form. That he was snoring incredibly loudly; and that the room stank of booze. He was still wearing the shorts he had been wearing when she got back here last night, but now a bottle of tequila was on the crate console.

'Ror?' She put a hand to his shoulder and when he didn't stir at all, lay down beside him, stroking his arm gently. Waiting.

Several minutes went by, but his unconscious form gave no sign of registering her presence. She might as well have been stroking the wall.

She checked the time. It wasn't yet eight. She felt she'd been up for hours already. Part of her wanted to close her eyes and go back to sleep, but the smell of alcohol on his breath was cloying.

With a sigh, she got back up and went outside. All the other hut doors were still closed, so she walked down the beach, enjoying the cool crush of the sand beneath her feet. There was a good surf today, the waves breaking several metres out, some ominously dark clouds on the horizon. She hadn't yet swum in the ocean, she realized. She stepped out of her shorts and waded out, taking care not to go too far. She had grown up with Jed warning her about the unpredictable currents here and, sure enough, as she trod water and looked back to shore, she could see him standing by the bar, watching her closely. He would run straight into a rip tide if he had to. He might get to reject *her* offers of help but at the end of the day, she was a Tremain, the big boss's daughter; nothing would happen to her on his watch.

They hadn't said a huge amount on the journey back. Once he had definitively rejected her help, it had seemed to stultify all other topics of conversation. She could feel his resistance to even her silent entreaties like a wall between them and she wondered what warnings Sarita had waved him off with as she had stood by the door to the hut. She could guess.

Tara walked back up the beach, picking up her shorts as she passed, and lay back in the striped hammock; she squeezed the water from her long hair and let one leg dangle over the side, propelling her, rocking slightly. She felt agitated still, but there was no headache. Inexplicably, it had gone.

'Hey, you're back already! How was it?'

She twisted to see Holly, hair wild and clutching a bottle of water, come over and slump in the neighbouring hammock.

'Awful,' Tara sighed. 'He's in bad shape.'

'Bad how?' Holly frowned.

'Pyrexia cachexia, palpable lymph nodes, hepatosplenomegaly.'

'Jaundice?'

'Not that I could see.'

'Bugger. Are you still thinking hepatitis?'

'I am, I think. There were some old scratch marks on his arms and stomach too and itchy skin is a key indicator.'

Holly's frown deepened. 'But?'

'But there were some old blood stains on the sheets by his head which worried me.'

'Nosebleeds?'

'Yes. And some bruises too.'

'Bruises,' Holly said in an ominous tone, nodding slowly, putting the pieces together. 'The bruises may not be relevant, of course. Could be a red herring.'

'Could be, yes. But if they are relevant . . . It could be acute myeloid leukaemia.' She gave a hopeless shrug. 'There's no way of knowing anything without a full workup. He'd need a liver biopsy, blood screen, ultrasound.'

Holly stared at her for several long dismayed moments – she loved her job and she hated it too – before she took a glug of her water. 'So what's the plan? Get him over to San José?'

'Nope. No plan.'

Holly coughed, spluttering on the water. 'What do you mean, "no plan"?'

'Just that. There's no plan. The parents say he's too sick to move, they won't listen to any advice to the contrary.'

'. . . So they're just going to leave him there, suffering untreated instead?'

'Oh no, he's being treated. By the Awa.' Tara couldn't keep the sarcasm from her voice.

'Who?'

'The shaman, remember? He's like the . . . doctor, village elder, wise man, all rolled into one.'

'Oh please, don't tell me . . . ?'

'Yep. *His* action plan is for the patient to exist purely on some . . . leaf sap. No medicine, not even any food. At all, for seven months. Basically starving it out of him.'

'What?' Holly was sitting up now, her body locked into a crunch position. 'Don't be so fucking ridiculous.'

'Hols, believe me, I hear you. I feel exactly the same. That child is going to die and . . .' Tara sighed, her voice breaking on the emotion. 'I feel so . . .' Her words ran out of shape, thinning into silence as she rubbed her face in her hands again. The powerlessness was what enraged her most of all. It was so unnecessary. Why couldn't Jed see she could help him?

Neither of them said anything for several minutes. They both knew how this went.

'Right, well,' Holly said finally, her voice thin with bitter defeat. 'Then that's that. Like it or not, there's nothing more to be done. You gave them your best medical opinion.'

'For all the good it did,' Tara snapped. 'It's not Jed who's resisting it. I think . . . I really think I could talk him round; it's his wife. She's Indigenous, she doesn't trust Western medicine. I mean, why would she? She doesn't have any experience of it. She thinks her son will suffer for no reason if we move him to a hospital. She believes everything the Awa says.'

Holly was quiet for a long moment. 'Look, we've both had situations like this before. Remember that Jehovah's Witness family I had in? The girl was trampled by a horse and they wouldn't accept the blood transfusion?'

Tara nodded sadly, not wanting to remember it.

'The number of times I have wanted to scream, watching as people's bloody *faith* makes them walk out of an A&E department and you know, you just know, they're going to drop dead in the street.' She gave a hopeless shrug. 'But at the end of the day, they have autonomy over their bodies. And even if we disagree, even if we know they're wrong . . . that is their right.'

'But it's so hard, Hols,' Tara said, talking through gritted teeth as she stared back at her friend with shining eyes.

Holly nodded. 'I know it is. It fucking sucks.'

'—would like some fresh coconut water?'

They looked across the beach to find Jed walking across the sand with two topped coconuts, straws sticking out at jaunty angles. It was a jarringly cheery image at such a downcast moment and all the more perverse given the tragedy was his.

'Thanks, Jedders,' Holly said, her voice determinedly even as she took one. Tara noticed Jed kept his gaze down as she took hers.

'Let me know when you're ready for a proper breakfast, okay?' he asked.

'Thanks, Jed,' Tara said flatly.

They both watched him walk back over the sand, towards the beach bar.

'See how he didn't look at me?' Tara murmured, sipping her drink. It was exquisite.

'Yeah. Well, that's a sign he knows, doesn't he? He knows it's the wrong thing.'

Tara sighed, looking out to sea, watching the waves roll in in a hurry. There was a definite storm brewing on the horizon, the sky dark and moody. '. . . So what happened here last night, anyway? Rory's out cold.'

Holly gave a groan. 'They had a session. Fire on the beach, music, dancing, the works.'

'Dancing?'

'If you could call it that. Stumbling, mainly. Jimmy was most unimpressed. Dev managed to stand on a bit of broken glass.'

'Ow.' Tara winced.

'Yeah.' Holly rolled her eyes. 'It was fun cleaning that out, I can tell you. Sand everywhere.' She took a sip of her coconut water. 'Hey, you don't have any antibiotic cream, do you? I'm already all out.'

'Yes. It's in my kit, in the bag.'

'Great. I'd better slather it on when he wakes up. He probably won't even remember – until he tries walking on it.'

'Was he that drunk?'

'They all were.' Holly glanced at her. 'Rory seemed right up for getting caned.'

'Mmm, doesn't surprise me. He's annoyed with me for being gone when he got back yesterday, and then going straight out again with Jed.'

'Poor baby. Is he feeling neglected?' Holly asked, pushing out her lower lip.

'Well, I am a terrible girlfriend, let's face it. I forgot our anniversary, worked through his birthday. Now I've abandoned him on holiday.'

Holly kicked her lovingly. 'He's hit the jackpot with you and he knows it. He's your perfect match.'

'Yeah, yeah, I know – me with a willy,' Tara said, rolling her eyes. 'But I don't blame him. You can see why he'd be hacked off. He's come all this way and we've scarcely seen each other. We may as well be in London, working.' She dropped her head back against the hammock, closing her eyes against the sun. And something else . . . 'Talking of which, I haven't had a chance to tell you yet – I had a call from Helen McPherson.'

Holly looked up. 'What?'

'They're doing an internal investigation, after, y'know . . . the other day.'

'The little girl?' Holly's head tipped to the side sympathetically.

Tara felt her throat tighten. 'Mmm.' She swallowed. 'Rory says it's standard procedure.'

'Well, he's right. But it's still a shitty thing to go through. Given her parents put her in theatre in the first place, there'll be a police investigation, surely?'

Tara nodded as the memories bubbled up, unbidden. 'It's been bad enough just trying to deal with losing her. It was such a shock. It all happened so fast, and . . .' She automatically pinched the bridge of her nose before remembering there was no headache to assuage. Her hand fell away. 'I mean, what were the chances of a blade falling loose? Have you ever even heard of such a thing?' She spread her hands wide in disbelief.

'Never.' Holly reached for her hand and clasped it in her own. 'Which is why you can't blame yourself for not thinking to check for it. It was a freak one-off.'

Tara stared back at her, wanting to believe her friend's words, that this was logic talking and not kindness. 'It's all just left me feeling . . . shaken, you know? Like everything's about to come crashing down. I mean, if they took my licence, I don't know what I'd do.' Her voice slid up an octave.

'That's not going to happen.'

'You don't know that.'

'Oh yes I do,' Holly replied calmly. 'You're the best they've got.'

'Rory says I'm their show pony.'

Holly's mouth tightened. 'You're the best they've got,' she repeated.

'He's always telling me I can't save everyone.'

'*That*, he and I can agree on.'

'But Hols, right now, I can't seem to save *anyone*.' She thought again of Paco, still lying on the mattress in the hut, the sound of the jungle alive and pulsating around him. 'They won't even let me help.'

'Look, you've tried your best, but you're fighting their emotion with logic and they're not going to hear you.'

'But he's going to die, Hols.'

'Probably, yes,' Holly agreed, looking angry again, her mouth flattening into a line. 'But if there's nothing they will *let* you do, then there's nothing you *can* do.'

The two women stared at one another, frustration in both their faces.

'We could kidnap him,' Tara suggested after a silence.

'Shit, I can't even tell if you're joking.' Holly gave an uncertain laugh. 'You probably actually know people for that kind of thing.'

Tara wasn't sure if she was joking either. The words had just escaped her. 'We could, though,' she pressed.

'I don't think it would end well. What if they shot you with a poison dart or something?'

'Oh that is just offensive!' Tara protested. 'This isn't . . . *Pocahontas!*'

'You're the one talking about kidnapping a sick kid.'

They smiled at one another, appreciating each other's dark humour. It had seen them through some hard times.

'Jed said the leaf sap the Awa's using is just a . . . backup remedy,' Tara murmured.

'To what? Tea-leaf reading?'

'Oh no, better! There's *another* leaf, apparently. A magical, mystical, unicorn leaf that only grows on a sacred mountainside two days' travel from here.'

Holly rolled her eyes. 'That's helpful. So when the kid dies, he can say it was because he didn't have the right kind of leaves?'

'Mmm,' Tara murmured, staring out at the horizon. She ran a hand across her forehead again. 'It's funny, though. He's given me some tincture that's really worked on my headache.'

'Huh?' Holly lifted a sceptical eyebrow. *'Really?'* She knew better than anyone how Tara suffered with them.

'Seriously. This morning, before we left, I had to drink something gross – I don't even know what it was – but it's really done the trick.'

'Why would you drink something gross when you didn't know what it was? Don't you know anything?' Holly scolded. 'Did you accept sweets from strangers too when you were a little kid? He could have been poisoning you.'

'I was being polite.'

Holly groaned. 'You and your sodding manners.'

Tara smiled, but gave a small shiver as an old joke resurfaced from the depths of her memory, tiptoeing across her mind and leaving little scorch marks. '. . . Anyway, it's just a coincidence.'

'Well, of course it is! Don't start going all voodoo on me now, girl.'

'Mmm,' Tara hummed. But it occurred to her now . . . she hadn't actually *told* the Awa about her headaches. Not a word. Nor about the child who had died, either. And yet somehow he had known both . . . And her headache, as much a part of her as her own shadow, was now gone. Gone after the drink . . .

'Just suppose for a moment . . .' Tara narrowed her eyes thoughtfully. 'Bear with me here – but just suppose there was something in it.'

Holly laughed. 'No.'

'I mean, I know it's highly unlikely. Of course.'

'Yes.'

'But us refusing to even admit to the possibility that this stuff might work . . . how is that any different to Sarita refusing to concede that our medicine might work?'

Holly shot her a stern look. 'Because we have science on our side. Provable, traceable fact.'

'Yes. But she doesn't know that. And for all we know, this shaman's got a complete history of all the people he's saved and how, too. Do you remember at Imperial? They told us Lamb's Ear used to be used as a battlefield wound dressing. And that it helps with sore throats and fevers too. That's not a million miles away from what he's suggesting.'

'Antibiotic properties are one thing, but you can't cure hepatitis with *leaves*,' Holly refuted.

Tara squinted, thinking more deeply as an idea came to her. 'But if we were to meet in the middle, agree to pursue each other's point of view . . .' Tara's voice trailed off as the thought began to acquire shape, heft.

'You've lost me.'

Tara's eyes widened. 'We could strike a deal. I get the mystical magical unicorn leaf from the sacred mountains and bring it back for the Awa to use, on the condition that when it fails – because of course it will – Sarita agrees to let us move Paco to San José for treatment.'

Holly stared at her. 'That is the dumbest thing I have ever heard in my life.'

'Do you have any better ideas?' Tara spread her hands wide.

'Don't be daft!'

'If we can't make her believe us, then we'll go with what *she* believes, on the understanding there's our plan as the backup for when it all goes wrong. It's a no-lose situation as far as I can see.'

'Not for her, maybe. But that poor boy spends another four days slowly dying whilst you trek through the mountains and back.'

'I'm sure when it comes down to it that there's a quicker way,' Tara said with a sniff. 'We could get a helicopter in.'

'Helicopters can't land around here, in case you hadn't noticed.' Holly waved her hand around idly. 'Trees. Lots and lots of trees.'

'We could—'

'What? Parachute out?' Holly laughed. 'Descend ropes, SAS-style? Please.'

'Fine. Well, even if it is two days of walking—'

'Each way.'

'Each way, yes. Then at least there would be some definitive action five days from now. But if we just do nothing, then nothing will ever be done and he'll still be on that mattress two years from now.'

Holly gave a derisive snort. 'He'll be dead long before then.'

'Exactly.' Tara stared intently at her friend.

They were quiet for a moment, before Holly shuffled back under her scrutiny. 'What? Why are you looking at me like that?'

'I want you to tell me it's a good idea.'

'No. It's the maddest bloody idea I've ever heard! And don't think you're roping me into it. I'm here on holiday with my family.'

'I wouldn't dream of dragging you into it.'

'Well, you can't bloody go on your own!' Holly argued, contradicting herself.

'I know. Jed can go with me.'

'Hang on a minute, why can't Jed just go on his own?' Holly frowned. 'It's his kid.'

'Because apparently the leaves have to be picked by a woman. At dusk.' She watched as Holly's eyebrows shrugged up in confoundment. 'I know, don't . . . I can't even . . .'

'So then why doesn't the mother go?'

'Because she has an eight-month-old baby and two other kids to look after. She can't just disappear into the hills for four days.'

Holly tutted, resting her elbows on her knees and blowing out through her cheeks. 'Rory will hit the bloody roof when he hears this.'

'He's a doctor. He'll understand.' Tara glanced back towards the red hut. 'Although he's so sparko in there, I wouldn't be surprised if he sleeps right through it.' She looked back at Holly, chewing intently on her lip. 'I think I should go and present the deal to Jed.' She scrambled up from the hammock, leaving Holly looking up at her, slack-jawed.

'What, now? Right now?'

'Well, if it's going to take four days, we need to get going as soon as possible. It's Dad's big day on Friday. I can hardly miss it.'

'But . . . we haven't even had breakfast yet.'

'Really? I'm going full Indiana Jones and you're thinking about your stomach?'

Holly laughed in disbelief. 'I just can't believe you're actually serious.'

'Unless you've got a better idea,' Tara shrugged, beginning to walk towards the beach bar.

Holly got to her feet and began running after her. 'Well, all I can say is you're going to need a hell of a packed lunch.'

Chapter Seventeen

The sky cracked in half, splitting like an egg, and the rain came down like glass bullets as they hiked through the trees. Tara spluttered as it streamed down her face, plastering her hair to her head in moments. There was nothing English about this rain. It wasn't a soft smudge of grey, a lingering drizzle. This was tropical – warm and heavy, persistent, everywhere.

'Here.'

Jed, just two steps ahead of her, reached down and pulled the knife from the holster – holster! – strapped to his knee. He bent down and with two clean hacks, detached a hand of banana leaves from low down the stalk. He held it above her head, providing an immediate umbrella. It wasn't foolproof – rivulets still caught her in the gaps, but it blocked most of the strikes. It even sounded like an umbrella, the raindrops heavy upon the leaves as they landed and bringing to mind – curiously – a forgotten moment of running down Kensington Gate a long time ago, when a copy of the *Evening Standard* had had to suffice. She could still remember the weight of a hand upon her waist as they'd run, their laughter . . .

'Thanks.'

They had been walking for a couple of hours now. It had taken her twenty minutes to convince Jed she was serious about the plan, another hour and twenty minutes to get back to the village and explain to his wife.

The Awa had been called.

Strangely, he hadn't seemed surprised when Jed had conveyed it to him, and he hadn't seemed perturbed either by the prospect of Paco being transported to San José if – or rather, to her mind, *when* – his treatment failed. Instead, he had begun to draw, on a piece of cloth, two things: an illustration of the black star plants they were looking for, and a map. Neither one of them looked distinctive or detailed enough to even navigate off her roof terrace, much less a two-day hike through the tropical rainforest. Nevertheless, it had seemed to resonate with Jed and he had listened intently as the Awa had spoken.

Their departure from the village after that had been swift. As Holly had predicted, there were no shortcuts to Alto Uren. This wasn't a money issue, but a tree cover one and the only way in was through, on foot. Everything about this trek, Tara had quickly realized, was going to have to be done the hard way – back in London, in anticipation of the luxury of a barefoot holiday, she hadn't packed walking boots, only the pair of Tod's trainers she had travelled in and that now seemed woefully inadequate, not to mention impractical; if the Italians could take on Costa Rican coffee, they certainly couldn't stand up to Costa Rican mud. It had been decided that rather than lose time going back into town to buy new ones, she and Jed would head for the rangers' base station several hours up into the mountains; Jed's father worked there and Jed knew there would be kit they could use.

The Awa had given her a long, narrow parcel wrapped in cloth and secured with vines, which was only to be opened when the black star leaves were being picked, and other than some wry advice not to pull on the vines and never to look up with her mouth open, they were set on their way.

She carefully walked in Jed's footsteps, carrying her banana leaf umbrella and backpack now stuffed with food. (Holly hadn't been joking about the packed lunch.) And as the footsteps spooled up into the thousands, and the jungle grew thicker and louder, she began to realize that the trek to Jed's village was nothing compared to the gradients ahead of them. The Talamanca mountains towered like purple shadows; sleepy rivers began to tumble and drop. Her breath came fast, her hurried mileage up and down the hospital corridors seemingly not counting for much out here in the wild.

The tension between them had eased with this proposal and Jed explained to her as they walked that their village was in fact but a 'modern satellite' in the foothills, the tribe's original village being another thousand metres higher up. Sarita had been born there and spent the first twenty-three years of her life living on the high plateaus, walking down weekly with the other women to barter goods and services with women of the other tribes. But it wasn't enough. Her brothers were lured by the inducements of modern life; they wanted to work in the towns, drive bikes, watch TVs, meet more people. In the old village, there were only twenty-four males and twenty-nine females – and over half of those were children. Moving to the foothills had been the tribe's own compromise solution, a way to preserve their culture, language and ways whilst being more accessible to the outside world.

'How did you meet her?' she panted, vaguely aware of the ground to their right beginning to pleat and drop away into a majestic gorge.

Jed gave an embarrassed laugh. 'I got lost. She rescued me.'

Tara laughed too. 'You're joking?'

'I wish I was. I was sent by my father to place some new wildlife cameras where some jaguar tracks had been sighted, took a wrong turn and within twenty steps was more lost than I have ever been.'

'And you're telling me this now? When *I'm* following *you*?'

Jed laughed again. 'Don't worry. This was all many years ago now, and the Awa's directions were very specific. I am confident I know the way. It is a place he has told me about many times. It will be an honour to visit it finally.'

They carried on planting one foot in front of the other, the rain still falling hard, the ground rapidly becoming soft underfoot. There was no real footpath to follow; just a vague animal track with broken branches and flattened leaves leading the way. Vines hung from trees in thick, twisted tangles, as thick as ropes; brightly coloured sticky flowers were blooming in the humidity, the chatter of hidden animals at their shoulders, but always out of sight.

'T-t, it is extraordinary to me that you are doing this,' he said after another few minutes, stopping suddenly and casually holding a hand out as a 'stop' to keep her back. She watched, horrified and fascinated, as a vivid yellow eyelash viper slid past between their feet, disappearing in the next instant into the undergrowth.

She swallowed. If he was calm, so was she.

She dared to lift her eyes and look back at him. '. . . Why? Your son is a beautiful young boy. He deserves to be given every opportunity to live his life.'

'No, I mean it is extraordinary you are doing this, even though you do not believe in it. You do not believe in the Awa's methods.'

Tara hesitated, not wanting to offend. 'Well, let's just say I don't fully understand them. The Awa cleared my headache when nothing – absolutely nothing – else has. I can't explain that, so I'm open to . . . other options.'

Jed glanced doubtfully at her and resumed walking. He had known her since she was nine. He knew when she was being *polite*. She sighed.

'Okay. Do I believe this plant we're looking for will help Paco?' she called, following after him. 'No, honestly I don't. I'm happy to be wrong; I hope I'm wrong! But for me, this is just a means to an end, a way to get *something* happening for your son – and that has to be better than nothing. As a doctor, it's my duty to pursue every path of possibility for my patients.' She squinted as something scampering through the tree overhead sent a shower of raindrops onto her, straight down her collar and running down her back. So much for her umbrella.

The background rush of running water became a sudden roar as they rounded an escarpment to face a dazzling waterfall. It was the sort of thing Tara had only ever seen on Instagram – water like horses' tails, rainbows catching as the sun darted in and out of rain clouds. A flock of macaws were flying around at the upper reaches, landing in the neighbouring trees. She wanted to stop and admire it, photograph it, swim in it. But Jed didn't stop. What before would have been the entire focus of a day of #gratitude was here just a footnote in their higher purpose, a pretty backdrop and nothing more. Within a few minutes it was behind them, the roar subdued to a gentle background rushing again.

Still it rained.

'How did Rory react when you told him you were doing this?' Jed asked over his shoulder, using his stick to beat back the plants that nodded over the path and making it easier for her to follow him. Well, easy-ish. He seemed to cover two strides to her one.

Tara grimaced, trudging behind him. 'He hasn't yet. I tried explaining it to him but I'm not sure he really took it in. He was like a bear with a sore head at me for waking him up. He's not used to drinking like that.'

'What were they celebrating last night?'

'Everything and nothing. Holiday vibes. I think they're just happy to be having time out. We all work pretty mad hours.'

'You work too hard,' he said simply, echoing the words he'd said to her yesterday morning too.

They kept walking, the path growing steeper, the mud becoming more slippery as the rain kept on coming down with no signs of stopping. Her feet were soaked, the tread on her trainers completely lost as the mud grew thicker with each step. Tara wished she had packed even just a cagoule – a cagoule! – instead of the expensive linen peasant blouses and silky dresses she had brought with her. Not that trekking on a mercy mission through the mountains had been on her radar back then – hindsight always came too damned late – and she was regretting the day she'd cut her old jeans down into shorts. She kept swiping at her thighs, not sure if it was insects or plants tickling them.

'So is he The One?' Jed asked, his voice more distant. Tara looked up and saw he was ten or eleven paces ahead now. She realized she was falling behind, tiring already in her inadequate footwear, feet sliding with each step, her socks sodden and her feet beginning to rub. 'Will you get married?'

'You already asked me that! Everyone always asks me that,' she called back. 'My mother's like a stuck record.'

'Sounds like a "no".' He pushed back a tangle of thick vines that hung from a tree like a curtain. They fell back in place behind him, snatching him from her sight.

'No, it's not a "no"; it's an "I don't know!" she shouted up to him. 'Because I don't!'

'They say when you know, you know!' he called back.

'*They* say bollocks!' she yelled. She heard Jed laugh at that – a distinctive belly-shaking sound – and it made her smile too, until a sudden commotion made her stop dead in her tracks. The jungle seemed to be shaking itself into activity, the constant twitchy, crackling torpor igniting into a frenzy of sounds, trees swaying, bushes shaking.

Jed?

She went to call his name, but a shout and the sound of muffled grunts made the word die in her throat as behind her, all around, a quick series of loud cracks made her gasp, jump and whirl round. What was that? Something running? Something approaching? She instinctively fell into a crouch, trying to make herself small as she strained to understand what was happening, her body held in a state of frozen tension, ready to run, but it was so hard to hear properly over the rain, to see through the grey haze and the mists that wound whimsically here and there. She felt horribly exposed. Jed had a knife but she had nothing, no way to protect herself. She looked around quickly for something, anything she could use, picking up a stick on the ground. It was just a stick, but it was green wood and bendy, with a sharp edge; an animal must have torn it off and dropped it. It wouldn't provide much meaningful help against seventy kilograms of muscle but it was something to threaten with, at least, a preliminary distraction.

Her heart pounding, her eyes wide, she remembered what Jed had taught her on their adventures out here when she was little: STOP. True, they'd never come this deep into the jungle, but he'd always told her to *Stop. Think. Observe. Plan.* Letting her umbrella fall from her hands – getting wet was the least of her worries right now – she fell still, became quiet. Began to *listen*. What was after them?

A hush contracted through the jungle, like the breath before a scream. Every living thing seemed to be holding its breath and the close, unseen presences that brushed right by her had stalled like stone statues.

The momentary quiet was broken by a bird flying into the trees in a scurry of hurried wing-flaps, followed moments later by a harpy eagle gliding in pristine silence overhead, looking for a meal.

Had it been that? She turned a full 360, looking behind her and feeling jumpy, eyes scanning the dense ground cover – there was so much to see, nothing could be seen. Everything was green, thick, tremoring as the rain continued to fall, the sky lowered so that it skimmed the treetops. The quietude held and, as suddenly as it had come, whatever it was, it appeared to have gone again.

She allowed herself to breathe. She could feel the sense of danger ebb away – or perhaps she had just over-reacted in the first place? A townie's nerves getting the better of her, every unexpected sound making her jumpy. She rose to standing again, feeling foolish, and grateful Jed hadn't seen.

But where was he? She had to get back to him.

She looked back to check nothing was approaching from behind. Their footprints of five metres ago, still suckered in the mud, were filling quickly with water, ready to overflow, lose shape, disappear. She attuned her focus further, beginning to pick out details, seeing now a bright green, red-eyed tree frog clinging to a leaf, the drooping head of an orange orchid, a sloth hanging from a branch ten metres away, chewing slowly on a shoot . . . It was surprisingly large, unbothered by her scrutiny. Had it been that she had heard, snapping off its lunch? Or something bigger? Something fast with sharp teeth? She remembered what Jed had said to Zac the night they'd arrived here, how the jaguars stayed inland. Well, this was inland. Deep, deep inland.

It came again, from the other side of the vines, another series of cracks that pierced the drumbeat of the rain, that sense of the jungle moving and rushing. Her pulse accelerated once more and her gaze felt primed to its sharpest setting as she scanned the undergrowth with forensic scrutiny, her heart banging hard against her ribs like it wanted to be let out. She wasn't imagining this. It wasn't an over-reaction. There was something out there.

The stick held like a wand, waving around warningly, she took a few steps forward, towards the knotted curtain. 'Jed?' she whispered, but her voice was overpowered by the rain falling like a symphony, orchestral, in the round. 'Jed?'

Slowly, she pushed through the vines, staring up at the path ahead. It was completely clear. Ferns nodded across the track like greedy hands, the vines hung from other branches forming rackety walls. Where was he?

A tree had fallen thirty metres ahead – not recently – but it created a substantial obstacle to a quick getaway. Clambering over trees wasn't the innocent activity of her childhood; out here, everything could bite, sting, elicit an allergic reaction. Surely Jed hadn't gotten past there already? She'd stopped for all of thirty seconds.

'Jed?' She shouted his name this time, raising her voice above the rain, not caring whether the big cats heard her. He had the knife, she just had to get back to him. 'Where are you?'

She waited for his jocular reply.

Nothing came.

'Jed, stop messing about. This isn't funny.' But she knew this was no prank. They were out here trying to save his child. He wouldn't muck about at a time like this. Neither of them was in this for fun.

She turned a slow circle, feeling eyes perpetually upon her back, her heart pounding heavily from the uphill hike through the mud, from the dawning panic that she was alone. Her skills to survive somewhere like this were rudimentary at best. Without him, she had no shelter, no weapons, no map, just a backpack full of cheese and ham sandwiches and some mangoes.

Then she saw it – a deep skid mark in the mud. She had been so busy looking ahead, looking out, it hadn't occurred to her to look down. She ran up, following where it went off the animal track and deeper into the undergrowth. A branch scratched her arm as she pushed past in a rush but she barely even noticed it.

'Jed?'

Pushing back the thick bushes, she caught sight of something.

'Jed!'

He was lying on the ground, his body crumpled, his face pressed in the mud. He was motionless, his arm thrown out at a grotesque angle. Blood was oozing from a wound to his head.

She stared in horror at the sight, hardly able to comprehend what she was seeing. In the space of mere moments, he'd gone from walking and laughing to this – broken and facedown in the mud. Who had done this to him? Or rather, what?

It wasn't over yet, she sensed that now, the scale of the danger dawning fully upon her. This was the jungle, no place for mercy, and a man down meant one thing: prey.

She looked up into the undergrowth again, still able to feel the weight of a stare upon her, cold eyes blinking through the leaves. She felt her blood still in her veins. Carefully, reaching down, she unsheathed the knife from Jed's leg holster and brandished it wildly, jabbing towards the bushes, seeing how the steel blade flashed even in the rain.

Her rage, courage, grew with every joust. The adrenaline was beginning to pump freely now and her body was telling her to fight. Her knuckles were blanched around the handle, her own body falling into a feral mode as she scanned the bushes.

Then it came again.

She jerked her head up with a loud gasp as behind her the rainforest suddenly shimmied and shook. She spun round and saw a streak of something moving through the undergrowth, ten metres away. She couldn't see what it was, only what it displaced as branches were pushed aside and snapped. But the cacophony was growing fainter, not louder . . . it was retreating. In the near distance, several howler monkeys began screaming as if tracking the predator, their shrieks carrying from the canopies across the gorge and down the jungled valley.

The knife began to shake in her hand as she sensed the danger pass finally – she had done it! Scared it off, whatever it was! – and she slowly, slowly, let her arm drop. She looked back at Jed. He was still motionless in the mud, water running around him like he was a rock in a river.

'Jed, talk to me!' she panted, getting down on her knees in the mud and putting her face near his. She felt his breath on her skin; he was breathing. She took his pulse. 'Jed, can you hear me? Wake up!'

There was a long silence; he was still out cold.

'Jed, what happened? Can you talk to me?'

He didn't respond, but on the ground beside him, she saw a large club. Like an old-fashioned policeman's truncheon, it had been carved from a single piece of wood. He had been hit with *that*? A weapon?

Who . . . ? Who . . . ? She looked around them desperately again. Had it been a *man* she had seen running away? Were there more? Others, watching her, even now?

There was no possible way of knowing. She just knew she had to get him to wake up, to move out of this wet mud, get away from the rain. She looked desperately around them. His forearm was broken, she could see that just from the angle of it. His shoulder looked dislocated too. Once he regained consciousness, she wouldn't be able to move him in this condition. He wouldn't even be able to sit up with these injuries. He'd pass out from the pain.

She felt her brain slide into autopilot . . .

She looked around her again. There was a bamboo plant a few metres away, its shoots straight and strong, and she went over and after a few clumsy hacks, cut down the straightest length she could see. Then she cut it in half.

Raindrops dripped from the tip of her nose as she kneeled beside Jed again, trying to keep quiet, wanting now *not* to wake him. His eyelids fluttered vaguely, too heavy to lift and she knew his semi-conscious state would be a blessing for the next few moments at least. Carefully, she lifted the broken arm and began palpating gently. She could discern two fractures to the radius. The shoulder was definitely out of place. Defence injuries.

She remembered she'd brought her small doctor's kit with her and she shrugged off the rucksack, scrabbling to find it at the bottom, beneath their food. It didn't have what she really wanted – which was a tank of morphine – but she had some basics that would help. Finding the strip bandage rolls, she placed the two bamboo lengths either side of the wrist and bound them to one another, splinting the arm. Then carefully, supporting the weight of the splinted arm, she slowly levered it to a ninety-degree angle.

Jed groaned, more alert this time, and she knew she had to act quickly. He was coming round. With the forearm now supported, she rolled him carefully onto his back, then placed her hands either side of his upper arm, above the elbow. She put one of her feet gently against his ribs and with a steady pressure, pulled.

She felt the joint click as Jed's eyes opened and a cry of pain left him like an exhale, his face pale with sweat, pain and fear. 'What . . . ?' He stared up at the sky, rain pelting his face, his reactions too slow.

'Don't move.' She scrambled back onto her knees so that he could see her. 'You've got a broken arm.'

He groaned in reply, disoriented and concussed.

Moving quickly, she stripped down to her bra and knotting her shirt in one corner, created a roughly triangular shape that would serve as a sling. Lifting his head, she knotted it behind his neck so that the arm was now splinted and strapped across his chest.

She needed something else though . . . saw his belt. 'Excuse me,' she said, as she pulled it from the loops of his trousers and carefully fastened it around his torso, going above the right arm rather than under it. It meant the injured limb was pinned down and would help immobilize the shoulder too.

'What . . . T-t?' He was coming round quickly now.

'Jed, can you sit up for me? I'll need to help you.'

He looked bewildered and, without free use of his arms, she had to get behind him to help push him up. His backpack had been torn off in the struggle, the strap ripped from the seams. She pushed it up behind him, as a lumbar support. He gasped with every movement, looking like he might be sick as he came to an upright position and she knew it was the head injury. 'Don't move. Take it slowly. Just breathe,' she said calmly, watching as his head hung, his eyes opening and closing drowsily.

'Do you know what happened?' she asked after a few moments, when it became clear he could cope with gravity, he wasn't going to pass out.

He gave a grunt that seemed to be an affirmation.

'Who did this to you?' He had no scratches, no puncture wounds. The wooden club clearly signified it had been a human attack and not animal. She remembered the streak she had seen through the trees and looked around again, just as another sound of twigs snapping came to her ears. She saw the knife she had left lying on the ground as she triaged him, and picked it up again, on high alert. She stared hard into the undergrowth again, knowing countless eyes were staring back at her. But the man, or men, who had done this – she didn't know how many there were, or why they'd done this, or what they wanted – were they still here, watching them?

For several minutes she scarcely dared breathe, the tip of the knife pointed towards every bush, every tree as Jed sat slumped, scarcely conscious. They couldn't stay here. A broken arm in the jungle was as dangerous as a broken leg in the Alps.

The rainforest pulsated and scratched loosely around them, with none of the quivering tension during the initial attack. Slowly, her grip began to loosen on the knife. Her nerves were frayed but her gut told her whoever had done this had gone.

Jed was beginning to come round, his head nodding as he tried to look up.

'Jed, listen to me – we can't leave you sitting in the wet mud. You'll get hypothermia in these conditions and that will leave you vulnerable. We've got to get you somewhere warm and dry.' But it was a laughable notion. Nowhere was warm and dry in the Costa Rican jungle, everyone knew that.

'Jed, the rangers' station. Where is it?' She supported his head with her hand, getting him to look at her, to focus. 'Where, Jed?'

He tried to look at her, but his eyes kept crossing.

'Where is the rangers' station?' she asked slowly. It couldn't be far surely? They'd been walking for a couple of hours already and it was supposed to be a 'base' station in the mountainous national park.

He stared back at her, both of them soaked in the pummelling rain. '. . . Map.'

Map. Of course.

She reached around him for his rucksack, holding his weight against her momentarily as she scrabbled for the map, drawn in a green dye on the scrap of cloth.

'Here.'

She replaced the bag and brought the map over, opened it up. There was little more than a few scratchings to go by, symbols that might mean something to him, but nothing at all to her.

He stared at it for several long moments, then with effort, with his good arm, he pointed to a space below a simply sketched mountain peak – halfway down. 'Us.'

Every word was a trial, he was blanched with pain.

He moved his good arm slowly, carefully, to a point only just above where he had said they were. 'Ranger.'

'Rangers' station?' she repeated. 'Above us? Here?'

She looked up but they were shielded by the sprawling bush that had blocked him from sight from the path – and now blocked her view again too. 'Jed, don't move. Just wait here. I'm going to look and try to see where we are.'

He didn't protest, just closed his eyes again, his head hanging. She scrambled back to the path and looked up the banking. Hectares of knobbled green stretched above and all around. The uniformity of it was dizzying, like looking into the deep blue when she'd gone scuba diving with Miles and her father in Belize. All scale was lost, nothing emerged from the all-encompassing black and green landscape.

Except . . .

She squinted, training her gaze hard on a single tiny, bright dot, several hundred metres up and along the path from here. It was nothing really, snagging the eye as just a break in the trees perhaps – a singular tree that had fallen. Or a building. It could be the roof of a building.

She kept staring. If that was the rangers' station . . . *if* it was . . . it was still a long way from here. She didn't think he could get that far. He'd taken a bad beating and she didn't know yet how many other injuries he might have.

But to leave him here and get help was a risk too. Big cats prowled these territories. There was nothing hypothetical about an ocelot or puma or jaguar chancing upon him, injured and defenceless. This was their territory. It was she and Jed who were the visitors.

She ran her hands down her face, hardly able to believe this was happening. This time yesterday she'd been swimming in waterfalls, enjoying a picnic with her friends. How had everything gone so wrong in the space of a few minutes?

She tried to think clearly. Empty her mind of emotion and pretend she was in theatre . . .

She would leave him with the knife, something to defend himself with. She would find herself a better stick and go to the rangers' station and bring help down to him here. The rangers would know the terrain, they'd be able to get back here to him in half the time it would take her to get there. The sooner she went, the sooner they'd have help.

She heard a sound behind her – the cracking of twigs again – and she spun round, startled, her eyes white with fear. She was jumpy and agitated.

Jed stood there, swaying and pale. Somehow he had managed to get himself to standing. The map was crushed in his good hand, which was also somehow holding the bag. He looked like he was going to either pass out or throw up. She stared at him in disbelief.

'Let's go,' he said finally, putting one foot forward. Then another.

'Hello? Help!' she called, her voice ragged with breathlessness as Jed leaned on her. He had one arm over her shoulder and was doing his best to support himself as they staggered in pitifully small steps over the rough ground, but he was fighting against recurring loss of consciousness and three times he had collapsed, bringing her along with him, her knees buckling from the weight of him as he went down. She would remember his howls of pain, as he landed on his fractured arm, for a long time to come.

It had taken them almost two hours to get here, the rain like an enemy pushing against them – stinging their faces, making their feet slip – but as they placed their muddied feet on the deck of the rangers' station, Tara felt a euphoric rush of relief. They had done it! Found refuge! Here, they could get help, get back.

'Hello! Is anybody here?' she called again as they staggered up the steps, leading Jed haltingly towards the low bleached timber building. It had several peaked roofs, covered in the traditional style with rushes, and woven window hatches pulled up against the rainstorm.

The station looked closed and worryingly uninhabited. She could feel its emptiness, the quality of silence and stillness upon it. She felt a stab of alarm. They couldn't have come all this way, only for nothing. Limping over, Jed's head hanging again, she tried the first door they reached. It was locked.

No. No, no. They had to get in. She would break in if necessary. Turning back wasn't an option. They went slowly around to the other side, Jed's weight becoming heavier with every step – he had depleted himself fully to get this far – and she was grateful for the firmness underfoot of the decking after endlessly slipping through the mud. She tried each window, seeing if she could get her fingers between the hatch and the walls, whether she could force them open; but they were securely fastened. They reached another door and she went for the door handle.

It turned. Unlocked. As simple as that.

'Yes!' she cried, wanting to weep with gratitude. She pushed it open and peered into the space. 'Hello?' She felt her voice sink into the walls of the office, swallowed into the silence. They were in, but still alone.

She scanned the room, looking for signs of how it could help them – two desks were covered with paperwork towers, a water cooler in one corner, several boxes stacked against one wall. She clocked a printer, posters of insects, mammals and birds on the walls, a phone—

A phone!

'Jed, come and sit down,' she said, guiding him carefully through the door. There was a chair where he could rest, finally, while she called for help; she could get them both some fluids, clean him up, find some dry clothes they could both change into; staying in wet clothes was one of the biggest risks right now. At the very least, there had to be towels. There would be a bathroom here, surely?

The outside door slammed shut behind them on a gust of wind, making her jump. 'Dammit,' she muttered, her nerves still frayed from the attack as she half-led, half-dragged Jed towards the chair behind the desk. Water was still running off her hair, down the bare skin of her shoulders, back and chest. She was smeared with mud, sweating and her skin was red and sore from where he was leaning on her. There were scratches on her thighs and countless bites.

'Okay, we're going to sit you down here,' she panted, trying to push the chair back from the desk with her foot for him, just as a sound outside came to her ear. She paused and looked up, still on high alert. The sound had a static quality, like the air was crackling, voices carrying as if on a tide. Radio?

She heard heavy footsteps come close across the deck, but then stop. She held her breath, aware every muscle in her body was tense as she stood hunched behind the desk, still supporting Jed's weight. The feet began to tread again, pacing now, a male voice drifting in and out of earshot – making no attempts *not* to be heard – the low timbre winking through the timber boards.

She breathed again, looking up at Jed with joy. 'The ranger's here!' she beamed. 'He's back!'

Jed looked back at her with an unfocused gaze. Her smile faltered. He was in a bad way. 'You hear me, Jed? Help's here. You're going to be okay. The hard part's done.'

The sound of static was right outside now, briskly advancing footsteps making the floor vibrate, and the door swung open in the next moment, letting in the pounding staccato of rain. The ranger stopped in the door at the sight of them – a mismatched pair joined at the hip, muddy, soaked, beaten up. The hand holding the walkie-talkie dropped down from his mouth, his mouth dropped into a shocked 'o'.

Tara felt the world cleave in two.

'. . . Alex?'

249

Chapter Eighteen

'Tara?'

Shockwaves shook the ground beneath their feet, uprooted the giant trees from their ancient roots, tossed clouds around the air, sent the birds flying for the stars.

Or maybe it only felt like that to her.

The silence that opened up between the two sides of the room felt yawning and endless, a void she might fall into and never climb out from. She didn't even notice that Jed was leaning on her now, that she was half bent and broken by the weight of him. She couldn't process what her eyes were showing her: Alex, right here, in the room, in this hut, in this jungle.

Ten years had passed since she had last seen him but it felt like a time-slip; it could have been yesterday. Only, how was it possible that he looked better than that last night in London? His wan, urban pallor was now replaced by a deep tan; his hair was longer, shaggier, and with a few sun-tinted caramel highlights; he had always been lean but he had broadened in the shoulders and thighs. He was a man now and not the man-child she had known.

Jed slumped suddenly, his knees buckling from the effort to remain standing, and she felt her own go too. Alex lurched forwards, moving from hologram to three-dimensional truth as he went to catch Jed, who cried out from the pain of his arm and shoulder jolting.

'Sorry, bud. I'm sorry.' Alex winced as, in a stroke, Tara felt Jed's weight being lifted off her as he was helped towards the chair.

'. . . What happened?' Alex asked her, his pale eyes burning with alarm.

'He was attacked by someone,' she said, watching now as he manoeuvred her old friend carefully into sitting down, taking care not to jog his broken arm again.

Alex looked back at her sharply. 'And you?'

She shook her head. 'Jed was ahead of me. I don't think they knew I was there.'

Alex stared at her with narrowed eyes for a moment as though debating whether he believed that. He looked back at the patient. '. . . Jed? Can you hear me, buddy?' Alex crouched down in front of him, looking more closely at the crudely splinted arm. For the first time, Tara realized she was standing there in just her bra and jean shorts.

'His arm's broken in two places, shoulder was dislocated. And he's badly concussed. We need to get him to a hospital asap. He needs a CT.'

Alex thought for a moment, then stood up, bringing his walkie-talkie back to his mouth. His thumb pressed on a button and the room filled with static again, like the swarm of a million mosquitoes. It was not an enticing thought and Tara scratched herself mindlessly, realizing a miniature army had feasted on her in the oppressive humidity, her shirt off, as she helped Jed stagger along.

'Base to Torto One, over.' Alex walked across the room, towards the door, waiting for a response. It came within moments.

'Torto one, responding to Base, over.'

'Medical emergency,' he said in easy Spanish. 'Mora and Jimenez back to Base asap. Bring the stretcher. Over.'

'Roger that. Over and out.'

Alex turned back to them, glancing at the pitiful scene, but he didn't say anything. He reached for the phone on the desk and punched some numbers in. Tension infused every movement. He looked almost angry, his jaw set in a firm position.

'Hello, yes,' he said, lapsing into Spanish again as though he was a native. He seemed so . . . at home here. 'This is Alex Carter at the rangers' base station in Tremain Talamanca Park. We have a medical emergency. One man, late-thirties, arm broken in two places, dislocated shoulder, head injury and concussion. Arm is splinted and stabilized. Requesting ambulance at Marzano Highway, junction nine, in . . .' His gaze went up to a clock on the wall as he made a mental calculation. 'Two hours twenty minutes.'

Tara felt her stomach clench at his words. Another two-and-a-half-hour wait before Jed could even be transferred to an ambulance. And then how long would it be to the nearest hospital? And what facilities would it have? Did it even have a scanner? Every minute counted with head injuries.

He put the phone down and turned back to them. 'Help's coming.'

Tara felt a burst of irritation. Help was coming? Like he'd done the hard part? He'd saved them?

He stood there for a moment, staring at her again like she was the one who'd been beaten up, then left the room.

Tara stared after him in bafflement. Now where had he gone?

Beside her, Jed groaned, his head rolling back.

'Hey, it's okay,' she said, taking his good hand and squeezing it lightly. 'Help's on the way. We're safe now.'

'Paco—'

'Paco's . . .' What could she say? 'Paco's okay. He's the same as he was. Let's just concentrate on you for the moment.'

'Nnnn . . .' Jed protested, his eyes fluttering. Without warning, he pitched forward and began to vomit.

Tara grabbed the desk bin and positioned it beneath him as he retched and heaved. This was a bad sign. 'It's okay,' she soothed him, slowly rubbing his back.

Alex came back in with a pile of uniforms, neatly folded. He took in the latest development in silence.

'Is there somewhere we can lie him down?' she asked.

'Yes, there's a bed in the back.'

'That would be better.'

She stepped back, allowing Alex to support Jed's weight and lever him back to standing again. She felt so weak now, her muscles stiff and sore from having supported eighty per cent of the weight of a ninety-five-kilo man for two hours.

They went through to a tiny room at the back of the building. It had no windows at all and was only big enough to accommodate a single mattress and a chair. They got Jed sitting down on the bed.

'We need to get these wet clothes off him,' Tara said. 'Hypothermia's a complication we could do without.'

But with his arm strapped and bound, there was only one way to do it. Alex went back to the office, returning moments later with a pair of scissors and a towel. They cut his shirt off and Tara dried him carefully. Then, lying him down, they took off his boots, socks and trousers. Covering him with the towel, she cut off his soaking-wet underpants too and covered him with the blanket. 'We need to keep him warm.'

'And you.' Alex swept a cautionary look over her, reminding her she too was soaked to the bone – and half-dressed. 'There's some dry clothes out there.'

Without another word, she went back to the office and rifled through the stack of ranger uniforms he'd left on the desk. They were the same as he was wearing, and exactly what she and Jed had been planning to beg/borrow/steal when they got here – utilitarian ripstop khaki trousers with useful cargo pockets, long-sleeved shirts. She stripped off her sodden clothes. She dried herself with the hand towel and changed into them, having to roll over the waistband of the trousers twice to get them to stay up.

She went back to the desk for her rucksack, then walked back into the small bedroom, to find Jed throwing up again. Alex hadn't been quite so ready for it and it was all over the floor.

'Mop?' she asked.

He looked up, hesitating at the sight of her dressed in the too-big ranger's uniform; she knew she must look feral. A Jungle Jane. 'There's some cleaning supplies in the cupboard beside the—'

She arched an eyebrow, stopping him.

'I'll get it.' He rushed past as she reached into her bag and pulled out her small doctor's kit. She put the stethoscope back on and listened to Jed's heart. It was labouring hard. She put the cuff on his good arm and took his blood pressure. Too high.

'Have you got a torch?' she called through to Alex, able to hear his footsteps coming back down the corridor, stop, retreat again.

'Here,' he said, a few moments later.

She took it in silence. It was far too big for what she needed, but better than nothing. She shone the beam into Jed's eyes. He winced, the pupils restricting.

'Good, that's good,' she smiled, rubbing his uninjured arm encouragingly. 'You're doing well, Jed.'

Alex began mopping the floor around her and she stepped out of the way. The smell of bleach was a welcome alternative to that of vomit. She watched blankly for a moment as he squeezed the mop head in the wringer. It seemed completely ludicrous that any of this was happening. That of all the people to have come into this remote outpost, it should be him. Or rather, them.

He looked up and caught her staring.

'There's some in the office too, remember,' she said.

'Right.' His eyes narrowed slightly.

'How much longer before help gets here?'

Alex checked his watch. 'Five minutes? Ten? We'll hear them.'

Hear them? 'What's going to happen?'

'When the other two get here, they'll stretcher him down to the road, where an ambulance can get near enough to intercept.'

'And the hospital?'

'Is about half an hour away from there.'

'Do they have the equipment? He's going to need a CT scan.'

'They've got good doctors there.'

It wasn't an answer. 'Good doctors still can't see a bleed inside a skull,' she said flatly. 'Do we need to have a helicopter on standby to get him to San José?'

He stared at her and she realized he'd never heard her speak this way before, referencing her easy access to resources that were out of reach of almost everyone. When they'd been together – so very long ago, now – it had been something she had gone to great lengths to keep hidden. As well they both knew.

'Probably. Yes.'

'Then I assume you can sanction that.' She stared at him levelly. 'Or would you prefer I do it myself?' She was pulling rank and they both knew it.

'I'll do it,' he said, walking out.

Tara felt the room decompress as he went down the hall and made the call; all the air seemed to leave with him. She looked back at her patient. Jed was lying stretched out, eyelids fluttering as he stared, unseeing, at the pitched ceiling.

'Just don't go to sleep on me, Jed. You must stay awake. For Paco's sake, and Sarita's, and all your beautiful children – stay awake.'

He groaned. 'Pah—' His lips pushed out, making the sound but not quite able to finish it.

'Paco's okay,' she soothed him. He wasn't okay, of course, but neither was it a lie. The child was technically in the same condition as when they'd left, the same as if they hadn't ever embarked upon this quest in the first place. She knew it had always been a long shot anyway, a desperate attempt to just do something.

Alex came back ten minutes later. 'Okay. Everything's arranged. There's a chopper landing in town that will take him straight to San José.'

'Good.'

His expression changed as he looked back at Jed. 'How's he doing?'

'His GCS score is nine, which I'm not happy about.'

'GCS?'

'Glasgow Coma Scale. It's a way of grading head injuries.'

'Oh.' He stuck his hands in his pockets and began to pace at the doorway. The room stank of bleach and her initial relief to be free of the stench of vomit was fading fast. The air felt toxic and chemical; she had a growing urge to stand outside and turn her face up to the rain.

The sound of something outside made them both turn their heads. It was a distant whirring, high-pitched and insistent.

'That's them,' Alex said. 'Let's help him up.'

He came over and pushed Jed to a sitting position.

'Let me just get him covered up,' she said, wrapping the towel around Jed's hips and securing it. Dignity mattered, even at times like this.

Alex draped Jed's good arm over his shoulder and managed to get him to stand. Tara grabbed the blanket and held the doors open as the two men staggered and limped through the narrow corridor, coming through again into the office. She opened the door onto the deck outside and saw with relief that the rain had finally stopped. A hazy sunshine now lit the sky, a gentle steam lifting up off the ground, the trees and bushes . . . The animals had come back out again too, birds trilling and shrieking from on high, insects buzzing and skittering furiously.

She could almost believe that the events of the past few hours had been some strange delusion – the shock of seeing Jed crumpled on the ground, administering first aid in a jungle setting, staggering through the streaming mud, Alex . . .

She looked up, not sure what the sound was that she could hear and was astonished to see a microlight coming through the sky. She watched as it approached at speed, then hovered at a point just above the station, before lowering into the trees.

Alex looked at Jed and patted his chest reassuringly. 'Nearly there, buddy. Hang tight.'

In a matter of mere moments, two rangers appeared, dressed in the same clothes Alex and now Tara herself were wearing. They were Indigenous men, well-built – she knew her father had made a point of ensuring the ranger jobs were offered to the Indigenous people first; they knew the terrain better than anyone – and they came running down through the trees and onto the deck.

'What've we got?' they asked in Spanish.

'Jed Alvarado.'

Tara saw the way the men's eyes widened at the mention of his name and they looked at him more closely.

'He's been attacked—'

Tara saw a knowing look pass between the three men.

'We need to get him off the mountain. There'll be an ambulance at the Marzano cross-section, ready to get him to the helicopter to take him to San José.'

Both men nodded, glancing at the slumped figure leaning heavily on Alex.

'We've got the stretcher,' one of them said, unfolding a portable red heavy-duty plastic stretcher and two harnesses. The men shrugged the harnesses on as Alex and Tara helped Jed to lie down on the stretcher on the deck, but he was becoming increasingly confused and distressed now, sensing change.

'Nnnno,' he moaned.

'Yes, Jed,' Tara said, guiding him gently down, pressing on his good shoulder to get him to lie flat. 'We must get you looked at properly.'

'Nnno—'

She draped the blanket over Jed's exposed body and fastened the straps to secure him in. 'Alex, translate to these guys for me. They'll need to pass it on to the paramedics.'

Her Spanish wasn't good enough for medical jargon. 'His arm is broken in two places along the radius,' she said slowly, waiting for Alex to translate and pointing to Jed's forearm to show the rangers what she meant. 'His shoulder was dislocated and has been reset, but it will still be unstable and very painful . . . I've immobilized it but you must still be very careful . . . Tell the paramedics he's scoring a nine on the GCS scale. They'll know what that means,' she added as the rangers looked back at her blankly, even after translation.

'Have you got that?' Alex asked sharply, seeing their vacant expressions too. 'Tara is an ICU consultant at St Thomas's Hospital in London. She knows what she's talking about.'

Both men nodded and she felt a tightening in her chest that her word could only be trusted on Alex's say-so. 'Okay.'

'Right, fast as you can then,' Alex said, chivvying them to get on.

'But steady,' Tara added as both men squatted down and connected the stretcher to their harnesses, the man at the front needing Alex's help to connect it to the back of his harness. They rose on a count of three.

Tara looked down at Jed; his head was lifting off the stretcher as he felt the sensation of being lifted and carried.

'Sar—'

'I'll tell Sarita, don't worry,' she said as Jed flailed to reach her. She grasped his good hand with hers, keeping him calm. 'And I'll get her over to San José to see you, don't worry about any of that.'

'Nnno . . . Paco . . .'

Tara swallowed, looking back apprehensively at her old friend. 'Let's just deal with first things first.'

'Pahhh . . . co.' He was staring at her now and she could

see the effort it was taking him to fix his gaze, to keep her in his sights. 'Paco.'

'Who's Paco?' Alex asked.

She glanced up. 'His son. He's very sick. We had come out here to get a remedy for him for the Awa.'

Alex's eyes narrowed. 'What remedy? Where, exactly?'

'We were heading for Alto Uren,' she muttered distractedly. What did it matter now? She looked back at Jed. 'The moment we know you're all right, we'll head off again,' she lied.

'Nnnno!' The word burst from him, his body becoming tense, resistant. He was strapped down but he was a big man and the rangers both struggled to balance as he began to fight.

'Jed—' She faltered, trying to calm him. 'I promise, we'll get Paco what he needs, but we must look after you first. We need you to get us there, remember? You and the Awa are the only ones who know what we're looking for and where.'

But Jed wouldn't listen. He began trying to sit up, to undo the straps tying him in place with his good hand, even though his co-ordination had gone, his movements flailing and useless.

'I know where Alto Uren is,' Alex said suddenly, calming him with a steady hand on his chest. 'I can go there.'

Jed stopped fighting. His head fell back on the stretcher as he looked back at Alex, and Tara wondered how well they knew one another. Alex had called him 'buddy', and Jed's father worked with Alex all the time. The thought that they might be friends felt like another loss, something else Alex had stolen from her.

'Tell me what it is you're looking for.'

Jed mumbled a word in Bribri that Tara couldn't catch – but Alex's eyes narrowed. Slowly he nodded. 'I know that plant. I've seen it there. You're sure that's what you're looking for?'

'Pahhco,' Jed repeated, the word almost a sigh.

'Then leave it to me. I'll get it for you. Don't worry about a thing. We'll protect your boy.'

Jed's body softened as if tranquillized and at Alex's nod the two rangers immediately set off. Tara and Alex watched as he was carried across the deck, down the steps and along the jungle path. Within moments they were gone, but she and Alex stood there, looking on after the red streak was out of sight.

She knew he was thinking the same as her, feeling the same sense of unease as they found themselves alone in the Costa Rican jungle, one question running through both their minds.

Now what?

She went back inside, remembering that in all the rush, she'd left her wet clothes in a heap on the floor. She picked them up and rolled them into balls, stuffing them back in her rucksack with all the food. She went through to the small room at the back and did the same with Jed's clothes too, although his shirt was in rags now and she put that in the bin.

Alex stood watching her as she moved about busily. 'Will he be okay?'

'As long as there's no further holdups, yes, I hope so.' Her voice was brisk, her eyes anywhere but on him.

He watched her fasten her backpack, frowned as she hoisted it over her arms. '. . . What are you doing?'

It was her turn to frown. 'Heading back. What do you think?'

There was a small laugh. '. . . What?'

She looked up to find Alex staring at her with an openly shocked expression. 'I'm heading back. His wife needs to be told what's happened. Why's that funny?'

'You can't go trekking through this jungle on your own!'

There was a pause. 'I think you'll find I can do whatever I like,' she said in an even voice. If he thought he could tell her what she could or couldn't do, if he thought he was entitled to talk to her as though he knew her . . .

'Tara, this isn't . . . Hyde Park!'

'I'm perfectly aware of that,' she said coldly, not appreciating his condescension.

'You have no idea where their village is from here.'

That was perfectly true. 'Don't I? And how would you know?'

He stared back at her, unable to tell if she was bluffing. He knew she'd come here throughout her childhood.

She tightened the straps on the backpack. 'Thanks for your help. I'll be sure to let my father know.'

She saw the insult register as she elucidated his place in the pecking order: an employee – albeit an important one – nothing more, nothing less.

She went to walk past but he blocked the door. 'Twig—' There was that shocked laugh again.

'*Don't* call me that,' she said sharply, feeling her composure shake as he stood close to her now. She felt at the edge of her limits, her heart banging too fast. She knew if she were to take her pulse it would be high 140s, maybe higher. This was rapidly becoming more than she could bear. Now that the initial urgency of seeing to Jed was over, the shock of suddenly coming face to face with the man who had all but destroyed her life was overwhelming. She had promised herself she would never set eyes on him again. It was the condition she had set – sending it out into the universe – that had enabled her to get out of bed again after those first few desolate weeks . . . But now here he was, right in front of her. He worked for her father, of course, so she had known he would be at the handover this week – she had spent months refusing to think about it – but to bump into him in the middle of the jungle, in a land area of almost 20,000 square miles . . . she had thought her chances of avoiding him were pretty good.

'Look. I'll radio Jimenez and get him to go to Jed's village and tell his wife, after they've handed Jed over. It's not that far from the handover point.'

She shrugged. She could see, even if she would not admit it, that that was a much better solution. 'Okay, fine. See ya.' She turned away again so that he had to jump almost in front of her, blocking her path.

'Tara, can we just . . . just take a second? Please?'

'For what?'

He gave another baffled laugh, ran a hand through his hair. 'Well, for one thing, I've not seen you in ten years. How are you?'

She blinked. And there it was – the easy lapse into pleasantries which in itself told her everything she hadn't wanted to know: that he was happy to see her and therefore happy without her. He stood before her fulfilled, a man at ease, those three simple words drawing fresh blood and confirming all over again her conviction that she had never been to him what he had been to her; she had simply been his way to realize his lifetime ambition by the age of twenty-three. Of course he hadn't looked back when he'd come here! Tasked with creating an entire national park, he wouldn't even have looked up!

The plain fact of it was no less painful now than it had been then, even though she had gone on to make such a success of her life, excelling in her career, embracing the privileges she had once sought to hide, taking her place among the fashionable, good and great. She was wanted at parties and dinners, at keynote conferences and skiing trips. She had had a string of lovers who had been just diverting enough and now, of course, Rory, who made her feel so settled and content. And yet, standing before this man, it all felt like a mirage, a glittering image of a life but without any real substance. Three little words and she was exposed.

'Goodbye, Alex.' She walked past him, pushing the door so hard on its hinges it flew back and hit the wall. She was halfway down the steps back to the path when she heard him call out after her.

'What about the boy?'

She didn't stop. 'There's nothing that can be done now,' she called back, not caring whether he heard or not. She just had to get away from here. She wouldn't stay another minute.

Her heart advanced to a gallop as she got to the rough path that would – supposedly, eventually – take her off this mountain and back onto the flats, and then somewhere after that, the road. She saw how the track seemed to disappear into the leaves, but hadn't they largely travelled in a straight line? She hadn't been aware of any sharp left or right turns. She was pretty sure she could navigate her way back. Or, might she be able to catch the rangers? They were only, what, five, six minutes ahead of her? They'd set off at an almost-jog but she could catch them if she ran. They were carrying a full-grown man and she had a past to outrun; she'd catch them in no time. It was her best bet.

'Tara.' Alex was staring at her like she'd gone mad, his hand on her arm. 'Could you please just wait?'

'Get your hand off me. I need to catch up with them.'

'Who . . . ?' He looked confused. Then surprised. 'Mora and Jimenez?' He gave a laugh. 'No chance! Seriously, none.'

'That's just your opinion.'

'No, that's my experience,' he countered with a look that told her he wasn't joking. He was still holding on to her arm, as though he didn't trust her not to make a break for it. She could feel the spread of his palm over her skin, the press of his fingertips. 'And besides, we have to discuss next steps.'

'There are no next steps. Jed's getting medical help and I'm getting off this mountain before it gets dark.'

'And what about his boy? He was distressed. We made a promise.'

'Jed's concussed, therefore promises mean nothing. He'll already have forgotten all about it. Nothing can be done now anyway.'

'But I know where Alto Uren is. I know the Guetares tribe and the plant you're looking for.'

'Oh! Well, good for you! Go get it then! Go be the hero!' Her sarcasm was out-out now.

His eyes flashed with sudden anger too. 'And in the meantime, what? Leave you wandering through the jungle on your own?'

'Trust me. I'm a big girl,' she snapped. 'I can look after myself.'

'Really? So if you encounter a cougar you'll do what exactly . . . ?' He pointedly looked for signs of a weapon on her, something that could be used for self-defence. He seemed to have forgotten that his hand was still attached to her arm, the two of them joined and wrestling like a two-headed snake. '. . . No? Nothing?'

'The chances of me encountering a cougar are low to nil.'

'As low as encountering me?' He stared back at her with a black light in his eyes. 'And how about the men who attacked you? What if you meet them again?'

'Why would I? Their issues are with Jed, not me.'

His mouth opened as he went to say something, then closed it again. He took several breaths and she watched him try to calm himself down. He dropped her arm from his grip and took a step back. Proximity had always been a problem for them, she remembered. They had never been able to think straight when they were too close. 'Look, this is an either-or situation, Tara. I can either get you off this mountain *or* I can take you to Alto Uren, but not both.' He planted his hands on his hips and blinked back at her. 'I'd lose my job if your father found out I let you travel through the jungle, unprotected and alone.'

It was the return punch to her own slight. To her, he was just her father's employee. To him, she was just his boss's daughter.

She stared at him, hating him. She wondered how it could be that she had ever thought she loved him, that she had been prepared to give up her career, all her own ambitions and dreams, to share a life with him. He was self-centred, selfish, power-hungry, vain.

He read the contempt in her face and took another step back. 'Just . . .' he exhaled, looking bewildered that any of this was happening. That after ten years of silence, they'd gone straight into a fight. 'Tell me about the boy. What's wrong with him?'

Tara looked away. She didn't want to think about that child right now. She didn't want to be reminded of his suffering. She wanted to get away from here, away from *him*. '. . . I think it's hepatitis, but it could be leukaemia and I can't be sure without further testing.' She kept her gaze well away, not interested in seeing the sadness in his eyes, his postures of compassion.

There was a silence. 'How old is he?'

'Six.'

'And you think his hepatitis or leukaemia is going to be treated by a herbal medicine?'

She whipped back to face him. 'No, of course I don't! But it was the only way I could get his parents to agree to trying my methods. They have to pursue all their options as they see them; they have to see those fail first. Then they'll let me intercede.'

He held his hands up in a gesture of surrender. 'I'm only asking because there's been some impressive reports about certain botanicals. I just didn't figure they were your scene, that's all.'

'You don't know what my scene is,' she snapped. Although clearly he knew some things about her. She remembered now how he'd reeled off her position and title and place of work to the rangers; it hadn't struck her at the time because she'd been more indignant that her professional opinion was going unheard, seemingly because she was a woman. 'I go where the science leads me. I'll do whatever I can for my patients. You're not the only one who'll do whatever it takes for their job.'

Anger reflected off every word, like sunlight on steel, dazzling him and forcing him back. They were quiet for several moments as she tried to recover herself. She wished she hadn't said that – referred back to their past and how he'd hurt her. It suggested she was still wounded by it when, in truth, there was only scar tissue there now. She was simply exhausted by this afternoon's turn of events, upset about what had happened to Jed. And now she had the shock of this to contend with.

'So what do you want to do, then?' he asked finally.

'I want to get off this bloody mountain,' she snapped again, unable to help herself. The sooner she got away from him, the better. She couldn't bear it. It was like some kind of sick cosmic joke.

He nodded, as if he understood, but he didn't. He never had. 'Then I'll lead you down. Just give me two minutes. I need to lock up.'

She stewed as she watched him head back up the steps again, still moving with that same languid lope, that easy SoCal manner. She felt furious, resentful. And guilty – because as much as he was the last person she had ever wanted to see again in this life, anywhere on this planet, as much as she detested him . . . she still couldn't put that above a sick child who needed her help.

His hand was on the door handle now, ready to get her off this mountain and back in time for dinner. Was she really going to allow her personal feelings to colour her professional actions? She well knew that in this medical instance, to do nothing would be to do harm.

She sighed and shut her eyes, feeling the resentment burn. *No. No. No.*

'. . . Alex, wait.'

Chapter Nineteen

Tara looked down from the microlight, her stomach feeling liquid at the sight of the jungle right below her feet. Giant, sprawling trees which from the ground blocked out the very sun, here looked like nothing more than broccoli florets. It was like travelling by bubble and felt no more secure, but Alex, sitting immediately in front of her, handled the controls with relaxed skill. Irritatingly, it made her feel safe. She wondered how many times he had flown one of these machines. Apparently, he had told her as they'd climbed in, it was the most efficient method for crossing the national park when the dense tree cover meant even helicopters couldn't land. It would take half a day off their trek, enabling them to land in a spot only thirty miles from where they were trying to get to; she supposed that had to be considered a blessing – so long as they weren't killed en route first. At a certain point, after they crossed the river, he told her, the jungle became a cloud forest, and there would be no hope of landing even a drone there; they would have to walk the rest of the way on foot. But half a day saved was half a day saved. She was grateful for whatever shortcuts they could find.

She looked down and as the minutes ticked past, began to relax. It was beautiful up here; the wind on her face stripped away the humidity momentarily, the mist of cascading waterfalls billowed above the trees, brightly coloured birds flew below and alongside them. She watched their own dramatic shadow glide silently over the ever-twitching, ever-shrieking jungle; her gaze traced the silhouetted peaks and folds of the land, saw how it pillowed up and sank again. Somewhere in her mind, a small voice pointed out that this was all hers – or technically, her family's. They owned everything the eye could see. It was a dizzying thought. Fantastic, overwhelming, visionary.

She wondered vaguely whether Alex thought the same thing when he surveyed it like this too; he had to be proud of the achievement, surely? It had been his dazzlingly simple, revolutionary idea, after all – convince a billionaire to invest his fortune in one global problem. Protect one of the planet's most fragile ecosystems by buying half a country! Why not!

She admired the concept itself. Philanthropy was big business, not just big charity, and there were always far too many egos and agendas, too many pies, too many middlemen. Her father had explained his reasoning for going with Alex's pitch many times over the years, and she always nodded and smiled and agreed that it was a great idea. She had let him assume she had set up the introduction because she believed in the concept; that she hadn't seen Alex since that night and their 'friendship' had suddenly dissolved simply because her part had been played, that that was why she hadn't even bothered to be around for Alex's pitch that weekend.

But she knew he – and certainly her mother – had suspicions too, wondering whether there was a connection between this legacy project and their daughter's abrupt withdrawal from them. Her father despaired that she hadn't been back to Costa Rica since, always citing weight of studies and work. He had no idea she had only agreed to come out here for the handover, ten years later, as a show of support for him, because she loved that he had done this and she loved him. That love was the only thing to outweigh the dread of seeing Alex at the ceremony and she had been careful to make sure she would have Holly and Dev and Rory by her side – not to mention Miles, who would deck him if Alex so much as looked in her direction. She didn't like to think how her brother would react to the sight of her sitting half a metre from Alex in a plastic bubble in the sky.

He pointed out the vague direction of Alto Uren and where they would be trekking. It looked much the same as all the rest of the park – a long way down, steep, lots of trees – and she wondered how exactly they were supposed to find this one special plant. She also wondered why, if Alto Uren was over there, they were now travelling in the other direction?

Further and further away they flew, finally coming to land in an area with enough clearance. It was a bumpy stop, and she had to suppress a small cry of fright as they rolled along the ground on their small wheels – more like bike stabilizers than aircraft equipment – only just stopping in the shadow of a large boulder.

Alex unbuckled his harness and jumped out, offering her his hand; but she ignored it and got herself out. She was an adult like that. She could do things on her own.

She looked at their equipment, now packed in two large rucksacks. They had had something of an upgrade from the first leg. Holly's enthusiastic Girl Guide packed lunch efforts had been replaced by something far more Bear Grylls. When she had given him the nod for continuing the expedition into the hills, Alex had gone into the station's Lost Property trunk and found her a belt (thank God!) and some walking boots in her size. He'd then disappeared into the stores, below the deck, and emerged forty minutes later with two huge ruck-sacks almost as big as her. They now had sleeping hammocks and tarps, camping towels, a camping stove, fire-starter kits, torches and head torches, water purifier tablets, and a selection of knives including some for her, 'in case we're separated' – the look he'd given her as he'd said that had suggested he half expected her to run off again. Now all they had to do was carry it all for thirty miles there and thirty miles back again. It was beginning to feel a little daunting.

Alex shrugged his pack on like he was a cool uncle giving a piggyback. Tara grappled with hers, almost toppling backwards when she straightened up too quickly without planting her feet square first. Alex laughed, but didn't offer to help.

'Uh – what about that?' she asked, pointing to the microlight as he went to set off.

Alex looked at it. 'What about it?'

'Surely we're not just going to leave it here?'

'What else would we do with it? I've got the keys. It's locked up so the monkeys can't get in and use it.'

He was being sarcastic. She exhaled impatiently. 'I meant, how will you ever find it again?'

He blinked. 'The same way I found it just now. This park is my playground, Tara. I know it pretty well.'

She glowered at him, hating his cockiness. He was always so sure of himself, he never felt any self-doubt.

They set off, Tara two steps behind again, her gaze on his heels, but unlike with Jed, they barely spoke. She wanted it to be very clear they weren't friends, this wasn't social. Also, Alex was a lot fitter than Jed and he walked at a pace that would have been tiring going downhill, carrying nothing at all, much less uphill with a small house on her back. Talking wasn't really an option at this speed. But her pride meant she refused to ask him to slow down and in spite of the inclines and humidity, she kept up, the sweat pouring down her cheeks, her back, her legs, in her hair, which was now roughly tied back in a ponytail.

She didn't know how much ground they were covering. It was hard going, having to fight back, with every step, the tangle of plants that might sting or scratch her, drop a heavy branch or be hiding something with teeth. The heavy morning rain had suffused an already saturated landscape, making their feet slide even in their big boots, and he kept stopping every so often to drink from the large, waxy leaves that had bellied out, collecting rainwater.

Without a word, she copied him. It was vital, she knew, to remain hydrated, especially as the last of the afternoon heat was making them steam like puddings. Dusk was already approaching and they would soon need to set up camp for the night before it grew dark. Sunsets were always fast here, with none of the lingering, bleeding skies of home. Within a space of minutes the sky would just ripen and bruise, and the day would die.

For the first time, she thought about the reality of sleeping out here. Everything had been so spur-of-the-moment, sitting in the hammocks with Holly that morning – had it really only been this morning? – that she'd considered only the steps they would take once the Awa's treatments failed. She'd thought ahead to the contacts she had in central America, and whether it would be better to fly the boy to Miami instead. Not once had she given any thought to what she actually had to go through first – sleeping on a hammock, in an open space with no walls, no roof, nothing to stop the monkeys crawling down the trees, tails curled in curiosity; nothing to stop the snakes slithering and spiders skittering along the rope ties . . .

'This is a good spot,' Alex said finally. She looked up to find him standing ahead of her, scanning an area that looked identical to every other patch of land they had just passed through. They'd been walking for ninety minutes or so, she guessed, and the light was already fading.

'The river's just over there and running quickly. Hear it?' he asked, but it wasn't really a question. He was just thinking out loud, his gaze on the ground, in the trees. 'No standing water nearby that I can see, so the mozzies won't murder us.' He turned slowly on the spot. 'And those trees look a good distance for the hammocks.' His eyes narrowed as he looked more closely at the leaves. 'I don't think it rained here earlier either, which would be a result.' He reached out a hand and rubbed some leaves between his fingers. 'Should hopefully mean we'll be able to get a fire going more easily.'

Tara wanted to unbuckle her backpack. She desperately wanted to take the weight off her shoulders, lie down sprawled on some fresh soft English grass, feel a breeze on her face, listen to some cows munching nearby . . . She swatted at a mosquito instead that kept bothering her, waiting for Alex's cue. She refused to let him see that she was struggling with this, to know that it had been a terrible idea to even think of doing this, much less to continue it when she'd had every excuse – every possible justification – to abandon the cause and go back to the beach. And her friends. And Rory.

Rory!

She realized she could have called him from the rangers' station to explain her plan; he would be up by now (surely) and she could have promised him a picnic at the waterfalls on her return, or a day on a chartered boat, just the two of them. But he hadn't crossed her mind. Her day had been too . . . eventful to be daydreaming about her boyfriend and she shook her head now, as though swatting away her guilt.

'You okay?' Alex asked. 'Mozzies bothering you?'

'Fine. I'm fine.'

'I've got some Deet if you need it.'

'I said I'm fine.'

He inhaled sharply at her brusque tone, looking irritated. 'Okay, well let's set up here then.' And he unbuckled his backpack. Without hesitation, Tara did the same, rolling her shoulders and feeling light as air as she shed its weight. A groan escaped her and she caught his head automatically turn in her direction at the sound.

She watched as Alex unrolled his hammock, fixing it to two trees that seemed very conveniently located, only having to hack at some low-growing branches that would otherwise poke him in the back. Then he secured a nylon line higher up the trunks and draped a large mosquito net over it, so that it fell on both sides over the hammock. Finally, using another fly line on a tree set just a little further back, he draped a tarp that angled above the hammock and fell behind one side of it, creating a wall.

Tara looked on, irritated by the impressive makeshift 'room' he had created – a bed that was off the ground, dry, protected from insects and any rain. He looked over at her. 'Want me to do yours?'

She scowled at him. 'I'm sorry – do I have "helpless" written across my forehead?'

He sighed, his hands on his hips, regarding her with an exasperated look she recognized, the one that he always used to give when she would remake their bed – plumping the pillows, tucking the fitted sheet, smoothing out the wrinkles on the duvet – straight after his own best efforts. His retort had always been to throw her on the bed and proceed to make it very messy again. Now, though, he looked away. 'My mistake.'

Swallowing hard and regretting her reflexive proud scorn, she did her best to copy what she'd seen him do – but her trees seemed further apart, stretching her bed tight like a trampoline, and the tarp tree was further away so that she was only half-covered from the dense canopy overhead. It was risky – Jed had forever warned her as a kid how monkeys liked to drop things like stones and fruit from on high – but if it was the price she had to pay for privacy, so be it; unlike Alex's tarp, which hung behind his bed, she had deliberately draped hers in front, so that it stretched like a wall between his hammock and hers.

She could hear his sighs grow heavier and more frequent as she tested his patience but she didn't care. What had he expected? A *bonding* exercise? That they were going to reminisce over old times?

He stuck his head around the tarp, watching for a moment as she grappled with the hammock ties; she couldn't get them to loosen. 'Do you want to dig the toilet or get the water?'

She stared back at him as if the question was a joke.

'Yeah, thought so . . . Just watch for crocs.' And he put a pair of collapsible rubber buckets on the ground. She looked back around the tarp to find he'd picked up a small shovel – like the type Rory had in his avalanche kit when skiing – and was pushing through the bushes, walking with the ease of a gardener making his way back to the potting shed. He disappeared from sight within a matter of seconds and she immediately, acutely, felt her sense of aloneness again. The afternoon's events had left her more shaky than she had appreciated and for all that she hated him, she had begrudgingly taken comfort in his company and expertise too; this had been his home for nigh-on ten years, after all.

She turned a circle on the spot, looking out for the neighbours, but she felt lumberingly conspicuous just standing there. It felt better to keep moving and she picked up the buckets and walked in the direction of the rushing river. She pushed tentatively through the bushes, startling as her eye glimpsed a tail flick through the leaves, by her feet. A pair of butterflies flitted in a dance, fluttering in a helix above the leaves of a bush with bright orange spiky flowers. The light had deepened in intensity, as it often did in the moments before sundown, and the bold, bright colours glowed almost neon, as if under ultraviolet.

There was no path to follow, just delicate animal tracks that meandered around trees, hanging vines to push back, the giant root-bed walls of upended giants to navigate. She watched where she put her feet, noticing how big the ants were, easily the size of grape pips. Bullet ants – Jed always used to point them out to her, and they were named for good reason; they had a nasty bite.

She stepped out of the jungle onto the riverside and took a breath as the world suddenly opened up again. She had a view, some breathing room; she didn't have to push at something to see past. She stopped by the water's edge and watched the river flow. It was a muddy torrent, the earlier rain having washed the land into the water, large branches sweeping along with pronged, leafy fingers, catching on boulders before releasing themselves again.

The river was wide here, but it didn't seem very deep. Rocks poked through the surface like the smooth humps of hippo backs, some mossy and slippery-looking further out; but there was no sign of any man-eating reptiles as far as she could see. There wouldn't be crocodiles this far upriver, surely? Alex had just been trying to scare her, to throw her off guard and keep her nervous, as if somehow in his debt.

He wished!

She stepped carefully into the water, grateful for the borrowed pair of walking boots; they were waterproof – possibly bulletproof too, judging by their thickness – and she was able to stand up to her ankles with her feet still remaining dry. It was a luxury she suddenly appreciated.

She stood there for several minutes, feeling the water pressure pushing against her planted feet, staring into space. Her mind kept asking her the same question, over and over: what was she doing here? It was complete madness to be out here, doing this, much less with *him*. She'd acted so impulsively and been so determined to save this child, as if it could make up for the one she'd failed when she knew nothing could bring Lucy back. If only she'd not been so rash, she could have taken time to think it through – Rory would have had a chance to talk her out of it, or he could have joined her too if she had just given him time to sleep off his hangover . . .

She allowed her mind to ponder, for a moment, how that would have played: her, Rory and Alex, out here together. She gave a shudder. She'd never even told Rory about him – why bother? Alex wasn't relevant to her anymore; he had been in her life for all of four months, ten years ago, but she wouldn't have been able to hide her contempt of him any better with Rory present than she could now when they were alone. She could only imagine how awkward it would have been with the three of them.

She stretched her neck, feeling the stiffness already gathering from the trials of supporting Jed earlier, and then carrying the pack. She wanted to sit and rest for a while – or a week. She'd been on the move all day, from the moment she'd left Jed's village, pretty much, and she already knew she wasn't going to be able to relax in her hammock with *him* on the other side of the tarp. A large boulder sat hulking in the shallows upstream and she waded over to it, setting the buckets down and bringing her heels in to her bottom, resting her chin in her hands, her elbows on her knees. Why was she here? Why was she here?

Paco.

She thought of the boy – still sick, still lying on that mattress – and how, while her landscapes had changed so much over the past twenty-four hours, he still stared at the same patch of ceiling from the same corner of the room. Just the endless monotony of it must make him despair. He had been sick and starving now for seven months, lying there all that time. It was hard to conceive – and even harder to forget.

Her resolve hardened. Why was she here? She was here for Paco. And not just him, Jed too. Like it or not, Alex had been right – she owed it to him to see through what she had promised to do. She just needed to keep a calm head. Too much time today had been lost, but all things being well from here on in, she and Alex would get to Alto Uren tomorrow evening. Then, if they made a really early start the morning after and pushed through, they could get back to the microlight and maybe even get to Jed's village late the same night. If she pushed hard, Paco's situation could finally change just two days from now – and she could rid Alex Carter from her life again. Just forty-eight hours, that was all she had to endure. She could get through that for a sick child.

She heard the buzz of insects start up suddenly and realized the sun was setting quickly now; the intense colours had dimmed too, and there would be only a few more minutes before dark. It would be even darker among the trees, of course, and she needed to get the water back, she needed to help Alex get a fire going for some light . . .

She got up from the rock and filled the buckets, turning back towards the trees, stopping as she regarded them afresh. She stared. Now that she looked at it from this perspective, from the river . . . she couldn't see exactly where she'd stepped out. There wasn't much to distinguish one tangle of branches from another.

How many steps had she taken through the water to the boulder? Fifteen? Or perhaps twenty? And they'd been big, right, as she waded through . . . ? She walked upstream for a count of ten. She frowned as she turned and tried to remember the exact view garnered as she'd first emerged from the trees, but on the opposite side of the river, there was nothing especially significant about this stretch – no caves, toppled trees, rapids . . . She swallowed as she realized she had mindlessly headed in the direction of the river – following the sounds – without ever thinking to notice any distinguishing features of where they'd set up camp either.

How would she find her way back? As soon as she stepped into the trees again, even if she was only ten feet upstream from where she'd emerged, she could easily bypass their camp and take herself further with every step, heading deeper and deeper into the jungle, into the night.

She stood motionless, a bucket in each hand, as she looked back at the immensity of the jungle. She felt both frightened and stupid. How could she have been so . . . distracted? This wasn't Hyde Park—

'Hey.'

She turned with a start to see Alex stepping into the river, ten metres upstream of where she stood. He crouched down and washed water over his face, the droplets refracting the dying light of the day.

'Hey,' she mumbled back. Had he been watching her? Had he seen her dawning panic as she stared, frozen, into the treeline? She had an unwelcome feeling the answer was yes – that he'd come to check on her when she hadn't returned immediately, that it had occurred to him that she might do something so stupid as walk blindly through the jungle without taking some stock of where she was.

'Want me to carry those?' he asked, straightening up again and holding a hand out for the buckets.

'No, I'm fine,' she said, walking back up to where he was.

'Of course you are,' he muttered with a careless shrug, shaking his hands off and turning back into the trees again. She followed quickly after him, not wanting to lose sight of him again and wishing she hadn't been so stubborn. At least if she'd given him one bucket, she would have had a hand free for pushing through the bushes.

She kept him in her sights at all times, noticing after a minute or so a white stripe – like a lick of Tipp-Ex – painted on some of the leaves every few metres; she saw how his hands automatically reached for them, as if he was counting them as he passed. Within minutes, they were back at the camp.

She stopped at the sight that greeted her. He had built a small fire that was already flickering red and orange. But not just that.

'What did you do that for?' she asked, seeing how he had moved her tarp to the far side of her hammock, effectively creating a little room in which they both now slept.

'Room for the fire, for one thing,' he pointed out. It sat between their two beds. 'Plus your own protection. Falling branches are the number one cause of injury out here.'

'If a branch is going to fall on me, I doubt that thing's going to provide me much in the way of protection.'

He blinked, refusing to be baited. 'Anything to break the fall is helpful. Besides, the monkeys will have a great time pelting you with God knows what if they see you sleeping unprotected.'

She saw now that her hammock had been adjusted too; it lay slack and inviting, something to roll into, rather than cling to. Ordinarily she would have said thank you. But nothing about this was ordinary.

'I'll take those,' he murmured, and she startled as he leaned towards her and took the buckets from her hands. For a moment, she felt his skin brush hers and the unexpected silky warmth of it gave her shivers. It wasn't personal, it wasn't anything to do with him. The jungle was just so spiky and scratchy and tickly and hot and wet. Skin-on-skin out here felt like cashmere on a November night back home.

She watched as Alex put the gas camping stove on its feet and poured some of the water from one of the buckets into a small pan. He added a water purifying tablet and both sitting on their haunches on opposite sides of the flames, they watched in silence as it slowly came to the boil.

'You should keep your sleeves rolled down,' he said, glancing at her rolled-up shirt sleeves. 'Everything will be coming out around now.'

She didn't reply. She didn't want even to roll down her sleeves – to reject his advice just to reject him was a pleasing thought – but there would be only one victim of that mindset. What was that Buddha quote Holly loved throwing at her? Holding on to anger is like drinking poison and wishing the other person would die.

She went to roll down her shirt sleeves, but he suddenly

reached over and held her arm still. 'Hmm, that looks nasty,' he muttered, examining it closely. She saw she had a scratch on the underside of her forearm, just down from her elbow, several inches long. It was livid-looking, a raised red weal, and she flinched as he placed a hand protectively over it, feeling the heat. He looked up at her. 'How did you get that?'

'I don't know. I didn't know I had,' she frowned.

'Really? It looks deep. You must have felt it at the time?'

He was right. They both continued staring at the wound. '. . . It must have been when Jed was attacked,' she said, thinking back. 'There was a lot going on. I was running, trying to find him, and . . .'

His eyes narrowed as he regarded her afresh. He looked . . . she wasn't sure what. Concerned? 'And you're sure they didn't hurt you?'

She looked back at him coldly. She didn't want his concern. Or pity. 'Do I look hurt to you?'

Mission accomplished.

He blinked, letting her arm drop. 'No. You look damn near armour-plated to me.'

Another moment passed in which they said nothing, just stared at one another, both of them fundamentally bewildered to find themselves in this scenario.

He turned away, checking on the water, and she examined the wound herself more closely. She didn't like the look of it either – deep, angry, hot – and she rolled her sleeve back down. With the heat, humidity and lack of washing facilities here, she would need to take care it didn't become infected.

The light had all but gone and the fire threw out a spreading, warming glow. Alex poured a packet of rice into the pan, added some black beans and began stirring it. She went over to her rucksack and pulled out her head torch and the crank-up flashlight he'd given her, putting them both inside her hammock. She fussed with her mosquito net like it was the drapery to a four-poster, hearing the flames crackling at her back. She resented how easy he made this all seem. She knew perfectly well that to be out here alone would have been a very different story; the lessons Jed had taught her in childhood wouldn't have covered much of what had happened on the journey so far.

'Jed must be a good friend, for you to be doing all this for him,' he said, still stirring the rice as she came back to the fire, nothing else to do. He had found and rolled some logs – of course he had! – for them to sit upon, and she sank onto the nearest one.

'Anyone would do the same.'

He frowned. 'Would they? This isn't exactly camping for beginners.'

'Well, I'm not exactly a beginner. Not completely. Jed used to take me and Miles into the forest for overnight trips when we were little. He taught us what to look out for, all the things not to do.'

'Sounds like fun.'

'It was. Our times out here were the best we ever had,' she said flatly; she didn't like agreeing with him.

'That makes it even more of a shame, then, that you haven't come out in so long.'

'How do you know I haven't?' Her voice was arch.

But she knew he knew. He looked at her and away again, their shared past and what he'd done forever sitting between them. It was there in every conversation, every look. He cleared his throat.

Something overhead, hidden in the shadows, made a sudden movement, sending down a shower of leaves and seeds. She watched Alex catch sight of whatever it was, his eyes narrowing as he tracked it with a keen eye along the branch. He caught her staring and shrugged his eyebrows. 'Capuchin.' His eyes fell to the gold chain around her neck; it had a clear glass locket and a single ruby inside it – a gift from Rory on their first anniversary. 'Be careful, they like shiny things,' he said with an even stare, as though he knew that too.

She watched as he took the pan off the heat and carefully ladled the rice from the water. Two enamel cups were passing as their bowls and he filled them, handing her one. There was no cutlery.

'I don't understand how you have time to be out here doing this when the handover is happening in a few days,' she said in lieu of thanks.

'I don't,' he said, not raising his eyes as he scooped the food with his hands, the way she'd seen the children do in Jed's village. 'But it's an emergency, right? A kid is sick. Who's gonna put anything above that? If this is the only way to get him help, it has to come first . . .' He shrugged.

She stared at him with quiet fury. So there was something, then, that he put before his ambitions? There was some sort of moral code he lived by? He could deceive and seduce her in order to get the introduction he needed, but he wasn't so calculating as to put his career before a dying child? He wasn't *that* bad?

He didn't seem to notice her contemptuous stare. He seemed to be enjoying his meal, in fact, and she stared down at the cup of dinner. She began eating with her fingers, tentatively at first, but it tasted so good, the starch stinging her tongue as her body realized how depleted it was. She was starving and she hadn't even realized.

'Besides, it's not like organizing a dinner party or something,' he continued, picking up the conversation as though he hadn't just eaten a meal between comments. The cup – almost empty – was just inches from his face as he ate. 'The handover itself is pretty much just a paperwork issue at this stage; the lawyers will be pulling some all-nighters, I guess, but for me it's all ongoing long-term projects that are going to continue next week, regardless of who owns the land.'

She chased a bean with her finger. '. . . Like what?' she asked in her most bored voice.

He glanced up at her. 'Like right here.' He jerked his head around, his gaze scanning the towering giants that loomed above them, interlocking fingers and creating intricate aerial playgrounds for the animals that lived within their reaches. 'These trees are only nine years old.'

She stopped eating. 'What?'

'Yeah. Found a guy out here cutting down the trees and planting coffee bushes everywhere. We kicked him out, rewilded the place.'

'But they look . . . ancient,' she mumbled, looking around them both too.

'I know. It doesn't take much for things to return to their natural states and thrive again. Nature will always prevail. It's just a matter of providing the right protections.' He watched her from across the fire. 'In the past decade, we've reclaimed and reforested over seventy thousand square hectares of land; and in protecting and nurturing those habitats, it's saved countless species from extinction.'

She heard the pride in his voice. The lack of regret. He was telling her it had been worth it, that he'd do it all again. 'Well,' she said after a moment. 'No wonder my father's so pleased.'

She stared into the flames, grateful for the dry heat; it was a respite from the rain and humidity that had left her permanently damp all day.

'Tara . . .'

She looked up to find him staring at her. She could see there were things he wanted to say, apologies perhaps that would make him feel better – *I never meant to hurt you* – but they wouldn't change a thing. Because he wouldn't change a thing. She knew he'd do it all again. What had happened had happened, and flames would always divide them. She looked away, cutting him off with her silence.

'We'll wash up in the morning,' he said finally. He got up and, taking her cup from her, placed both in the pan of starchy water. 'This'll keep the bugs at bay till then.'

It was far too dark to go back to the river now and even the white-striped leaves would be hard to locate by torchlight. It might only be half past six, but it may as well have been three in the morning. The day had been gruelling and very, very long. She yawned and stretched, unable to stop herself.

'We should sleep,' he said.

'I won't argue with that,' she mumbled, walking over to her hammock and putting on her head torch. She turned it on and looked back at him. 'Where are the . . . facilities?'

'About twenty metres over there,' he winced, almost blinded as her torch beamed straight onto him. He pointed. 'See that red cord on the bush?' She looked over and saw a length of red twine tied to a bush, draped over the leaves and extending out of sight. 'Just follow it along. It'll take you straight over.'

'Huh.' Wasn't he just the Boy Scout! The simple ingenuity annoyed her. His constant mastery over somewhere so wild as this . . . At every turn he proved how he could thrive anywhere. Without her. Without anyone.

She felt the twine run through her palm as she walked carefully along, leaves and twigs rustling and snapping in the dark. She checked behind her several times to make sure the way really was clear before she unzipped her trousers, peeing faster than she ever had in her life. The jungle still teemed with activity, tiny rustles making her jumpy, the constant sound of flickering static in the air as insects chattered and scratched.

She hurried back again within minutes, stopping only as the glow of the campfire lit up the scene before her. She switched off her head torch as she approached, although she was quite tempted to 'accidentally' dazzle him again with it, but something in his movements made her stop walking. She stood hidden in the trees, watching as he shook out her hammock, sending multitudes of catkins and seeds that had fallen from the branches to the ground. He pulled hard on the ties of her hammock, checking they were secure. He pulled the mosquito net back across and tugged the tarp to make sure she was covered—

A twig snapped somewhere close by and the sound made him freeze and look up. She realized he couldn't see her in the shadows – the firelight was too bright – but he strode back to his own hammock and began rifling in his rucksack instead. She stepped out of the trees a few moments later and he glanced at her casually. 'All okay?'

'Of course.'

He disappeared the way she'd come. She knew without being told that they were going to have to sleep in their clothes despite the humidity; bare skin was to the jungle insects what roadkill was to buzzards back home. She pulled off her boots and climbed into her freshly swept hammock, refusing to be grateful for his secret kindness. A groan escaped her as her exhausted body finally stretched and became heavy. Her eyes closed almost immediately.

In spite of her earlier fears that she wouldn't be able to sleep near him, she knew now she would drop off quickly. The day had depleted her and her breathing was already heavy and slow . . .

Only distantly did she hear him come back a few minutes later, his footsteps pausing as he saw her already in bed, motionless. Feeling far away, she heard him move about for a bit, busily rearranging things, checking his own bed, kicking the fire apart and smothering the embers with damp leaves and soil so that it smouldered. There was another pause, a long one, then she heard his footsteps come over, closer. Right by her.

Her eyes were still shut – the lids leaden – but her heart was pounding as she felt him stare down at her, watching her sleep through the twilight hum. There was a slight rustle as her mosquito net was pulled back and something light traced over her hair, pushing back a tendril on her cheek. The touch felt shocking, almost electric, but she didn't stir.

There was a sigh, then his footsteps retreated again and she listened to the sounds of him pulling off his boots and getting into his own hammock a few metres away. She heard him settle into position and listened to the sound of his sighs begin to slow. She opened her eyes and stared into the remains of the fire, watching embers still flickering, refusing to burn out.

Chapter Twenty

She was woken by, of all things, a tapir snuffling about under her hammock. It took her a moment to understand what she was hearing before she opened her eyes, and then another moment to recognize what she was seeing. It was walking, nose down, through their small camp, having seemingly investigated and abandoned the promise of the starch-water pan and two cups within it. The pan was now tipped on its side, the water seeping into the earth.

She watched from behind the gauze of her mosquito net for several minutes, entranced, but also wanting to delay what was dawning on her again – the reality of her ex-fiancé, sleeping just three metres away.

She looked up to find Alex already awake, his eyes trained upon her like he'd been guarding her all night. She supposed she was precious cargo of a sort – an heiress; the daughter of his billionaire boss. His meal ticket.

'Morning.' His voice was thick with sleep, his accent seeming stronger first thing; she remembered that about him, pushed the memory away again. 'Sleep okay?'

'Yup.' She rolled onto her back, silencing any further encouragement for conversation and stared up, her overhead view of the trees blocked by the silver-backed tarp. It wasn't an Instagram moment, but it appeared to have kept the dew off her; it was literally dripping off the leaves all around them.

Blessedly, it wasn't raining – at least not yet – but the prospect of another long, hard day like yesterday, stretching before her, felt overwhelming. She was sweating already, her clothes clinging to her limbs, and one pat of her hair told her it was like a tangled birds nest. She gave a small groan and let her arm fall across her face like a strap. She wasn't sure she had the energy for this. She felt completely drained, besieged all over again by doubts over what she was doing out here. This wasn't her life; it wasn't her story. Somehow she had just . . . strayed into someone else's drama. *Her* story, right now, was supposed to be ten-hour sleeps and lie-ins and dancing on the beach and lots of sex with her handsome boyfriend. That was the point of holidays – normal life and all its unwelcome tribulations went on hold. It wasn't supposed to get *worse*. She should be having cocktails for breakfast and surfing under a full moon; not sleeping in a hammock, opposite the person she hated most in this world, with a giant herbivore snuffling underneath her.

Alex must have felt something similarly bleak because he rose with a sigh, checking his boots and scooping out a very large millipede before he put his feet in.

'There's some bananas for breakfast,' he said, going over and pulling one from a large banana hand that had been put on the tree stump. When exactly had he foraged those? she wondered in disbelief as he came over and held one out for her. 'Eat as many as you can. You'll need the energy today.'

As many as you can? She took it with a bemused look. Did he think she was going to eat five bananas for breakfast? As if.

She watched in silence as he picked up the pan and bowls,

grabbed the camping towel and headed in the direction of the river. She began to eat. Lucky for her, she loved bananas. Rory hated them. She thought of him as she chewed and wondered whether his hangover had gone, or if he'd decided to overlay it with a fresh one. He was going to be livid with her when she finally got back, she knew that. This wasn't the holiday he had signed up for – nor her, of course – and he wasn't going to be persuaded by her argument of finding leaves on a remote mountain spot in order to treat a child who quite possibly needed a liver transplant. She was going to be going back to a fight, she knew that.

The banana eaten and the tapir long gone, she swung her legs awkwardly out of the hammock; it was harder than it looked, and she was stiff as hell. She checked her boots too, before sliding her feet in. She itched at her arm absently – in spite of the net, plenty of mosquitoes had still found her, it seemed – and winced as she caught the edge of the nasty scratch again. Peeling back her shirt cuff, she took another look. It was even redder than before and definitely showing the first signs of infection. It was very hot to the touch, swollen and had what seemed to be tiny pustules or cysts developing in the most tender part of the wound. The humidity, no doubt, was accelerating her response.

She went to reach for the antibiotic cream in her kit, remembering only as she rummaged fruitlessly that Holly still had it for Dev's foot. 'Ugh, bugger,' she groaned. Just her luck. She would need to get it treated the moment they got back. The irony wasn't lost on her that she'd brought a dozen boxes of the stuff over for the clinic, but still had none for herself.

Her hands found something cool and unfamiliar in the bag, and she pulled out the small leaf-wrapped anti-mozzie ointment the Awa had given her yesterday morning. She had forgotten all about it, but the mozzies had found an easy target in her last night; something had to be better than nothing, surely? And if it was anywhere near as good as his headache drink . . . She realized her head was still clear – no vice-like grip at her temples, no stabbing pain behind her eyes.

He had told her to put the cream on before getting dressed. She glanced round but she was alone, Alex still at the river. Nonetheless, she turned herself so that her back was facing that direction as she quickly took off her shirt and bra. There was still a full bucket of water that she'd collected last night and, kneeling down, she splashed water onto her face, neck and torso, trying to wash herself as best she could.

It felt so good, even if only for a few moments, to have her skin clean and cool. She opened the parcel of leaves wrapped with vines; the ointment inside was thick and pungent and she rubbed it over her skin quickly. It was sticky and she waited impatiently for it to absorb into her skin. She couldn't wait long. The man who had once known every last inch of her body would be coming back any moment.

Sure enough, after several minutes, she heard the sound of footsteps coming through the bushes again – twigs snapping, leaves brushing – and she just had her bra clipped back on as he emerged with the clean pans. She kept her eyes down but she heard him stop at the sight of her, back to him, shrugging on her shirt. Her fingers kept fumbling with the buttons, not quite fast enough, but she reminded herself this was nothing he hadn't seen yesterday. She had reintroduced herself to him in exactly this look.

The fabric clung in patches to her sticky skin, hardly appealing when the shirt was already a day old. Finally, she looked up with defiant nonchalance, to find his dark hair was wet and slicked back like an otter's; she wasn't the only one who'd cleaned up. Unable to stop it, an image of how he used to look coming out of the shower, a towel around his hips, flashed through her mind.

Without a word, he took the now gleaming cups and pan over to his rucksack and began carefully repacking everything. They dismantled their tarps and hammocks, wound the rope back in. He collected the red twine and made sure the fire was completely out. Tara was struggling to fold her hammock down to a small packable size.

'Let me.' He held out a hand.

'No, it's fine, I can do it,' she replied, snatching it away from him.

'I know you *can*. But it's just a question of how quickly you want to get this done.' He stared at her evenly and after a moment's reluctance she handed it over, watching with intense irritation as he got it down to the size of a pillowcase again.

'Okay then,' he said several minutes later, with what she thought sounded like a note of weariness. 'Ready?'

Their backpacks were on and apart from a few oddly striped leaves, there remained no sign they'd ever been here.

'Yes.' The sooner they did this, the sooner they could get out of here. Back to Rory and the land of antibiotics.

She kept her eyes on his footprints as he walked, as determined as yesterday to keep pace with him and not to moan about the rubbing on her heel that started up almost immediately. Her boots might have been broken in – just not to *her* feet.

Within twenty minutes, their bathing efforts were undone, sweat rolling in rivulets down their skin and both were breathless as the humidity rose. She had no idea of the time;

she had been without a phone for two days now but, strangely, she was increasingly less in need of a clock. What did it matter if it was six o'clock or nine? The rules were simple – if the sun was up, they could walk and when it set, they stopped before they were pitched into another black, chattering jungle night.

Still they walked. She listened to the animals' conversations and tried to see them in the branches, she heard their songs rise with the sap, she noticed how the early sparkling sunlight sent golden shafts through the trees down to the forest floor, so that it was like walking through the place where rainbows end. The colours were intense – ten thousand shades of green, leaves that had felt blackish and mulchy in the rain yesterday now waxy and bright. The ground was firm underfoot again, shadows trembled with sharp edges and, in spite of her tiredness and resentment and developing blisters, she became aware of a strong feeling of gratitude, a recognition that life was beautiful.

It was even getting hard to keep hating him. Her gaze kept rising to him – obviously, he was her guide – but she saw the energy in his movements, his connection with this place. She wondered how many times he had walked this trail, watching as his hand would shoot out occasionally to brush against a particular plant, his fingers sliding over the leaves or flowers, looking up inquisitively beneath the canopies of particular trees. He seemed to see stories within the habitat, he could 'read' what he saw and understand the tiny, unseen lives that were being lived there in fragile balance. He moved with such self-assurance that she was able to relax; she didn't need to think or orienteer. She just walked and followed. Mile after mile. One foot after the other. Up the side of a mountain, right to the very top and back down the other side.

After several hours, Alex stopped and pointed. 'Over there.'

She followed the line of his finger, looking for something distinctive, but the land kept rolling away from them in grassy peaks, anonymous and endless.

'Okay,' she said tiredly, a trace of sarcasm lining the words. What was she supposed to be seeing exactly? 'If you say so.'

He seemed irritated by her response. 'I do say so.'

She arched an eyebrow, surprised but also somehow pleased to have got under his skin. 'Okay. What do you want? A round of applause?' He had about as much chance of that as forgiveness.

She saw the irritation bloom into anger behind his eyes. He resumed trekking again but his speed immediately began to feel punishing as he walked at a faster and faster rate as they went downhill. She half expected him to break into a jog and just openly run the rest of the way, but she refused to ask him to slow down. Was he wanting her to *chase* him? Was he trying to provoke her into asking him to stay back with her? To help her? She wouldn't do it, she wouldn't play the helpless little woman and let him be the hero in this. She simply kept up, kept on, matching him stride for stride, mile after mile, a stubborn silence jostling between them like a storm cloud as they headed down the valley.

She could hear a river close by – the rushing sounds growing louder; they were seemingly heading towards it – and she allowed herself to feel some relief as he finally began to slow down. They would stop now, have some lunch and rest for a while. Thanks to their silent battle, they had both pushed hard and must have covered some good ground. But her feet were killing her and she was exhausted; he'd been right – one banana had not been enough for her breakfast.

They stepped out of the trees, blinking several times as the open sky and bright light rushed at them. This part of the river was a different beast to the section they had camped by last night, or perhaps it was an entirely different river altogether? Ten times as wide and seemingly three times as deep, the water looked silken and elastic, a dark greenish-brown; it slunk heavily like an eel. She swallowed at the sight of it. Now *this* was crocodile country.

Downstream, she saw a deer drinking at the water's edge. Careful, she thought, seeing its ears twitch and then its head lift as their scent carried over on the breeze; in the next moment, it had gone.

The water was running clear, stretching out of sight. She glanced over at Alex, waiting for his cue for their next step. Clearly crossing here wasn't an option and she didn't much like the prospect of lunching beside these waters either, not with the natives lurking in places she couldn't see.

But, to her disappointment, it seemingly wasn't food that was on Alex's mind. He appeared to be looking for something. Standing on the river's shore, he had turned his back to the water and was peering back along the banks with a look of concentration.

'What are you looking for?' she asked, turning back too.

'I'm certain I left it here,' he muttered.

'Left what?'

His eyes narrowed, his voice distracted. '. . . A boat. I traded it with the Cabécar tribe about a year back.'

Tribes. Trades. These were insights into his life now. 'What did they trade it for?'

'Some radios. They're mountain people, pretty remote, but even they want to be a bit more connected – especially for after the handover.'

Tara frowned. Why did they need more contactability after then?

297

'It's a good boat,' he mumbled. 'Especially useful for me to have some way of getting about that doesn't involve walking a hundred miles. There's a lot of gorges in this stretch; it's hard going.'

'So you come here a lot, then?' It was a sardonic take on the age-old question but he missed her sarcasm. His eyes were still on the banks.

'Reasonably often,' he said distractedly, after a pause. 'There's a young female jaguar that we've been tracking and it quite often crosses around here.'

A jaguar? Tara looked around them again nervously but there was an ominous stillness to the trees. Only the river rushed past, in a hurry.

'Well, could someone have taken it?' she asked as he began walking along the shore, leaning into the bushes. He pulled out and straightened up again, unaware a leaf had become caught in his hair. Her gaze went to it but she resisted the urge to pull it free.

'It's possible,' he mumbled reluctantly, as if even to talk was a waste of precious energy. 'But unlikely. We're pretty deep in the jungle here and I pushed it right into the bushes so it couldn't be seen. Clearly I pushed it too damn far in.' He squinted as he looked up at the horizon and did something with his hands, as though pinpointing markers. '. . . I was certain it was in the crease . . . opposite the . . .' he muttered to himself.

Tara looked to the opposite bank, but saw only trees. Trees, trees, more trees.

'Ah!'

Suddenly he moved, walking with purpose towards a spot a hundred yards downstream. A tree was hanging slightly forward of all the others, one of its roots exposed from the riverbank like a lover's knot. Alex ducked as he reached it, pushing back the foliage and seconds later giving a shout of victory. He seemed very pleased to have found it and it occurred to her the rest of the journey must be gruelling if *he* was looking for shortcuts. She watched as he reached up and began heaving and pulling, slowly bringing out the prow of a very long and narrow wooden canoe.

'Feel free to help!' he called over to her sarcastically.

'Ugh.' She ran over and together they began dragging it off the bank, down towards the water. It was incredibly heavy and appeared to have been dug out from the trunk of a single tree; she could see the knife markings against the grain, a ladder of single seats carved across the width. It was crude and naive, but also beautiful. Sculptural, almost.

The canoe wobbled precariously as the near end was freed from the bank and nosed into the water. It reminded Tara of those old-fashioned wooden skis – so much longer and narrower than the modern designs; she didn't know how anyone used them without breaking their legs.

After much heaving and ho-ing, they pulled the far end free too and it landed heavily in the water with a splash. Alex pushed it fully away from the bank as the canoe began to float. 'Climb in,' he said, unbuckling his backpack and letting it slide off his shoulders, falling into the hollow of the boat behind him. 'I'll grab the oars.'

Carefully, wanting to get in before the water went above her boots – she didn't want wet feet again after yesterday's trainers debacle – she grabbed both sides of the narrow boat to try to stabilize it, and climbed in. It rocked alarmingly and she felt nervous; she was still wearing her backpack and feeling cumbersome and off-balance. She kneeled awkwardly, waiting for the boat to stop lurching, then straightened up, still on her knees, and quickly unbuckled the backpack. It was immediate relief, again, to get the weight off her shoulders, and the boat pitched and rolled as it fell heavily into the hollow behind her. Gripping both sides again, she turned, twisting herself onto the seat—

'Alex!' Her voice was a cry and he turned from where he was standing in a split stance, reaching up the riverbank into the undergrowth. He had one oar by his legs and was holding the end of the other, a vine seemingly having wrapped itself around it. She saw his expression change, his face instantly pale and his mouth fall into a perfect 'o' as he took in the sight of her – already heading towards the middle of the channel and drifting quickly away.

'Tara!' He instinctively dropped the oar and ran into the water up to his thighs, but the river was thirty metres wide at least. He could never wade out to her in time.

'Alex no! Get back! Get out of the water!' she cried, trying to stop him from following. The water was murky and thick – anything could be below the surface. 'The oars! I need the oars!'

They would be long enough to bridge the gap between them, something for her to grab at so he could pull her in again. He turned and ran back to the shore again but she was drifting quickly, ever further from reach and within seconds she was too far for the oars – even tied end to end – to reach. It was already too late. She was ten metres away, now twenty, the canoe gliding through the fast-flowing silky water like a cut reed. It had been made too well, by people who knew too much.

Alex was standing in frozen horror, up to his knees, knowing all of this. 'Twig! Get out of there! Paddle back! Use your arms! Paddle!'

She leaned over the edge and stared down into the unsee-able depths, but the sides of the canoe were low and even with just her transfer of weight, water slipped over easily, quickly, soaking her thighs and making her cry out.

'I can't!' she yelled. 'I'll capsize!'

She watched as Alex's mouth opened but no words came out. He didn't know what to say, how to help her – because there was no way to help her. For once, he couldn't do anything. '. . . Tara!'

She scanned the hollow of the boat for something she could use – something to throw over the back to act as a drag and slow her rapid progress – but there was nothing except a half-coconut ladle that would barely dole out soup. She thought fast about what they'd packed in their rucksacks, but it was just camping stuff – sleeping and cooking equipment.

She gave a whimper of terror, feeling her fear grow in waves. There was nothing they could do. Not her. Not him. Her grip tightened on the wooden hull as she looked back. Alex was already a diminishing figure, growing smaller by the second as the canoe slipped into the pleated central channel, as the river sped through the mountain pass. He was sprinting along the riverbank now, his momentary shock thrown off for action. The look on his face was no longer visible, but his shouts carried over, betraying his fear. She heard her name carry into the sky, up with the birds, pretty and useless.

She looked ahead again. The river – broad and smooth – stretched ahead like a silver mirror, deceptively benign, but she felt the incredible power of the current beneath the boat, propelling her along. The sun was still shining but the sky had grown hazy during their morning trek, and in the next moment, a cloud took the light away again, like the closing snap of a fan. She felt the shadows slacken upon her face, a cold chill rippling over her sweaty skin.

She glanced back. Alex was still running, his arms and legs like pistons, his shouts still carrying to her, but he was falling further and further behind. There was no way he could keep pace with her. The boat was now settled into the centre seam of the water and sailing along like a car on rails, smooth, fast and unimpeded.

She was alone. He was calling her but she couldn't hear even her own name anymore and she had to twist now to see him – and to twist meant rocking the boat. She just wanted to be still, as still and small and light as she could possibly be. She wanted to close her eyes and pretend this wasn't really happening. She wanted to curl up in the hollow of the canoe and just lie there till somehow, safety came.

The canoe rocked gently in the slipstream. There was nothing she could do. She was at the mercy of a river that was vast, fast-flowing and crocodile-infested. It stretched out peaceably, calm and deceptively tranquil, and had she been on the riverbank – bathing, washing up, filling buckets – she might have said it was beautiful. Instead, she warily watched the banks for company as she was led downriver, eyes searching for a ripple on the water's surface, bubbles popping, footprints in the muddy banks. But she was no expert – she didn't know the warning signs of what to look for, the specific areas these river predators might choose to lie in wait.

Alex was out of sight now. She looked back as best she dared, but even if he could have kept up with her, he couldn't have kept his line running along the water's edge. The landscape had begun to change as the miles slipped past, the stony shore now submerged as the river abutted the banks, the shallow tree-topped embankment growing ever taller, mud swapped for rocks. He would have been forced back into the trees, losing sight of the river's edge.

She had no idea how far she had travelled already. Two miles? Three? More? It was impossible to track. She saw Alex's pack lying in the front of the boat and realized what that meant for him too – with no supplies, he was as defenceless as her. He would have nowhere to sleep, no food—

Then she remembered. The small shovel he had used for digging the toilet! Could that work? As a paddle? Or even just as a brake? Could it slow her enough to allow her to steer her way back to the shallows?

She crawled forward on her hands and knees towards the pack. There were two bench seats between her and it, and every time she scaled a seat, the canoe rocked precariously, the waterline lapping the edges. Her nerve was failing her, her fear mounting as the boat continued to slice through the water, seemingly frictionless and hydrodynamic.

With one seat between her and the pack, she kneeled on the bottom of the boat and reached over for it, but the bag was heavy – twenty kilos at least. She heaved and strained as hard as she could, but she couldn't kneel on an unstable base and lift that weight above her head. She would need to get in beside it to unfasten the clips.

With a deep breath, she steeled herself to climb over the last seat, keeping her body low as she swung one leg over. Water slopped over the sides from the jerky movement and she watched it deepen the growing puddle along the base. Carefully, scarcely daring to breathe, she sat astride the bench and leaned down to unfasten the bag, sliding her arm down the back of it. Her hand groped for the narrow handle amidst the kit but everything felt industrial and unfamiliar . . . Was that it? Her fingers closed around a hard stem. She glanced up distractedly and in the corner of her eye, caught sight of something. Her head jerked up as she focused – disturbances to the water's surface were breaking up the serene banner of silk. The river was beginning to change, to shift, the cool smooth waters beginning to gurgle and chatter ahead. She peered into the distance and made out some rocks beginning to protrude again, as they had by the campsite. That meant it was becoming shallower – but it also meant obstacles, things to hit.

She tugged at the shovel – if that was indeed what it was – but the hammocks and tarps were tightly wedged in and it wouldn't budge, the spade seemingly caught against the saucepan at the bottom. From her newly elevated position on the bench, she started seeing the hazards that had been hidden as she kneeled in the hull – the tree branches submerged just below the surface, detritus that had been swept downstream in the torrents now catching on the riverbed. Just ahead, the tip of a rock jutted from the water almost imperceptibly, but it was what lay beneath that concerned her.

Behind it was another one, much larger, a white lace of skittering water spinning out behind it. She was being swept along at a rate that made missing it impossible and within moments the canoe was upon it, the prow propelled onto the hump as the water surged around it. The impact dislodged her from her precarious position astride the bench and she fell back into the hollow, hitting her head on the wooden seat behind. She lay there dazed as for several long moments the boat was stranded on the hummock, rocking erratically as water surged against it on one side and the river continued to rush underneath. She could feel it pushing against the stern of the boat with insistent force, dislodging it centimetre by centimetre, slowly nudging her off . . .

She cried out as the boat suddenly freed itself from its perch, floating sideways down the fast-rushing river for several metres, gaspingly cold water frothing over the upstream side again, before the canoe corrected itself and the prow swung back to nose through the water.

But there was no respite. The rocks were dotting the river like miniature islands now and two seconds later, she hit another one. Momentum meant the boat carried over it for a fraction before becoming wedged again, its prow out of the water, the river rushing around her on all sides.

She looked downriver and, at what she saw there, began screaming. She started hollering, yelling for someone, anyone – *Alex! Alex!* – to save her. She was screaming not because she wanted to get off this rock in the middle of the river, but because she wanted to stay on it. Because she could see now what had been hidden from sight before – that the rapids up ahead, seemingly shallow rills that might tear the bottom from the boat, actually preceded something far worse – a mist rising like a steam where the river dropped away, out of sight. It just . . . disappeared.

She could feel the force of the water still pushing against the boat, like hands and winds and wheels beneath it, relentless in its pursuit. It felt personal, merciless, as steadily the canoe began to shift in tiny increments. She looked about her wildly but there was nothing to hold on to, no tree branches to grab . . .

The rushing river ahead was now a rolling thunder so that even her screams were swallowed up as the canoe came free again. It skirred over the shallow rocks, hitting each one roughly and throwing her about but not stopping, the momentum too great. She tried to sit up but the boat was being tossed about as the water roiled and frothed, its prow caught and spun like a pinball by half-submerged rocks. She was travelling side-on again, water sloshing over the low sides by the gallon and sinking her ever lower. She could hear the boom of the water, see the smooth rock walls along the banks . . . But she couldn't see ahead, only up.

The boat hit another boulder, a huge one, the impact slamming her body against the hull, and this time she heard a crack that told her it was all over. Suddenly she was in the water, the boat spinning away from her in two pieces. There was no time to scream. Her hands reached for the sky as she went under, she felt the smooth ancient rocks buried under tonnes of pressure as her body was swept like a rag doll's over the edge. For a moment she was contained within the body of liquid, almost embryonic, suspended, protected . . .

Then it dispersed into a million tiny crystals and she felt herself fall.

Chapter Twenty-One

It was both endless, and over in moments. The pool below was deep and clear, the debris of the boat pushed under the surface and bobbing up seconds later, several metres downstream. She had landed hard, the breath knocked from her lungs so that she surfaced with a gasp. But her lungs wouldn't inflate. She was winded, quite literally breathless.

The spray from the falls made it impossible to see, a hard-falling rain that pounded down on her head, forcing her straight under the water again, her body sinking easily without the buoyancy of full lungs. Even below the surface she could hear the roar, feel the immense power tumbling above her and pushing her down. Her body was heaving and buckling, her lungs screaming to be reinflated and she knew she had to move away somehow, get to anywhere but here. Her limbs were flailing with conflicting instincts – to surface, to breathe – but she somehow co-ordinated herself enough to kick for three, four strokes, out of the way of the central chute.

Almost immediately, the water became calmer. Calm. She broke through the surface and the air was a slap against her skin like her primal first breath, oxygen filling her lungs as she coughed and wheezed, the spray misting her face. She kicked her way blindly towards the edge, catching hold of a rock and hugging it, sucking in the air in desperate gulps as though she was trying to strip the pigment from the sky. She pulled herself up enough to lie sprawled on her stomach, gasping like a landed fish until gradually she felt her diaphragm relax out of spasm and her body recover. Shock had her in its grip; she was shaking too much to stand, her limbs as weak and trembling as a newborn fawn's. She hardly dared look back, look up . . . What had just happened? It had all been so fast . . .

When she saw it, she cried out. She had come over *that*?

A drop of twelve, maybe fifteen metres, the water shot out like jets, the immense pressure pushing horizontally before it began to fall. Perhaps that was a mercy – it meant she had missed any rocks at the base.

She lay there shivering and shaking convulsively, her mind feeling unwieldy and shapeless too, as though she had lost her edges, like the water. But a voice, an instinct, was telling her to get out of this river and get warm. She wasn't safe yet.

Hauling herself up with effort, getting her legs out of the cold water and onto her hands and knees, she crawled over the rocks, sobs escaping her as her elbows buckled suddenly or a knee slipped, sending her crashing again, bruising her, dropping her back into the water. Nothing was working properly, her body disconnected from her brain, her limbs shaking violently. It seemed to take an age to cover any distance at all, the clamour of the falls pounding her ears and reminding her of their power, making her quake. She didn't want to go back in that water again. She couldn't get wet.

She was so close to safety, almost at the riverbank but for a narrow channel of water that slipped between the rocks. On any other day, she could have hopped it, a girlish leap with her arms in the air. But today she had almost been killed. Today she had cheated death. There was nothing left in her, adrenaline left her like a rag. She stopped where she was, unable to go any further.

The voice in her head was telling her she had to get dry but it was an impossible task now, too much to ask. The rock was flattish beneath her, almost like a ledge, soaking up the sun's heat. Just getting here had depleted her and she lay there, shivering in the sunlight, feeling its warmth steadily seep into her bones as she curled up into a tight ball. She let her head and limbs become heavy, watching the river glide past her at a stately pace, now that the excitement was over.

She stared impassively back at the falls. The cliffs rose up like a gorge on either side from where she lay, smooth and dark and completely impassable. Already it was impossible to believe she had come over the edge of it. She couldn't forget that feeling of falling, of her arms and legs flailing as she tore through space, the moment of impact . . . She couldn't forget the utter terror of thinking that she was going to die. She couldn't forget that as she waited for oblivion, her last thought had been of her first love.

The voice was distant, dream-like. Her fingers twitched against the rock, her mind resisting the call back to wakefulness. She wanted to stay under, stay still. There was solidity beneath her. No movement, no rushing. As long as she didn't stir, she would be safe. Nothing could reach her here—

'Tara!'

Her eyelids fluttered open, even though she felt pinned down, tethered to a force that was pulling her into the earth. She heard the heavy sound of footsteps running, panting drawing closer, the crash of water. And then her body was being lifted, being held, cradled in warm arms.

'Tara?' Alex's voice was torn velvet, his eyes wretched and desperate as he stared down at her, looking for signs of life, of injury. 'Tell me you're okay.'

It was a demand.

'I'm okay,' she mumbled, staring up at him, unable still to move. She had never felt so heavy. Her entire body felt filled with lead, her limbs stiff in their bent foetal position.

'I can't believe . . .' But his voice trailed off as he looked back at the falls. He immediately paled as his heart forgot to beat. She watched his Adam's apple bob up and down as he swallowed, imagining.

He looked back at her and she felt like a child. Tiny in her father's arms. Safe again. She felt a feeling that she hadn't felt in so many years now as his eyes settled upon hers. It was like a lock turning within her. Or perhaps unlocking. Fundamental bolts and slides moving into position, giving her shape. She felt tears begin to stream from her eyes, silent and endless – fear superseded by relief. Now she was safe.

His hand smoothed over her face, pressing against her skin, taking a gauge of her warmth. 'You're freezing. We need to get you out of those wet clothes.' He stared at her tears as they raced like raindrops down a window. 'Christ, I can't believe . . .' His voice was hoarse. The apple bobbed again. He cleared his throat. '. . . Can you sit up?'

She could feel his heart pounding against his chest. It sounded like a racehorse's, one of her father's winners at Cheltenham. Had he run all the way? How many miles? Had he known these falls were here? Surely he must have done – that was why he'd looked so scared as she'd been swept away. He'd known this was where she would end up. Could he have conceived that she would survive it?

She couldn't. The sensation kept ripping through her still, her body falling through space as the body of water broke apart into tiny droplets and just . . . let her go. It wasn't an unfamiliar feeling, she realized. She felt like she had been falling for a very long time, bracing for the landing and knowing that when she did, she would break apart.

'Come.' Gently he gathered her up, bringing her to an upright position. 'We've got to dry these clothes while there's still heat in the day.'

She felt his fingers against her skin as he unbuttoned her shirt and peeled it off. He did the same with her trousers too, unlacing her boots and pulling off her socks so that she was in only her underwear. Yesterday, Jed. Today, she was the patient.

'You have a guest,' she heard him murmur and she glanced for long enough to see him detach a leech from her calf. '. . . They get in everywhere. It'll itch for a bit, but don't worry, I know something for that.'

She didn't respond. He quickly unbuttoned his own shirt and pulled it on over her, bending her arms through the armholes, buttoning the buttons; she seemed unable to help herself. 'There, that'll keep you covered. Sunburn is the last thing you need right now.'

'I'm okay,' she mumbled, her voice just a faint shadow, surprising even her.

'No. You're in shock.' His hands ran over her head, smoothing her hair as he gazed down at her. She felt little again. He looked back to the falls as if magnetically drawn, his despair silent but tangible, like a dog's mournful melancholy. She sensed he didn't know what to do. He looked around them, stiffened suddenly. 'Hang on . . . Wait there.'

She wasn't going anywhere. Where was there to go anyway?

They had no provisions, no shelter. She could hear him in the water, his legs wading in long, slow, powerful strides. They receded and then, after an absence, drew near again.

Something red came into her field of vision. Slowly, she looked up. He was dragging the rucksack – one of them.

'It got caught on that branch!' he said, his voice infused with an incredulous wonder. She watched on blankly as he took it to the shore and unpacked it. Litres of water spilled onto the stones, staining them dark as slowly, methodically, he began opening everything out and laying it all in the sun.

Hammock. Tarp. Lines. Stove. Sheathed knife. Collapsible buckets. A few packets of dried noodles. Even the strange package Don Carlos had given her, which she hadn't had enough time to open, her curiosity going unanswered. He sat on the stones beside the river, next to their worldly belongings, his elbows on his knees as he waited for everything to dry. He watched her in silence. She curled back into her foetal position on the rock – still shivering but less than before, still wearing his shirt – and watched him back. Neither one said a word, her blinks steadily becoming longer, her heart rate slowing. The river had become a tranquil place again, a beauty spot where dragonflies danced and toucans squabbled for fruit in the trees. It was an idyll, a tropical paradise. Nothing bad could ever happen here. It was a beautiful day. The last thing she thought, as her eyes closed again, was that the sun wasn't even yet at its highest point in the sky.

Chapter Twenty-Two

They set off when there were still two hours of light left. Alex was sure they could make it. Their morning's speed-hike, coupled with her runaway ride and his riverside sprint, meant they had covered far more ground than he had anticipated and he was confident they could get to the village before nightfall, even though they were walking at half the speed of the morning leg.

He kept turning back every few paces to check she was still there, still okay. She saw now, as she followed in his footsteps, that his clothes were torn and ripped in places, that he had some nasty cuts to his forearms, a vivid grass and mud stain along the seat of his trousers as though he'd gone sledging without a sledge. He looked like he'd been in a fight with something a lot bigger and more vicious than him. She wondered again what he'd been through, getting to her.

Everything had dried now, including her clothes, which were stiff and crackly, and her second sleep had been powerfully restorative, somehow effecting a profound change. Perhaps knowing she was protected, her mind had been able to relax, but when she had woken – under his watchful gaze for a second time today – she found her nervous system had calmed, her strength had returned, her body was responding to cues once more and the fizzing bitterness between them had dissipated. If they weren't exactly friends, they were no longer enemies either.

They talked easily as they went, feasting on fruit for lunch – fresh mangoes he harvested from some trees as they walked, some bananas. 'There's more bananas in this country than there are stars in the sky,' he declared, using his belt as a strap to help him shimmy up the tree trunk, the way she'd seen Jed do when she was a little girl.

'You've gone native,' she said, as he climbed down with ease and offered her one.

'No, I always was more feral than civilized,' he shrugged.

The statement puzzled her. 'That's not true.'

'Sure it is. You just chose not to see it.'

'You weren't *feral*,' she argued. 'Just because you grew up on farms, it didn't mean you were—'

'I wasn't ever going to fit into your world, Tara,' he said simply. He stared at her with an inscrutable expression, before setting off again and leaving her watching him in confusion.

They walked like they were strolling in the park, the tense hurry of last night and this morning now replaced by something softer, kinder.

'Don't lick that,' he said at one point, pointing out a tiny red frog perched on the underside of a giant palm leaf.

'I hadn't planned on it. I'll have you know my frog-licking days are behind me.'

His laughter rolled through her. He pointed out birds – scarlet macaws of course, but also kiskadees, orioles, woodpeckers; and her favourite, the toucans, who made a wonderful clacking noise as they tried not to bump into trees with their oversized beaks. He identified plants. 'This one's called the anaesthetic tree,' he said, getting out his knife and hacking away a small twig.

'Ah, the famous propofol tree. Yes, I've heard of it,' she quipped drily.

He shot her a look. 'Chew on that.'

She chewed on the twig. With minutes her mouth and tongue were tingling, all taste gone. 'Huh. Could be handy I guess.'

'It has been. Many times.' He began walking again.

'For you?'

'Yeah, once or twice.'

'Like when?' she pressed.

'Well, there was one time I was out looking for some quetzals that we'd heard were nesting here. They usually stay on the Pacific side of the Talamanca mountains.'

'So quetzals are . . . birds, then?' she clarified. He always had assumed everyone had a PhD in biology.

'Yes, very famous ones,' she could almost hear him rolling his eyes. 'Although now sadly nearing extinction. They're beautiful – dark green wings, scarlet stomach, really long tail feathers and a cute little buzz cut. They're hard to spot. I'd been out here for three days looking and was just giving up when I had an unfortunate encounter with a protective mother peccary and ran straight into a manchineel tree.'

He looked back at her to see if she understood the meaning.

'You lost me at buzz cut,' she shrugged, wearily picking her way over a tree trunk.

'The manchineel tree is known as the Tree of Death.'

She shrugged up her eyebrows. 'Are we getting a little dramatic?'

'Their fruit looks like small apples. If eaten, they cause vomiting, fever, ulceration of the throat, haemorrhage of the upper digestive tract, slowing of the heart, coma and death.'

She nodded. This was her kind of language. 'Wow. Impressive.'

'Clearly, I didn't eat the apple. But the bark and leaves are toxic too – they give you lesions, blisters. You shouldn't even sit under the trees in the rain because the drops carry off the toxic resin.'

'Nasty.'

'Yeah, and I basically ran up to it and gave it a hug.'

'Whilst running from a close relative of the pig?'

'Hey!' he protested, laughing. 'I'll have you know it was a nasty incident! I managed to get some anaesthetic leaves and rub them on quickly, but I've still got the scars – look.' And he took her hand and pressed her fingers against his upper chest and neck.

Ten years contracted to a single breath as the sudden contact of her skin upon his made her own laughter fade. She could feel the scars beneath her fingertips, skin she had once known so intimately now marked by events experienced in her absence, and it made her wonder – how much had he lived without her? How many stories and adventures; how many women . . . ?

She felt a white flash of pain sear inside her, memories she had long ago suppressed shooting up like fireworks. 'Alex—' She tried to pull her hand back but the pressure on her hand increased.

'Tara.' His voice split and at the sound of it she instinctively looked up. A mistake – the passion that had surged between them from their first ever meeting was there still, impossible to deny; like an underground shoot reaching for the light, she understood now that it hadn't withered but had simply been buried. 'Tara, you have to forgive me.'

She swallowed. 'No.' The word was unequivocal.

316

'I know what I did, the way I hurt you.'

She looked straight back at him, forcing back down all the feelings that wanted to surge and be seen, acknowledged, felt. '. . . You don't know anything.'

'You have to forgive me,' he repeated. 'It's been ten years!'

'I know,' she said simply. 'Our child would have been nine.'

Her words, softly spoken, were like thunderclaps and she watched as the confusion ran over his face. His hand dropped from hers and he stumbled back, away from her, as though she'd hit him.

'. . . *What?*' His voice was a whisper.

'I was pregnant. I'd planned on telling you after the engagement.'

She spoke quietly but with power. How many years had she waited to say these words? She saw the pain travel through him, an electric current she had been able to shoot across from her heart to his, leaving him trembling. But there was no joy or satisfaction to be had from it. It didn't mitigate her loss. She felt only dismay that the secret she had so excitedly wanted to tell him in bed one night, all those years ago, was instead being revealed like this, here, a world away. She could still see her and Holly's ghosts standing on the bridge in Hyde Park, both thinking they knew their own futures. They had each been so utterly wrong.

She looked straight back at him, determined to answer the next question before he even asked it. 'I miscarried nine days later.' The intimation was clear.

'Tara—'

'It's why I can't forgive you, no matter how much time passes,' she said simply. He looked broken, but she was resolute. *The heart vibration is weak. You lost a child.* She had spent ten years living with this and the pain was still the same. She didn't feel any less empty, and unburdening herself of the secret didn't make her feel any less haunted. He knew now too, that was all. He understood, at last, that they had lost so much more than the last decade, that there was no way back, whatever chemistry told them otherwise. 'What you took from me, you can never give back. And no matter how kind or generous you may be – now that you've achieved what you wanted – we're not friends. I just need you to help me help Paco and then we're done.'

He stared at her in an anguished silence. She could see the words and arguments climb into his eyes and onto his lips, only to be discarded again. They would have had a child, nine by now? There was nothing to counter that.

She watched as he swallowed and looked away, his body turning as if in slow motion. He put one foot in front of the other and they resumed the trek in silence.

There were no more jokes or stories now, the miles ticking along as the sun charted its descent. The jungle was growing blacker in the fast-fading light, birds like bats against the dusk, an eerie grey mist beginning to wind through the trees.

'That's it over there, in the cloud forest,' he said finally, stopping at the edge of a dramatic, narrow gorge, a pass between two mountains. The land dropped away steeply between the cliffs, down to a river fifty metres below. A single-path rope bridge connected one side to the other, looking as intricate and fragile as a spider's web; the treads were simply split logs. Tara looked down again, not sure she trusted putting her weight onto it, but Alex stepped out and walked across without hesitation, so she followed. In this, at least, she trusted him.

She felt the change in habitat on the other side immediately. Three steps into the trees and the sky became a notional thing, completely blocked from sight by interlocking canopies that soared thirty, forty metres high. Low-sailing clouds bumped around the trunks, the ground cover reduced, making it easier to walk. Within minutes they were panting again from the steep gradient.

'What's that?' she asked, as a sound came to her ear unlike anything she had heard since her first step into the jungle. In contrast to the cacophonous sharp shrieks and calls, cries and shouts of the animals that lived here, this was soaring and melodic: a clean, mellow whistle that seemed to wind around the trees, beckoning her.

'Pan pipes.'

It was haunting, especially in the gloaming, and it stopped abruptly as they reached a grassy clearing and stood by the edge of the trees.

'This is it,' he said simply.

She looked at him. They were here? Just like that? After a trip in which Jed had been attacked and seriously injured, in which she had been ambushed by her past, where she had cheated death . . . they had made it? Somehow, it felt anticlimactic.

She looked on at the conical huts fully thatched to the ground with rushes, similar in style to those in Jed and Sarita's village, but more dispersed. A man was standing by one of them, staring back, as if he'd been waiting for them. He was wearing Western trousers but with a fringed rush tabard over his chest, and in his hand was a small set of bamboo pipes.

Alex stepped forward, speaking in a language she didn't recognize. He gestured back in her direction, the man's gaze coming to her and off again. He smiled, revealing gappy teeth, then gave a laugh that sounded surprisingly *matey*.

Alex gestured for her to come over. 'Tara, this is William, the Awa.'

'William?' she repeated in surprise. They'd just trekked two days to get here. They were by anyone's definition in the middle of nowhere, and the Awa sounded like a public school boy from the Home Counties?

William regarded her with a look of open scrutiny, as though he was somehow reading her. Could he see what she'd been through to get here? Would he even believe it? Her face was sunburned on one side from where she'd slept on the rock, she had cuts and bruises, she was covered in mosquito bites, her leg itched like mad where the leech had stuck on. Did that tell him enough, or was she wearing her terror – and exhaustion – like a dress too?

'He's reading your energy,' Alex said in a low voice, as the Awa – as in Jed's village – took her hand and held it, his eyes closed for a moment. 'Standard greeting here.'

William opened his eyes after a few moments and stared back at her, nodding as though she had confirmed something for him. He reached forward with his other hand and placed it on her forearm, right above her wound. She immediately winced. The scratch that had been showing signs of infection felt significantly worse again.

William took a closer look at it, peeling back her sleeve, and she wondered how he had known it was even there. The infection was setting in fast, the pustules growing larger and whiter. She stared at it, trying not to panic. The jungle was no place to accrue an infection, clearly, but she reminded herself she would be back to civilization in less than two days. That would be enough time, surely?

William walked off into the trees a few metres away, without a word, returning several moments later with a clutch of leaves.

Of course, more leaves, she thought to herself, obeying

320

politely as William beckoned for her to follow him. She trailed him into the largest hut, her eyes widening in amazement at the sight that greeted her. It dwarfed the scale and grandeur of Jed's Awa's hut. Carved wooden masks hung from the walls, bows dangled by their strings; decorated gourds and carvings of animals she almost recognized, but not quite, were placed on tables and makeshift ledges propped against the walls. Hides of snakes and deer hung drying from lines, and some loosely woven twine hammocks were suspended between the giant wooden struts.

He put the leaves down on a table and, with a small knife, chopped them roughly, releasing the sap and grinding them into a paste. He worked quickly and efficiently. No one spoke. Tara just watched, too tired to protest; there was something hypnotic about his sense of purpose. Within a few minutes, he had created a bright lime green unguent and began applying it to her arm. It smelled foul but didn't sting at least, Tara watching on sceptically as he took one large, waxy leaf, different from the others, and stuck it over the mixture like some sort of plaster. He pressed it down with the palm of his hand, holding it there for a count of ten and then stepping away. It didn't budge when she moved her arm. He murmured something.

'It'll feel better tomorrow,' Alex translated.

'*Gracias*,' was all she said. She could feel the ointment already sinking into the festering wound and a distant part of her could hardly believe that she – a doctor – had allowed a complete stranger, without any proven medical credentials, to treat an established infection; he could easily make it worse; he hadn't taken a patient history, he didn't know whether she had any allergies, contra-indicated conditions . . . But the day had stripped her of any mental rigour. She had never been so tired, her accident and then the sad showdown with Alex leaving her fully drained.

The villagers had begun to come into the hut now, gathering at the threshold and staring at them with curious eyes. A babble of chatter quickly grew as the crowd expanded, almost everyone's eyes on her, for they seemed to recognize Alex. Then, as if on an agreed cue, the children ran forwards, excitedly surrounding him and pulling at his trousers, asking to be picked up, their eyes wary upon her all the while. Tara watched the way he gave them high-fives, greeting them with smiles that for once didn't reach his eyes.

'Beauty,' one of the women said, coming closer. She was dressed in a dark red skirt and blue cotton top, a young child swaddled to her chest, its legs poking out the bottom of the sling. Slowly she traced a finger around one half of Tara's face, but looking back at Alex. 'Very beauty.'

Some of the children were edging closer to Tara now, seeing that she didn't bite. Their hands were reaching for her legs, as if to touch her was to see she was real. One little girl in particular was staring up at her with almond-shaped eyes and Tara instinctively stretched out her arms to her. She lifted her up and the two of them looked at one another with a mutual curiosity.

'Hi,' Tara smiled. '*Hola*.'

'*Hola*,' the girl whispered back, shyly.

'You doctor lady?' one of the women said, coming closer too.

Tara was surprised, and not just because she could speak some English. How could she have known what Tara did for a living? '. . . Yes.'

'From England?'

'Yes.' She looked over quizzically at Alex, now standing

there with a three-year-old on each hip, an inscrutable expression on his face as he saw the questions buzz through her brain: how did they know she was a doctor? How did they know she was English?

The laugh that she'd heard earlier, outside, cackled behind her again. 'Alex spent many months here,' William said, as if that explained it.

She was dumbfounded. '*You* speak English too?'

'Of course.'

'But why didn't you say so when I arrived?'

'You would have been disappointed, I think?' He smiled, his eyes twinkling mischievously as he brushed a hand over the tabard. Had that been for her benefit, then? 'When our friend here first became the . . . big boss man . . .' William rolled his eyes. 'He wanted to learn the ways of the jungle from the Indigenous peoples.' He gave a shrug. 'So we bartered. He taught us English and in return, he could live with us and learn our ways.'

'Oh.' It was another insight into the life he had found After Her. So different to the one she had built After Him. She wondered how long he had lived here with them, and when? Was it a month after he arrived? A year? Six? It was another clue as to the adventures he had had without her, the life he had lived without her by his side, and she felt a fresh pang of loss, another mourning for the life she hadn't had. He had asked her to marry him, to share her life with him . . . they might have had their child. But instead they had diverged – an ocean between them and not a word in ten years.

Tara watched Alex put the wriggling children back down again and they ran off, laughing and shrieking, as he ran a hand through his hair. He looked older. Tired.

'Well, talking of the "big boss man", Tara's father is *my*

323

boss,' Alex said pointedly. William appeared to absorb his meaning as Tara saw his expression change before her eyes.

'Then what are you doing over here?' William asked him. 'The ceremony is soon.'

'Yes, three days from now, I'm aware,' Alex sighed. 'Tara has come to help a friend. They need the black star leaves for a medical treatment.'

William's brow furrowed deeply. '. . . It is the spider disease?'

'Apparently,' Tara nodded, still holding the curious little girl on her hip.

Alex went on, 'William, we've had a hard journey to get here and Tara's exhausted. She and her guide were attacked yesterday, down by the rangers' station, and clearly time is of the essence. We'll need to leave again at first light tomorrow.' He lapsed into the Awa's language again and as he finished speaking, William met the gaze of an older woman standing by the door and nodded to her. She came over and William spoke to her in a low voice.

'She's going to get the black star leaves before the sun sets,' Alex translated.

'Oh. But shouldn't *I* . . . ?' she began, before stopping herself with a wry smile. Did she honestly believe it made a difference who picked it and when? But she thought back to how her headache had cleared . . . 'Wait, I've got something from Don Carlos.' She got up and hurried over to the rucksack, retrieving the wrapped parcel he had given her on her departure. 'Apparently this has to be opened only when the leaves are being picked,' she said to him. 'I don't know what it is.'

'It's a talisman, believed to optimize the healing qualities of the plant.' Alex took it and handed it to the woman, who accepted it with a look of understanding, as though she had been expecting such a thing. Without a word, the woman slipped from the hut. If only out of curiosity, Tara would have liked to have gone with her and watch the obscure ritual, but the woman would need to be quick. They had only minutes of daylight left.

'Come. You are in need of food and rest,' William said, and with a sweep of his arm, he led them over to the communal area where wooden stools – old tree stumps – were arranged in a circle around a low-flickering fire.

Tara put the little girl back down, sending her off with a wink, and sat where she was put in front of the fire, watching as the villagers began to busy themselves with hospitality. She was too tired to object to anything and she gratefully accepted the drink which was placed in her hands; it was a deep amber colour and smelled as potent as brandy.

'What is this?' she asked Alex.

'Aguardiente. Or "burning water",' he replied, watching as she began sipping eagerly. 'Careful, it's strong stuff.'

She shrugged, feeling grateful for anything that took the edges off her day. It had been one to remember, for all the wrong reasons. The sensation of falling still kept jolting through her as though her mind was stuck on a trauma loop, and her heart ached from disturbing long-held secrets. She noticed Alex wouldn't quite meet her gaze now either. Their past, which he had tried so hard to pretend could stay in the past, pulsed bloody and raw between them now.

William sat down opposite them, but the teasing quality she had briefly discerned in his eyes on arrival had gone – the revelation that she was a Tremain and no mere eco-tourist appeared to have changed things – and he looked once more like the Village Elder of her stereotypes. 'Who was it who attacked you?'

She was surprised by his return to the topic. 'I don't know. I didn't see them. It was my friend Jed who was hurt, not me.'

She saw William's gaze lock with Alex's. '. . . What?' she asked them both.

'There's been a lot of trouble lately, that's all,' Alex said with a dismissive tone, still with his eyes down. 'Certain ranchers and plantation owners don't want the handover to go ahead, so we've been seeing an escalation in . . . problems.'

She remembered the ranch worker's hostile stare by the truck, the way Jed's car had been hemmed in, the slashed tyre, almost being run off the road . . . 'What sort of problems?'

He hesitated. 'There's been some thefts, fires, intimidation tactics . . . Petty stuff. But it's all in hand.'

'Petty stuff?' she echoed. 'Beating a man of Jed's size into unconsciousness isn't petty stuff. It's serious assault, if not attempted murder!'

He lifted his gaze to hers at last. 'Like I said, we're dealing with it. They're just scare tactics. Nothing is going to stop the handover going ahead on Friday.'

But Tara saw a bleakness in his eyes she'd never discerned before and for several moments they stared at one another in a silence that was louder than their words.

William, she noticed, seemed troubled too. She wondered how much he knew and if there was anything he wasn't saying either. She had a strong suspicion Alex was downplaying the issue.

'Alex, is there something going on that you're not telling me?'

'No.'

'Has a threat been made?'

'It's fine. They're all talk.'

Wasn't that exactly what Jed had said? And look at him

now! She didn't blink as she stared back at him. 'Are they going to do something on Friday?'

'No!'

But he had answered too quickly, too vehemently. 'Is it targeted at my father?'

'Tara, I've told you—'

'You tell lies, Alex! I don't believe what you tell me,' she snapped. 'Is my father in danger?'

He stared back at her, looking shocked and angry. 'We've informed the security teams. Your father's PPO is aware and we've briefed the relevant government offices. I give you my word that nothing is going to happen to him. These people want to make a point and they're out to make a scene, but there's no way they'll get anywhere near him. We both know a man like your father is incredibly hard to get close to.'

It was his counter-strike, the verbal slap back. 'Yes. I'm very aware,' she said quietly.

He stared back at her for several long seconds, then looked away, the ball of his jaw pulsing rhythmically, words unsaid. But she knew what he wanted to say to her: that in spite of what she'd told him, he could justify what he'd done, that he still fervently believed he'd been right to sacrifice her – them – for the greater good.

Was he right? How many hours had she spent listening to her father over the years, expounding the virtues of his legacy project? It would bring in billions of dollars in eco-tourism, protect the wildlife habitats as well as the Indigenous cultures, promote reforestation, reduce carbon emissions . . . She could list the benefits in her sleep. Her broken heart had been the only fly in the ointment and there were times she had half expected her father to be nominated the patron saint of Costa Rica. So how could it be that he was now under personal threat, and their friends and staff were being attacked?

An eruption of dirty laughter, a universal sound whatever the language, made her look over. The women were bustling about, preparing the food – peeling, chopping, slicing, glancing over surreptitiously in the direction of their unexpected guests every so often, some of them giggling with their heads together. She wondered whether she was the butt of their jokes as curious eyes crept upon her.

The woman came back into the building and walked straight over to William. She opened her hands to reveal the bundle she was carrying – a large bunch of freshly picked leaves, now wrapped in soaked muslin. Alex looked on with bright eyes, glancing over at her with an intense look. So this was the great cure they had come searching for?

'Good,' William nodded, examining the leaves carefully, picking up a few and sniffing them deeply. He glanced at her, seeing how she watched him. 'They must be picked at dusk, when the sap is falling.'

'Ah yes, dusk,' she replied politely, remembering the Awa's instructions as they had left Jed's village. She had almost lost her own life trying to get these herbs, in the full knowledge they would be as effective against hepatitis as drinking lemon juice or only bathing on days with an easterly wind.

It's a means to an end, she reminded herself, as her mind went back to Paco and the thought of him lying on that mattress. It was for him that she was sitting here, being hosted by an entire village and sipping something so strong, her own brush with death was beginning to feel like just a warm and fuzzy dream.

She watched Alex, seeing how easily he smiled as he talked to William, the way he stretched his legs in front of him, crossing them at the ankles like a Victorian gentleman in his parlour. It was true that wherever he lay his hat . . . He could talk to anyone; from a tribesman to a billionaire, he treated them all equally.

A young woman, very pretty, came over with some chopped fruit and berries arranged on banana leaves. Tara saw the way her eyes rested on Alex, waiting to meet his gaze as he looked up with a grateful smile. A moment held between them. He glanced over at Tara but she looked quickly away, remembering how Jed had told her yesterday morning about the tribes' polygamous culture. It was disingenuous to think that, if he'd lived here for several months, Alex wouldn't have formed a relationship with at least one of the women. Was that what the women's laughter was about? Her heart ached a little harder.

William was watching her too and he seemed to smile knowingly as she caught his eye. 'Are you married?'

It was the inevitable question, the one any woman in her thirties – or even approaching thirty – was asked every time she met someone new. Even in the jungle. 'No.'

'No? This is impossible to believe!' William laughed, suddenly jocular and slapping his thigh like she'd told a great joke. 'Has not Alex Carter tried to make you his wife?' He looked incredulous, as though surely the two Caucasian people in the hut must marry each other?

Tara looked between the two men and wondered again what Alex had told them about her; definitely something, she knew. She was the doctor lady from England. But what else? Former fiancée? The one who got away? Just an ex?

She decided to get her account down, too.

'Well, as I'm sure you must know, he tried, a long time ago,' she replied lightly after a pause. The retort was relayed back through the crowd in a verbal Mexican wave as the villagers – some translating for others – erupted into cheers and laughter at the boss's expense. Perhaps they hadn't known *that*.

'But you said no?' William gasped, enjoying himself immensely.

'I should never have said yes,' she said simply with a little shake of her head, as though it was but a trifling thing. She could feel Alex's stare like hot coals on her skin as she forced a smile, the drink – *burning water* – scorching her throat, making her chest tight.

'Well, then, perhaps you would like to consider one of our fine men? They are fast and strong and make big babies.'

At his words, Tara felt the world stop spinning. She saw Alex's face freeze in her peripheral vision. '. . . That's a generous offer,' she said, recovering herself. 'But I fear my boyfriend would take exception if I returned from the jungle with a husband.'

It was the kind of flippant retort she would use back home and William was laughing uproariously. They all were, even the children, who surely couldn't understand what was being said but were excited by the novelty of tonight's guests. The hut reverberated to the sound of hilarity.

Tara wouldn't look at Alex, but she could feel her cheeks burning under his continued scrutiny. They were even, her point made. If he had had lovers, so had she. He knew, now, about Rory, if he hadn't known before – and she wondered just how discreet her father was on his visits out here, talking easily about 'the family'. How else could Alex have known about her career?

At least he would understand now that she had someone to hold her, to miss her. He would know that when she told this boyfriend about Jed's attack and her accident, he would be horrified and angry and upset; her new lover wouldn't be able to bear that she had suffered like this. In a funny sort of way, Tara couldn't wait to tell him, to see the love on his face. It would be so . . .

She remembered how ragged Alex's voice had been as he found her on the rock, the look in his eyes as he'd evaluated her for injury, the feeling of his hands smoothing her hair in the hammock, how he had sat on the bank and watched over her as she slept.

Slowly, she looked up. Alex was staring at the ground with a look that made her body limp. Her words, sharpened to a point, had hurt him, drawn first blood.

The little girl Tara had lifted earlier came running over, holding out something. It was a necklace, wound from grasses and interwoven with dried seeds and seed pods. 'For me?' she asked in a hollow voice, raising another smile. Polite as ever.

The little girl nodded happily, dancing on the spot as Tara carefully took it and lowered it over her head. 'It's beautiful! I love it.' She pressed her fingertips to it. 'Thank you.'

She watched as the child ran off and hid behind her mother's legs. The food was being brought over now – chicken, potato, yucca – and the smell made her mouth instantly water. She hadn't eaten a proper meal in days and terror had suppressed every appetite in her, but it came back now with a fury. The villagers ate with them, children sitting on the floor by her feet, voices clambering over one another in excitement and rush. Tara ate till she thought her stomach would burst, delighting everyone with her rabid hunger. The aguardiente had done a fine job of numbing her, making the hut swim and sway a little, and she watched the proceedings as if from behind a gauze curtain, a step removed.

A crackle of static made her look up and she saw Alex reach for the walkie-talkie in his thigh pocket. 'Alex Carter, over,' she heard him say, sticking a finger in his opposite ear as he tried to hear above the noise. He got up from the stool and walked towards the edge of the hut. '*Hola?*'

He stood, his back to the room, staring out into the darkness of the jungle for a moment, then he stepped outside. Tara stared at the space where he'd been standing; the room felt empty without him in it.

She saw him pace past the door, his body erect. He looked tense as he talked to the person at the other end and she stiffened too. Was it the rangers? Did they have news about Jed?

'Excuse me,' she said to William, carefully putting her banana-leaf plate on the ground. 'I just need to talk to Alex. I think he's got news about our friend who was attacked.'

William nodded, watching her go.

She stepped out into the jungle night. The sky was a rich sapphire blue, the stars so numerous they joined hands and slipped through the air like sparkling streamers. A background chorus chattered, invisible, all around.

The conical huts were now silhouetted as giant geometric shapes in the twilight and she saw Alex standing with a hand on his hip, his back to her. His body language was spiky.

She began walking towards him, feeling her own tension rise. What had happened? Had Jed arrived at the hospital in time? The delays had been undesirable and concerning—

She drew nearer, hearing the static of the radio and then, only just overlaying it, a voice: '. . . *was trekking into the mountains with Jed Alvarado, who was attacked. He was taken*

332

off the mountain but I need confirmation that she is okay. I need to speak with her. Over.'

'And I told you, I don't know who you're talking about . . .' Alex snapped, his voice rising.

Tara stopped walking. Wait, what?

The static crackled again, jarring in the soft night.

'*Dr Tara Tremain—*' the voice came down the other end, patient and insistent.

Rory?

'*—She was last seen at the rangers' base station. She is thirty years old, Caucasian, English, five foot eight, dark hair, hazel eyes. Have there been any reported sightings of a woman matching that description? Over.'*

She watched, dumbstruck as Alex's arm swung down away from his ear, the walkie-talkie gripped loosely in his hand. He looked like he might drop it at any moment.

Tara couldn't move. She couldn't process what she was seeing. Was it the drink? Why would Alex deny knowing her? Refuse to admit that she was here and okay?

She took a step forward, silent, she thought, but he must have heard – sensed – something, because in the next moment he whirled round, eyes wild, a dangerous look on his face.

'What are you doing?' she asked, her voice little more than a whisper.

'Tara—'

'That's Rory.'

As if on cue, the radio crackled again. '*Hello? Are you there? Over.'*

Alex looked at the radio in his grasp, then back at her. 'Now just listen—'

'Why won't you tell him I'm here?' she asked, walking towards him again, stopping just a metre away.

His mouth opened, but no lie was fast enough.

'Alex? Tell him I'm here,' she insisted. 'He's worried about me.'

'Just give me a chance to explain,' he said quietly, his eyes burning into her so that she felt she could levitate from the ground.

'Go on, then. Explain,' she said, her voice shaky as a silence opened up. But no words dived into the silence. He couldn't think, couldn't think fast enough why he could reasonably deny telling her boyfriend that she was safe and right here, when there were other words that were going unsaid.

'Give me that,' she said suddenly, lunging forward and reaching for the radio in his hand. He shot his arm back fast, holding it up above his head, far out of her reach. 'Alex!'

She struggled for it, not noticing how their bodies pressed together, her eyes only on the radio so that she didn't see his head dip down, his mouth find hers—

Time stopped. She felt the world stop spinning, gravity loosen its hold on her, the trees, the grass beneath their feet . . . She felt like she was floating into space, up into the thick frothy galaxies, into the cocooning silence . . .

'*Hello? Is anyone there? Over.*' The crackle of static flickered between them like a taser.

'No!' Tara pushed him away, breathless, furious. 'No!'

He stared back at her, his eyes shining. 'That's why!'

'No!' She couldn't stop saying it, her only defence. She was undone by a kiss.

'Yes. Nothing's changed. You know it hasn't.'

'*I've* changed! I don't want you! I hate you!'

He blinked. 'No. You want to hate me.'

'Don't tell me what I want! You don't know me!'

He saw how her hands were clenched, the whites of her eyes

334

reinforcing the veracity of her words. Her chest was heaving from the effort it took to stand there and hate him, her entire being willed into a force field, repelling him away from her.

'What I did—'

'No!' She put a hand up as if to stop him, even though he wasn't moving. They were only words coming from him, but they were words intended to pull down walls, dig up the roots she had laid for a new life. The one without him.

'—What I did was unforgivable,' he said, his voice steady and lower now as he regained control of himself, his calm dismantling her chaos. He stared at her, as still as she was shaking. 'No excuses, I saw an opportunity and I took it. It wasn't personal. I never set out to hurt you and I never set out to fall in love with you.' He swallowed. 'I just thought I'd get close enough for an introduction and that was it. A shit move, I know, but I had my eyes on the prize. When I saw you in that newspaper article, I knew you were my only way to get in front of one of the few people on this planet who could actually do what needed to be done.'

'There were other ways!' Her fists clenched again. He couldn't justify his way out of what he'd done!

'No. Believe me, I had tried them all – the letters, the lobbying, the networking. That gets you only so far. It's easier to get close to the President than it is to Bill Gates, or Jeff Bezos, or your father.'

'Don't be ridiculous.'

'No? Look at Attenborough. He had an audience with Obama at the White House – but what actually changed? There were some headlines and photo ops, but what the planet needs isn't slogans or posters or promises. It needs cold, hard *cash*.' The word was a sneer. 'There's only a handful of people in the world who can write the big cheques – and

I mean the really big ones – that translate into action. The moment I actually got to talk to your father, he got it immediately. That was all I'd ever needed. An hour with the Big Man!' His eyes shone suddenly. 'My brilliant plan worked, except for one thing: you weren't just a face in a newspaper article anymore.'

'Spare me your sorrow. We both know you'd do it again.'

He hesitated. '. . . It's true I thought eventually I'd get over it.'

They stared at one another as the unarticulated 'but' hung in the air, but she didn't reach for it. She left it dangling like a dream catcher in a window, catching the light and offering to sweep away all the proclamations that had gone before.

He took a single step towards her. 'Look, I'm not making any excuses. I stand by the decisions I made, and the reasons I made them. It was always bigger than the two of us. You know it's not an exaggeration to say that the consequences from this project will impact millions of lives. I thought you and me . . .' His shoulders slumped, as though his soul was wriggling free from his body. 'But there hasn't been a day since when I haven't wished it could have been different.'

'Well, that makes me feel so much better. You'd do it again but at least I know you feel bad,' she sneered. 'You asked me to *marry* you, just so you could hurry things along—'

'No. That was real. I never planned it.'

'I don't believe you!' she cried. 'I don't believe a single word that comes out of your mouth.'

He fell quiet, staring at her under the night sky. '. . . Do you remember what I told you my mom used to say to me?'

'No. I made a point of forgetting all your lies.' Her tone was withering, her eyes cold as the lie tripped off her tongue easily. It was her only weapon.

He blinked. 'The people who are meant to be in your life will appear in it, twice, without trying.'

'*This* isn't twice,' she replied, shaking her head, instantly knowing where he was heading with this. They weren't *fated*.

'Yes it is. What were the chances of—?'

'No. Because you *were* trying. The first time we met, you had engineered it. You did your research, found out one of your targets had a daughter round about your age and you tracked me down. That's stalking, not serendipity!'

He stepped towards her, forcing her to take a step back. 'Tara, you can throw your sarcasm and your hate and your anger at me, and I'll take it because I deserve it. But we both know you're lying. I still love you, and you still love me.'

'No.'

'I'm not going to let you go again.'

'You don't have a choice! When are you going to hear what I'm saying? I hate you.'

She turned to walk away but he caught her by the elbow, swinging her into him and kissing her again, setting the world on fire.

'Fine,' he said when they finally separated for air, eyes burning, hearts pounding. 'Hate me, then.'

She lay in the hammock, wretched and sleepless. She had gone against her own nature, defying every instinct to listen to his words and believe them, and now her heart couldn't rest. She was at war with herself, the lies she had told herself over the years falling to ashes on her lips.

Even here, alone in the middle of the night, she didn't want to admit the truth that her entire life since that fateful day in her parents' home had been a charade. That she had smiled, laughed and achieved without feeling any of it; that she was an excellent doctor and a brilliant friend; but a distant daughter and only a good-enough girlfriend. She had moved through the motions of her life according to the path of least friction, watching her friends live life on her behalf – throwing confetti as they married, babysitting when they had kids. They had no idea that she envied what they had – houses that were homes, lives bursting at the seams with anniversaries, arguments and school term dates. It didn't matter that they worked first and foremost to pay the mortgage, and any career satisfaction was largely incidental. She had climbed to the top of the tree to show the world she was more than what Alex Carter had deemed her: just a rich man's daughter. But she could never save enough people to feel truly needed. She could never trust another man enough to believe she was truly wanted.

In the wake of his betrayal, she had excised him from her life like a tumour – a clean, surgical strike – but she saw now that stray cells had been left behind, multiplying in silence, hidden from sight and constantly sabotaging her efforts to move on. He moved through her bloodstream like an infection and she would never fully recover. He made her febrile and shaky. *Hate me, then.* She couldn't trust herself. She couldn't trust herself not to trust him. The pull towards him was gravitational, his kiss making undeniable a truth she had refused to admit to – she only wanted to hate him.

She lay there letting the simple fact settle, finally, within her bones. She would admit it to herself at last – that she loved him and she always would. Nothing could be done about it. A decade of running hadn't outpaced it. Neither one of them was free from the other's shadow. Right now, he was lying in a hut ten metres from here. Was he awake too?

She closed her eyes for a long moment. If they headed off

early, before dawn, there was a good chance they could get back to the microlight before dark and fly out of the park; from there, they could arrange to drive to Jed's village and undertake the short hike through the trees. This time tomorrow, if they could get through without incident or disaster, she would be back with Rory. She would be back in his arms and back in her own life and all of this could be locked in a box and quietly stored in a deep, dark part of herself. The truth she was facing here would become just another little secret to keep and – bar the handover ceremony, with Miles and Holly as her gatekeepers – she would never have to see Alex again.

Never again.

She felt the finality of it. This was the end.

Minutes passed.

This was the end. She would never see him again.

Never again.

Her heart pounded against her ribs as she swung her legs out of the hammock, remembering only as her toes went into her boots, to check them first. She upended the boots and flinched as a red spider fell out. She was trembling, her fingers fumbling as she readied herself, then tiptoed out of her hut. The village was asleep, even the jungle quiet. The moon's light painted the scene silver as she walked over to the hut William had pointed out when he had come to check on them earlier, oblivious to the scene he was interrupting.

She stood at the door for several moments, telling herself she could still turn back, knowing she wouldn't. This was inevitable, how it had to be. She lifted the latch on the door and peered into the darkness.

'It's me,' she whispered, stepping inside.

Chapter Twenty-Three

Holly, lying flat out, wriggled her bottom and shoulders a little deeper into the sand and, for the twentieth time that hour, took a deep sigh of gratitude. She could hear Dev and Jimmy in the water, trying to stand on their boards. Failing, from the sound of it.

She lifted her head and looked over – just to check they were okay. One of them might get biffed on the head by the board or catch a rip tide; the locals kept telling them to keep an eye out for rips, that the Playa Cocles beach was safer, bigger, better, but they all liked it here. The small bay felt more private. Apart from a few locals first and last thing, hardly anyone came over here, to the extent that they had even taken to leaving the doors to their huts open as they lay on their towels on the beach.

She examined a leg, pleased that she – even she! – was finally showing hints of a tan. Her freckles were joining up and she was feeling good on all the juices she'd been having.

'Hey.'

She looked up, shielding her eyes to take in the sight of Rory silhouetted against the setting sun. Even blacked out, he looked rough. He'd spent most of yesterday in his hut, had hardly said a word at dinner, and today he'd stayed away again, not even making a show at lunch. As sulks went, this was top-tier stuff.

'Mind if I join you?' His voice sounded like he had sand-paper in his throat.

'Sure,' she said, as he sank into the sand beside her. 'How are you today? We missed you earlier.'

He shrugged in reply, arms draped languidly over his knees, looking out to sea.

'I know, jet lag's a bitch,' she muttered, glancing at him sidelong. He had bags she could lance under his eyes and he hadn't shaved for days, a golden stubble covering his jaw and cheeks like a harvested wheat field. The poor guy looked truly terrible. She sighed. 'Ror . . . you've got to stop seeing this as something more than it is. She'll be back any minute!'

'It's been four days.'

'I know.' Holly couldn't quite disguise her own disappoint-ment. She had missed having her friend here too and their group didn't quite work without her as a central figure. 'I don't think she planned on it taking so long. Well, she didn't plan any of it, let's be honest. She just took off on this crusade. But she's just off being a doctor. Doing doctorly things and trying to save a life. That little girl dying on her really shook her and with the hospital's investigation on top . . . she's never been in trouble in her life! It's pretty obvious she's just trying to exert some control because she feels powerless.'

Rory glanced down at her, his expression severe. He looked like he was going to say something but the words seemed to sink back down again, unspoken.

'Listen, I get where you're coming from but the helicopter's coming for us in two hours and there's no way she won't be back for that. I know Ta. She adores her dad; she wouldn't let him down for his big day. Come hell or high water, she will get back here in time.'

Rory didn't reply but he didn't seem unconvinced either;

341

he too knew how much Tara admired her father. Holly leaned up on her elbows, joining his gaze as he watched her two boys playing on the water. Jimmy had caught a wave and was 'popping up' – there had been much teasing over Dev's pops; he didn't quite have their son's rubbery bounce. The sun was beginning to set and Holly caught her breath as she watched her silhouetted child, arms spread wide as he straightened, finding his balance, riding the wave into shore. Dev was sitting astride his board, further out, whooping and cheering like a maniac.

Holly smiled. Daft man.

'So tell me this, then – who's Alex?'

The question floored her and she looked at Rory so quickly, her own hair slapped her in the face. 'Alex?' she repeated, moronically.

'Yes. And before you pretend you don't know – don't.' Rory shot her a look that told her he would brook no bullshit.

Holly sat up fully and took another deep breath, this time with significantly less gratitude. This was not a conversation *she* ought to be having with this man. '. . . He's Tara's ex. From ages ago. Like . . . a decade! . . . I can barely remember him, to be honest,' she lied. She had watched her best friend living with the man's ghost every single day of those ten years.

Rory didn't reply immediately. He was still staring out to sea but Holly sensed he couldn't see Dev belly-flopping on the board, losing his balance and falling in with an almighty splash and a shout.

She swallowed, feeling nervous and not liking the vibe that sat upon him today. He'd been grumpy all week; it had hardly been the tropical holiday of dreams that he'd anticipated and Holly had had a lot of sympathy for him, frankly; she'd have been pissed off in his shoes, too. But this felt different. Any mention of Alex Carter in relation to Tara was never a good thing. 'Why d'you ask?'

'It came up in conversation,' he shrugged, looking evasive.

'With Ta? You mean you spoke to her?'

'Not exactly.'

He was talking in riddles. Holly put a hand on his arm. 'Ror, what's going on? Talk to me.'

There was a long pause in which nothing happened, then his whole body sagged, his head dropping. Holly felt a bolt of alarm. This wasn't like him; he didn't collapse or fall apart at the seams. He was stoic and dependable and resilient. A little dull perhaps, for Holly's taste, but nonetheless a good man. Decent. Not deserving of this.

He looked back at her. 'The other night, I had a brainwave.'

'Oh yeah?'

'Thought it was such a good idea.'

'Tell me, then.'

'You know when those guys came to tell us about Jed?'

She nodded, frowning hard. 'I know. It was so terrible.'

'Yeah . . . Well, I decided to go back with them.'

'What? Back where?'

'To the conservation park. Where Tara's gone.'

'*When?*'

He sighed, irritated by her lack of understanding. 'They told us Ta had continued the expedition with another ranger, so I asked if they had any way of contacting him. I was worried about her and wanted to know she was alright. They said they had some radio equipment that works within a certain radius, but it was back at their base station. So they took me up there. I had to sleep on the bloody floor.' He stretched his neck.

'But I thought you'd gone out with Miles and Zac!' Holly muttered, shocked as she tried to think back. The days were all beginning to run into one now. As she recalled, she, Dev and Jimmy had gone into town for tacos and to hear a reggae band playing. 'Jesus . . . So, did you get hold of this guy?'

'Oh yeah.' He stared back out to sea. Jimmy was paddling back out on his board, lying on his stomach, arms wheeling in strong arcs.

'And? . . . Oh shit,' she whispered, getting it at last. 'Alex is the ranger.' Her entire body became tense. 'Tara's in the jungle . . . with Alex.'

Rory winced at her response. 'And that's exactly why I wanted to know who the hell this Alex character is. I've tried ignoring it – I kept telling myself I just need to trust her – but I know what I heard. She's in love with him.'

'What?! No!' Holly's brain was struggling to catch up with this development. It made no sense. How on earth could Tara be out there with *him*, of all people? She knew he worked for Tara's father – everyone who'd been there ten years ago knew that – but for them to have just randomly met in the jungle . . .

'You don't have to cover for her, Hols . . . I heard them. I know the score.' His words seemed to have an echo to them, ringing in her head. This was all wrong. And bad. Really bad.

'Rory, what do you mean, you know the score? Tara hasn't seen Alex in almost ten years! He was an absolute bastard, he completely used her! The entire affair was a disaster for her, the worst thing to ever happen in her life. You're the best!'

Rory squinted against the sun, staring past the horizon. 'There's unfinished business between them.'

'What . . . ? No!' she blustered. 'You're wrong. Why on earth would you think that?'

'Because I heard them! I keep telling you, I heard them over the radio . . . He must have kept his finger down on the "speak" button. I think the bastard *wanted* me to hear them.'

Holly stared at him in utter disbelief, her mouth agape. 'Ror, listen to me,' she beseeched. 'Tara hates him. She totally hates him. I can't stress that enough. No one can even mention his name to her.'

'And that alone doesn't strike you as odd?' he asked bluntly. 'It doesn't seem weird to you that she has never mentioned this person to me, not once in the fifteen months we've been together? If it's been ten years, why isn't she over it by now? His name should hardly register, ten years later – surely?'

Holly swallowed, feeling out of her depth. It wasn't for her to be having this conversation with him. 'Look, it wasn't a straightforward breakup. Other things happened too. She was completely devastated. She didn't leave her bed for three whole weeks.'

But Rory wasn't listening. 'I think he kissed her. Right there.'

'No,' Holly protested again. 'There's no way Tara would have done that.'

'She didn't. I think *he* kissed *her*, because she was really angry afterwards. She kept saying no. That she hated him. All the things you've just said.'

'So then what are you worrying for?'

He looked at her again. 'Because she was protesting *too* much. I know Tara. I know when she says she's happy to have steak, but really she wants *aglio olio*. She's never been a good liar. She doesn't hate him. She just wants to.' He gave a bark of mocking laughter. 'Alex even said that to her. He knows it, too . . . She still loves him.' He looked away sharply. 'Which is why she doesn't love me.'

'Rory, stop!' Holly was on her knees now. She was going to beg him to believe her.

He stopped her with an honest gaze. 'Hols, we both know it's true. What I thought was . . . *reserve*, that feeling of distance she has about her . . . it's not distance. It's absence. She's there, but also not.'

Holly stared at him. Her mouth felt dry, her heart rackety in her ribs – but could she really deny it?

She looked at him guiltily, then away again. Now that she was on her knees, her back to the sea, she had a full view over the beach, towards Jed's beach bar, those evil trees at the edge of the sand that had made Dev's skin blister when he tried picking one of the apples.

'Oh for fuck's sake,' she groaned, seeing the bar hatch had been opened and a man was standing behind the bar, talking to a customer. 'What's he playing at? It's far too early for him to be up and about again.' She tutted as she looked back at Rory. 'It's Jed. He's turned up to work tonight. It's like he wants a bleed on the brain!'

'Mmm,' he said distractedly. 'That is too early.'

'Look, I'm going to go over and tell him to go straight back home. Just stay right here. Don't move. But I'll get us some drinks while I'm there and we'll talk about this, okay? Things are not what you think.'

She got up to standing, doing a quick visual check on her boys before she went. She turned back. 'Right. Won't be a jiffy,' she said, patting the sand off her bottom and watching as the customer Jed had been talking to began running over the sand. Straight towards them.

'Oh, fucking hell!' she cried, looking down in panic at Rory.

He scowled. 'What's wrong?'

She couldn't find the words to tell him. Instead her arm stretched out, pointing towards the man approaching them. 'It's Alex. He's coming over.'

'*What?*' He was on his feet in a flash, staring in disbelief as Alex stumbled over the sand towards them. He was wearing a khaki uniform that was ripped and stained and completely filthy. 'The fucking nerve!'

Within moments Alex was right there, panting in front of them. He seemed exactly as he had the last time Holly had seen him. Time had skipped lightly, fairy-like, over him, his hair just longer perhaps, the tan more weathered, some softening of the skin around those pale celery-green eyes. He was still far more attractive than was decent.

The two men stared at one another in silence for a few seconds, then Rory pulled his right fist back and punched Alex square on the jaw.

Alex didn't even try to duck. He lay sprawled on the sand, his nose bleeding, stunned for several moments, before looking back at them defiantly. No one spoke for several moments. Holly could feel the tension between the two men. Not a word had been said but they each knew what the other represented. 'I need to speak to her.'

What?

Alex began pulling his legs back in, getting up again. He had looked exhausted and battered even before the punch. He stood again, right in front of Rory. 'I'm sorry, man,' he said, staring his rival straight in the eye. 'I am. But I'm not going till I speak to her.'

Rory's hands were no longer bunched into fists. Holly watched as though everything was happening in slow motion. She felt the sand draining away from under her feet, as if it was being washed down a plughole.

Alex looked between the two of them, his own confusion growing. '. . . What? What's wrong?'

Holly swallowed, hardly daring to even ask the question as she saw now the desperation in his eyes. 'Alex, are you telling us – Tara's not with *you*?'

347

Chapter Twenty-Four

'This can't be right.'

But William was too far ahead of her to hear.

'William!' she called.

He stopped and turned, waiting patiently, his carved walking stick pressing down on the head of leaves that otherwise obscured the faint animal tracks. She dropped her hands onto her thighs and let her head hang. She was pouring with sweat, blisters – real blisters – oozing into her socks as her feet were rubbed raw. This was their second day of walking and the light was fading again. Surely they should be there by now? Perhaps it had been over-optimistic to think they could manage it in a single day, but after two full days of non-stop hiking . . . ?

Of course, they didn't have the microlight that had made such a difference on the way out, but that had merely recouped the time lost following Jed's attack anyway. And after their pre-dawn start yesterday, it was reasonable to expect to be back in time for nightfall tonight. Every summit they crested, she looked out hopefully across the interlocking canopies, scanning for some landmark or something she recognized from the outbound leg. But it was just trees, trees, more trees. The sea was now visible, though, and she gave an exhausted nod as he pointed towards it. That way. They had to keep going.

Her feet began moving on autopilot again. They had been going for several hours yesterday, the sun still climbing into the sky, before she had even remembered about the black star leaves, and the realization she had left them behind had stopped her in her tracks. Such had been her desperation to get away from Alex, the entire reason for being there had slipped from her mind and her failure to deliver what she'd promised felt all the more acute because of it. She had placed her needs above that poor child's.

She could only hope Alex would bring them back with him. Once he'd realized what she'd done – forced, by his actions – he would have headed back too, surely? He wouldn't leave them behind to spite her? He might be many things – ruthless, ambitious, unprincipled, uncompromising – but spiteful wasn't one of them.

She tried not to think about how he had found out she had gone – she tried not to imagine the look on his face when he'd checked in on her hut and found it empty. Maybe he had waited a while, letting her rest properly and sleep in, or perhaps too ashamed of how he'd behaved – drunk on exhaustion and aguardiente and nostalgia – to rush to face her again. But then, eventually, he would have had to; he'd have seen her things gone. It would have gone around the village that William – his old mentor, guide and friend – had gone too.

He'd have put two and two together and . . .

That was the moment she kept envisaging as her feet moved, left-right-left-right . . . She saw the change in his eyes, the growing slackness of his lips, the paling of his skin as he understood she had abandoned him, walked away again. She saw in microscopic detail his feelings of hurt, of rejection. And anger too. *Hate me, then.*

349

She wondered what time he'd left, and how far he was behind them. Would he take the microlight? He couldn't catch them on foot, of that she was pretty sure. William didn't walk as fast as Alex but they must have had a head start of at least three hours and she had a feeling – but couldn't be certain – their route back was different.

It had still been pitch black when they left. The head torch – which Alex had chivalrously given her the first night in case of midnight loo trips – had been the only way for her to see as they picked a route through the trees. William needed no assistance at all; even the sliver moon appeared to be, for him, merely decorative, an ornament in the sky. Rather, he moved as if by instinct, understanding the sway of the land, its stories and secrets, an inner compass guiding him through the landscape of his ancestors. She trusted him implicitly.

They had slept the night before in a cave, behind a waterfall. Perfectly dry. She had been too terrified to approach at first, explaining to him what had happened to her with the canoe and going over the falls and he had seemed strangely unsurprised by it, almost as though he might have expected it. Because of her naivety? Her Westernness? He had simply held out his hand and led her onwards, behind the furious water, where not a drop touched her.

He hadn't brought anything with him, only a hunting knife sheathed on his belt, his walking stick and a bag of stones that appeared to be important. A shawl, knotted diagonally over his shoulder by day, had been wrapped around him as a blanket while he slept. That was all.

He had checked the wound by her elbow for her, explaining that what she had thought was just an infected scratch had in fact been invaded by an insect, which had laid its eggs in her skin. Left untreated, he had said, those eggs would have turned into a worm. Instead, the leaf sap he had rubbed in and covered with the leaf when she'd arrived had killed the worm within two hours – that was the 'activity' she had felt, and the wound was now healing quickly. It both grossed her out and fascinated her. Even steroid cream couldn't work that fast.

She looked ahead to the sparkling strip of sea stretching along the horizon. The lights of faraway ships twinkled at the earth's edge and she knew somewhere, beyond where she could see, lay Jamaica. Jed's family had originated from there, coming over the Caribbean Sea to hunt turtles here back in the thirties and forties. He found it both ironic and pleasing that he now worked for a man whose foundation was set up specifically to protect those creatures, and many others.

Jed. She wondered still how he was and again sent her fervent wishes into the sky that he had reached hospital before any brain swelling became problematic. She wondered if his family knew. If *her* family knew. Was her father aware there had been serious problems out here with the ranchers? Alex's tone on the matter – like Jed's – had been evasive, eye contact averted; he clearly hadn't been telling her the whole story. But her father, writing the cheques and putting his name to the project . . . he had to know, surely? Unless Alex was keeping it from him too.

She would need to talk to her father when he got here. She frowned, trying to think when that would be. The handover was happening Friday, and today was . . . today was . . . ? Everything had become such a blur, what with no phones, no clocks, no watches . . .

Was today Thursday? Or Friday? No. It had to be Thursday . . . Or perhaps Wednesday?

She began thinking back, counting the days since they'd

left England on Saturday evening . . . It was Thursday. The handover was tomorrow, which meant her parents would be arriving today. They were all supposed to be flying up to the Lodge tonight. Right now! Her, Rory, Miles and Zac, Holly, Dev and Jimmy. All of them. There was no way she couldn't be there. Her father had taken his fortune and committed to giving away ninety-five per cent of it with the brushstroke of a pen. It was a historic act of singular philanthropy. Even Chuck Feeney, the co-founder of DFS and her father's old friend, had taken decades to give away his $8 billion fortune; her father was doing it in less than one. That was what he had liked so much about Alex's proposal: the purity of the project, its sheer simplicity. One problem, one man; one cheque, one decade, one solution.

She had to get back to Puerto Viejo as soon as possible. She would walk faster, she had been walking through the pain for days now anyway. Summoning an energy she didn't know she had, she broke into a run, closing the gap between herself and William.

'William, how much further? We've got to get there tonight,' she panted, catching up with him.

He didn't turn. 'No.'

'We have to. You don't understand, I have to be back for tonight. We're flying up to the Lodge for the handover. My parents are arriving today and I can't not be there.'

'It is not possible.'

'But—' She frowned. *How* could it not be possible? It was a two-day hike to Alto Uren from the foothills of Puerto Viejo. Jed had told her that, and she and Alex had managed it in a slightly shorter time thanks to the microlight. She and William had already been travelling for almost two full days too. Surely they should have arrived by now?

'Look, I'm sorry if it's a push.' She gave a tight smile. 'I've lost track of time the last few days and been distracted, but there's no way I can't be there. We *have* to keep going, even after sundown if necessary.' She shrugged. 'It's not like we didn't start in the dark. We can finish in the dark too. I don't mind.'

'It cannot be done.'

She stared at him, confused about why he was being so . . . obstructive. He seemed like a different man here to the one she'd met in camp. He hadn't smiled since they had started the walk; there was no trace of the easy-going, jokey manner he'd had when she'd arrived with Alex. She had put it down to him concentrating on navigating. Even for someone with his bank of knowledge, the jungle was still a place fraught with danger; he had to concentrate.

Then it occurred to her. His was a bartering community; she had to haggle.

'Ah. You want more money.' She shrugged. 'Okay, that's fine, I can pay more.' She had thought the sum she had offered him to get her off this mountain and back to the beach had been more than generous; although frankly she couldn't imagine what use he would have for her money full stop. The village was entirely self-sufficient.

'No.'

He turned and began walking away again.

'William!' she barked to his back. She ran again, getting ahead of him this time. 'I'm sorry if I haven't made myself clear but this isn't negotiable. I'm not asking you, I'm telling you I need to get back to Puerto Viejo tonight.'

'And I have said it cannot be done. Puerto Viejo is four days from here.'

'Four . . . ?' Her voice trailed off as she looked around them with a new alertness, a dawning panic beginning to creep through her bones. She had trusted him solely on the basis that Alex did too, blindly assumed he would help her simply because she had asked (and paid) for it. But now she saw the situation clearly. For the past two days, she had put her faith in a complete stranger, a man whose manner, now she reconsidered it, was more than diffident – it was quietly hostile.

She took a step back, feeling her entire body go cold. 'Oh my God, where are we?' she whispered. 'William? What's going on?'

'They've fucking kidnapped her!' Miles gripped his hair with his hands as he began pacing the length of the beach bar.

'We don't know that for sure,' Holly said, trying and failing to keep him calm.

'What? You think it's just a coincidence that she's disappeared in the jungle the day before the world's press gathers to witness Dad's grand gesture?'

Holly swallowed. 'We—'

'Jed got jumped!' His arm swung towards the man sitting – at Holly's insistence – oversized on the small stool. 'How do you know that wasn't a failed attempt to grab *her*? For all we know, it was her they were after, not him!'

'To be honest, that's what I thought too,' Alex agreed. He looked over at Rory. 'And it's partly why I didn't tell you she was with me. You'd identified her as heading for Alto Uren. If the guys who jumped Jed had been listening in on those channels . . .'

But Rory's eyes narrowed. 'Partly?' he asked pointedly.

Holly saw the tension billow between the two men again, and Miles was no better. He kept glowering at the guy who had destroyed his sister's life – he had been shaping up to

354

punch Alex himself when he'd been blindsided by the news that his sister was missing.

'No. They were after me,' Jed said quietly, sitting on the stool. He was still weak and Holly was keeping a close eye on him. He was constantly pushing his luck, doing too much too soon. He ought to have gone straight to San José on Monday, as Tara had tried to arrange, but no one had been able to get him out of the ambulance – the suggestion of not getting home to his wife had raised his blood pressure to a degree that was more worrisome than the head injury. To placate him, they'd been forced to divert to the local hospital instead. It had been sheer luck that it was just a bad concussion after all. His arm had been set in plaster, the shoulder checked, and he'd been home again that same night. 'I know the guy who jumped me. He's a rancher who's been giving us lots of trouble.' Jed glanced at Alex, his hands fiddling nervously with the damp muslin-wrapped parcel Alex had handed over to him when he'd arrived at the bar. 'Miguel D'Arrosto's henchman.'

Alex gave a nod that suggested he knew exactly the man.

'A rancher,' Miles echoed, planting his hands on his hips. 'And why should a rancher be giving you trouble, Jed? Is it personal? Do you owe him money? Did you sleep with his wife?' Jed's head jerked up, his eyes glowering in a flash. 'Or is it because you and your family work for my father?'

Jed's heavy silence was confirmation of the latter. It was all the proof Miles needed that Tara had been taken.

Holly looked over at Alex, who was rigid and pale-faced. His eyes kept darting everywhere as though his brain was firing off thoughts and theories that flitted like dragonflies, dancing and uncatchable. Holly had seen the look that bloomed on his face when she'd told him Tara hadn't come back here . . . It was a look she knew all too well. She saw it all the time at work when parents brought in their sick and injured children, husbands their wives . . . It was pure fear. Pure love.

'It can't be William,' Alex muttered. 'It can't.'

There was a silence as everyone tried to work out who William was.

'. . . Who's William?' Dev asked blankly, on behalf of them all.

'The shaman in Alto Uren. He's a friend of mine.'

'How good a friend?' Holly asked sceptically.

'I lived in the village for nine months shortly after I moved over here. He was my mentor. There's no way he could be involved in this.'

'So then why are you suggesting he might be?'

Alex hesitated. 'Because he wasn't at the village yesterday morning either.'

They all looked at one another in horror.

'But that doesn't necessarily mean he's with Tara,' Alex said quickly. 'He could have gone picking leaves for his medicines. He often gets up before dawn and goes into the jungle alone.'

Holly stared at him. 'But when you realized that Tara had gone, and then him too . . . what was your initial instinct?'

Alex swallowed. 'That they were together. I assumed she'd asked him to help her get back here.'

'That would seem to be the logical thing,' Rory said evenly. 'As we all know, Tara is a rational woman. She lives by order and rules. Anything . . . *unpredictable* frightens her.' His words were loaded, his gaze openly hostile. They both knew what he'd done to startle her.

'It's weird that she would leave without you, though,

356

Alex,' Dev said. He had missed Holly and Rory's initial conversation about Alex. He had only come out of the sea when he'd seen Rory punch Alex to the sand, a figure from all their pasts. 'I mean, after you went to all the trouble of helping her get there, why leave while you were still asleep? That would surely suggest she was . . . taken, rather than that she left of her own accord.'

Holly sighed, knowing this wasn't the time for tact. 'What Rory's referring to is that Alex kissed Tara the night before she left,' she said with her usual brevity.

Dev's eyes widened. 'Oh fuck.'

Miles's eyes narrowed, for he had missed the revelations earlier too. 'You did what?'

Rory's hand had pulled into a fist again too, but Holly reached an arm out and patted his arm. 'Not right now. You can all knock ten bells out of each other later. We need to concentrate on finding out where Tara is first.'

Zac stepped into the conversation: an impartial observer, he knew nothing of Tara and Alex's traumatic history. 'Okay. Let's look at what we know,' he said, trying to summarize with his usual legal clip. 'She left the village at some time in the night, either voluntarily or she was taken. This William guy is also gone, so he may or may not be involved. But you think not, Alex.'

'Not in a sinister way, no.' Alex shrugged. 'As soon as I realized they'd gone, I took off. I didn't see anyone else, it was still early. I thought I might be able to catch them up.'

Zac thought for a moment. 'Is there any way William could have been helping her back here, but they got lost?'

'Would it be possible for you to get lost walking down one end of Sloane Street to the other?'

Zac frowned. 'Of course not.'

357

'Precisely. That's what this place is to William. Getting lost is not an option.'

'. . . Okay. I'm just trying to cover all angles,' Zac muttered, not appreciating the sarcasm. 'Could they have had an accident?'

Alex stared at him for a moment and Holly could see the panic swimming in his eyes, his face paling before them. He looked away sharply and began to pace. 'I would have . . . I would have seen them.'

'*Would* you, Alex? Surely there's more than one way up or down those mountains?' This time it was Miles throwing sarcasm.

Alex shook his head, as though he didn't even want to hear the suggestion. 'You don't understand. William is a part of the jungle; he knows the animals that live in it, the trees and flowers and bushes that grow in it. He knows what heals and what poisons. He knows the gorges and the rivers. The seasons. The weather. He can read it all.'

'But accidents can happen to anyone, at any time. That's what makes them accidents.'

Alex stared at Miles darkly. Their bad start ten years ago hadn't mellowed with time. No one spoke for several moments, all painfully aware they were completely blind as to Tara's predicament. She might have been kidnapped, or maybe not. She might be safe with William and injured, or unsafe with him and injured; she might be uninjured and safe with him, or uninjured and unsafe with him. She might be alone and lost and injured . . . The possibilities were endless.

'We should get a chopper up there, looking for them,' Miles said decisively. 'Start covering some ground.'

'Miles, even if you were standing in the trees immediately beneath the helicopter, you wouldn't see it,' Alex sighed.

'The canopy cover is absolute. You won't see anything at all from the sky.'

'So then what?' Miles cried, throwing his arms out in frustration. 'We just do nothing and wait here for her to come back – or not? My parents land in an hour. What am I supposed to tell them? That she's lost and we did nothing?'

'Of course we're not going to do nothing,' Holly said, stepping in again to calm frayed nerves. 'We just need to keep coming at this logically. Tara's not an impulsive person. There will be a . . . *traceable* train of thought to her actions.'

Rory's stare slid towards Alex again. They all did. Alex turned away with a gulp of air, his face turned towards the ceiling, his eyes squeezed tightly shut. *Hate me, then.*

'But that is precisely my point. If this wasn't to do with *her* choices,' Miles said, his voice tremoring with suppressed fear. 'If she didn't choose to leave but was taken . . .' He let the intimation hang in the air. There would be nothing to follow; how would they ever find her out there?

Holly swallowed. 'Well, then if she was taken, there will be a ransom demand,' she said calmly, with a poise she didn't feel. 'And if so, we will know soon enough.' She looked around them all. 'So we should all keep our phones charged and to hand and try to stay where there's signal. You especially, Miles, as her brother.'

He nodded, looking grateful that someone was listening to him at last. He suddenly looked younger than his twenty-eight years. 'If it is that . . . if they did take her . . . she'll know what to do. We had kidnap training when we were kids. Well, teenagers really.'

'Kidnap training?' Holly echoed.

'Yes. Our father arranged for the SAS to teach us what to do in the event of a kidnapping.'

'Fuck,' Dev whispered, looking appalled.

Alex looked like he was going to be sick. If he had thought he was used to his employers' extreme wealth, it was a different ball game to see how it played out in family life. Holly wondered if he was beginning to see now why his lies had been so devastating for Tara, why his betrayal had been so much greater for someone who struggled to trust.

'So she'll have a good idea of knowing what to do to get away,' Miles said, his eyes brightening at the prospect as though this alone meant everything was going to be okay. This course, taken twenty years ago, was going to save the day.

'I'm not sure we would want her to get away, in the middle of the jungle,' Jed said quietly, his gaze on the floor. 'Not without . . . equipment.'

He said 'equipment' but Holly suspected he meant 'weapons'. Or survival kit. 'Tell us about the trouble you've been having with the ranchers,' she said. 'What exactly has been going on?'

'They don't like that they can't expand their farms,' he shrugged. 'They say the land belongs to Costa Ricans, not rich foreigners. They refuse to recognize the authority of the land purchase.'

'Refuse, in what way?'

'They grow their acreage secretly – felling a few trees over here, more over there. They start fires and say they were natural. They ignore fines. Intimidate and harass the rangers. And their families.'

Holly frowned at the stress in his voice on the last word. '. . . Yours?'

Jed's gaze met hers. He nodded.

'But your son . . .' She remembered what Tara had said about it not being safe to move Paco, Tara's desperation to act when she'd returned from seeing him, Jed's own agitation to return to them and not be helicoptered out of the region to San José; he'd been trying to protect his family. They were especially vulnerable, left alone.

She kneeled down in front of him. 'Jed, I know you've been trying to protect Tara by keeping from her how bad things have been, but I saw how those men hemmed in your car at the clinic and I know we didn't get that flat from a sharp stone. Trust me, I work in A&E, I know intimidation tactics. But you need to be honest with us now – when you were attacked, do you think they might have been looking for Tara?'

Jed swallowed and she could see the sense of failure in him. '. . . Perhaps. Things have got a lot worse since she arrived.'

She felt her heart rate quicken, her mouth become dry. 'Could they have followed her, do you think, after you were taken back down the mountain?'

'I don't know. I don't remember much.' He fiddled again with the wrapped leaves, clutching them tightly like a talisman.

'But they *could* have stayed there, watching her . . . ? Maybe they deliberately hurt you to separate you both, knowing she'd be easy pickings on her own?'

Jed stared back at her with a haunted look.

'But she wasn't on her own,' Alex interjected. 'I showed up at the base station and found them both there. We got Jed back down to safety, and she and I continued up to Alto Uren together, to get the medicine for Jed's son.'

'So then they followed both of you,' Miles said.

'No. We took the microlight for the first leg. There's no way they could have kept up with us on foot. They couldn't have known where we were unless, as I said, they'd been listening in on the radio channels.' His glance only skittered in Rory's direction.

'But you were worried enough about the possibility of that, that you deliberately kept quiet,' Holly argued.

'Only *partly*,' Rory said with sharp sarcasm.

Alex didn't reply for several moments. He looked like he was trying to keep calm; there was a haunted look behind his eyes. '. . . I didn't have any sense that we were being followed.'

'But were you looking?' Holly pressed. 'Or were you just enjoying being with her again? Maybe you weren't concentrating in the way you ordinarily would?'

Alex's eyes narrowed. 'There wasn't much that was enjoyable about any of it! Tara wasn't exactly thrilled to see me. She barely even spoke to me for the first day.'

Rory straightened up, hearing the subtle distinction. 'But on the second?'

Alex hesitated. '. . . There was an incident that changed things.'

'What kind of incident?' Miles stepped in, looking fierce.

'I had a boat I'd hidden away along a particular stretch of the river. It's a fast-flowing stretch but we were driving each other mad. I decided we could make up time if we covered some miles on the water. But the boat came unstuck as I was getting the oars and she . . . was swept away.'

There was a disbelieving silence. 'Excuse me?' Miles asked, his voice hoarse.

'She was okay,' Alex said quickly. 'I mean, the boat was carried over some falls and broken up, but it wasn't . . . I mean it was, but . . .' He stared back at them all with wide eyes. 'She was okay. Just in shock for a while.'

Holly couldn't speak. She could scarcely believe this was happening. While she'd been lying on the beach the past few days, her best friend had been enduring . . . all this? Quite literally, hell and high water?

'After that, things between us improved. She realized we had to stick together and work as a team. Things were okay—'

'Till you kissed her,' Rory interjected furiously.

'It's not his fault,' Jed said, a look of quiet intensity on his face.

Everyone turned to look at him again.

'Oh, I think it is!' Miles cried. 'Thanks to him jumping my sister's bones, we have absolutely no bloody idea if she ran or was snatched!'

'It's the curse.' Jed stared back at them.

There was an astounded silence.

'Curse?' Dev repeated with his characteristic mildness, as though this was a reasonable explanation to enter the conversation.

'You need to understand – to the Bribri people, the river *is* life. It is fundamental to their culture, their entire way of being. Their lives respect and preserve Iriria, or Mother Nature as you would say. Every living thing should be kept to Mother Earth, even the fossil fuels – oil, coal, gas, they are all the remains of ancient plants and animals and should remain part of Iriria's body. That is what the Bribri believe.'

'Okay. But what does this have to do with Tara disappearing?' Dev asked.

Jed was quiet for a moment. 'A curse has been cast. That was why the river took her. It was no accident.'

The silence that greeted these words was deafening.

'I don't understand,' Miles said finally, looking to Zac for help. 'What . . . why is he saying these things? What curse?'

'The project has been cursed,' Jed repeated.

'The *project*? You mean the park? That makes no sense,' Zac said with obvious scepticism. 'The Tremains are the good guys here. Conservation, preservation. They're the reason there's no more ranching, no mining. Why, Costa Rica now has a reputation on the global stage as the world's first country to be run completely on renewable energy. *Why* put a curse on them . . . if such a thing is even feasible?'

But Alex straightened up suddenly with a look of intensity on his face, as though he knew why. He looked like a man who understood, at last, the game. 'Who placed the curse, Jed? Which tribe?' There was urgency in his voice.

Jed blinked, looking unhappy, like a spy being forced to reveal his secrets.

'Tell me!'

'. . . The Guetares.'

Alex slumped, and Holly somehow instinctively knew what that answer meant.

William.

Chapter Twenty-Five

Day sprang at her like a cat, silent, soft and unforgiving, a beam of sunshine winking past a banana leaf and splashing over her face like water. She blinked a few times, trying to gather her thoughts and process where she was, but it was hard to think; everything ached from lying on the hard ground and she felt peculiarly absent, as though her body was a shell and she was but a shadow flitting inside it.

Her gaze settled on the stone a few inches from her face. It was perfectly smooth and domed, another one placed twelve inches further along, arranged in a form too symmetrical to be random. In a flash she remembered—

She sat up and looked around her with a gasp. The stones were placed around her body in an oval, far enough away not to become dislodged if she turned. William was sitting on a tree stump, seemingly whittling something from a stick.

'There is tea,' he said without looking up, and she saw a half-coconut filled with a green tincture just outside her stone perimeter. Without a word, she reached for it, sipping tentatively. She didn't want to drink it; she didn't want to accept 'hospitality' when she was not a guest but in effect a prisoner – but she also knew she needed fluids. The humidity levels meant dehydration was a constant risk and though she didn't trust him, she assumed he had had some of this tea too. He might be able to navigate this jungle without compass, map or phone, but he was still a man – seventy per cent water; he needed to drink too.

'What are those for?' she muttered, nodding towards the stones, extending a leg and deliberately scuffing one so that it rolled a few centimetres out of position; the jarring asymmetry was pleasing. She crossed her legs, staring at him defiantly over the top of the coconut as she sipped the tea.

But William didn't look up. 'Protection. No predators will move past the stones.'

She gave a snort of disdain – the only protection stones could provide was defensively in the form of a blow to the head – but it struck her that she hadn't stirred all night; she had slept heavily, even though her eyes had closed against her will as she yearned for the luxury of a string hammock and fretted about pale green eyelash snakes slithering over her in her sleep, the exploratory bites of leaf-cutter ants, the warning stings of scorpions . . .

She watched him whittle with the knife; it was made from bone, one edge looking as sharp as any of her scalpels. If she could get it off him, she would know exactly where to cut . . . not to kill him, but certainly which tendons to slash to immobilize him enough for her to get away. It didn't matter that she wouldn't know where she was going. She didn't know where she was now *with* him, and though she knew his skills kept her safe, she was also inherently unsafe in his company. She still didn't know what he wanted. Money appeared to hold no sway now, even though he had reacted quickly enough when she had gone to his hut and offered him a small fortune to get her off this mountain and back to Puerto Viejo. It was odd. Now when she mentioned money, the numbers going up in ten-thousand-dollar increments, he just seemed to look at her with pity.

She knew she had to get away from him, and she knew it had to be today, before she grew weaker. She hadn't eaten enough in the past week to sustain full-day treks in smothering temperatures; her feet were rubbed raw and in this weakening state, she was becoming more vulnerable to accident or infection the longer she was out here. She had no idea how long he intended to keep her here for.

Did her family know yet what had happened to her? Surely they must do. She couldn't bear to think about it. Her mother would instantly dissolve into a puddle of hysteria. Miles would freak out but in a different way. As for her father . . . it would be his worst nightmare come true. He had always done his best to shield them from the harsh realities that came with wealth such as theirs; he had tried to give them normality; he had even prepared them for just such an eventuality. 'Unfortunately, what we've got makes us targets,' he had explained when they were barely teenagers, just as several members of the SAS walked in to the drawing room. But was it really possible to anticipate this? Her kidnapper was a sixty-something tribesman in a blanket, sitting on a tree stump, whittling a stick. Take them out of the jungle setting and in any other scenario, he'd be far more at risk from her than the other way round.

'So . . .' she said, putting down the coconut. 'What now?'

He slipped the bone knife and the stick carving into the waistband of his trousers, then got up and carefully, almost reverentially, picked up the stones from the oval and put them in the bag. He took his walking stick from its place propped against a branch and finally, he looked at her.

'Now we walk.'

*

The beauty was lost on her. Twenty thousand different shades of green, monkeys looping through the trees, exotically coloured birds perching on branches and chattering loudly as they passed by . . . She didn't care. It was raining again (although no banana-leaf umbrellas were offered this time), the temperatures soaring, the relentless din grating, air so thick she could bite down on it. She longed for her bedroom in London, the dim light as the louvred shutters were closed, the silky smoothness of her sheets, the puffiness of her duvet and firm but yielding mattress . . . A bubble bath in the room next door, the scent of rose otto oil delicately tracing the cool air, a chilled glass of fizzing champagne, music on low, dinner cooking, Alex moving about in the kitchen . . .

Was she hallucinating? Or just dreaming? Would she ever get back to it? It felt like an impossible task. She couldn't imagine ever getting out of here, stepping away from the towering trees, seeing an open sky again. How much had changed in under a week? A little girl had died, a little boy had gone unsaved and it was her life in London that felt like the paradise escape now, not this.

Wait.

Her feet stopped moving as she caught up with the mental mistake.

Alex? She had meant Rory.

Rory.

She was just confused. And soaked. And tired.

She resumed walking, falling into autopilot.

Rory.

Rory in the kitchen.

Wearing just his jeans, the tea towel tucked into the waistband, a leaf in his brown hair as he pulled the chicken pie out of the oven . . .

She stopped again, raindrops falling from the end of her nose, her hair. Her mind was playing tricks on her. She closed her eyes and felt his lips press against hers, so vivid, almost real . . . *Hate me, then.* All this had happened because she had tried to get away from him, deny a truth that was plain to them both. If she had just stayed . . .

She watched William walk on ahead, pulling further away with each step and it occurred to her – for the first time – that she could just . . . turn around. He didn't have a gun to her head. She could simply walk in the opposite direction and go back the way they'd come. He walked mile after mile after mile without ever turning around to check on her; she could be ten miles away before he even noticed she had gone. Sure, she would be lost within ten metres, but what did that matter? She had no idea where they were heading to anyway. And what was he going to do? Stop her with that little bone knife?

She glanced behind her and then ahead again.

'I wouldn't.'

Tears gathered in her eyes, frustration and fury marbling in her blood as she saw William had stopped and was watching her. He hadn't so much as twitched in her direction in over two days of walking, and yet the first time she even *thought* about turning around, he caught her?

'Why the hell not? I'm not scared of you!' she yelled, her self-control snapping in half finally. 'I'm not your bloody prisoner! And you're not my captor! You can't make me do a damn thing!'

He didn't reply, the benign villain with a carry-bag of stones and a walking stick. He just stood there for a few moments, then turned around and continued on his way. Almost as though he agreed with her. He couldn't make her.

Tara's mouth opened in disbelief. That was it? He was going

to leave her there? 'What do you even *want*?' she cried after him. 'Tell me! Tell me what you want!'

But he didn't turn back and she watched as the leaves and branches began to flutter back into place after him, steadily taking him from her sights in chunks. Within moments he was gone. Just like that.

She turned on the spot – breath held, heart clattering – as she felt the same overwhelming, terrifying aloneness she had felt on the canoe, when the river had rushed powerfully beneath her.

With a sob, she broke into a run after him. 'William!' she cried, rushing blindly past the branches, feeling them scratch and claw her as she ran too close, too fast—

He had stopped in a clearing, a rainbow winking in the sunlight even as the rain continued to pour.

'. . . What . . . ?' she faltered, taking in the sight. She had never seen anything like it. She reached an arm out and walked over to the rock in front of her. It was vast – as high as she was tall but at least two metres in diameter and perfectly, completely spherical. Her hand brushed over its smooth surface in awe. How on earth had something so huge and precision-sculpted come to be here, in the very middle of the jungle?

And not just one of them, but . . . she counted them . . . twelve in all. They were of varying sizes but their symmetry was perfect. There was no way the vehicles needed to transport boulders of these sizes – fourteen, fifteen tons, surely – could get through these trees; and they were days away from anywhere. There were no roads for miles.

She walked into the middle and turned slowly on the spot. The gap in the trees allowed the sun to break through, beaming onto the grass with dazzling intensity even as the rain poured. 'What is this?' she whispered.

'Our most sacred spot. Our church, you would say.'

She looked back at it. There was indeed a spiritual presence here; she couldn't describe it exactly but the space felt full somehow, as if loaded. The air seemed to sparkle, the rocks to bask. She expected to see fairies flitting with butterflies, fawns nosing the grass.

'We believe they are over two thousand years old.'

Tara's eyebrow arched. 'That's pretty . . . pretty old,' she murmured. She kept wanting to touch them. 'Is it okay that I . . . ?' she asked, holding her arm out.

He nodded, watching her as she walked slowly around the circle, touching each sphere in turn. They all felt different. Some felt older and more 'scarred' or marked than others.

'They are . . .' He reached for the word '*Gabbro* . . . ? From inside the earth. Melted . . .' He frowned.

'Magma?' she supplied for him.

He nodded. 'Magma. Magma.'

'How are they so perfect?'

'They were carved by hammering and grinding with smaller stones . . . There are three hundred throughout the land.'

'Three hundred,' she marvelled. 'It's incredible. I've never seen anything like it.'

Actually, that wasn't strictly true. Stonehenge inspired a similar awe and confusion, but there it was the scale of the stones that held the power; here, it was the beauty and symmetry of the spheres that set them apart.

She looked back at him, seeing how he watched her, seeming to appreciate her reaction. 'William, why have you brought me here?'

'Come.' And he walked to the centre of the circle and sat down, inviting her to do the same. There were two flat stones in the centre, like discs, and she was grateful for them, the ground already soft and muddy, rainwater running freely past their feet.

She settled herself, almost sighing with relief to rest, becoming steadily aware of the birdsong again, the slanting light through the trees. Beauty reasserted itself, along with hope. She realized she no longer felt frightened.

William looked at her with his brown eyes that seemed to see more than just what was in front of him. Like the parrots that could see ultraviolet, so she sensed he could read her beyond the normal spectrum. 'Your father is a rich man.'

She was still. '. . . Yes.'

'He is a good man.'

'Yes.'

'And you . . . you are good too.' They were statements, not questions.

'I try to be. I've made helping others my career.'

'Even when you did not need to have a career.'

She shrugged. Not many people noticed that.

'Is Alex good?'

The question startled her. Alex was William's friend. The very query of whether he was a good person seemed like a betrayal, a suggestion that he was not. But how was *she* to answer? Could she respond in all honesty that he'd been good to her? He had possibly never harmed anyone as much as he had harmed her.

Her mouth parted, no obvious reply coming to her lips. 'I believe he has good intentions,' she said finally.

William stared at her, waiting patiently for the 'but'.

She took a sharp inhale. 'But he doesn't necessarily go about things the right way.'

'He is too ambitious.' It was another statement.

'Yes.'

'He hurt you.'

Just talking about it hurt her. '. . . Yes. But it was a long time ago. It's all blood under the bridge now, as they say.'

'Do they?'

'Well, some people.' She shrugged again. It seemed to be raining even harder – if that was possible – and yet she noticed it less. The water was warm; it felt somehow . . . cleansing.

William was quiet for several moments. 'I believe his intentions are good too. I do not believe he deliberately intended to do us harm.'

Tara frowned. 'Do *you* harm?'

'My people. His vision is big, he wants to save the whole world, and if that means sacrificing a few people for the greater good, well . . .' He shrugged and looked at her meaningfully. 'You. And us. We are disposable to him.'

There was a brutality to the statement, as well as finality. But was it true? She had seen how Alex's eyes had shone with pain as the 'but' had spun between them too. *I had expected to get over it.* She didn't think she had been so disposable after all.

She shifted her feet closer to her bottom, feeling a kernel of worry begin to worm into her stomach. 'William, God only knows Alex and I have had our issues and I'm not his greatest fan, but I don't understand what you mean about him doing you harm? He's not a bad man and I know how important you are to him. I could see it in the way he laughed and spoke with you. He came to live with you.'

'Yes. We welcomed him as a true friend.' He nodded slowly, looking around the space they sat in. He closed his eyes, rocking very slightly for a few moments. He opened them again, looking straight at her. There was something about his gaze she felt so unlike anyone else's – prescient, almost not quite human, or perhaps more than human, she wasn't sure which.

'It is hard for you to understand, I know, that I am able to communicate with animals, and the spirits of the jungle.'

'I . . .' She stammered. 'We don't have an equivalent facility in our culture. I'm sorry.'

'Don't be. It is you I am sorry for. We are sitting here now and I can feel the presence of my ancestors. They are all around us.'

Tara's eyes swivelled, trying to 'see' the sparkling air and not just the rain.

'In our village, in Alto Uren, each family has lived on the same piece of ground as his ancestors for three thousand years. Older even than this sacred site.'

'That's wonderful.'

'Yes, it is. We grow over one hundred crops for our food, building materials and medicine. We need nothing from the outside world and we take nothing. We live as we always have done, in rhythm with the forests and the seasons . . . So I am sure you can understand that I have a duty to protect my people.'

'I do.'

'We have a saying: that it is better to be a skinny dog, than a dead lion.'

Tara was quiet for a moment, not fully sure she understood. So much of what he was saying was oblique to her. Was he telling her all this because he was suggesting Alex was somehow working against the tribe? 'William, you do know that the entire point of the project is about safeguarding Indigenous cultures and communities such as yours, as much as it is to do with protecting the rainforests, stopping mining and all that?'

A small smile spread over William's mouth, but it did not reach his eyes. 'No mining, that is right.'

'Exactly. Projects such as this national park mean mining will never be allowed. Your country is leading the world in terms of renewable energies.'

William tipped his head to the side, interestedly. 'How exactly?'

'By using hydro-electricity instead of fossil fuels.'

'Yes. Hydro-electricity.' He looked her straight in the eye, and Tara had a sudden sense of being ambushed. Led into a trap. 'And when the handover happens today and the land is given back to the Costa Rican people – specifically, the government . . .' His downward inflection on that word left her in no doubt of his view on them. 'They will start to build a dam that will flood thousands of hectares of land which are sacred to my people. The places where we have lived and worshipped for thousands of years will be destroyed. Our villages will be underwater. Our monuments' – he swept an arm to indicate the stone circle – 'will be underwater. Our entire culture will be lost, our people will be displaced. And no one will care, because it is far more important to be seen to be using renewable energies.'

Tara stared. 'But surely . . .' She frowned. 'No. There are laws in place to protect your rights.'

'Laws can be changed. And once the land is made the property of the nation, the laws *will* be changed.'

'But I remember my father . . .' She strained to remember the details of all those many dinner-table conversations she had tried so hard to avoid or block out. 'I remember him saying there's a government body specifically set up to protect the interests of the Indigenous communities. Co . . . ?'

'No one from Conai has ever come to our village. It is just a face to show to the world. They pretend to consult us, but nothing changes. I brought you here because I wanted you

375

to see this, feel it and understand. If it is lost, it will be lost forever.'

Tara bit her lip, staring around at the clearing – ancient and hidden, secret and sacred. There was so much she didn't understand out here and never would . . . but she couldn't deny things had happened that she couldn't explain. Her headaches had gone; she had seen plants heal wounds that would have taken weeks at home; both medicine men had intuitively read her psyche in a way no GP or therapist ever had. And there was something unequivocally spiritual about this place. It felt more reverential than any church she'd ever been inside.

'William, I want to help you. I honestly don't know if what you're saying about Alex is true – I can't say with certainty that it *isn't* – but I do know my father would want to help you if he knew.' She sighed. 'But we're miles from anywhere and the handover is today . . .' She gave a hopeless shrug. 'It's too late to do anything now.'

He reached into his bag and pulled out something large and rectangular, like a black brick.

She frowned as he handed it to her. 'What is that?' she asked. She turned it over and her eyes widened. '*You've* got a satellite phone?' she gasped. 'But . . . how?'

'Alex,' William shrugged. 'We bartered.'

She looked up at him with wide eyes. 'What did he get in return?'

'A goat.'

She was silent for a long, drawn-out moment. A phone for a goat. She couldn't stop a smile from climbing into her eyes as she remembered a whispered conversation in the night, many years ago . . . 'He always wanted a goat.'

William watched her with an enigmatic smile of his own.

She looked back at the prehistoric phone. 'You'll have to show me how to work it,' she said.

'You will speak to your father?'

'I will. But I still don't know what can be done at this stage. Getting the national park ready for today has been a huge undertaking. Hundreds of people are involved – rangers, ecologists, consultants, lawyers. It's a juggernaut. Trying to delay it now would be like turning a battleship.'

'I've never seen a battleship,' he said simply. 'But all ships and boats – no matter how big – can turn.'

She smiled. 'Well, that is true.'

'Get him to listen to you, Tara. Then you can go home.'

There was a long pause down the line; so long, Tara half wondered if they had been disconnected.

'So let me get this right,' her father said finally, his voice clear and authoritative. 'You're telling me the ransom demand is a . . . clause?'

She looked at William, sitting cross-legged in the circle, whittling his stick – and winked at him. He gave her a gap-toothed smile in return.

'Dad, it's not a ransom. William wanted to bring me here so that I could see for myself what is at stake. Once you hand the park over, it'll be too late. Their rights need to be protected and written into the contract that no area of the park will ever be flooded or developed in any way to allow for a hydro-electric dam. There can't be any loopholes. It has to be completely watertight.'

'No pun intended, of course,' he said, but neither of them laughed. Tensions were running high and they were all stretched thin by the events of the past twenty-four hours. 'Tara, it has taken years for those contracts to be drawn up and agreed. Even if I agreed to putting the clause in, it couldn't be done in time today. You are aware the handover ceremony was supposed to be in three hours?'

'Of course I am! But there's still time. Zac's a lawyer. He draws up contracts all the time. Get him to do it. It's one clause.'

'Tara—'

'Or delay the handover. If it's a deal-breaker for the government – who, let's not forget, are being *gifted* all this land – then perhaps you should be asking yourself whether the handover is even a good idea?'

She heard him sigh. 'It's not that simple.'

'Dad, I know it's not. Nothing at your level ever is. But if you could be here and see this too, you would understand why I am asking this. Your vision is going to make a tangible difference to the health of this entire planet because you are a great man. But you're an even better father, and you, me and Miles know you've also created this legacy because it will protect a place we all love. Please trust me. I'm asking you to do this – for me.'

'Piglet . . .' Her father's voice was pained. There was a long pause and she could imagine him rubbing his temples, as he always did when he was troubled. The silence extended. '. . . Okay,' he sighed finally. 'I'll get Zac onto it right away and see what can be done. Tell your friend William we've got a deal.'

'Yes!' She looked over to William and gave him the thumbs up. 'Fantastic! Thank you.'

'But we'll still have to delay the handover.'

'Really? For just one clause?'

'It's not just the paperwork. I want you to be here, beside your mother and me, when we do it. This is a legacy from our family, not just me.'

'. . . Okay.' It meant seeing Alex again, assuming he had

made it back. Part of her had hoped that it could happen without her there. Things would be simpler that way if they could just never see each other again.

'Are you sure you're all right?'

'I'm honestly fine. My feet are sore but . . . they'll heal soon enough.'

'Most things do, Piglet.' His tone had changed and she had a feeling he wasn't talking about her feet anymore; she wondered again what conversations he'd had with his technical director over the years, the casual updates he'd given about the family back home and specifically, how she was doing. 'So now that the conditions have been met, tell me where you are. Where can we send help to come and get you? Your mother's beside herself and Miles isn't much better.'

'William says we're about two hours from the nearest place you could land a helicopter. But I'll call when we get there, I promise.'

Her father gave a sound that wasn't entirely happy.

'Honestly, I'm perfectly safe. There's no one better equipped than William to bring me back again.'

'Well, you'd better. We'll be running the clocks down. Bailey's getting the co-ordinates from this call and if we don't hear from you in two hours, they'll disperse a land search and rescue team across the radius area. You know that.'

She did know that. Simon Bailey had headed her father's personal protection team for fifteen years now. 'Really, Dad, I'm fine. I'll be back soon.'

'You sound tired.'

'More than you could know,' she sighed.

'Well, just hang in there . . . Oh wait, your brother wants to talk to you. I'll hand him over. We'll see you shortly . . . Bye, Piglet.'

'Bye, Dad. Love you.'

'. . . Make it quick,' she heard her father say, his voice more distant. 'She needs to get going.'

Miles came onto the line. 'Twig?'

'Hey,' she smiled.

She could hear him exhale with relief. 'Are you really okay?'

'I'm honestly fine. Just completely knackered.'

'We've been freaking out here.'

'I know. I'm sorry.'

'When that son-of-a-bitch Alex Carter pitched up here without you, all hell broke loose.'

It was her turn to go quiet. She closed her eyes, not wanting to think about how Rory had reacted to meeting her ex, a guy he'd never heard about. 'So Alex is there, then?'

'Well, he was. But he's gone again.'

'Gone?' Her eyes flew open and she felt her heart quake at the thought of him slipping from her life once more. 'Gone where?'

'Who cares? He went off to find you. He said he knows where you are, but that's bollocks.'

She frowned. 'He can't possibly know. *I* don't know where I am! And I'm here!'

'I know, it didn't make sense to anyone but him, but we couldn't stop him. He thinks you're at some sacred site.'

Tara went very still. Her gaze swept over the stone circle again. 'But . . . how could he possibly know that?'

Miles sighed. 'Don't laugh, but Jed said there's a curse on you.'

'A *curse*? On *me*?' She gave a shocked laugh. She didn't know which part of that statement was the more ridiculous. 'But . . . who? . . . I mean, wh-why?'

'Some voodoo spirit man trying to stop the handover, I don't know,' he muttered.

She looked slowly across at William again. He was still whittling away at his stick, quiet and still. Almost serene. Was it possible he was the architect of so much chaos? 'That makes no sense, Miles,' she said in a quiet voice.

'You're telling me!' he laughed, mirthlessly. 'Jed said it had something to do with the river being the tribe's lifeblood or something? That's why you had that accident in the canoe, supposedly. The spirit of the river was . . . enacting the curse. Anyway, it's all horseshit but Alex wouldn't listen. He took off before anyone could stop him.'

Tara stared into space, a bad feeling spreading through her like black smoke.

William had placed a curse. On her. That was what Jed had said. It was what Alex believed . . . But William hadn't even met her when she'd had the accident.

You. And us. We are disposable to him . . . We welcomed him as a friend.

He had used the past tense. Were they not still friends, then? They had seemed so when she and Alex had arrived at the village. But in her experience, the truth often lay in what *wasn't* said.

I thought I would get over it . . . but I didn't.

We welcomed him as a friend . . . but he betrayed us.

It was Alex's canoe. He was supposed to be on the boat, not her.

'Twig? Are you there?' Miles asked as she looked up to find William watching her. He had stopped whittling now. It was so quiet she could actually hear the forest breathe.

'It's not me who's cursed,' she said quietly, staring into the Awa's deep brown eyes. 'It's Alex.'

Chapter Twenty-Six

'William, you need to lift it,' she said to his back. They were walking again, heading for her freedom, the direction of home. But she wasn't interested in that now. She would stay in these trees forever if she had to.

It was heavy going. The rain was still falling, the ground underfoot sodden and making their feet sink, water running like tributaries down the narrow paths and animal tracks.

'It is not so simple,' he said, reaching for a plant as he passed and picking a leaf. He rubbed it between his fingers and sniffed it. Then he picked a few more and slipped them into his bag.

'William!'

He turned to face her, the embodiment of calm.

'You cannot let Alex be living under a curse.'

He regarded her with one of his ancient stares. 'I thought you did not believe in such things as curses and plant medicines.'

She was taken aback. 'I never told you I don't believe in them.'

'You did not have to say it.'

'But . . .' She stammered. She didn't believe in curses, of course she didn't. She didn't believe in ghosts or fairies or the Easter Bunny either. She was a scientist and she went where the evidence took her – but she couldn't deny things had happened out here that science alone couldn't explain. Headaches dispelled, auras read . . . and she had felt the relentless power surging against the canoe. Even in her terror and panic, she had sensed, she thought, something more than just a river current at play. It had felt not like it had drifted away, but been *spirited* away.

She swallowed. 'The whole point of me being out here was to help Jed's son by bringing back plants the Awa thinks can help him.'

William gave a small smile and walked again. He wasn't fooled by her elastic words, the illusion of action over belief. 'Do you know how long it takes to train as an Awa?'

She sighed, not interested in the slightest, but knowing he wouldn't be deterred from telling her. He had a gentle manner that was paradoxically forceful. Somehow, he seemed to get his way without appearing to try.

'Fifteen years,' he continued. 'I began learning when I was eight. Our clan has always been *awapa*; it was my uncle who taught me the *suwoh*.' He strained for a moment, trying to find the right English words. 'Knowledge that is told, not written?'

She nodded impatiently.

'He taught me the songs to help connect with the spirits. He showed me how to find medicine in these forests by accessing the spirit trinity – the spirit of the plant, of the disease, and of the patient. He gave me the knowledge and the wisdom and the power to *help* my people; I do not do harm.'

Tara was jolted by the echo of her own Hippocratic creed.

'The curse was placed in defence of my tribe, not in contempt of Alex. But he is the body through which this project lives. His intentions are good, but they will involve our sacrifice and I cannot allow that. He must do his work, and I must do mine. The curse, once it is set, cannot be lifted until it is fulfilled.'

She ran ahead of him in the rain, blocking his way, stopping him. 'And by fulfilled, you mean . . . ?' She dared him to say it, silently begged him not to.

'Until he is stopped.'

Did that mean dead? She stared at him, remembering her terror as the boat had spirited her away down a rushing river, sending her over a waterfall that even now made her knees weak when she thought of it.

'But you've got what you wanted,' she cried. 'The clause is going into the agreement and the handover will be delayed until it's sorted. My father has given you his word. I'll introduce you! He can personally pledge to you your protection. I guarantee it.'

'I believe you, Tara. But nature will run,' he said, not unkindly. 'It cannot be stopped.'

She saw that he wasn't lying to her. An unstoppable chain of events had simply been set into motion. It was as out of his hands now, as hers. 'So what, we just have to wait?' Her voice split, rain running down her hair and into her shirt. She didn't notice or care. She could see only his expression confirming her worst fears. '. . . How will it happen? What's going to happen to him?'

'I do not know. It is sent out to the spirits. I am only the medium.'

She felt a well of despair open up in her as he led the way once more, but his walk, she saw, had become a trudge. He was saddened by this – not devastated, not feeling like the world was beginning to split apart, the ground trembling beneath his feet as it was hers – but he was unhappy about what had to happen.

Her blood rushed with a speed that felt dizzying. She could hear it blasting through her head as a feeling of impotence flooded her limbs. So that was it? They just waited for something terrible to happen to him? Alex's ambition was going to get the better of him after all. The revenge she had dreamed of in those early years after his betrayal was now going to find a form and hurt him in ways she could not. She didn't doubt that it would. She wouldn't have believed in such a thing before this week. A curse? She wouldn't have given it a moment's credence. But she had been in that boat, in that river. She had felt it for herself.

She closed her eyes, trying to control her raging emotions, but she was weakened by exhaustion, pain and now fear. Her mind was in torment, going around in circles. How could he fight a curse? Should he even be told? She staggered through the mud, struggling to keep her footing and her mind straight. He would laugh at her if she told him. He was a scientist, like her.

William, ten or so steps ahead, was partly obscured from her view by the reaching branches of ferns, vines dangling down like gym ropes, so that she had to negotiate her way through a slack weave of foliage. She saw that he had stopped walking, his back as erect as a twenty-year-old's as he stared at something ahead. Instinctively she faltered, approaching carefully from behind. William was still and clearly hyper-alert. He seemed woven into the fabric of the cloud forest, an intrinsic part of its daily rhythms.

'Stay back,' he said in a low voice as she reached him.

'What's . . . ?' But her voice faded into silence as she saw what he was looking at.

The sight was shocking. Horrific. A vast expanse of nothingness, stretched out before them – no colour, no life, no sound. Just acres of desolation, an unsightly scar upon the most pristine landscape, an open wound left to fester. No pictures, no amount of foreknowledge could have prepared her for the reality of the sight. She knew ranchers and farmers and loggers illegally cleared land in protected areas – of course she did – but to be faced with the merciless violence of it, the sheer scale of the destruction . . . She had spent the best part of the last week living 24/7 in these jungle and rainforest habitats; it was so all-encompassing that at times she had felt claustrophobic. There was no let-up, ever, in the sounds and noise and humidity; nothing was ever easy out here and she had felt trapped in a giant green biosphere with no way out. She had longed to be clear of their shaded embrace, to have a view that stretched for miles, to see any colour so long as it wasn't green . . .

Or, she thought she had.

But to be suddenly faced with this brutal, wanton reality prompted a reaction that was visceral and completely primal. She understood now that what she had seen in William's body language was in hers, too; his wasn't a tribesman's response, just a human one. This wasn't the middle of nowhere – it was the middle of Everywhere. This wasn't just the beating heart of the planet but its pumping lungs too, and for something so immaculate and ancient to be pillaged like this . . . It somehow seemed worse that one or two toppled trees remained on the ground: abandoned, unnecessary, surplus to requirements but felled anyway. The mud that remained was a bright, bilious red-yellow, like guts had been pulled up. Great sheets of water were running unimpeded over the face of it, not even tree roots remaining to catch, break up and redirect flow. The scene felt apocalyptic, like the end of time. A desecration.

'No.' His voice was a whisper and she looked to see what he was seeing, for it wasn't just the carnage. His keen eyes read detail far more astutely than she and he had seen – barely visible, several hundred metres away down the steep slope – emerging from the tree cover lower down . . . a man.

Tara's brain processed the sight with a slow-dawning disbelief. He was still wearing the same torn, filthy, ragged clothes she had last seen him in. Even from here, she could see he now had a beard. Behind him was the microlight.

'*Alex?*' The cry burst from her, a sob that contained her sorrow and fury at this desolate site, her relief at seeing him, her amazement that he had found her here.

She saw his face turn up and search for her in the trees. Find her. 'Tara?!'

There was a moment in which they stared at one another in amazement. Could it really be? Then he began running up the wall of clag; she saw how he slipped, his hands planting straight down into the mud as he sank to his ankles. He got up again but could find no traction, his feet sliding away from him at every step.

'Alex, wait! I'm coming down!' she shouted.

'Tara—!' William spoke again, his arm reaching out towards her, too late. She was already running along the side of the treeline but it scooped away from her, away from Alex, and she began to cut across the wasteland instead to get to him faster. Suddenly every minute mattered. The years they had lost together, the decade of their lives gone forever, bore down upon her with an urgent realization that nothing else could be delayed. Not for a moment.

'No!'

William's voice was like a flare in the sky, interrupting the instincts that were propelling her over the scarred earth towards the man she loved to hate. She stopped and looked back. The expression on his face brought an arrow of sheer terror to her heart, for it was more than fear she saw there. It was doom.

She looked back to find Alex still on his knees, but his arms were above his head, as if he was trying to flag down a helicopter on a desert island. He was waving at her.

'No! *Tara, no!*' His voice was ragged, hoarse in his determination to be heard, to stop her too.

Why were they both . . . ?

And then it came to her ear: the background rumble – which her subconscious mind hadn't considered relevant a few seconds earlier – was now a roar. The ground shaking beneath her feet wasn't a hallucination. She saw a flurry of birds of all sizes, all colours, pitch into the sky. She heard the monkeys scream as they swung branch to branch, tree to tree on the borders, trying to escape.

Her mouth open, her eyes wide, she looked down to see the ground coming unstuck from beneath her feet. Not just there. The vast bank of mud – turned over, despoiled, denuded and now left unprotected against the full battery of tropical elements – was cleaving from Mother Earth, Iriria. From higher up, above where they stood, it was already beginning to slide down the mountain, an unstoppable tide gathering speed at a rate that she couldn't believe.

Even before William yelled at her to get back, back into the trees, she had begun running, managing two, three, four paces before her feet were swept from under her and she fell backwards. She heard the men's shouts as she felt the ground pulling away beneath her body, trying to take her downhill with it. Her hands grabbed automatically for anything within reach, finding only a sinewy vine that trailed down from a surviving tree at the edge of the clearance site. She was lucky – it was sappy and strong enough to slow her speed, and she was still close enough to the edges that the breakaway was shallow here. For a moment, all she could see was sky – grey, heavy and low – as the mud spun her around and she clung to the vine, but then she felt the force lessen and she could push herself up just enough to sit; the ground still rumbled and shook beneath her splayed palms but she was no longer at risk of being dragged along; the main body of the slide had broken free and was now heading . . .

Heading for Alex. He had been at the very base of the clearing, bottom and centre. He was still there.

'Alex!' she screamed. She couldn't understand why he was continuing to stand there. The mudslide was heading straight for him.

'*Tara?*' She saw his head turn and for the briefest moment, there was eye contact and she realized he had been looking for her. He had been waiting to see her, to know she was okay.

'*Run!!*' she screamed, with a force that she thought might turn her inside out.

He began moving, scrabbling, sliding, back towards the trees. But it was impossible to escape – the sheer speed, the terrifying velocity . . . *Nature will run*, William had said, and she screamed again as in the next instant, the mudslide picked him up and whisked him from sight. The wave slammed into the trees and the forest screamed as if in pain, giant timbers creaking and cracking from the force, their roots being lifted like weeds in a dahlia bed.

Tara couldn't stop screaming. She couldn't accept what she

was seeing. Nature roiling and frothing, breaking and destroying itself. The frightening power, the noise, the putrid smell of the ripped-up earth . . .

And then, almost as quickly as it had come, the thunder subdued, the fury spent. The mud tide was dispersed and broken up, its speed slowed, its force lessened by the tangle of trees, stopped by the forest . . . until there was only a haunting silence. No birds crowed; not even the monkeys shrieked. All life felt wiped out. Eradicated.

A sob wracked her as she stared at the vacuum that remained, the space where Alex had been now glaringly empty. As if he'd never been there. Her body folded as though she was going to be sick. She felt convulsed by pain, racked by horror as the image of him being snatched and thrown repeated itself in her mind. It was unsurvivable, she knew that. As her own feet had been swept from under her, she had experienced the same feeling she'd had in the canoe – of a great unstoppable force working against her.

William ran, sure-footed and agile, across her field of vision, down the mud with a speed she never would have anticipated. He was silent and focused. She knew what he was trying to do. But it was pointless. He knew as well as she that the curse had been fulfilled.

She sank back, unable to support herself. Even to breathe felt hard. Her heart didn't want to beat. It couldn't support the pain that was spreading through her like a poison. Alex was gone and whatever pain she had thought she'd known before, it was nothing compared to this. She was oblivious to the cold, wet mud oozing around her, through her hair, into her ears, down her shirt. She was aware of nothing but a searing pain. She felt consumed by a white light that was burning her from the inside. To have found him, only to have lost him . . .

No!

Her heart wouldn't accept it. Her brain was numb, the self-recriminations jabbing at her as she remembered how she had refused to show him the slightest mercy, telling him secrets that she knew would haunt him as they had her, guarding her heart with a grim and ruthless determination until she had been able to escape him again, just as she had ten years ago in London. She had got exactly what she wanted: Alex Carter out of her life.

He was the man she had loved to hate, and she had *loved* hating him! He had put the fire in her belly to succeed and thrive, to show him she had gone on to a better and happier life than anything he could have given her. She was the woman she was *because* of his betrayal. She ought to have thanked him for it. She had everything.

She closed her eyes, remembering the longing that had shone – unbidden, unwanted – in his eyes as Rory called for her over the radio waves. She remembered his smile like a sunbeam when he'd found her in that tiny office, a room in the jungle, the contrariness of it all seeming to him a sign that they were destined – when all along they were fated. Ambition, curses, either or both, the universe always conspired to keep them apart.

She remembered how she had stood on the grass in the moonlight, knowing she had to make a decision – and she had nearly, so nearly, gone to his hut. She had almost succumbed to the hunger for him that she'd told herself was purely a chemical reaction, the strange alchemy that sparkled between them. They could have had one night together, she had told herself. Just one. Old time's sake. Revenge sex.

But she had known one night wouldn't be enough. That

she could never have enough of him, and therefore it was better to have nothing. She had gone to William's hut and paid him to get her out of there, because she had known that once she took one brick from the wall the entire fortress would crumble and she would be exposed again to the man she loved to hate – and hated to love.

She didn't know how long she lay there. She couldn't feel her arms or her legs. Her body felt as if it was sinking into the earth, as though she was being reclaimed by Iriria. Strangely, the thought didn't alarm her. She thought she could happily never move from here again. Let the cloud forest claim her. She could no longer picture herself in her old life now anyway – sitting in the canteen with Holly, tepid orange food eaten off trays; the smell of antiseptic, the glare of the surgical theatre lights and the snap of rubber gloves, the sight of a tiny body on the table before her . . .

Little Lucy. It was a week since she had died. How much living had that poor child been denied? How much had Tara herself lived, even in that short time?

Distantly she remembered the call she had never made back to the hospital's clinical director – the investigation that would be going on in her absence and the eyebrows that would be raised on hearing she was 'on holiday'. She knew she ought to care, but she felt nothing. No one would ever understand what she had been through out here, chasing hope for another child on the other side of the world and failing at that too.

She closed her eyes, feeling heavier with every breath. She didn't think she could move if she tried. Her body felt set in the mud and she was dimly aware the rain had stopped, that shafts of sunlight were winking past the clouds sporadically and beaming them onto the forest like blasts of grace. The birds were flying again, criss-crossing overhead in the gap created by the hundreds of fallen trees. She felt insects burrow and wriggle beneath her splayed palms. Life had resumed, as though the momentary horror of the mudslide was already forgotten, if not forgiven.

She felt far away, almost below the earth, as the insect came into view. It hovered high above her in the sky, silhouetted black against the haze. It stared down at her as she stared back at it, then began to descend, growing ever larger and throwing out a wind that made the trees bend and her hair blow against her face. She squinted as her brain stirred from its torpor . . . Still, she couldn't move. Her body no longer obeyed instructions. She could no sooner get herself up from the ground than could a stick.

The helicopter lowered quickly, landing somewhere down the slope, out of her frame of vision again. Perhaps she hadn't been seen after all? It didn't really matter. She was happy to lie here. The mud had begun to feel like an embrace, the earth holding her, and she took comfort from the way it moulded around her body. It had been so long since she had felt truly held . . .

She closed her eyes, remembering just that spark of it down by the river . . . Alex's embrace as he had found her. A small smile ticked up the corners of her mouth as she felt herself moved, then lifted; the earth's suckered release of her was followed by a cold chill along her back. She opened her eyes to see two faces bearing down on her. They were wearing helmets and moving quickly. Efficiently.

'Don't worry, ma'am, we've got you now,' one of them said, seeing her distant gaze fasten upon him.

'How . . . ?' But the word was as shaky and thin as a puff

of smoke and in the next instant, she felt herself rise up several feet in the air. She realized she was being stretchered. She was being rescued . . . It was all over.

She stared at the sight immediately above her and as she was carried beneath the empty patch of brightening sky, she had a sudden longing for the shaded embrace of the trees again. She wanted to catch just one more ray of light heroically winkling its way through the leaves to a small patch of earth; she wanted to see a macaw preening its feathers on a branch, to watch a sloth hang in blissful sleep.

Instead, the return to her world had already begun. She watched the bobbing of her rescuers' perfectly round helmets as they navigated the slope, saw ahead the precision engineering of the helicopter's blades, spinning at speeds faster than her eye could see, ready to whisk her from here—

William.

He was there, suddenly. From her prone position, she saw for the first time a tattoo on his neck, the deep wrinkles in his skin that paradoxically appeared fleshy and youthful.

'Exhaustion. She must eat a little, and rest a lot,' she heard him say to one of the men.

'Will—' she faltered as they began to move her. Tears suddenly slid from the outer corners of her eyes. She felt desolate, terrified to be leaving him. This was it, yes, the rescue she had yearned for, the escape she had craved – but she wasn't ready to go. What she had thought she wanted and what she actually wanted were worlds apart. She was a queen at lying to herself. 'William!'

He looked down at her and smiled one of his gap-toothed smiles. He just nodded as he placed his hand on her forehead and said something she couldn't understand in his native tongue, his eyes closed, the other palm raised to the sky. When he had finished, he looked back at her again. 'It's all going to be okay now.'

'I don't want to go—'

'Then come again soon,' he said, giving her a wink before stepping back, out of her line of sight.

No! Didn't he understand? She wanted to stay here, near Alex! She wanted to be there, with him, in the earth . . . But her body was inert and as empty as a husk. It wouldn't move. Even without the straps binding her down, she felt paralysed and powerless.

She felt the wind beat upon her as they moved into the downdraft. It was like lying beneath the wings of a phoenix and she was forced to close her eyes, feeling herself lifted into the body of the aircraft.

The sounds inside immediately changed, the battery of wind ceasing like a hairdryer being switched off. She felt whatever tension, whatever fight remained in her body slacken. How many helicopters had she flown in, in her lifetime? And yet none like this – no stitched leather, no fridge with a bottle of Bollinger chilling inside. This was an alien landscape, sterile, medical. The walls were lined with life-saving equipment – an IV drip, a defib machine, oxygen masks . . . She didn't care! She didn't want to be saved, why couldn't they see that?

Tears streamed down her cheeks, over her temples, into her hair as the doors were shut and she felt the first tentative hops of take-off. She thought of William watching from the trees, of Alex somewhere under the mud, broken, destroyed, lost . . . and she began to sob, unable to bear it, the pain coming in sharp vicious waves that she had managed to hold off as she numbed herself in the mud. She had lost him for good and she would never even be able to make her way back here, she would never find this place again and be able to sit by the spot where she had last seen him, checking for her, before he was spirited away.

She felt hysterical with grief, she wanted to rip the skin from her body, pull her hair from her scalp, anything that would hurt less than this. The paramedic said something over her to his colleague, coming back into her field of vision as he observed her distress. She couldn't hear his words but she caught the shape of his mouth and one word: sedative.

'Take me back!' she cried, shaking her head from side to side. 'Take me back!'

She felt the other paramedic on her far side reach for her hand.

'No!' But she couldn't pull her arm away, she was strapped down.

'It's okay, ma'am,' the first paramedic said, leaning closer so she could hear him better. 'You're safe now. We've got you.'

The other paramedic was still stroking her hand, trying to calm her.

Oddly, it was working. Had he injected her already? She felt something deep inside her begin to settle as his fingers clasped hers, brushing over them with his thumb. There was a gentleness to the gesture that touched her, like he was soothing her troubled soul. It only made her tears come faster; kindness was more than she could bear.

He couldn't understand that she didn't want to feel, that she didn't want to *be*.

The grip tightened fractionally around her fingers, a small squeeze equivalent to a parent saying 'there, there', and as her thumb slid against the side of his hand, it felt the raised edges of . . . a small moon-shaped scar.

She felt the breath leave her body.

She turned her head as far as she could and took in the sight beside her. Completely caked in mud so that only his eyes were visible, an oxygen mask on and an arm and leg both splinted, Alex blinked back at her. She felt a sonic pulse jolt her world back to life. If her thumb wasn't feeling for itself the ridges of that little scar, she wouldn't have believed what her eyes were showing her.

He was weak, the other paramedic administering morphine in the very arm whose hand she was holding. She couldn't imagine the pain he must be in. She gripped his hand harder now, as hard as she could as they stared at one another, unable to speak over the noise; but steadily his grip weakened, the drugs taking over. His eyes flickered, as though he didn't want to lose sight of her again, until finally he slipped into unconsciousness.

Tara kept on holding his limp hand.

The pilot radioed ahead as they cut through the clouds, the forest at their feet. She felt its vastness and fragility all at once, its beauty and horrors. It was a land of rainbows, where even as the rain fell the sun still shone. Only by being lost there had she found herself.

Found him.

For the second time.

Epilogue

Two months later

'A good speech is a short speech, I've always said it,' Holly said, clapping enthusiastically as Tara's father folded up the sheet of paper in his hand and invited the President to join him at the podium.

'You have always said that,' Tara agreed, her eyes upon the stage.

They were sitting in the front row – along with her mother, Miles and Zac – of a small but illustrious crowd in which formally attired dignitaries sat with the park rangers and staff. Most of the Alto Uren tribe had come down the mountain too and were looking on with pride as William took his place beside Alex, beside her father.

Holly glanced at her, seeing how Tara's eyes never left the players on the stage. 'He looks well,' she whispered slyly, feeling no need to elucidate which 'he' she was referring to. He was on crutches now, his arm seemingly healed.

'Yes.'

'Good suit.'

'Yes.'

'Always was a good colour on him.'

Tara didn't respond.

'. . . They've obviously been looking after him well,' Holly persevered.

'Yes.'

'You're obviously nuts about him.'

Tara wasn't falling for her friend's tricks – she knew them all too well. She gave Holly a look. 'Behave,' she hissed.

'What? What'd I say?' Holly asked with mock surprise.

Tara straightened up. 'I haven't seen or spoken to him in seven weeks, you know that.' She kept her voice low, not wanting her mother, to her left, to overhear.

'Oh, I know it. I sure know it, but I don't frickin' understand it!' Holly hissed back. 'They concluded the investigation weeks ago. Total exoneration.'

Tara nodded sadly. 'I know.' It still didn't make her feel any better.

'So? You could have come back out.'

'I know I could, but I also knew I'd be coming out for this anyway.' Tara shrugged lightly, but in truth she had needed every last minute before getting on the plane. No matter what her heart said, she couldn't just run into the sunset with Alex when she had a whole life in London, with Rory. It was simplistic to think she and Alex could step straight into a happy ending after everything that had happened between them – and *to* them.

She saw Alex's gaze cast up and settle upon her again. She was easy to find in this crowd, of course, front and centre, but she sensed he would find her anywhere: a crowd, a jungle. Twice. His eyes kept coming back to her, like a bee to a favourite flower, and each time it happened she felt that electric jolt . . . If she had tried to talk herself into doubting her feelings in London, they melted away here. She could feel the connection shimmer between them, the gravitational pull between his sun and her moon.

A riot of flashbulbs went off as her father and the President shook hands, sealing the deal that had been ten years and two months in the making. So many sacrifices had been made to make this happen – had it been worth it? A wave of cheers rose up and the applause lifted again as, with the formal ceremony over, people got up and began to mingle.

Miles and Zac went straight off to congratulate her father, leaving the three women happy to stay where they were, well away from the international press photographers.

'Well, wasn't that marvellous?' her mother asked, turning to them both. 'He's finally done it. Maybe now we'll get a little more peace.' She was holding a small handheld fan and Miles had a tiny canister of mineral water in his jacket pocket to mist her on her cue; she didn't take well to non-air-conditioned environments.

'Congratulations, you're almost poor, Mrs T,' Holly grinned.

Samantha Tremain laughed. 'Well, relatively speaking.'

'Hey!' Holly smiled suddenly as she saw someone approach them and Tara turned to find Jed making his way over.

'Jed!' she cried, throwing her arms around his neck and hugging him. 'How are you?'

He knocked his head playfully. 'Well, it hasn't fallen off yet.'

She grinned. 'I'm very glad to hear it.' Miguel D'Arrosto and five members of his team had been arrested the week of her rescue. Thanks to testimony from some of the other rangers – and film footage from some nature-watch cameras in certain trees – the charges against them had ranged from arson to theft, criminal damage and grievous bodily harm.

No one had held out much hope for substantial prison sentences – in most cases, the evidence was purely circumstantial – but Tara hoped the severe fines issued might hurt more anyway. This had always been about money for them, as they came after anyone they believed to be getting in the way of their profits.

'You?' He looked down at her feet, in soft backless mules.

'Raw feet, but make it fashion, am I right?'

He laughed at the sight of her red heels. She had been in bandages for three weeks in the end. The wheelchair had felt dramatic when they'd first brought it over to her, but even she had been stunned when she'd seen the state of her feet. Infected blisters and a cluster of leeches from where she'd lain in the mud had not made for a pretty sight.

'T-t, I've got someone who'd like to say hello to you,' Jed said, turning slightly so that she could see past him. Sarita was standing there, and holding her hand . . .

Tara fell to her knees, feeling overcome. 'It's lovely to meet you properly, Paco,' she said quietly, in Spanish.

The boy smiled, dark-haired, big-eyed, pale as milk. He was still short for his age, and very thin – but not of the skin-and-bones quality she'd seen a few months earlier.

'You look better. You are eating, I can see.' Softly, she reached out and, with the crook of her finger, pushed against a plumping-up cheek.

Sarita gave a proud laugh and said something to Jed.

'He is always eating!' he translated. 'Now he has started, he won't stop.'

'Well that's wonderful! As it should be. He will grow into a strong, handsome man like his papa.'

'*Gracias*, Senorita Tara,' Paco said, and he held out a small plant, its roots carefully wrapped in a muslin cloth.

'What is this?' she asked in amazement.

'For your heart vibrations,' Jed said for him. 'The Awa says this will make them strong again. When the sadness comes, take two leaves and rub them fast between your hand. When they are warm, place them on the chest, over your heart.'

Tara reached forward and kissed Paco on the cheek. 'You see? I helped you and now you are helping me. Thank you.'

Sarita put a hand on her son's shoulder and Tara understood it was a sign they had to go.

'He must rest,' Jed said by way of explanation. 'He is still building his strength.'

'Of course.'

'I'll come and see you before you go,' Jed said.

'Great . . . Thank you, Paco,' she said again, as the child was led away.

Her mother was watching closely. 'I take it he's the child I almost lost *my* child for?' It had taken days for them all to calm her mother down. The talk of kidnappers and ransoms, curses and then hospitals had left her nerves in a friable state.

'Yes. He's Jed's eldest son. He'll be seven soon.'

'Well,' her mother nodded, watching his dark head move through the crowd. '. . . I can see why you went to the effort.'

Tara smiled. If her mother couldn't understand the impetus to work, she could certainly understand the need to help.

'What was the diagnosis in the end?' Holly asked, curiosity glinting in her voice.

Tara turned back to her. 'Cholestatic hepatitis, but presenting as myeloid leukaemia.'

'*Really?*' Holly's eyes sparkled. 'So then you and the voodoo guy were both right.'

'Yeah,' Tara grinned.

'And you got all this confirmed how?'

'Once he started responding to the leaves we brought back – enough to build his strength – Jed got Sarita to agree to some blood tests at the clinic.'

'So then your madcap scheme actually worked,' Holly chuckled, shaking her head. 'You brought them over to the dark side.'

'Not really. As soon as leukaemia was conclusively ruled out, he went back to the village and he's been treated entirely by the black star leaves ever since. Not an anti-biotic in sight.'

'Shut the fuck up!'

Her mother looked surprised by the foul language, but she had always had a soft spot for Holly. She patted Holly's arm consolingly. 'I'm going to go and check on your father,' she said to Tara. 'Make sure he's not hatching any more deals to give away the rest of our money. I'm planning on spending what's left.'

'Go, Mrs T!' Holly cheered.

Tara looked around at the assorted guests. Her father was still talking to the President, each of them holding a glass, and their body language infinitely more relaxed now the official duties were completed. William appeared to be talking to someone with medals.

A hand suddenly closed around her bicep. 'Oh my God. Do not move. Incoming,' Holly breathed, stepping in closer to her. 'Total fucking hottie, six o'clock.'

Tara fell still, unable to see but knowing exactly to whom her friend was referring. The moment she had lived and breathed for during the past two months was almost here – as she had known it would be. Like a satellite in space, it had been spinning towards her for years. Nothing could throw it off course now.

'He's not too hot on those crutches though,' Holly murmured, watching on Tara's behalf.

'Is he in pain?' She could hear the concern in her own voice.

'No. I'd say he looks more . . . pissed off. People keep stopping him to talk . . . Oh. Oh. He keeps looking over. Don't move.'

'I'm not moving.' Tara felt his gaze upon her back. She could still remember the feeling of his scar beneath her thumb, the shock and euphoria of discovering he was alive . . .

'Honestly, just look at him—' Holly whispered. 'No! I said don't move.'

'You just said to look at him!' Tara pouted.

Holly's eyes narrowed, watching his slow progress. 'He always was far too handsome for your own good. And cocky as fuck, using you to get to your dad so he could talk him into buying a national park. You know, as you do. Everyday stuff.'

Tara grinned. 'I've sort of forgiven him for that now.'

'I'm not sure I have. *I've* got PTSD from dealing with the bloody aftermath.'

'You're fine,' Tara chuckled.

Holly looked at her, suddenly serious. 'Am I, though?'

'What do you mean?' Tara frowned, watching as the jokes faded from her friend's eyes. It was always worrying when Hols grew serious.

'. . . Sometimes I feel so guilty.'

'About what?'

'About me getting what you wanted so badly – Dev, Jimmy, all the stuff I gave you crap about.'

Tara was stunned. It had never once occurred to her that Holly might have felt this way. 'Hols, no! I never resented you for it. Not for a minute.'

'Really, though?'

Holly looked back at her and for the first time Tara saw the scar tissue in her friend too, the twists of fate that had spun them all around, throwing their crystal-clear career paths, life goals and thrusting ambitions into complete disarray. None of them were living the lives they would have predicted for themselves ten years earlier – and yet somehow, against the odds . . . hadn't things largely worked out? 'Really.'

'Oh God. He's nearly here.' A secretive smile crept onto Holly's lips. 'Just stay calm.'

'I am calm. You're the one who needs a sedative . . . What's that smile for?' Tara asked suspiciously.

'I was just thinking how sweet it was, the way he came down a mountain looking for you that day and then went straight back up it again – he was like Rambo in chinos! Even after Rory biffed him on the nose.'

'Rory punched him?'

'Fully justified if Alex was going to kiss his girlfriend *and* make him listen to it, let's be honest,' Holly shrugged. 'At least he got to restore his honour.'

Tara grinned and Holly watched her, seeing how she couldn't quite bring her mouth down from a smile or dial back the light in her eyes. She gave a heavy sigh. 'So this is how it's going to be from now on, is it? He's really the one?'

Tara looked at her. 'You know as well as I do – he was always the one.'

An enigmatic look came upon her friend again. 'Well then, in that case . . .' And she leaned in to whisper a secret.

'You came back.'

She turned to face him and the electricity zipped between them, quicksilver, making a mockery of words. 'Of course.'

They both let the words hang for a moment, both adjusting to the other's proximity again.

'. . . I didn't know if you'd be here today,' he said finally, looking out at the crowd and then back at her again. Leaning on the crutches brought him down almost to her height. He looked hesitant, almost nervous, and she realized he didn't remember that she had sat with him for the three days before she'd had to return. Internal injuries had meant he had been sedated and largely unconscious at the hospital. He must have thought she'd just . . . gone.

'How could I miss it? This is the big day,' she said, watching him trying to read her for sarcasm or rebuke. 'Are you pleased?'

'That you're back?'

She smiled. 'That the handover's happened.'

'Oh.' He nodded, looking embarrassed. 'Yeah. I am.'

'Me too.' Her eyes roamed his face. It was so good even just to see him again. She longed to reach over and stroke the curve of his cheek, to trace the contours of his profile, to smell his hair, to nuzzle in the crook of his neck and tickle him, to make real what hadn't yet been said between them.

He looked down at the ground and back at her. 'You know, I was going to come back to London the second they cleared me to fly.'

She paused for a moment, seeing the desperation in his eyes.

'Well, that would have been unfortunate.' Her own eyes sparkled. 'If I'd been over here only to find you'd gone over there.'

He gave a squint of confusion. '. . . You over here?'

'I had to go back to work my notice and . . . see through some processes. But I would have been pretty hacked off to do all that and get back here, only to find you'd gone.'

Emotions ran behind his eyes, fast and light. 'Ta, are you saying . . . ?' His voice thickened and he cleared his throat. 'Are you saying you forgive me?'

She remembered the sight of him standing in the path of the mudslide, endangering himself to check she was safe. 'I'm saying, no more apologies,' she nodded.

He seemed unable to speak for several seconds. He stared at the ground, at her painted toenails in her backless sandals. He looked back at her. 'You've really worked your notice?'

'I've got a clinic here that needs me more.'

'Not just the clinic.' His eyes burned into her and the embers that forever smouldered between them ignited into small flames. 'But what about—?'

'Rory moved out within a week,' she said simply.

'He did?' Alex looked surprised.

'He said he'd heard all he needed to hear.' She arched an eyebrow. 'Apparently someone left the "speak" button on and he heard every single word of our conversation. As well as the bits where we . . . weren't speaking.'

She watched as his lips parted. Busted. No excuses. 'Well . . . all's fair,' he said finally, that familiar gleam coming back into his eyes. 'What did he expect? That I wouldn't fight for you?'

His hand, his good one, reached for her, pulling her closer. They stared at one another for several long, languid moments before he leaned forward and kissed her, right there.

Someone – they both knew who – whooped from the crowd as they pulled apart with shy laughs.

'Finally. I get to do that again,' he whispered.

'You do.' She watched his gaze fall to her lips again, and she felt their magnetism draw them in close, closer to one another, everyone else forgotten. They succumbed to another kiss, just the first of many, they already knew. Holly whooped again. '. . . What?' She saw his eyes had narrowed with curiosity.

'What did she say to you just now?'

'Who? Hols?'

'Yeah. She whispered something as I was coming over.'

'Yes. Because it's a secret,' she smiled coyly.

He shook his head faintly, pinning her with those light green eyes. 'There's no secrets between you and me. Never again.'

She felt the goosebumps ripple up and down her skin as his eyebrow arched quizzically, just a little, drawing it – everything – from her. 'She's eight weeks pregnant.'

His eyes widened with surprise. 'Really?' he smiled. 'Well, that's pretty great.'

'Yeah. Conceived in Costa Rica, in fact. I'm so happy for them.'

He was still watching her. '. . . And?' he prompted, still watching her closely. 'What else did she say?'

'How do you know there's more?'

'There's always more with Holly.'

She caught her breath and looked away, but he turned her back to face him again. 'Tell me.'

She shook her head. 'No.'

He leaned in closer, his gaze drawing her into him. 'Tell me.'

'. . . She said we could catch them up.'

Time refracted like a cat stretch, arching its back, moving through space. 'Well, she's right. We could.' A smile drew slowly across his lips. 'Although we'd need to get practising. There's not a minute to lose.'

'How? You're broken,' she grinned. 'Literally broken.'

'Not *everywhere*. A couple of broken tibias, a fibula, a few ribs . . . Everyone knows ribs heal quickly. You're a doctor. You should know that.' He reached forward and kissed her again and this time she felt the crowd fall away completely. She didn't care who saw. It was just the two of them, just as it had been during those long dark nights in London.

He pulled back eventually, both of them yearning for more. His eyes shone with a smile that began to play on his lips. 'Thing is, though, I'm a pretty conservative guy,' he said. 'I had an unconventional childhood, as you know, and I would want our baby . . .'

Our baby. *Our baby*. The words glittered like they'd been cut from diamonds.

'. . . to have more security than I had. I would want him – or her – to have my name.' His eyes were sparkling, a mischief she could see. 'But I wouldn't want you to, y'know, agree. Just to be polite.'

She had to suppress the bubble of laughter rising up in her. 'I don't understand,' she said contrarily. 'What would I be agreeing to?'

'Marrying me.'

'You want me to marry you?'

'I wanted it then. I've wanted it ever since . . . Will you, Tara, marry me?'

She stared back at him for a moment, as long as she could manage, before stepping into him and wrapping her arms around his neck. 'Absolutely,' she beamed. 'Thank you so much for asking.' She kissed him, feeling his smile curve against her own. 'How kind.'

Acknowledgements

My regular readers will know there's an army hard at work behind the name written in bold type on the cover. The team at Pan Macmillan are the very best at what they do, but they always make it such fun! This year has been different for us all – meetings held over Zoom instead of our usual lively meet-ups around a conference table, everyone (not just me!) working from home – but they've still done an incredible job of making sure the books are as finessed, polished and widely available to you as ever. Pan people, thank you, you make it look easy but I know it's not.

To my editor Caroline Hogg and my agent Amanda Preston, I feel our team just gets stronger and stronger. You are the start and end point of every book, and your insights and inputs are completely invaluable. Thank you!

Finally, to my family – everything I do is for you and because of you. You are my whole world and I feel like the luckiest person on the planet to live life with you. Thank you for inspiring me to work harder, to keep trying to do better, and for supporting me in all the ways you do. I love you to bits.